WHAT PEOPLE ARE

# COBALT BLUE

Gorgeously lyrical, *Cobalt Blue* ventures into dark psychological territory before the light finally rises. This is a bold story, dealing with frightening hypersexuality, unwanted religious experience, and hard-won transcendence. With its Jungian underpinnings and exotic settings, this beautifully written novel will appeal to anyone fascinated by boundaries, taboos, obsession and mystery.

**Anna Jean Mayhew**
*The Dry Grass of August*

*Cobalt Blue* is an engrossing story of the spiritual awakening of a painter who becomes so obsessed with sex that she nearly loses her sanity. Payne strips away the barriers to female passion; she entices the reader to vicariously experience the artist's hot and sensual fire.

**Barbara Hand Clow**
*The Liquid Light of Sex*

"A zesty, well-paced read—quite entertaining and rich in detail."
Pulitzer Prize winner **Oscar Hijuelos**
*Thoughts Without Cigarettes*

*Cobalt Blue* is entrancing and unsettling: a novel that gets at the marrow of sexual and spiritual experience. Peggy Payne is one of our most gifted writers.

**Angela Davis-Gardner**
*Butterfly's Child*

# Cobalt Blue

# Cobalt Blue

## Peggy Payne

Winchester, UK
Washington, USA

First published by Roundfire Books, 2013
Roundfire Books is an imprint of John Hunt Publishing Ltd., Laurel House, Station Approach, Alresford, Hants, SO24 9JH, UK
office1@jhpbooks.net
www.johnhuntpublishing.com
www.roundfire-books.com

For distributor details and how to order please visit the 'Ordering' section on our website.



ISBN: 978 1 78099 808 4



A CIP catalogue record for this book is available from the British Library.



Design: Stuart Davies

Printed in the USA by Edwards Brothers Malloy

Revelation

Sister India

The Healing Power of Doing Good
(with Allan Luks)

Doncaster: A Legacy of Personal Style

For my loyal, helpful critics who read multiple drafts of this novel as it evolved: Christina Askounis, Joseph Burgo, Dorrie Casey, Angela Davis-Gardner, my husband Bob Dick, Georgann Eubanks, critic-in-chief Laurel Goldman, Peter Filene, Ardis Hatch, G.C. "Pete" Hendricks, Carrie Knowles, Linda Orr, Randee Russell Bieler, and Dan Wakefield.

# Acknowledgments

So many have helped me with this novel, in addition to those in the dedication. I want to thank them all. Here's the list: the Sherwood Anderson Foundation, Jodi Barnes, Bonnie Bell, Sarah Compton, Emilie Conrad and Continuum, Barbara Hand Clow, Rebecca Dnistran, Michael Eha, Anne Fabbri, Claire Gerus, Judy Goldman, Kathleen Gruer, David Guy, Maria Herrera, Oscar Hijuelos, John Hunt, Dominic James, Rosemary James and the Pirate's Alley Faulkner Society's Words & Music, Ruth King, Betsi Koszalka, Linda Lankford, Gayle Lowry, Katherine Manger, Elaine Markson, Cathy Martin, Anna Jean Mayhew, Amy McDougall, Paulette Mitchell, Omega Institute, Elaine Orr, Dr Bob Phillips, Mamie Potter, Novie Ragan, Sam Ryburn, Linda K. Russell, Ruth Sheehan, Dr Nicholas Stratas, Brenda Summers, Nancy Tilly, Julie Tomlin, Jane Wallace, Victoria Wilson, Naomi Wolf, and Jan Yopp. Thank you again.

The author can be reached through www.peggypayne.com.

"The heaventree of stars hung with humid nightblue fruit...."

*Ulysses*
James Joyce

# 1

Andie sat poised to reach for her portfolio; she was the next item on the agenda, set to follow Parking Lot. Not exactly star billing. All the more reason to get fired up, to look alive. The club's private dining room had been turned into a boardroom for this meeting; midday sun glared hard against the French doors. She sat up straighter, breathed faster to get herself going. It takes energy to sell yourself.

"Now," said Tripp from the head of the table, in his warm-butter Southern-patrician accent, "let us move to the most delightful of today's new business."

She put on her happy game face, prepared to be delightful.

"At my request," he said, "George invited in Ms. Andie Branson, the noted painter, who also claims the distinction of being a lifelong Pinehurst resident." A flirty wink in his tone, but she couldn't manage just now to glow back at him. She knew by sight most of this long tableful, had been in school with the guy, Richard, in the round horn rims.

"Let me jump in here," said George, the head pro, "and quickly tell the board..."

She forced herself to wait. On the sheet before her: Spring 2002 in a fine-lined angular font, like tennis nets and racquet strings. The millionth in a line of hack jobs, this one, if she got it, would be far better than average: a mural on an outer wall of the tennis club's pro shop. She so needed the money. In recent weeks she'd let work slide, ignoring phone calls, invitations to bid and the no-rush project that was all she had on her schedule. As if cash would simply appear. One house payment remained in her account, and nothing more.

George was talking about posters she'd forgotten doing, and her one portrait of a college president, the watercolor of a Duke-Carolina game. She pictured a line-up of pet portraits and waiting room art, grimly repeating itself into the future, like the grapes-and-dead-fowl wallpaper border running around the top of the room. "She's top-ranked," George said.

He was wrapping it up; again she readied herself. "Not to mention," said whiskey-voiced Eloise Merrill, "that she's the daughter of that glamorous pair, Zack and Daphne Branson." Andie felt her scalp shift: prickly tone to that comment. But Eloise, stubby with a bulldog face, probably had suffered a lifelong crush on Zack. Everyone did. She too had a crush on him. In fact, she was in love with both of them, her parents.

The ever-appropriate Tripp ignored Eloise's interruption. "Andie?" he said.

She was on, finally, her jaw muscles tense from waiting. "A generous exaggeration, George, and I thank you for it." She unzipped her portfolio. They were scraping back chairs, crowding at her end of the table to look at the large photographs of her work, though she'd brought a small set of copies for each person. Tripp had said no need to set up the "PowerPoint, slide show rigamarole." People pressed close. "This, you probably recognize, is the billboard of the 6 o'clock news team."

"I don't like the idea of people you could identify," Eloise said.

Andie stifled irritation: she hadn't been suggesting likenesses. "Generic figures are the best way to go, I do agree." Faces and shoulders hovered, brushed against the ends of her stray hairs; the barely-there contact made her want to bat away gnats. "This is on a brick wall next to a playground in Charlotte. They wanted a natural background, trees, something to make the place look bigger and give it a little mystery."

"We don't need any mystery," said the man who owned beauty salons, his name she couldn't remember. Her hand paused on the page; best not to risk a reply to that.

"One thing we've got to have," George said, "is for the figures to demonstrate proper form of each stroke."

"And showcase the lines we carry," the shop manager said.

Okay, it's their wall, I'm used to this, it's all reasonable. But she wanted to put her forehead down on the table. "That's fine," she said, not quite loudly enough. "I can do that."

People were starting to drift back to their seats. Had she wowed them? No telling how many artists they were considering. This was her livelihood, as well as what passed for her identity.

"Andie, my dear." Tripp's voice had that warm sheen, like beautifully polished wood. Probably he'd say he loved life, as apparently one was supposed to do. She couldn't remember the last time she'd felt that way; probably the first few minutes after coming out of a feel-good movie, however long ago that was. "How about bringing us an estimate?" he said. "Let's include the mural and then one smaller project I almost forgot to mention. We'll want all the little niceties, the paper goods, etcetera, to give a unified image or brand, if you will, a nice monogram adaptable for towels, cocktail napkins and such."

Cocktail napkins? She felt her face go slack. Is he serious?

She cleared her throat to be sure she could speak. "That's fine, Tripp." She heard her tone, dead flat, and tried again. "I'll put that together, thanks." They set a time for her to come back and report to a committee.

As she got up to go, Tripp said, "Tell that man of yours hello for me. He did beautiful work on my house." Her gaze paused low on the side of a chair as she scrambled for what to say, and in front of all these people. Before she could get her mouth open, Tripp winced at his blunder: "Tell you what, I'll say the hello myself."

She attempted a philosophical shrug, a smile: "All things fade," she said. He looked so embarrassed she felt sorry for him. As she left, the conversation reverted to paving, gravel, ecological alternatives, with the man who didn't need mystery insisting: "...I know for a fact, concrete will give you the best value...."

Outside, she headed quickly down the steps. Rushing, as if

she could escape the feeling about to overtake her.

This is what my life has come to: napkin jobs. And nothing else.

She'd done none of the work that was hers to do, in 15 years since school. How did I let this happen?

A ball whammed against a backboard somewhere close by, bouncing off the court, the board, the court, the board… She wanted to scream at it to stop. She gripped the handles of her sample book, and hurried, pain pressing like a sharp knuckle at a spot between her eyes.

The sun was barely down when she gave up and went to bed. The afternoon's busywork had failed to distract her. Whether she got the tennis job or not, she'd failed herself. No point in staying up. Or in getting up tomorrow for that matter; nothing was going to change. Ridiculous to imagine she could get herself to do anything different; far less likely now that she'd realized she was 15 years behind. Tonight she hadn't managed her usual routines: her crunches, the crossword in the Raleigh paper, getting the day's Diet Coke cans out of the car… The pitiful drabness of the list, it was putting her to sleep….

Moonlight was all over the room when she woke, the board floor grooved with shadows. She was in an instant fully awake. Surely such brightness didn't come in at this hour every night, or every full moon, the air full of a wafting happiness that passed through her again and again. Tears sprang up in her eyes; such startling joy: she felt awash in liquid light.

Last night's clothes that she'd thrown over the back of the chair, jeans still holding the curve of her hips, blue-and-white top, dangling bra, together formed an image of falling water, a torrent seen from a distance.

Her bed seemed floating in light as palpable as clear brilliant water. And in the center of the room a loose coil of shining blue spun. Spiraled upward. Gone. A trick of moonlight against the mirror? In the reflection there, she saw clearly her face, the full upper lip, almost smiling, wide-set heavy-lidded eyes, narrow shoulders, the tops of her breasts.

She widened her gaze to take in the room. What she saw stopped her breath. The sharpness of every object, the jar of mascaras and eyeliner pencils, her canvas shoulder bag on the doorknob: astonishing, as if instantly made real from what had been merely a sketch. Her eyes lingered over each detail, memorizing its new face, awash in gratitude for its existence: the windowpanes, the half-open door to the closet, the woven light and dark of the straw hat she never wore.

Her normal dry routine, daily work schedule, her silent house, the plodding line of clients and errands and repeating scenery had shrunk to no more than a vantage point, a place to stand to take in what was before her.

Her body, naked against the sheet, thrillingly naked to the air, felt boundless. Weightless. Prickly desire to rub her mouth over all she saw, to drink the colors, to die of sex, made her stomach quake, the need in itself a pleasure. She wanted to dissolve into the sensation. She willed it, begged it, to push into her, enter her through every pore…

When she woke again, the bedroom looked ordinary in the grey pre-dawn. Well, of course; what had she expected? The full-moon extravaganza had ended. What she could remember felt dream-like: bright light that was somehow exciting. She sat up, chilly, on the side of the bed, sheet clutched around her against the damp air. She was ungodly thirsty. Her hand, reaching for last night's water glass, trembled.

"Stop it. I mean it, stop." Again she'd spoken aloud. To no one. No sleeping hulk waited to rouse and mutter a response. Not for almost 3 months now. No Charlie to reach half-blind from the pillow for the mug of coffee she'd brought him.

Still 2 hours before the alarm would blast, sitting here wide-awake. Though in recent days she'd stayed in bed hours late, dozing and staring. She stared at the pillow; it didn't beckon. Her legs were jumpy. The studio was starting to pull at her. First time in as long as she could remember. She'd already begun work in her mind.

This itch to get there, to melt onto the canvas as if she were made of paint: it wouldn't last. She should go, though, get something done before the rising urge faded, as it would.

She pulled on yesterday's clothes, the need to work intensifying, in her right hand and the length of her arm, in the dry-feeling rims of her eyes. Stepping bare feet into clogs, she put on glasses instead of contacts, grabbed the first thing, windbreaker with the broken zipper, for the April early-morning cool. No, she hesitated, then put it back; she wasn't wearing this today. Reaching to the farthest hanger in the closet, she pulled out her old satin Shenyang jacket. She'd neglected this once-favored item: tart chartreuse with red lining; it had seemed to require more energy to wear than she'd recently had available. She slipped it on. Much better.

No time now to make peanut butter toast; no more time to waste: she had to get to the canvas before this wave let her go and she lost her nerve. There was no question which picture; recently it had been afloat again in her mind.

On the porch, the still night air felt moist against her flushed face. She drove a fast four miles to town, pictured her clunker of a car as lunar-powered, running on the night's white moonlight. Her face, her cheeks had not begun to cool by the time she slowed through the meandering lanes of Pinehurst, then wheeled into the dirt parking lot.

Inside her studio, she flipped on the overheads, making the windowed opposite wall into a dim mirror. Out of the corner of her eye, if she looked, she could see herself lift the wide horizontal canvas she'd feared so long, locking it into her easel;

could see the rust-colored blur of her hair, her compact youngish shape moving quickly to get set up. She imagined her parents, Mom and Zack, hovering out there beyond the window, confidently watching. And she a nervous child before her first piano recital. She mustn't get self-conscious now or she'd tighten up and wreck everything.

She unscrewed a tube, squeezing yellow out onto the plate, unleashing the aroma of oils. In front of her, charcoal scratches crisscrossed the white. That much she'd done, long ago, years ago; she'd painted so many commissions since then. And done anything else she could do to avoid this picture. Now here she was, propelled out of bed to paint it; she'd say it was her calling from God, if she believed in such things.

The picture itself was going to be ridiculously simple: an open yellow umbrella shot through with sunlight.

She slopped the first wet color onto the middle of the canvas, reckless, as if she were throwing off weighty binding. Getting this done was going to bring her back to life; it already had. Something had. Some piece of the night's strange uproar was back: she hadn't felt so juiced-up and excited in years.

A few strokes, and she'd fallen into the rhythm, hand in steady motion. The subject of an umbrella wasn't innately upsetting, or shouldn't be; it had no more depth or threat than the jobs she worked on every day. Yet she'd let this canvas sit, edge visible, taunting her from the far back of her rack for so long. She felt for her paint knife without pulling her eyes away. Sometimes she'd imagined that the rough sketch vibrated, or hummed, like an alarm heard from deep inside sleep. Now she was the one who hummed, but quietly, more like a steady light rain or a purr. As if she'd been literally "turned on", an electric switch flipped in the night. She felt a calm and ease of heart that was shockingly unfamiliar.

This switch was going to stay on; she'd make sure of it. It was her new purpose in life. The door clicked open behind her. "Go away," she said, and heard the latch click shut. Then, after a moment, open again.

"Go away?" Otis's voice, but she didn't turn. "Since when are you so unsociable?" he said. "Where's the sarcastic wit?"

She felt herself waver. But she didn't dare look away from the canvas. What if she fell out of this state she was in? Lost her flood-tide momentum? The plate holding the blobs of paint felt like her shield, the color-loaded brush a laser.

She waved him out without breaking her trance. "Later, Otis."

A couple or 3 hours must have passed, she guessed, as her hand continued to work, at least that long, based on how much she'd done and the angle of the daylight and the tube of chrome lemon she'd already squeezed flat. The image was taking on a peculiar striated effect, like the shadow of the louvers on the cement floor of the room in *The Lover* where the couple had sex in the afternoon, only the window slats separating them from the traffic of *tongas* on the street.

Not until the canvas was covered did she pause, the usual low clatter, hallway voices, clashing music of CD players from other studios, breaking into her awareness for the first time.

She stepped back to look at what she'd done. The tautness of the umbrella's yellow nylon, you could feel the pull. She felt it in her body, as if the tug were reaching all the way around into her back.

An odd sensation there.

A slow ripping. Peculiar. As if parts of her were coming loose inside.

She gripped her middle, with both hands, both forearms, trying to stop whatever was moving, see what it was. Now a prickle, rising in jerky motion, up through her center. A muttering, hissing stripe of neon buried in wet muscle, moving upward. She wanted to reach into her chest and grab it. She stood straighter to give it room to move. Heat! Such delicious heat! Climbing up her insides, last night's light sharpened to a laser.

And a wild feeling, a bird loose against the inner walls of her chest. God! Was she dying? But it felt better than anything…

A damp spot of excitement in her crotch. Her heart beat as if she'd just sprinted a mile and could run ten more.

Her hips moved, testing the sexual sensation that was starting to fade. Gone, her breath rushing back in….

She'd been hit by something invisible. Toxic fumes from her materials? It wasn't a stroke: she could still move. In the mirror she looked the same, hair a mess, paint on her chin. She steadied herself against the lavatory.

A spark of blue light popped just in front of her face, a tiny camera flash, a blip. Like static electricity. She waited, to see if there was more. A minute passed, or two. She gave up waiting, ran cold water on her hands and splashed it on her face, dripping dark spots onto the wood floor.

From the corner of her eye she could see the easel. The gleaming yellow crescent of umbrella seemed to hover in front of the surface, on the edge of flashing into motion. She'd gotten down some portion, at least, of what she'd long imagined and dreamed in the night. The image was electric; she pictured it spinning demonically, slicing at the air.

Looking again, she started to smile: this was what she'd hoped for, a seriously good start. Maybe after all it was possible, what her teachers had predicted long ago: she'd become someone people collected, not somebody they hired and bossed around.

But it wasn't just the picture. She dropped into a seat. The ferment, the sense of shaking loose inside – she could feel the engine of it still, an almost-physical vibration. She resisted the thought but couldn't stop it: this was what people meant by "mystical", getting swept up by the turbulent outer edges of some force. It wasn't at all what she would have imagined.

Out in the hallway, she banged both fists on Marian's glass door, though it stood propped half-open, and she could see

Marian was on the phone. She did a jogging victory-dance, both arms in the air. Marian, long-skirted and large, gliding the room with phone to her ear, made a deep nod of congratulation, not that she had any idea what this was about. Andie waved, started on down the hall. Marian was giving her a puzzled stare; she probably looked a wreck. Lights were off in Otis's studio and Caitlin's. Nobody home. Too bad. No chance of bumping into Caitlin's sweet boyfriend, Tim.

She burst out the front foyer of the building. With all that had happened, it was still barely mid-afternoon; she did a skipping step. The air felt perfect, a soft early-spring day, only a whisper of coolness, and she as clean and tender as a butter bean just shelled, as if she were 8 instead of the worn 38-year-old she had somehow let herself become. Maybe next she'd paint a close-up of a bean, the palest thinnest greens and new translucent skin stretched tight over the meat underneath. She'd use the tender grass green that made you think of Easter egg hunts, made you feel refreshed and alive. Easter had just passed; she'd ignored it, as usual. Though here she was, reborn anyway.

A tiny silver plane passed over high above. What had hit her in the studio wasn't ordinary and human-scale. That much was unmistakable. Pausing, she watched the jet drawing its widening white line of smoke stream across the sky. Two and a quarter years into the new century. She needed to make a note of the date of this day: her strange rebirth on April twenty-something, 2002, when she became someone who did disturbingly good work and felt strange and overwhelming sensations.

She headed toward her own mud-brown Caprice. Big and outdated as it was, it looked like a wide raft, floating on four oilcans. A dog was barking, the sound muffled. Over there, in that backseat. She ambled toward the car.

"Hey there, boy," she said, approaching. The dog was barking himself hoarse. A mutt, part German shepherd, the poor fellow by himself.

He stared hard at her through the glass, muscles so tight he was quivering. "There's nothing to be scared of, poochie." His black eyes fixed on hers. A big animal, though not as tough as he was pretending. "All you need is a good scratching, right there behind your ears."

She reached in through the opening above the window glass, slowly, to be sure not to scare him. He stopped his prancing and shaking, settling down pretty-as-you-please. Arm hooked awkwardly over the glass, she rubbed his head, scratched. "That's a good doggie." She smoothed the warm fur down to his collar and his eyes began to close as if he were falling asleep in the sun. She shifted her arm to get a better angle and her reflection caught her eye. Her hand fell still on the dog's head as she looked at the image on the glass.

Her face was positioned so it fitted over the eyes and mouth of the dog. The circle of her features, her skin verged into a thick neck covered with stiff black hair. And the ears, long and pointed, black. A wolf with the face of a woman.

In the reflection, the lips pulled back in a grimace. Her lips! her face! on the head of this animal. She moved and destroyed the image. Yanking her arm out through the crack of open window, she felt a pull in her wrist as her hand bent wrong against the top of the frame.

Pain moved fast, like something spilt.

Her right hand was hurt, her painting hand. Behind the glass, the dog growled, head lifted, teeth bared. "Shut up, you," the words choked off by a sob.

Cradling the wrist, she ran toward her car, crawled in and, left-handed, shut the door. From behind her came the barking, the dog frantically aroused. Over the sound of the engine cranking, she could still hear the crazed animal. She pulled out without looking, skidded the car forward, bumped the radio up louder until it blotted out the yowl.

# 2

The tennis committee, which had turned out to be half the board, was gathered at the buffet, stirring coffees, surveying the cantaloupe bites and little sticky buns.

Andie could feel the motions of the bodies around her all the way into her pores. She stepped away from the heat of the cluster. With her left hand, she managed her cup, her wounded right wrist held stiff by an old Ace bandage.

"I certainly like what you presented here," the tall strawberry blonde said, sidling up with her coffee. Anna, the architect.

"Thanks. How soon might the committee take action?" She'd gotten the idea they'd decide at this meeting. But they could be interviewing a whole line-up of people.

"Not today, I don't think." She looked a little startled at the question, as if a decision was simply too much to expect for a project roughly equivalent to the Sistine Chapel. An architect should know how frustrating this is, waiting to hear if you have the job.

George, the pro, appeared to be giving a mini-lesson to a couple of men, other members turning to watch as he stepped into a backhand, repeated the motion. One guy was making slight, perhaps unconscious, movements over his whole body, a restrained imitation of George's sweep: knees, shoulder, elbow, flick of wrist. The big sleeves and wide armholes of her loose "artsy" meeting blouse let the uppermost part of her arms brush against her bare sides: surprisingly rousing. The air of the room in this last hour seemed full of pheromones, faint arousal triggered by nothing. Doing without sex was unfamiliar, not that they'd ever set the bed on fire.

People had drifted away from the snacks, leaving cups and crumpled napkins. Napkins! That could be my work lying wadded up there. "Folks," Tripp said in a call-to-order voice, "let's walk out and take a look from spots that will have a view of the mural." Good. Maybe I'll still come out of this meeting with a job.

When they stepped out into the sun, Andie shaded her eyes. It was almost noon, perfect North Carolina blue sky. A shout went up from spectators at the sidelines of the most distant court, and a soft spatter of clapping. Tennis players in the morning, my own work in the afternoon: that would be the perfect balance.

In ones and twos, the group followed the narrow path toward one of the fenced court enclosures, all pausing as Tripp did. Sun lit the back of the nearest player's knotty-muscled legs, the neat square of the man's shorts; he raced forward across the white-on-green line. Her eyes followed. He paused at the net, wiry hair shone gold on one tanned wrist and forearm. Her head went woozy: the sudden feel of afternoon concerts in college, drinking vodka and pineapple outdoors in the heat, making out on a bedspread in broad daylight. She'd still had spirit in those days.

She stepped closer to the fence, the metal links broke the players on the other side into bits and pieces: an elbow, a crouched leg, the curve of a racquet. Where the wire twisted close to her face. a metal hangnail. The metal almost touched her face, she could smell its tang, imagine it wrapped around her. She was caught naked in a coil of fencing, bare skin against the wire. Now lying in the path, her hair in the dirt, legs around the man with the knotty calves who was humping her into the ground. Standing at the fence, she forced herself to hold still, scared of moving or making a sound.

The need started to ease, leaving a physical ache, plus a murmur of sensation at the bottom of her spine. A sense of danger skirted.

This fantasy, so public, so degrading! She felt assaulted. As if a stranger had come out of a crowd and hit her, then run away.

She glanced quickly toward the board members. "From this corner of the courts," Tripp was saying, "we have a view that takes in not only the shop, but one arm of the pool." All were turned toward Tripp. She kept her eyes pinned on him, as if listening. If she'd done anything weird or out of place, no one had seen. But she'd never done anything weird in her life; nobody would believe it if they did see.

Upstairs again, as the others took their seats, Tripp put a hand on the back of her arm. "Could you stay for a moment? I've got something else I'd like to mention to you. We should be finished here shortly."

"Sure. That's fine." His hand slowly drifted off of her as he moved away, leaving a warm blurry imprint. Maybe the weeks without Charlie, the absence of any human physical contact, had led to this sensitivity, to the bursts of craving.

She waited while the committee discussed how to handle prizes in the new little-kid competitions, how many port-a-potties for an upcoming demonstration match. Charlie would be at a construction site now in his mud-crusted boots with his clipboard, his hair so black and straight he was like a Cherokee. Good-looking. Sexy, if you liked impassive; every hard-muscled, farmer-tanned detail of him as familiar to her as her own short, paint-roughened hands. She'd stopped loving Charlie somewhere along the way, or at least that's what he said had happened to them; and so he'd called it quits. All she knew was: for so long she'd felt herself winding down and down.

The meeting was breaking up, she'd barely noticed.

"Always a pleasure to see you, Andie," Tripp said, pulling a seat closer to her as the room emptied. She and Tripp sat nearly knee-to-knee: faintly thrilling, but in a normal way, nothing out of the ordinary. "And I must say," giving her a searching second look, "you are positively aglow today. You must tell me sometime where to find your fountain of youth." He waved the subject of her looks aside before she could make any rejoinder. "Today we have business," he said. "Here's what I want to propose to you.

There's another project soon to be jobbed out by a panel I'm on. I'd like you to think about it."

She held his gaze, waited.

"We want to hire you to paint a portrait of Senator Billy Sylvester."

Her head fell back. "You're not serious."

"Of course I am."

She pictured Sylvester: his right-wing smirk. The man was a racist and had only recently bothered to hide it. They didn't need a portrait; they could use one of his sanctimonious campaign photos: the wet-lipped smile, the yellowish-grey hair laid just so across his pate. Dear God! Billy Sylvester, a notorious North Carolina senator. Billy, as everyone called him. He'd publicly praised the Baptists who voted wives should submit to their husbands. She could feel a wild laugh building. He thinks I'm going to sell my very soul.

"This will be an extremely high-profile undertaking," Tripp said, "extremely desirable. The portrait is a much more pressing matter, frankly than the club projects." Out of politeness, she let him go on. "I must count on you not to whisper a word to anyone. The senator has set a time to announce his resignation from the Senate, to tell the people he won't run again. I'm trusting you to keep our secret until he's ready to release the news. This painting, we feel, can be the monument to his legacy, a symbol evoking all that Billy stands for, like the Lincoln Memorial. The USA needs something like that right now."

He dares to speak of Lincoln in the same sentence.

"This is no billboard, Andie. We're looking at locations for a classical structure to house this portrait and his papers. This will be an enduring national landmark."

"Wait, Tripp."

But he lifted one long-fingered hand to stop her. "It doesn't matter whether you've voted for him." He smiled, wry and conspiratorial. "We all know artists tend to lean the other way, and that's just fine."

"Was the work for the club just an excuse? To get me over here?"

"No, no, we want that done, but the board tends to move very slowly, as you may have noted." Again his beautiful Kennedyesque smile. "This project on the other hand, has, as I said, a shorter deadline, and being privately funded by a number of generous donors, it doesn't have to go to bid. We want a first-rate job by someone experienced in this kind of work: we're prepared to pay you $100,000."

She stared. "You're joking."

"You need to develop a better poker face, Andie," Tripp said, leaning back, his eyes shining with amusement.

"Why are you coming to me with this?"

"Because the senator particularly admires your work. He has an eye; you may not know, he collects, mainly those Hudson River boys, those waterfalls and lake vistas. Then too, for obvious reasons, he could only use a North Carolina painter. Of course you're versatile, as I told them, you can handle any subject matter. There would be no problem."

She looked down toward the far end of the room: at the lighted case of trophies. Versatile, he'd told them, when what he meant was obedient, a trained poodle; she'd do anything they paid her to do. She felt creeping shame that they'd thought they could ask.

"I believe when you've had a day or two to think this over, Andie, you'll see what an opportunity it is."

# 3

Andie veered out of the way of the crates at the freight elevator door, rounded the corner into the room: Elliott was sprawled like a 14-year-old on the sofa talking on his cell, Marian at work at her easel, as she rushed in. "I need y'all to help me with this." Andie fell into a chair. She never should have driven away from there without giving Tripp her unequivocal no.

"I'm listening," Marian said.

"I got an offer," Andie said. "From Billy Sylvester. To do his portrait."

Marian's brush stopped.

"Belinda," Elliott said into the phone to his girlfriend. "Got to go." He sat up, in hiking shorts, long legs splayed. So young, he was barely 25. She felt a twinge of protectiveness toward him, but he was too serious and responsible to ever need it.

"Andie, you're not!" Marian came over, perched in the seat of her armchair instead of settling her substantial weight back in her usual serene way. Marian, the earth-mother-sexy Buddha, uncharacteristically perturbed. She also had a glop of magenta on one honey-blonde curl.

"No. Of course not," Andie said. Though the size of the fee had begun to sink in. She'd kept pushing it away during the whole speedy drive from the club. With such a large offer in hand, she felt suddenly more daring, more capable of anything.

"Then what's the question?" she said, as Elliott leaned forward with a paper towel, neatly wiping the paint out of Marian's hair. His narrow face, still faintly acned across his forehead, was worried.

"They're offering a lot: $100,000."

"Whoa!" Elliott fell back. She saw his envy for seconds, then just as quickly the somber beginning of disapproval. The dorm fridge in the corner was making its little mosquito noise.

"The senator sure knows how to bait a trap," Marian said

finally. "It's probably worth it to him for the humiliation value alone, to be able buy himself an artsy liberal."

"He'd be buying a portrait, not an artist."

"It would be up on a public wall," Marian said, "your name on what amounts to a piece of his advertising."

"Public wall? It should be that modest. They're planning a Parthenon to hold it."

"He supports Milosevic," Elliott said, "who just went on trial for genocide." Mass graves found in Yugoslavia. She'd heard it on public radio. "Also," Elliott said, "Sylvester's the one who's made a crusade out of the playwright from Trinidad. Keeping him in jail and still no charges brought, no trial set."

Andie put her face in her hands, as if that would keep her from hearing or picturing the scene. In Boston to premiere his play that criticized U.S. wealth and warmongering, then attempting to board a plane home with a set of manicure tools in his carry-on. Akeem Desmond, a distinguished man in his seventies, black, mentioned for the Nobel, hustled to a waiting police car. Her underarms felt damp with sudden sweat.

"It's been weeks, I'm pretty sure," Elliott said. "For questioning, they claim. I've heard that in person Sylvester is usually polite and courtly. To me, that makes him creepier."

Andie let her hands drop to her lap. "This much money," she said, "would buy me nearly 3 years to do my own work. I'd like to see what either one of you would do with the same offer."

But she couldn't face 3 years wide open to do her own work. It was too scary. Her bold start hadn't lasted one full day. Then she'd managed to hurt her hand.

"I can't take this job," she said, "and I can't turn it down." On the news as recently as last week, she'd seen Sylvester, smarmy and threatening: saying, "this Caribbean man's brand of dangerous talk requires a gag..."

Her throat locked, fighting imagined pressure. Desmond had had the guts to speak out at least; whereas she'd gagged herself, let years pass without doing a single piece of her own work. There lay the source of her long-running disgust with herself, or some of it anyway.

Grunting with the strain of getting up, Marian went over and put the hot coil back in her teacup. This room, at least, was comforting: Marian's homey embracing style. The tatty old armchair gave off the almond smell of her health brew. It'd be nice to stay on in this space, sitting quietly, instead of going back to work in her own. Her room felt full of straight lines and hard surfaces; nothing she did seemed to make it more inviting. Marian was talking: "Have you asked your friend Otis what he thinks about you signing on to work for a rabid segregationist?" Her friend Otis, who she could no longer flirt with, since Marian had hopelessly fallen for him.

"Segregation is over, Marian. Billy is an old man, won't be in the Senate forever."

"When is it they want to know?" Marian's tea was boiling so hard you could hear it across the room, like pasta cooking. It would be difficult enough to do this job; she couldn't stand it if everybody was going to be against her.

"I think I have a few days."

"Have you already decided?"

"No." Which was true. Sitting with Tripp, she'd felt only shock after shock. She cast an eye at Elliott, his hard-set expression, jutting chin: no let-up in his stubborn opposition. "Don't judge and condemn me yet," she said, getting to her feet. "It hasn't even been an hour since this was sprung on me."

Her wrist rested on the side of the tub in an ice-packed towel. It felt good: the warm bath, the ice-bathed arm, not to mention being home in the middle of the afternoon. Her arm needed babying, *she* needed babying, to get her bearings after the last 2 days, as well as some time to think, to steel herself to tell Tripp no. That was the only acceptable course, so really there was no need to think.

What she should have asked Marian was about sudden electric surges hitting you out of nowhere. And sudden bizarre lust... She wanted those first surges of good feeling, in the moonlight and then in the studio, to come again, but without the weird backwash of dog-faces and debased sex beside a tennis court. Whatever had produced those first moments felt huge, she wanted to turn herself over to it, let it break her out of her tight mental container into the full-color open air where everyone else seemed to live.

As a child was when she'd been happiest, most confident. Eight years old, at a theatre in London's West End, her parents and their friends making a fuss over her at intermission: she'd felt heated by all the eyes on her, warmed, like a berry ripening. Now *that* was sexy; and she'd sensed it, almost known it, at the time.

Being her parents' child had been far too delicious: the glow of their extraordinary attention, and then the sophisticated nomadic life the three of them had led through Zack's import business. Those years, the love, not to mention all the room service, the jungle riverboats, silk traders, streets roofed like tunnels, all the swarthy men, turbaned men with their dark watchful eyes, so much beauty and intensity, had ruined her for ordinary living.

She was drifting: the three of them in India... Her dad, Zack...she loved calling him that...had been buying rugs on that trip. The air, rich with smells, had wrapped around her the moment they'd stepped off the plane onto heat-softened tarmac. She sat up in the tub, water sloshing. She'd almost let it happen again: her memories, the sweet drug of back-then, slipping over her, fogging out everything else. It had to stop, especially now that she was alone.

But she could hear the sound of her footsteps in the halls of that big old hotel in Delhi, long marble corridors where, at almost eleven, she'd been too sophisticated to run. And the view from the window that first morning: those gardeners below in the yard of the hotel, one cutting roses, his head wrapped in a rag turban. And on the street, a man on the corner frying big puffed bread-things, big as a soccer ball, in hot oil, the tall bendy neck of a camel swaying over the crowd. The women in saris, grown-up women with their bare stomachs showing.

Zack was still sound asleep, Mom taking a shower as Andie tiptoed in from her adjoining bedroom. With the window slats closed, their room was dim, shadowy grey-white, like the tangled sheets. She needed to tell them to look out the window. He was breathing slow and loud. One bare grown-up foot, all its bumps and hard places, stuck out from under the sheet. He looked too big for the bed, and his hair was standing up from the way the side of his face was pushed down into the pillow. She touched...no, almost touched the sole of his foot with the tip of her finger. Close enough to feel warmth coming from him, but not to wake him up.

Her mother stepped out of the hotel bathroom, enveloped in steam, her hair wrapped up in a towel. She had on her little satiny robe. "Hey, sweetie," she said. "You're all dressed."

Zack rolled over on his back then, stretched his arms out wide, reaching past both edges of the narrow double bed. "Good morning," he said. Then seeing Andie: "How's my baby?"

She pointed to the window. "Did you look out there?"

"Not yet," he was yawning. Mom sat down next to him on the bed, unwinding her hair. Zack put a hand up and started rubbing her back, his fingers going up and down the long dipped-in part where the backbone was. His eyes closed as if he was going back to sleep. Andie watched his hand rise and fall, slow and lazy, felt almost as if she was going back to sleep too, or swinging in a slow swing that carried her up so high...she felt the motion sway her insides.

Then Zack was getting out of the bed, Mom going to her suitcase, everybody all at once getting ready to go. They were exciting, her parents, none of her friends had parents who were exciting. She was proud of them.

"Little darling," Dad had said as he passed her, hitching up his pajama bottoms, giving her a sideways kiss on her forehead. She could feel the imprint of the kiss, coolish and damp in the middle, warmer around the edges.

As if waking, she found herself motionless in her tub. The bathwater, gone chilly again, curved downward ever so slightly along the line where it touched her skin, making a long oval around the knee that emerged into the air. The surface lay still, as if she were installed here permanently, entrapped in a clear gel. She might as well be. She *was* stuck, glued to her hometown, wasting her life in memories. She'd let herself fall back into it; it was irresistible, seductive.

She again reached for that moment: soothing low light of the hotel room, the window louvers, sleepy rhythm of Zack's hand, her mother's vast calm. She had never been at such ease with anyone else, friend or boyfriend. The scene fell away from her, fading out. Here she sat, in water she'd let get cold. She couldn't get it back: the feel of being there, the cozy, and yet reckless, sensation of the three of them, folded into each other until she wasn't even a separate creature.

# 4

Ordinary, complacent midmorning light shone on the driveway gravel and the dirt-patched yard. With her uninjured left hand, Andie managed to shift into drive. Two days, and she still couldn't paint with this sprained wrist. Neither was she going to stay out here in silence.

Her mind, in increasing ferment, kept flickering weird images at her. Last night she'd dreamed a wall of water, twenty feet tall and teeming with creatures, had rushed across the neighboring field and wrapped around her house, trapping her inside, leaks starting to push in through the cracks and corners. Whatever had fired her up to tackle the umbrella had completely turned on her.

She hit the gas, hungry for noise and people, the usual back-and-forth in the hall, somebody other than herself to pay attention to.

Up ahead at road's edge a golf cart putt-putted slowly as the driver scanned the edge of the piney rough for his ball. In only minutes she was going to walk back into the room, look at the canvas and know in an instant it wasn't anything special. Or worse, that it was good and she was faced with having to finish it without wrecking it. She could still turn around and go back home.

She was procrastinating, taking the long way, driving these streets she already knew by heart, the picturesque little walls, oaks big with low-hanging branches, the order of the houses and who lived in a lot of them, parents of her friends who'd grown up and moved away, couples whose love for her since childhood still reached like a generous protective canopy over her head, though she never saw them except in passing. In her family, it was the parents, not the kid, who'd moved away; off to London, once they'd finished giving her a quasi-American childhood. She was the one still hanging around, as if there were something in particular to wait for.

Almost there. the two-block "rough" side of town: the laundromat, the carwash, the beer joint, the studio building. This was where she belonged, in today's dark mood anyway, with the night's grisly images batting against the underside of her brain.

She pulled into the parking lot. At the door to her space, she fumbled for the key. Through the glass, she could see the easel, from behind. Turning away, she leaned her back against the doorjamb, facing out into the hall. She could actually feel her heart beat. Ridiculous.

Across the hall: Otis busily at work toward the back of his space. If he looked up… But he didn't. A scorched smell leaked into the hall from the chemicals he used. She had no business interrupting anybody who was working.

She shouldered open her door, keys in hand, walked across the high-ceilinged space to stand in front of it: wide yellow arc. A taste like a lemon zinc cough drop came up in her mouth, then a rush of hope that seemed to go all the way to the top of her head. She wanted to cry with gratitude that it could at least do that, could evoke in her mouth the sharp tang. The piece wasn't close to finished. She needed to suggest more about the space underneath: the tight nylon should not only shelter, but needed to bulge with the force of whatever it was hiding.

Her eyes skipped from rib to rib, checking each of the graduated shadows. Wait, what was she seeing? Blue? Hints of an undercoat of cobalt blue. She'd have sworn she hadn't touched this canvas with blue, but it seemed part of what was giving the picture such force.

Her hand throbbed. She sat down at the table. She was scared to pick up a brush. And she hadn't begun the sketches for the Virginia school. In her current state, those too could turn into images that scared her, if an umbrella could.

She checked messages, wrote down numbers.

Didn't reach for a brush.

When she was a kid first starting to draw, being an artist

seemed sure to be the best possible way anyone could ever live. A hurt arm couldn't have slowed her. Sitting on her narrow bed in her little room, which was itself like one big window seat with a slanted roof, an alcove with a door, she drew over and over what she could see from her window: the oak tree, the gutter pipe and the overhang of the house next door, the abandoned tricycle on the bit of sidewalk visible in the Sanders' front yard. Often, before she drew, she'd sit and stare, and then was shocked to see that 15 minutes or half an hour had passed. Curled up there on the bed, in her own room, her sketchpad propped against one knee, she felt surrounded by a layer of soft air as big as the house itself. It felt good against her skin. She'd wanted to draw even the air, to pull everything in the world closer to her with her pencil.

Simply trying to feel that way didn't work. The yellow canvas...she was scared of it. Facing the window behind her, it seemed to gather in the light from the room, leaving the rest of the space dim. Fatigue drifted over her. She could almost see a cloud of tiredness in the room: a fine haze of dust, familiar as her pocketbook. When did she start living inside this smog?

Rousing, uncertain how long she'd sat, she got to her feet, flung her keys onto the table and crossed the hall, pressed herself, as if imploring, against Otis's glass the way she'd done a thousand times. Pain ran the length of her forearm.

Finally he turned and waved, his welder's glasses pushed up on his forehead.

"What'd you do?" Otis said, coming to the doorway, nodding at her bound arm. His T-shirt, from Jimmy Walter's where he tended bar, stretched tight across his chest. You could faintly see his dark skin, almost African black, through the weave.

"I don't think a doctor wrapped that," he said, smiling his slow way, certain of his gorgeousness. Marian suffered torments over him, never mind her 52 years to his 31; he never seemed to notice her longing.

"It's not a fracture. But I can't use my hand."

He shook his head, giving her a dubious once-over. She looked down the wide cavernous hallway. "Is anybody going to lunch?"

"Baby, it isn't but 10 o'clock."

"I mean after a while."

He nodded. "In the meantime, you might want to look out down the hall. Elliott's model cancelled. You could go sit, get him out of a tight spot."

"I'll check with him."

Otis was turning in his broad-shouldered way back toward his own door. Now was when ordinarily she'd toss back some light reflexive bit of banter. Today that lever wasn't working. Her brilliant moonlight flicker of excitement, and what followed, seemed to have shorted everything.

She found Elliott standing in his doorway talking with his next-studio neighbor, lanky, bare-midriffed Caitlin. She and Elliott up ahead in the hall, both so tall and slender, looked attenuated, a pair of Giacometti figures. For a second, she'd hoped it was Caitlin's boyfriend; she always felt cheerful, exhilarated even, after running into Tim. Elliott started shaking his head no before she'd finished her modeling offer. "Andie, the class is tonight and it's life drawing. Nude."

She felt an excited tremor and then another, like a wave, close behind it. "I'll do it!" She started at hearing herself. What was she thinking?

"You sure?" Elliott looked worried.

But the thought of modeling made her brazenly confident; she could feel her eyes sparkling hot. Her vision did a funny jump. She imagined herself rising, bodily, in a slow-turning spiral upward toward the hallway ceiling. She put out a hand to steady herself against the wall.

"Andie, I'd be happy to have you sit if you're sure." His voice had a note of authority. Muscles deep in her gut quaked inward and down, squeezing out her breath. She could feel herself pulling the sweaty band of his boxers down. She blanked the image, made her face hold steady. She wasn't, had never been, attracted to Elliott. This is not me.

"Keep in mind," he said, "that someone you know could turn up in the class." Such a grave tone, and he was trying not to look shocked. Of course anyone who knew her would be surprised. She'd never once modeled nude in school. She was the girl who was a virgin until first semester senior year of college, though her suitemates wouldn't have guessed.

The thought of standing naked in front of a random group sent another ripple through her body. "If some surprise visitor shows up," Andie said, forcing her breath to slow, "I'll be sitting pretty. Completely at ease in the world."

# 5

Her white terrycloth robe belted loosely around her, she walked in a zigzag path amongst the seated students and their sketchpads to the model platform at the front of the room. Here was the stool. Sweating under her arms, she let the robe drop off her shoulders, to the floor, the shock of air against her breasts, her whole body.

She tried to kick the robe aside; it wouldn't kick, only an arm of it moved. She started to bend over, thought better of it. The varnish of the stool felt coolish and sticky against her ass; she gazed off into the distance as she settled herself, as if this were something she normally did and knew exactly how to do.

Her peripheral vision extended as far as the knees, the laps of people in the front: jeans, sweats, spattered khakis. She glanced once high enough to catch the glint off a pair of glasses, a fiftyish woman, graying. There might well be someone she knew in this crowd, some friend of her family's: that thought should not be exciting, yet she wanted to press down, rub herself against the stool. Her nipples were hard, and her breath: she couldn't make it slow. She glanced fast across the faces; no one she recognized. Good. She was relieved to be relieved.

"That's perfect, Andie," Elliott's voice, she couldn't see him, "that glance to the side. Let's hold that for 10 minutes," his voice carefully level and matter-of-fact. Her breath started to ease. The difficult part was over. The student she could see well from this angle was seated at the side of the room: a strawy-haired man in his sixties. His eyes followed the line of her hip, his hand inching along the paper. He never, while she watched, took his eyes off her. For him, she moved, ever so slightly, lifting her chest. His lips parted. He noticed. She didn't dare look at Elliott.

Not since her mid-twenties had she stood naked in front of anyone but Charlie. This airy bare-skin feeling brought back their earliest months, maybe that time had only been weeks. Days after the breakup, she'd gone back to his house once, knowing he wouldn't be there, to get her belongings and leave her key. She'd gathered up underwear, jeans and T-shirts, books, her shampoo. She'd walked room to room, run her finger down the stack of four sensible ironware plates on the kitchen shelf, looked into the freezer, shook the half-empty half-gallon of vanilla double cream to feel the rattle of the serving spoon he kept inside. In the den, she'd stood at the side of his recliner, pressed her face against the fabric of the headrest that almost held the smell of him. That had been one of the moments when her face seemed to open from pressure inside, like two heavy doors, letting out a gush of grief she couldn't put a name to.

"Okay, Andie, that's 10. Give us something different, some sense of motion."

She stood, raised her arms overhead; she'd left the grubby wrist bandage in the back of the room. Clasping her hands together, she leaned backward as if she were stretching and locked into position. This job wasn't difficult, once you got past dropping the robe. She felt shockingly at ease.

But the position hurt. A V-shaped burn from the sides of her neck crept down her back. What had possessed her to hold her arms overhead? Her head, tilted slightly back, was starting to feel as if it was going to snap off. She stared up at her hands, two dangling white fish. This was the posture of someone imploring: let me paint, don't make me paint.

"Time's up," Elliott said, just when she'd thought he'd left and gone off to have a beer. "Andie, take a break, while I talk a minute." Her arms dropped. She half-expected to see them lying in pieces around her on the floor. She hoisted her robe, dusty on one side, over her shoulders, hurried out the door, into the hall, as if she'd find her normal self out here, walking around waiting for her.

Her studio was four doors down on the left. Through Otis's glass wall, she could see the dim shape of a large metal figure, vaguely human. On the other side, Marian had a light on over one of her Caribbean scenes. The light needed repositioning; the bottom of the canvas disappeared into shadow. Although the encircling dark made the pale blue seascape more compelling. But who am I to judge? She'd demoted herself from artist to model. She envied the passion of the others who rushed from day jobs or night jobs, eager to get here and work. Except for the blip of umbrella frenzy, she'd turned dry as an old can of house paint. She thirsted for that feeling of eagerness.

She was coming up to her own door. Out of habit, she groped for her keys, her fingers finding only terrycloth. A few teasers hung on her display wall, a portrait no longer needed when the couple separated, two sure-sell spec golf scenes. The closest canvas, deep green grass, red sweater. You could look at it and feel the dampness in the air. You could hear the click of the ball. It was good work. Yet these images couldn't haunt you. Not because golf was the subject, but because they all had a neatly formulated look. These pictures looked complete, tame, smoothed off at the edges. They gave no hint of the mysterious.

Footsteps behind her, aimed her way. She looked back over her shoulder, her chin brushing the collar of the robe. The strawy-haired old guy was coming toward her, a purposeful smile on his face. "You had the same idea I did," he said. "Walk along and see some of the art in these gallery windows."

"Feels good to move." She felt again that slight thrust of chest that she'd thrown in his direction; she avoided his eyes.

"I would imagine," he said. He stood tilted back, as if he were seriously studying one of her golf paintings. "And I was wondering," he said. "If you and I might have dinner some time. I'd love to take you out somewhere real elegant."

Real elegant: the suggestiveness of that...

"The Carolina Hotel," he said. "Or wherever you want to go. Sky's the limit."

No question: he thinks I'm a hooker or the closest thing to it.

Simplest to play innocent. "I appreciate your inviting me..."

"Of course I can understand a lady like yourself being busy," he said. "But if you should get free..."

"Thanks." She should be offended. Instead she was excited, disturbingly aroused.

"Andie." Elliott stood at his door, down at the other end of the hall.

"Coming." One quick glance: she could see an edge of the umbrella canvas from the back, sticking out from behind the wall that divided her gallery space from her studio, a reminder that it was waiting in the near-dark. She clutched the robe around her and hurried back to where Elliott waited, the man following, as if casually browsing the studio windows behind her.

She could feel Elliott trying on and discarding things he could say to her. "That pose didn't look too comfortable. I almost called time early."

"Good of you," she said, breezing past him. "This time I'm going to do it the easy way." She was taking charge of this modeling business. She didn't slow down. She marched straight to the front, through the scattering of seated students. Throwing the robe onto the stool, she flopped down on her side on the second tier of the platform, lay back against the pile of canvas tarp and a mildewed pillow, lolling, gazing at them at their eye level. A Rubens pose, and she had the rounded body for it. She looked out across their faces, half a dozen women, three men and over at the side, Elliott, who said, hesitantly: "Let's give this one 10 minutes. And keep your pencils moving. Don't stop to think about how a hand or elbow is supposed to look, just let your pencil record line and shadow."

It wasn't a Rubens pose she was thinking of; it was Manet's "Olympia," the naked courtesan, a prostitute, stretched out on fat pillows, wearing only her fluffy high-heeled mules, a dark string tied in a bow around her neck.

Somewhere real nice, the man had said. Sky's the limit. He'd thought she was buyable; the thought sent a surge through her again. She wanted to sit facing them and slowly spread open her legs. Something in her, something altered or new, was urging her to do it! do it! Turn herself inside out for them.

She stopped the racing thoughts, concentrated: Stay perfectly still. Think of anything else. She'd been in school when she first saw "Olympia". Sitting in the dark, hearing the slide projector click, she'd seen the girl arranged on her bed like a gift just unwrapped. Her stomach, round and dimpled, her ankle thick.

Elliott, across the room, had stepped into view. Weird excitement was crawling up through her body. She made herself concentrate on the remembered painting: the girl's calm face, her hair pulled back, the hibiscus tucked behind her ear. Elliott, his back turned to her now, was holding up a student's drawing, talking.

She could be that courtesan in the Manet, arranged on her daybed, naked. A whore, the deepest core of her available to anyone. Pleasure rushed through her, turning the room almost dark.

Her eyes came into focus, sweat popping out all over. She'd stopped short, she'd made no sound. She ventured a frantic glance, to see what they'd noticed. The old guy who'd followed her was watching, touching the end of his pencil to his lip, the edge of his teeth. One older woman looking intently away. Thinking these thoughts, lying here naked…

She grabbed for the robe, so excited she ached and, at the same time, horrified: She'd turned into that animal with her face, the image in the car window.

Elliott turned. "Okay Andie," he said, "That's fine. We're done. You can get dressed." Her legs shook as she stepped down from the stand.

# 6

Afternoon light hit full force across her big studio table; the sun had moved out from behind the old Beacon Printery building. Her wrist still out of commission, she'd tended to business, returned all phone calls, stirred up some interest in the golf pictures from a bank branch in Hilton Head. So now what? The dust on her windows looked awful; and white drips of pigeon shit, how had she not noticed? With her good left hand, she could clean the crud off the glass; find some newspaper and a blue squirter and set to it. It wouldn't be a total waste of time; the physical work would be good for her, restore her to some semblance of normal.

In only a couple of hours, the studio was clean down to its paint-spattered bones. She'd managed to do the scrubbing in the same room with the canvas, though moving near it felt unsettling, as if she were sweeping around a dead body. She headed down the hall to take Archie's workbench vacuum cleaner back to him before it did more harm; it had sucked up the tape of a cassette a foot away, eating it as if it were a string of spaghetti. If she complained, he'd tell her to update to a CD player; being a cabinetmaker, he worshipped good tools. Otis back behind his glass was bent over something. Goggle-free, he was thus available to talk. He caught her eye, came to the door.

He nodded toward her wrist. "You still wearing that thing?" The edges of the arm wrappings were dark with paint dust and grime from all her cleaning, never mind that she'd used her other hand. A grease spot on the loosened top layer looked like food, or linseed oil. "That's like the rag of a blanket my sister's baby drags around to suck on."

"I was doing some cleaning."

"If there were anything much wrong with your wrist," he said, "it would need a whole lot better wrapping than that. That mess you rigged up can't be giving any support."

"How about a little sympathy, Otis?"

"I'm sympathetic," he said, "whatever it is that's ailing you. Going over to Caitlin's in a little bit?"

"To play volleyball? Have you been listening to me? The wrist?"

"You don't have to play. Just hang out. Keep us company."

Of course. I can spend a few minutes with Tim.

The grass was damp under her legs at Tim and Caitlin's place. Potato salad and chips and a charred hot dog had slid together in the center of the flimsy paper plate. Three people, new to the studio, sat around her, talking about the town's various garage apartments. A smoky meat smell hung over the yard from the grill. She'd been here an hour, but Tim had been dashing back and forth, in and out of the back door, doing things with the ice chest and the charcoal fire, then vanished from sight. She'd have looked silly and obvious trotting after him, but she so badly wanted a hit of his warmth, his heft, to stop feeling so adrift.

From the other side of the house came a mock coyote howl, a child's trailing laughter, one of his nephews. That was where she'd find him. She got to her feet, balancing the plate with her good hand, rounded the corner to the front, where Tim galloped and whooped across the yard carrying a toddler piggyback. "Batman!" the child called between jouncing peals of laughter. Again: "Batman!"

Making a big circle, Tim loped back to the front porch, lowered the boy to the ground and picked up the next kid, an older one, a four-year-old peeping over the wall of shoulder. Turning, Tim caught sight of her, walked to meet her, still trundling the kid. He was graceful for such a big square-ish guy; she'd seen him sling a leg over his motorcycle and crank it in one smooth movement, then take off like a low-flying bird. "Hey there, Ms. Andalusia."

"You're on uncle duty," she said.

"Playing at it." Of course it would be play for him.

"Looks like fun." Bland, boring remark. She always got stupid around him, never mind that she had no romantic ambitions.

"Yeah." He grinned and his face lighted the way the briquettes had when he'd stirred up the embers.

She wanted to tell him what had happened: waking in the night, the modeling, the rushes of sensation with a sexual charge…

She sucked in a breath. "So…" she said.

He was waiting, sprawling black eyebrows ever-so-slightly raised.

But of course it was impossible: even if she knew how to start into it or could say anything with this kid staring at her. Much too intimate: he's Caitlin's boyfriend.

"I wasn't going to come," she said, with a nod toward her wrist, her excuse for everything. "Otis reminded me I didn't have to touch a volleyball."

"I'm glad he convinced you." He seemed so at ease saying mundane ordinary things: no pressure to do better. Anyway, he probably wouldn't understand such difficulties. He didn't seem to second-guess himself.

"Couldn't miss your cooking." I should have stayed on the other side of the house, or not come at all.

The child hammered his heels against Tim's ribs: "Go, horsey!"

"Horsey's taking a break." To Andie: "You need to come out and have supper with us some night when I'm doing my specialty chili."

Not too late to blurt something out, ambiguous so the kid wouldn't notice. To say: I'm being abducted, Tim, from inside.

But now the topic was growing a tall hedge around it. "That'd be great," though she didn't love the thought of an evening at home with the two of them. She'd feel extra, an intruder. He shifted the weight of the boy, resettled him. His eyes were unnervingly warm. His heavy beard, close-shaven and yet such smooth fair skin, so that his complexion was like pepper in cream. The back of her good hand brushed slow against his cheek. She snatched it back.

I didn't mean to. Her heart was beating at emergency rate. She still felt the contact on the skin of her hand. The kid scowled at her, pressed his chin possessively into Tim's shoulder.

But Tim, a toucher, apparently saw nothing amiss.

Her heart wouldn't slow down. "Horsey," she said. The word came out husky. "I think you better go. Your rider is in a hurry."

He gave her face a careful looking-over, then seemed to put his own questions aside. With a grin and a whinny, he loped safely out of her reach.

At home post-party, Andie stood in the bright fluorescent bathroom light, undid the safety pin and started to unwind. As if taking this wrapping off would untangle whatever was going on: you can't go around fondling people. Not like that.

The layer of bandage underneath startled her, it was fresh-looking, relatively, an even eggshell-brown. She lifted her wrist to her nose and smelled the dangling rag: warm and soiled as a dishtowel. She unwound it into the trash.

What could Tim have told her anyway? How could he know anything? He was 23 years old. She'd just wanted to be near him.

She flexed the joint: stiff but the swelling was gone. Spreading her fingers: the stretch felt good, still there was a twinge…yes, definitely soreness still. The studio gang didn't take it seriously, that she'd hurt herself in such a vital place. Did they think she was faking? Or exaggerating?

She didn't feel ready to go back to work yet. For once, she could imagine becoming as the lilies of the field: no sewing or spinning. That would make a nice dream: turning into a stalk of white blooms with such a light sweet perfume. A flower, not a primitive woman-faced beast. She felt again the prickle of Tim's cheek across the back of her hand. Nothing so strange about an affectionate pat, except not knowing she was doing it.

What she needed was a vacation, away from people. It had been at least 2 years since she'd taken a substantial break. Plus her hand still wasn't right, whatever Otis thought. It felt tingly, the fingers too red. If there was any part of herself she knew, it was this hand. It needed another day, just to be sure. Or 2 days, to relax and sort things out.

Her bare foot on the pedal, Andie braked down to 30 for another of the crossroads towns. She loved the old brick buildings in the business districts; they were sweet-looking, the lines inexact as if they were home-made. It was an old-fashioned highway, this back road to the coast, only two lanes wide and winding. Though around the gateway to the military base she'd seen the sleazy "adult" establishments. Another coming up on the right: "Exotic Dancers, Private Rooms," the sign said, in front of a rundown house with boarded windows.

The beach was close now; she smelled the salt, felt the heavier weight of the dampness in the air. She flexed the fingers of the hand she'd sprained, and the image flashed again: the canvas, its acid yellows that could burn an image in the very air of the room, peel veneer off the cabinet doors down to the raw pine. She wasn't going to finish it; who was she kidding? Getting it done was less likely than ever; the longer she waited the truer that was.

My life is nothing…the thought jabbed at her from nowhere…not even failed. I haven't turned out. Haven't begun.

She steeled herself against hopelessness. I'm going to figure things out, get a fresh start.

She propped her elbow in the frame of the open window, held her hand out in the spring air and let it wash between her fingers. A blond shirtless boy, nineteen maybe, was walking along the shoulder on the other side, a shell necklace lying across his collarbone. He looked listless. She could fix that: dropping to the gravel in front of him, right here by the road, for anyone to see...

Again! These degrading fantasies kept appearing, as if she'd poked around in pond muck and set the silt and rot to floating. Made her think of the smelly water in a vase where flowers stems had rotted. Nasty. A good thing gone bad. She pictured a sweep of high-gloss white paint rushing across her mind: her trick for dealing with worries.

Up ahead the light was brightening on the metal roofs, the white of frame houses, glare rising by the second. Riding into a town, the long-awaited Swansboro, jump-off point to the Outer Banks' bottom tip. The beach was going to fix everything. The road swung right and all at once sun sparked off water on every side, the blast of light so gorgeous it felt like a high piano note all around her.

She wanted to slow and bask in the sensation but the traffic carried her out onto the bridge. Seagulls skimming and diving off to the right. So much to see and all of it shockingly vivid. *This* was how she'd felt in the studio: exultant! She had hold of it again. Such a swoop of delight, expansiveness...As if airy spaces had opened between her cells, as if she'd physically lightened.

But already it was slipping away: the fullness and ease. She was sinking, colors around her going dull, her vision darkening. Plummeting back into ordinary. Or worse.

She let out a shaky breath. The feeling was gone. And so quickly. She pushed down disappointment. Because, after all, the feeling *had* returned, a trace of it, a few seconds of the unearthly surge of well-being. Tears of gratitude rose in her eyes. Now she knew: it could come back.

A bird, an everyday physical seagull, flapping hard, lifted off the water with a flash of silver in its beak. She wanted to reach a long arm out and help him rise. As if, having felt for an instant such overflowing health, she had the strength to keep birds in the air.

The poor scrounging creature, diving for food over and over. She and the gull had similar work habits, both of them fast moving and steady-at-it. She could slap down an image almost as fast as a rubber stamp: press against ink pad, then onto paper. Presto! A picture. She imagined herself as the stamp, her whole body 3 inches tall, held neck to ankles in the grip of a huge hand: all control of herself given over. A sickish thrill passed through her. Such creepy desire in the wake of the joy, the two wound somehow together.

She forced her mind back to the driving: still on the bridge, in heavy traffic, almost at the island side.

To give up self-control, though, let everything go: there could be relief in that.

The feel of the tires against the pavement abruptly altered as she drove back onto land, the inland side of the barrier island. She pulled in at the first stopping place: Dudley's Marina, selling gas and tackle. Jamming her feet into her worn-to-grey Nikes, she got out, stretched her legs, one and then the other, sturdy old cheerleader calves. The damp air felt divine. She wanted to lie down on it. She yawned a great gaping head-clearing yawn.

Shoelaces dragging – she wasn't going to be here long – she walked around the corner of the store to get closer to the water. Behind the building were the docks where sailboats and yachts were tied. She breathed in the mixed scent of bleached shells and mud, salt, creosote and the fumes from the gas pumps. This was what she had come for, a whiff of this.

The scene out beyond the boats was sky and water and the high white dune on the other side of the channel. A ski boat was passing with two young guys standing up at the helm. Funny to have the urge to draw a place because it smells good. She leaned back against a waist-high oil can somebody had painted Gulf-Stream-blue. Her checkbook was the only paper in her bag; she'd made a point of not bringing a sketchpad. She pulled off the top check, 4437. Drop a 4 and she'd have the balance in her account, about $437. Even if she took the Billy job and used it to travel, she'd never live in the delicious way she had as a child.

The family romance was over. She'd known that for a long time, of course. But the absence of Charlie made every other absence feel tender again. At moments, her solitude felt huge, inescapable, as if she were trapped alone in an empty airplane hangar, even as she sat out here in the sun.

Her hand moved slowly across the wavy pastel of the back of the check, as if she were making a cut with a scalpel. She'd stop at the first flicker from the injured wrist. She roughed in the tops of the distant trees, the edge of the channel, the sand bluff. A light wind was running through the marsh flattening the grass for a second in spots here and there. And the water: moving fast. The tide must be going out.

"Hi there, little lady." A man stood almost at her side, a big guy in canvas boat shoes, his neck and face sunburned a red so dark it hurt her to look at it. Inside his collar, beyond where the line of red stopped, he was white as a hard-boiled egg.

"Hi," she said, turning back to her drawing. "Though you shouldn't address a woman as a little lady." Three swipes and she had the channel marker and the water sweeping past it. "That kind of talk isn't fashionable, you know."

"Is that so?" He had a nice laugh that echoed off the wall and out toward the marsh. "You're full of beans," he said. "I admire that. What are you drawing?"

"All that I survey." She kept her attention on her paper, then on the curve of the marsh, adding a boat that wasn't there and made no sense at all. It was way out of proportion to the rest of the scene. As soon as he was gone she would throw this away and start over.

"That's a large order," he said.

"I'm up to it. Some days."

"I'm Mike Sebastian. I'm bringing my boat up from Georgia."

"I'm Andie Branson. Where are you taking it?" She'd talked to nobody all day except the fast-food drive-through guy who'd said "My pleasure" when she thanked him for the chicken sandwich; she'd wanted to run past the window again just for the friendly voice. For a moment, she could overlook that this man in front of her would probably vote for, even bankroll, Billy Sylvester.

"Just on a joy ride. I'll get up into Virginia, or wherever another couple of days takes me and then I'll turn around and go back. You live right around here?"

"About 3 hours inland."

"Where?" He took off his cap, rubbed his forehead with the other hand, put it back on. His hair was short, sandy grey. He'd be at least in his late fifties. His conversational style was more 1950. Even so, not bad.

"Pinehurst," she said.

"Well, damn. I've been playing golf there for years."

"Lot of golfers in Pinehurst."

"How'd you settle on the back of a filling station as a good place to sit and draw pictures?" She could feel his eyes on her, quick, thorough, touching ever so briefly on her mouth, on what Charlie used to call her "spunky-sexy" compact body.

"I pulled over as soon as I saw the water."

"You could see it better from the deck of the Ne'er Do Well."

She smiled in spite of herself. If this guy were a painter, he'd have produced a whole line-up of yellow umbrellas by now.

"My boat," he said, as if this needed explanation. "Come on out and sit in the stern and have a daiquiri with me. The view's just as good and we have deck chairs. You can't be comfortable leaning on that barrel."

She looked at the way he stood, legs wide apart, his cap pushed back on his head. It would be difficult, if not impossible, to hurt his feelings. Nothing could faze him.

"Okay." She stood up. A little idle conversation would be good, help to settle her.

"Well, damn," he said again. "I didn't think you'd budge."

Checkbook and pencil in hand, Andie walked out onto the long dock, Mike Sebastian leading the way. "Now that boat you see there," he said, pointing to a sailboat down below them. "It hasn't got the deep hull you need. It rolls mighty bad. I wouldn't have it."

"I would. Where's yours?"

He pointed down the dock to the end. "Right there."

The big one. Andie glanced at him to be sure he wasn't kidding. This boat was huge, a long white building parked at the end of the dock. Her eyes traveled from one end to the other, down the row of windows with lined drapes, up to the high white canopy at the top, down to the open deck and the flagpole that pointed off the back. Sleek.

The door to the inside of the boat opened as they stepped aboard, and a wiry black guy in a red and white striped T-shirt came out. "Andie, this is Terrence."

Terrence smiled, flashing a gold front tooth, old-fashioned solid gold, not a rapper-style diamond-studded grill. "Good afternoon to you." In addition to his pirate get-up, he had a Bahamian accent. Only a few minutes ago, she'd been in her own car.

"Hi," she said. He was already on his way, hopping up onto the side of the boat and following the catwalk toward the bow.

"Terrence could have put Magellan out of business if he'd been born a little earlier. He's a one-man crew," Mike said, patting his own stomach with a satisfied air. "I'll go whip us up a strawberry Icee. That suit you all right?"

"Sounds perfect." Andie settled back into the deck chair. The sun felt restful on her face. She should probably put on more sunscreen, but it was too far to go back to the car and get it. She wanted to stretch out here in the sun, langorous as a cat. Waves slopped against the side of the boat from the wake of a passing motorboat out in the waterway. She listened to the water hit and closed her eyes. Ropes squeaked and pulled against metal up in the masts of the sailboats docked nearby, ropes banged against the length of the masts like Chinese wind chimes. She kicked off her shoes, stretched her legs out in front of her. Sitting here reminded her a little of the way she'd felt as a child, traveling with her folks, contentedly led by those two lovebirds to places that turned out to be Morocco or Bombay. Traveling the way they had, it was like flying along above the marsh, their magic threesome buffered by a layer of air against any intrusion.

Mike opened the door and came up onto the deck with the drinks on a round tray. The way he concentrated on not spilling was endearing.

She laughed. "You look like a brochure for a cruise."

The drinks each stood about a foot tall, dazzling pink and full of decorations: parasols, cherries, swizzle sticks, everything on the bar.

"A cruise is what this is," Mike said. He handed her a drink, took one, fell back into his seat, obviously his regular.

The red of the parasol seemed to leap where it bordered the pink. She'd left the umbrella when it was still in such a delicate stage; whatever she'd told herself, it was still possible to ruin it.

That sensation: Here it came again, a rising drone inside her lower back. Gone. But with no rush of joy, no excitement. This time the feeling was quick and faint; she wasn't sure if she'd felt it or merely thought of it. Yet again she felt altered, as if a strange electricity had buzzed up through the seat of her chair.

"Now," he said. "I want to propose a flowery toast." He leaned his head back as if he were preparing carefully for this. He was appealing in his way.

He raised his glass. "To the artist, Andie Branson, who I am honored to welcome aboard."

She felt her gaze warm. "To the captain. I'm happy to be here."

She sipped, then held it away from her and took a breath. For a drink that was dressed as a floozy, it was strong stuff.

"I thought you were fixing us a lady's drink," she said.

"I seem to recall you don't like that word."

Andie smiled, taking another sip. "Thanks for reminding me."

The water and marsh had taken on a gold tinge. "The light is fantastic," she said. She could feel her spirits lifting and lifting. Could be the same rush again, happening slower this time. She could feel an echo of the vibration along the damp backs of her legs.

"I told you this would be a good place to paint a picture. You paint too? Or do you just draw?"

"I paint." A white boat was passing in the distance out on the waterway. The marsh in the foreground blocked her view. All she could see was the deck, the people, the outriggers sailing above the grass.

Mike said, "Do you ever take a ride up the Waterway? Sit and watch the scenery go by?"

"No. Am I about to be invited?"

"Lordy," he said, laughing. "What in the world have I run up on?" His gaze made a quick sweep of her body. Her stomach did a sky-diving free-fall. She gave the parasol in her drink a spin; it sank deeper into the melting pink slush.

Her heart beat audibly. "What you have..." A deep flush was spreading all through her. She didn't feel right. She needed to leave, but didn't stir. She tried to put the scene at a distance: sitting on the boat deck, her turquoise top, sunglasses... Tried to blank her mind with paint. But recklessness was growing, a force massing inside her. Now a rising tide of heat.

He sat with a card player's face, waiting.

"I was sitting there sketching, that's all." The heat... Was it the sensation again? or shock at the thought that was rising... His face had blurred, as if he were behind something, couldn't really see her. "I'll do it," she said, her breath roaring inside her head, the dock and inner wall of the boat gone wobbly all around her.

"A thousand dollars. A day," came out of her mouth, her heartbeat slamming like a fist behind her collarbone. Excitement made her brain roll inside her skull. She gripped the arms of the chair.

He looked her up and down slowly, as if she weren't seeing him doing it, pulling at his lower lip, eyes wandering over her breasts. Billboards had shown balloon-breasted women, waists pinched down to nothing, like on the mud flaps of trucks. He was going to say no.

He said nothing, one foot half out of his boat shoe, blue and purple maps of blood vessels under the skin of his instep. She imagined biting that place, lightly. Her legs trembled, her whole body on the verge of shaking: What have I done?

"Little lady." She could barely hear him. He said, "I believe we're in business."

# 7

The yacht slid sideways away from the dock, Mike up on the bridge steering and calling out directions to Terrence. The strip of water between boat and pilings was widening, three feet, five feet. She could yell: stop! let me off! He'd do it. He would. The deep rumble of the engine came up through the legs of the deck chair, repeating in the back of her throat: thousand-a-day, thousand-a-day… She'd heard herself say it in a sleep-talking voice. Her face hot. There: a man washing the deck of his sailboat; he should throw the bucket of suds over her, shock her back to normal.

She scanned the marina lot trying to catch sight of her car. Barely 20 minutes ago she'd gotten out and stretched, ambled toward the smell of salt water. From the bow, the end of a line flew through the air, casting them loose. This man could be or do anything. And there were two of them, Mike and Terrence, when all her life she'd known not to so much as get into a taxi alone with two strangers. What possessed her?

A monster gear shifted and diesel smoke burbled out of the churning water behind. They were moving, the shoreline sliding past.

A week ago this couldn't have happened. Never in her life…

She pictured her body, bloated, washed up in the marsh grass, her parents' grief, the shock back in Pinehurst on hearing the news. People would think she'd been abducted, they'd never imagine… Her throat tightened. Still she couldn't move; could not call out Stop!

They'd cruised for nearly 3 hours before anchoring, had eaten the steaks that Terrence, who was also apparently the chef, grilled in the open air. The smell of lighter fluid and singed fat hung around the back of the boat; it was dark, no moon, almost no breeze.

"You better put on some bug spray," Mike said. "The no-see'ums have already started their season. They will eat you alive before you know it." Andie took the can, sprayed until her arms and legs were wet. The big live oaks on the shore beyond the marsh were silhouettes, barely visible. She could see his face, deeply shadowed, in the glow of the boat's parking light. He hadn't touched her once since helping her down into the boat, not a single accidental brush; his careful distance only made the tension build. From below came a faint muffled sound of Terrence clattering around, the rest of the boat empty and silent. She liked it when he made noise, so she knew where he was. They sat for minutes not saying much. Her legs felt jumpy. She could get out of this. If she wanted to. He'd still let her go if she insisted, take her back to the dock, unless he was a criminal, and he didn't seem to be.

"You have kids?" She hesitated. "A wife?"

"Sort of."

"You don't want to talk about it," she said, sorry she'd asked. She didn't want to hear about a wife.

He laughed. "Are you asking me or telling me?"

"No, it's okay. I mean, whatever." If he were single, his manner would be more current, he'd be updated.

More silence. He should grab her, or she him. The need was pressing on her.

Finally: "You've probably heard the same two or three stories," he said, "a lot of times."

"No. I never did anything like this before."

He frowned, no doubt assuming she was lying. The way the light hit him she could only see half his face. A slight breeze as the boat swung on its anchor made his hair lift back from his forehead, as if somebody, his mother, had brushed it back. She felt like a child herself, in the wrong place, on the back of a runaway horse or a wild animal.

"So you took one look at me," he said, "and you decided you

wanted to go into business."

"I don't know what's possessed me." The sound of Terrence from below had stopped. She imagined him standing somewhere close in the dark, without her knowing.

"I guess artists have a pretty hard row to hoe, moneywise."

"Tell me about it."

"So money's the reason then?"

"Maybe it's what my high school history teacher used to call the surface cause. You know, the way slavery supposedly was for the Civil War. With a surface cause like that, who needs to think about the ones underneath?"

"You don't talk like a hooker." He stretched his legs out in front of him. He had a reasonable body: hard-looking, except for the sag under his chin. His face looked tired. She felt a sneaking fondness for him, uneasy; they were both caught in this. Time for him to do something: make his move. She wanted to get to the mindless sex, ease the craving to be fucked senseless, fucked into oblivion. Since when did she want senseless oblivion?

"Well, I'll tell you something," he said. "I never paid before. Not outright, anyway. I have no idea how hookers talk."

She laughed. Her spirits jagged upwards. After all, she was single, a free agent; she wasn't betraying anyone. It was only sex, what she was doing. But for pay! The thought spun her downwards again.

"Suppose I'd said 'no' to your offer," he said.

"I was starting to get worried." By now she'd have unpacked and gotten comfortable in a hotel room, private, her own safe space. She saw herself slipping out of that room, though it was late, going downstairs to the bar, telling herself it was just to get a Diet Coke. In a hotel at least she'd have been able to get away, if she wanted to get away.

She glanced once around the deck: nobody there except the two of them. When he wasn't talking, he was blank-faced, unnerving, his legs a vague whiteness in the dark.

The water made a steady whisper, washing around the back of the boat. She wanted to calm down, feel ordinary desire, not this strange queasy need: to be taken over. "Do you usually make this trip by yourself?" she said. "Up and down the waterway?" Her voice sounded normal.

"Terrence and me. Sometimes a full staff, and guests." He lifted out of his chair for a second, to get a look at the anchor rope. "I use the boat a lot for business."

"I guess that lets you write it off."

"Well, sure."

"I write off turpentine and rags."

"And trips to the beach to draw pictures," Mike said.

"I hadn't thought of that."

He shook his head. "You need a manager. For both your businesses." He massaged his hand, the web of flesh between one thumb and forefinger. He'd said he was a manufacturer, kitchen appliances.

She cleared her throat. "Does your business have a lot of pressure to it?"

"It does."

"Like people not buying enough stoves, or deliveries that get there late?"

"And people wanting too large an order at once. Maybe I'll quit and take up painting. I used to like that sort of thing as a kid."

"Talk to me before you do anything rash."

He turned and looked out across the water behind him. All she could see out where he was looking was the light from the boat glimmering on the crests of the choppy water. Little fingernails of light, and beyond stood solid darkness. The conversation had flickered out again, her stomach muscles tightened; her own excitement, its strangeness, frightened her.

He turned back toward her, his mouth already open to speak. Here it comes, she thought.

"Well," he said. "Shall we…?" But it wasn't a question.

She picked her way down the stairs into a lower hall, Mike behind her. This passageway felt stuffy, not enough air down here. He didn't turn on the light. A door up ahead was ajar; she headed toward the strip of moonlight from the windows of that cabin. His arm came around from behind, stopped her short. She stood still, both arms now pinned. His breath touched her neck. He smelled like wet straw, like rope. They were still in the narrow hall, so cramped she felt suddenly as if trapped under a building. She tried to move the two of them into the bedroom; he held her tight. Nothing she could do. A surge of excitement, and she felt herself give up, slide into abandon, her insides loose and swollen; I'm coming apart.

He pushed her toward the door, then lifted her; and she flopped over his arms as if she were something lifeless, arms dangling, one thump of pain in the wrist as it knocked against the jamb of the door.

He lay the top half of her across the bed, legs hanging off, her knees almost touching the floor. His hands left her; she waited motionless the split-second until he was on her again, sliding up the skirt that hit her mid-thigh. Nothing there but the white strip of thong. Another wait: make me wait. Then her pants slid down. The air felt alive, touching her. Her breath came out almost a groan.

From behind her the quick rip of a condom wrapper. Her face pressed forward, almost at the wall. If he pushed hard, she would hit it.

"Do it," she said.

He slapped her ass with his hand.

Not hard. Just hard enough.

Then she felt him go in.

Her eyes opened, searched the dark room, Mike asleep three feet away on the second bed; with his face slackened, she wouldn't have recognized him.

Out on this boat. She waited, expecting herself to fly into action. to jump up from here, scramble into clothes, jerk him awake and tell him to keep his money, take her back to her car. And no, tomorrow wouldn't be soon enough: take me home now.

But she didn't move.

Instead, her dream rolled over her: A dog was exploring the sidewalk in front of the studio, thin legs trotting, sharp ears alert, walking between its owners. The animal darted this way and that, tags jingling from the collar; she'd felt a pressure at her own throat, the tug of the leash as she'd planted her weight. She was low, close to the pavement that glinted in the sun. A sudden oily feel to the air brought her up short. There! the crumpled bag on the pavement near the wall, crumbly-rich smell coming out in gusts as she nosed at the paper, her rear legs wide, shoulders tense. Pain pressed up from the base of her hand; she must have waked then, the weight of her head on her sprained wrist.

She looked at the length of herself under the sheet, sunk so deep into the mattress that her lower half made only the slightest rise in the cover. In the quiet, she could imagine not being here; she'd never come here at all.

Mike, asleep on his back, made a snuffling sound and turned on his side, away from her. She hated him. Best to get away from here this minute, get off this boat, swim to the bank, slog through a mile of marsh; she could, if she weren't held here needing to do it again, finish it…be used up, consumed.

She held perfectly still, fought off the need. So quiet she was bodiless; that was better, safer; now she was nothing but eyes, a gaze that traveled around the room, round the ceiling, out the dark window, moving without limit until her eyelids started to close and the tight ball of lust let go and she finally drifted back toward sleep.

Andie sat cross-legged on top of the padded engine case at the back of the boat, waiting for Mike to draw a card. "Your turn," she said, not bothering to suppress her hostility. They were playing gin rummy and drinking, the two piles of cards, three-masted sailing ships on the backs, sat in front of Andie's bare feet. Mike had pulled his chair up in front of her perch on the stern, as if he were dragging a chair to a table. She pictured Leger's Card Players, the human figures made of cylinders and pipes; a cold, ominous image. This trip was an illness she'd come down with that was going to run its course in a couple of days. She didn't know what else to think. She'd gotten one thing clear, though: what invaded her in the studio hadn't been any doing of God, nothing divine. Instead she'd had, was having, some kind of emotional crash. Brain hormones gone awry, landing her here.

Mike took a swallow of his drink, spit the ice back into the glass, adjusted the waist of his faded shorts.

"It's not like this is chess, you know," she said. She'd fallen into a sarcastic tone with him. Her plan was to coast through this, as if all were normal, as if she were capable of quitting at any time; then she'd streak for home, untouched by any of it. Beneath that intention, though, the hunger was probably lying in wait, for the feel of being taken over, as if that would lead to something good.

"This is gin rummy," Mike said, "on the deck of a vessel, which is at least as worthy of contemplation as chess." He slapped down a card. "I'm starting to think this might really be your first time." He shot her an amused glance, affectionate almost; she saw it coming and glanced away. "A pro," he said, "wouldn't mention anything funny or odd about what I like."

Andie laughed. "I see. Well, maybe I'll get the hang of it after a while."

"Maybe not. Your go."

She picked up a red jack, put down a three of clubs.

Perhaps she'd had a sort of orgasm in the studio. Some weird spontaneous variation. Maybe she'd been going around desperately ravenous, needier than she knew; and this of all places is where she happened to strike. And yet it felt inevitable: that she would have found her way to this place, this position.

Terrence came down the ladder. "What's for lunch?" Mike said to him, without looking up.

"Fresh salmon, Cap'in." He had such a lilting accent, her fellow slave. Not that Mike was responsible for the kind of sex they were having. She'd set it in motion, asking for money, putting herself in this subordinate position. Such submissiveness wasn't something that she'd ever wanted, at least not beyond the mildest of fantasies. She rolled her weight from one hip to the other, slowly shifted back. She'd needed a break from herself, but not this.

"Salmon sounds first rate," Mike turned to Andie with his same wry smile. "Suit you alright?"

"Absolutely." Terrence had already gone back downstairs. Terrence wasn't pretending: he knew she didn't count, a thought which, oddly, felt relaxing.

Mike studied his cards. Beyond him, close there at the edge of the marsh, sand fiddlers ran across the grey mud, each with one heavy claw held ready, darting up out of a hole, then vanishing again. The air smelled of salt mud. This was the smell that had made her decide to stop and draw, which is what got her here.

She took a sip of the scotch and water Mike had handed her an hour ago, fire on the tongue and it wasn't noon. Little as she'd drunk of it, she felt eased, luxuriant. Mike should be the one who was waiting on her, bringing her what? Chilled satin pillows, a parasol, rosewater, a surfer-dude in a pair of those drawstring shorts, a rime of salt on his sun-warmed hard-muscled shoulders. Once on a college spring-break trip to South Beach, she'd waited in line at a newspaper stand behind a stunning young black woman and the clammy-looking, awestruck man who had obviously hired her. People in line had exchanged meaningful glances, grins. The man didn't seem to notice, repeatedly asking the tall beauty, "Do you want anything? Is there anything I can get you?" That was how it should be.

She rubbed at a spot where sea salt had dried on the waterproof cover. From last night, she had two small bruises, fingerprint-sized, high on one thigh.

The best approach with Mike – maybe it wasn't too late – would be to wrap herself in the queenly manner of that woman long ago in Ecuador. They'd crossed the Guayas River, she and her parents, in the motorboat taxi well before dawn. Lights from the town had made long gleams across the water with dark places for the tangled mats of water hyacinths that looked like clusters of snakes. Across the river in Duran, they'd run to catch the train that was about to leave. Vendors in the shacks around the station were just lighting their stove fires. She had looked into the open window of one of those huts. Inside the room, no bigger than a booth at a fair, two women were starting their cooking. At least one of them was. The younger, darkskinned in a red dress, stood with her arms raised, brushing her hair with long, languorous strokes. Posing before what must be a mirror there on the back of the post, she tilted her head, lifted her chin to let the glossy hair fall straight. She, not the cooking fire, seemed the source of the shack's red-gold glow.

The older woman hoisted a heavy iron pot, straining to get it onto the fire. The harsh light from the overhead lantern made the lines in the woman's face dark; and her hair, pulled back tight, looked brittle. All these years, since she was 11 or 12, Andie had kept the sharp image of that dried hull of face, the thin arm lifting the pot for, no doubt, the ten-thousandth time. She had told herself she would never let that happen; she would stay radiant and alive, simply by will; by concentrating, she would have that fiery light.

"Your go," Mike said. "Come on. Pay attention to me or I'm docking your pay."

"That running gag is getting stale. I don't want to hear it." She swung her legs around, let them hang off the engine case. Her mother was the one who had that fire, had it still.

"Having second thoughts?" Mike said.

"Having thoughts."

"I'm not surprised." He shaded his eyes with his hand and squinted up at her. "We'll call this off if that's what you want."

"No thanks." She wanted none of his warmth. Mike was down in the well of the boat looking at her up on this platform, this auction block. "How do I know you're going to pay?" she said. "I could get stiffed."

He laughed; she could feel his eyes, still trying to charm her. "Where'd you pick up a word like that?" he said.

"In the art business."

"I can imagine. Okay, then," he stretched himself out long to reach into his shorts pocket, took out his checkbook, popped out the point of a ballpoint pen. "Sure you want me to do this?"

"$1000 a day," she said. "We're up to 2 days."

"One day, my friend. It's the nights that count."

With her tongue, she caressed the swollen part of her lower lip; didn't answer. His hand, writing the check, looked confident, moving in quick zigs and zags, as if he were used to signing autographs. Across the water and islands of marsh, sunlight was sparking off everything. The check in her hand. She felt light-headed; she didn't have to keep it. But all she'd done, she told herself, was have sex, everybody had sex. The money seemed part of a mind game, coming from some deep-sea part of her that hadn't seen light before.

That night there was no breeze at all, no air coming in the open screen windows of the cabin; she felt as if she were breathing warm water. Mike was on top, his sweat trickling down both her sides, his whole body slipping and sliding on her. He'd been at it a while, and she hadn't been giving him much help. She put one leg across his back, imagined her arms pulled tight over her head, hands roped together at the top of the bed. Five or six men had brought her here, tied her up, their faces were dark, they were Indian, one of them Terrence; she could see their white teeth, the shapes of their slight bodies, hear their low laughter in the dark. They had pulled the clothes off of her, pushing and rolling her, touching each new part of her they exposed, so many of them at once, thin fingers pinching at a nipple, hands and mouths darting at her out of the dark.

She *wanted* this swarming, this invasion.

Mike picked up speed, humping hard, the side of his face pressed insistent against hers. She spread wider underneath him, lifting. Mike's mouth against her ear, the way he moved inside her, shifting and shifting as if he were trying to touch everywhere.

Under her fingers, she felt the skin change on his back, leaking out a fresh sheet of sweat. Then the sound like a cough, and a second cough, he was done, rolling off. She rolled with him, seizing his leg between her thighs, humping faster, faster, the long cry starting out of her, pulling at every organ, brain turned to drifting smoke… Relief! Dear God…

She was slumped over him: Mike. She lifted her head, shoulders; dry-mouthed and sweaty, her breasts slippery one against the other. His hand rested light on the small of her back. She felt grateful; she couldn't help it.

When the boat headed back in to the dock the next day, she was up on the bridge, Mike at the wheel beside her, wind in her face. As they slowed, she took off the Steelers cap he'd found for her, one of his, damp with her sweat.

The side of the boat moved at a diagonal toward the dock. "You're going to hit it," she yelled. Mike was working a lever back and forth, dancing this way and that to try to see the bow and the side of the boat at the same time. She covered her eyes and waited for the crash, the wood splintering; she'd leap to the dock if she had to.

She heard the slopping of water and the sound of ropes and wood creaking. She looked again. The boat was almost in place, coming parallel to the dock, a few yards from the pilings. Engine exhaust rolled up out of the water. Over on shore was the back of the gas station where she'd sat to sketch. The woman she'd been in that moment had had no idea what was coming, what she might do. Whatever had altered within her was forceful beyond her understanding. Now they were easing along side the dock. "I was sure you were going to wreck it," she said over her shoulder to Mike.

"I've got too much in it." Boys on the dock were pulling at ropes, and Terrence ran the length of the boat making sure everything was tied. The motor shut off; all was quiet. Andie could feel herself still trembling with the thrum of the engine. It was only that: engine rumble, not any uproar of her own.

"It'll be strange to be on solid land again," she said. She wanted to skip the farewell, jump straight back into her old life and lock the door behind her. "I hope my car's still there."

"Probably is." He had pushed his cap back, was wiping his forehead. The sunburn he'd had when she'd met him had faded to a tan. She could have simply accepted his invitation for the boat ride, never made her proposition; and she'd be facing the awkwardness over where it would go from here. The second check was folded in her pocketbook with the first.

"Well," she said, moving her legs around to the side of the chair, getting ready to get up. "I guess it's about that time."

"Time to put you back on the road, is it? Where're you going?"

"Home."

He sat with his hands on the wheel, facing straight ahead as if he were still driving. She stared at his hands. This was the end of the adventure. Two nights. Forty-eight hours. Once in a lifetime. Probably most people had at least one wild episode in their lives. She imagined him one last time making her bend over, lift her hips. The moment she stepped off this boat, she was finished with this sick craving that had come from nowhere.

"How about you?" she said. "Going on home?"

He nodded.

"I don't know what's going through your head," he said. "But I'd say you didn't do half bad for your first time out. Nice boat ride and all. Could have been a lot worse."

"I had a good time," she said. It came out of her without her thinking. "Mostly."

He scratched the back of his neck. "I did too. Not that you're an easy one to get to know." His eyes roamed her face.

Time to end this.

"You in the phone book? In case I play golf there sometime."

She nodded. If she so much as spoke... But she didn't know what she feared. Or what she might do.

"In a hurry to skeedaddle, are you?"

She stood up; her head was still bent over because of the canopy. Leaning, she kissed him on the mouth, fast; his lips didn't have time to move. He tasted of sweat and suntan lotion; his skin felt old.

"Bye," she said. He gave her a pat as she turned to go. She felt a pang of sadness.

Backwards, so she was facing him, she started down the ladder, keeping an eye on him for as long as possible, as if he were the one who was dangerous.

# 8

Andie dug into the family-sized bag of M&Ms lying on the passenger seat. The road ahead had narrowed to a corridor through the tall pines. Almost home. She sucked on the mouthful of chocolate, its shards of broken shells.

In no time, these days would seem no more than a stupid escapade. Him with his big spotted hand, fondling in her pants on deck in the daylight, acting as if he were indulging her. He knew nothing about her. At least she didn't have to worry about word getting out. Mike was too old-school. He and Terrence wouldn't exchange a glance. She did know that much now about him.

She scooped up another handful of chocolates. She'd bought two bags. Strange to be alone, the car big and vacant. At some point, what she'd done was going to crash down on her.

She hit the brakes. The car in front of her had slowed, the lane of traffic nearly stopped.

Damn! A horse show.

Cars were turning right up ahead: the harness-horse stables. On a path toward the grassy parade grounds, a trainer was having difficulty with a skittish chestnut stallion that wouldn't be led. The horse reared back, snorting. Andie wheeled onto the dirt road between the barns.

She hadn't known she was going to swerve in here, barely slowing for the turn. Was she avoiding going home, as if judgment would fall on her there? A few minutes' stop would be a good buffer; would slow the re-entry; otherwise she might burn up hurtling back into the normal atmosphere. Besides, she did have the horses-in-the-pasture assignment for the Virginia school, so this was research.

She came to a stop in the grassy parking area. You couldn't see these fields at all from out on the road, hidden as they were by the brushy pine woods, a private clearing in the forest for pagan, animal rituals. As she got out of the car, her motions felt slow and tentative, like an old person's. The air was damp, on the verge of rain, which she would welcome: she needed to be washed clean. Arriving at the edge of the crowd, she soon sensed herself safely surrounded.

In front of the judges, making a turn, was a black carriage, pulled by four immense draft horses. A mythic stirring sight, the men straight-backed and slender in their top hats and tall black boots, standing out there in the middle distance in a mist that looked as if it had blown in from the British Isles. And the horses, tarted up with braids and ribbons and bits of silver. "Now show a strong trot, please," said the voice through the loudspeaker, and the horses stepped along at a perky pace.

At the edge of the fence, a fabulous animal, mahogany-colored, pranced and tossed his head between the shafts of a sulky. To be harnessed that way, like the horse, a belt cinched tight just below her breasts, forced to give up all control. She felt a flicker of excitement, started, shocked as if a hand had reached between her legs.

Where was it coming from again! this kind of desire? She glanced around for something to hold onto, a tent pole or the back of a chair, for balance, but there were only the spectators. She planted her feet. Onto the field now, that rich brown horse and a woman driving. Watching closely as if she were going to paint them, that would steady her breath. The dull light there hitting the horse's coat, the moving muscle of his haunch shifted color ever so slightly, the motion of fire within embers. See? Already she was calming.

"Andie!"

She jumped. There, down the row: it was Mrs Carlisle, heading this way, ever elegant, and smiling. Her stomach turned over. She should have known this would happen, the mother of an old friend. No escape, she'd have to manage a couple of minutes of talk, when she was so aroused it could show on her mouth, her eyes.

"Well, darling? I never see you." Elga Carlisle hugged her, wrapping her in a delicate scent. "You are just the cutest thing," she said, holding Andie at arm's length. "You always were."

"That's kind of you." Andie put a hand to her ratty, wind-straightened hair. Mrs Carlisle's blonde chignon shone. "I was just coming in from a trip to the beach, stopped on a whim." A wild impulse rose: tell the story, be purged of it. "I'm a terrible smelly mess," she said, "got to run, nice to see you." Andie was already stepping away.

"Down there by yourself?" without waiting for an answer. "We're all so proud of your artwork."

"Please tell Amalie hello." She could have said she'd been working, sketching beach scenes. If she started talking, she might not stop. Whose business was it? She didn't have to account for herself. Amalie had teenage children, a husband she was in love with, a law practice; she had turned out well.

"I'll tell her, sweetheart, and you come by and see us, I mean it."

Nodding, waving, Andie made her escape to her car, then out of the complex of stables and sandy lanes, back to the hardtop.

Anybody else on earth would have been easier: Elga Carlisle was truly nice, from back when they were a pack of 7- and 8-year-olds running and sliding in sock-feet on the polished hardwood floors in that house. She hungered to be back there now, in that time.

On either side of the road golf courses rolled and dipped, off to the right in the distance, the long white colonnade of a clubhouse. Several little sex scandals had happened there, or gotten off to a good start. Maybe hers wasn't too much worse than some of the others.

There were no doubt people in town who would enjoy having her humiliating story to toss around. Most would be horrified, frightened for her. They should be. "The physical danger, if nothing else," she imagined Emma Westig saying in her Kentucky accent. "The police could have found you washed up on shore." Henry Westig would get out his checkbook and sternly insist she take money, on the promise she'd never do such a thing again. Her parents would do all of that and more. The wounded disbelief from one and then the other. Her father would somehow manage to hold Mike responsible. Her savvy mother would know better. They'd want to send her to therapy, to grad school, to church, or more likely, take her on the road with them. They would search their own souls, each assuming all blame. There would be bursts of hurt and outrage: how could you? How could you *risk* yourself like that? She cringed from forehead to shoulders. Tears were starting.

She wasn't worth what they'd invested in her. Crying in shudders, her vision blurred, she gripped both hands onto the wheel.

Without slowing, she passed the road that would take her out to the house. Apparently she was going straight to the studio, unwashed. Unless she took some other turn, which obviously could happen.

She pulled into the dirt parking lot, cut off the engine. The town hadn't shut its gates against her. She slumped, mind-weary, weak, as if some ailment had let go its hold. Except it hadn't let go, she was faintly aroused still, the sensation strong but barely discernible, like the deep hum of a furnace in the floor of a building, like all the soundless vibrations that had risen in her these recent days. She wanted no more of them. They brought trouble.

At the front door, she glanced up at the fort-like brick palisade. The checks were securely tucked in with the cash in her billfold. She didn't need money that badly. She didn't have to sell herself: not to Mike and not to Billy.

She'd almost let Billy slip out of her mind.

If she were desperate she could let her parents help her, give up the pretense of adulthood. Better to be a whore than a 38-year-old child; at least it offered independence, which was what you were supposed to want. Money wasn't why she'd done it, though. She didn't know why, or if she even wanted to know.

The door to the building fell shut behind her. She dreaded having to act like herself. She couldn't manage cheery, or wry. She imagined falling face-down on the glossy hallway floor, letting out a long cry. She could feel the shape of it lodged in her throat.

No one in the hall. The accelerating burr of a power drill from Archie's open door, then silence, followed by his murmured swearing. Inside her studio, she walked without pause to the easel, the canvas. This umbrella, this very spot, was where the first strange feeling occurred. No, that wasn't true; it had begun the night before. The over-vivid moonlight that now seemed half a dream, then waking up with the image clear in her mind, and the rush to get to town to paint… Before that, she'd been…well, certainly not happy, but normal.

She took in the whole canvas at once, as if it held some answer. Luminous, but rough, a lot still to do. No answers here. Nothing to do but finish it and get it out of her sight. She twisted off the top off the nearest crumpled tube, a yellow, just to get the first stroke over with. Where the fuck was a regular medium-sized brush? She'd hidden the brushes. Yanking open the cupboard of cans and jars… Whatever was good in the piece was an accident. She couldn't make it happen twice.

Grabbing a fresh new brush, she started laying on paint, feeling the momentum of the motion carry her as she tried to stay clear-headed. The image of an umbrella, of all things…it made no sense, but had traveled to find her, wafted by unnamable emotions. Done right, the picture would give off feeling the way swamp gas rises. How it felt to be her at this moment. She let her hand drop, the tip of the brush driggling its way off the bottom edge of the stretcher. There could be other dangerous desires waiting.

With one sweep, she drew a yellow circle on the largest panel of the umbrella, then a line across it, diagonal. No, it said: No Painting Here. She sat down at the table, hands lying loose on her lap. She couldn't do it.

The sky out the window looked white; no season, any season. Half her life slipped away. This was where all her time and efforts had brought her. Even the room smelled stale, air unbreathable.

She got to her feet slowly, crossed the hall. Cranking up a measure of jollity, she flung her arms up against Otis's glass in her signature clownish posture of please-let-me-in. It was that or wilt against the window, starting again to cry.

Otis waved, welder's glasses pushed up on his forehead. He took a second look, then came to the door, gave her a studying look with his eyes half-closed. "Where've you been?"

"To the beach. I gave my wrist a few days to heal."

"A likely story."

She managed a tight smile, glanced away down the wide cavernous hallway. She wanted to tell him that all of it, with Mike, had erupted out of her, she hadn't been able to stop. That was what terrified her. "Going to lunch?" she said.

"Sure. A couple more people were wanting to eat late too."

She felt a heavy sinking at the thought of a crowd.

"You can tell us all how it was on the coast," Otis said, "make us jealous."

The diner smelled of burned bacon. Globules of fat in the air. A foursome, with Marian and Elliott, for lunch.

"Nice tan, Andie," Marian said.

"She's been at the beach chasing boys," Otis said. "Now that she's single again."

"You guys be nice to me for a change. Don't ask me about Billy either. I haven't called yet." She saw glances exchanged.

"If we were any nicer to you," Marian said, "we'd be cleaning your brushes." Before the beach, she'd tried to reach Marian, got her machine. But if they'd talked, nothing would have changed; for one thing, Marian wasn't one to discourage adventure. Probably nobody could have kept her from heading for that marina. She must have been on fire already and not known it.

Which meant that trouble might be building again even now.

The weight of Otis's arm settled across her shoulders, he tugged her a little closer. Her body leaned into him, just for a moment, long enough to seem normal. Then she eased herself away. How could she know what else she might do? It would take years of self-control before she'd trust herself again. If ever. When you couldn't rely on yourself in the most basic ways, there was no safety anywhere.

Elliott was staring out into space, as if impatient with a bunch of children.

"We wouldn't need to take shots at you," Otis said, "if you weren't our star player, our onsite advisor."

The lift and drop of wave motion seemed almost to tip her: a leftover from the boat. She should have deposited the checks, one for each night, first thing, gotten that over with. Putting her feet solid on the floor, she took a swallow of water. Sitting in this tight space and she hadn't had her bath. She could tear up the checks, or hold them. But she wasn't going to do either one.

"You know, I think that's my water you're drinking," Otis said, "and I have a summer cold."

"Fine. Bring it on. I'll stay home in bed."

"You are touch-y today, girl," Otis said, in his Sea Island accent he loved to slip back into. He nudged at her with his elbow. Her shoulders let go. There was no need to worry at this moment at least; she wouldn't proposition Otis sitting here at the diner table.

"Somebody put a powder on you?" he said.

"Enough, Otis," she said. "I mean it."

"What kind of powder?" Marian said.

"Not a love potion," he said. "A hex is more like it."

Andie leaned her head back, eyes shut, against the wall of the booth. "You guys talk," she said. "Pretend I'm not here." She heard Elliott start in, haltingly, about the deadline for some juried show, his voice overwhelmed by Marian laughing, teasing Otis about his voodoo charms. This was the cure: to hear their same old voices washing back and forth, no matter what they said.

At home, where she'd come from lunch, she poured bath salts into the tub, the rest of the contents of the jar. Looked like clean sand on the well-water-stained bottom. She added bubble bath to foam a white layer over the surface. Good that she'd stayed on the pill, and had Mike's condoms. Hot water, soap: that was what women who'd been raped wanted.

Making the deposit at the drive-through hadn't bothered her, was no big deal; but the fact of such ease was sobering in itself. Marta, the teller, hadn't thought to ask any of her sweetly unprofessional questions about what kind of painting she had done for this Mike Sebastian.

Steam was filling the room, the mirror clouding over. She should have come here first, scrubbed up to start. She sat, blanking her mind, as the bubble bath foam melted away into a few white drifts and the brown stains on the tub came back into view, as well as her own roll of stomach fat, made worse by this slumped position. She didn't want to look at herself, her body.

She pulled at the corner of the towel hanging nearest, yanked it off the hook. Laying it out as well as she could on the water's surface, she positioned it so she was hidden. The white towel half-floated, starting to sink down around her, its waving loops of terrycloth moving against her. She'd never imagined for one moment that she wanted to act on that kind of fantasy, rarely had she ever even thought of such a thing. It was the submissiveness, the self-surrender even more than the money, that went against everything: against her independence, dignity, her whole view of herself. She'd acted like she was no more than a part of him, an arm or leg or foot, doing whatever he said. The muscles of her lower abdomen pulled tight, forcing the air out of her, a wave of pleasure, rolling upward, even as she told it to stop, overtaking her lips and the lids of her eyes. She sank deeper into the water.

# 9

Tripp picked up. Sitting on the edge of her bed, she pictured him at his desk, reaching sideways to get the phone, while still talking to someone leaving his office. "Andie. I knew it would be you." There'd been no moment when she'd consciously made a decision. "Right on time," he said, "scrupulously professional. So what's the word, my dear?"

She hadn't said hello. She cleared her throat. "I'm going to do it. As you probably knew I would." If she could take money from Mike, she could take it from Billy. "I did have one of my folks draw us up a contract. You've made the right decision. And I'm going to bet you'll find the senator quite interesting, whether you agree with him or not."

She had no reply for that. "What's your time situation?"

"Soon. The senator's got a couple of his image guys nailing down details: exactly what this picture should project, the match with the building design, that sort of thing."

"I'm to be handed a spec sheet?"

"We leave nothing to chance or guesswork."

"Or the artist either, I gather." The usual situation, but she felt oddly free to complain.

He laughed. "No second thoughts, now. We're going to have a good time with this. You wait and see."

They signed off. She fell back on the bed, hands clapped to her eyes. The yellow umbrella flashed to mind, as if impact with the bed had jarred it loose. And Billy's fleshy face in motion, ranting, damp-lipped, the piggishly upturned corners of his eyes.

She was still lying on the bed when the phone rang, so close and loud her shoulders drew up against it.

"Hello?"

"Andie, Tripp again. A piece of good luck's fallen in our laps this morning. I've just learned that the senator is unexpectedly in town and wants to see you."

She took a long deliberate breath. "Alright, how about Thursday?" she said. "Any time that day."

"He's here for a few hours today, wants you to ride with him in his golf cart for a quick nine holes, just to meet and get acquainted before you start on the painting. He likes to get a sense of anyone he'll be working with."

"I would join his foursome?"

"It'll be the two of you. His tee-off time is in," he paused, "40 minutes. I wish I could have given you more notice."

Alone with Billy Sylvester on a golf course! If she'd known it was going to start this fast… Only yesterday she was out on that boat.

"Andie?" Tripp said. "You'll be there?"

She made a sound that was the start of an objection.

"Great," he said. "I knew we could count on you."

The grass was still wet, spiky underfoot even in shoes. The sturdy cleats she'd once had were long gone; that kind wasn't allowed on courses anymore. He, the senator, the famous Billy, was lining up a chip shot, doing the little hip jiggle you do before drawing back to swing.

He was compact and solid, more than a little bow-legged. From the back, he seemed ordinary enough in his red knit and khakis, if you didn't know.

Six holes still to play. She felt fresh relief each time he turned his attention away from her. He was pointedly taking his time, not pressing the foursome ahead.

A flash of metal, the click, the ball traveled fast and low, then dropped neatly onto the green. He turned with a grin she'd seen in the news a thousand times. "Put that in your picture, Miss Andie."

"I may." Doing his wide-legged strut back toward the cart, the look on his face was unabashedly gleeful, as he held the club by the neck, his eyes seeking her congratulations. You couldn't help smiling at his delight. "Nice shot, Senator." Her mouth felt awkward saying it.

He slid onto the seat beside her, swigging on the green Gatorade. His face was beefy, like a drinker's, she was close enough to smell his sunscreen, feel the buzz of intensity around him. The man was a crackling force-field; that was what no one had said. But nearly old: up close you could tell.

"You know I told you to call me Billy." It wasn't Billy he'd said, instead Billeh, a short "e" on the end that trailed off into breath. It made the name sound sleazy.

He switched on the cart and put them in motion. The visor clamped his yellow-grey hair in place. She'd already seen at a distance her own insurance agent Mark Dudley teeing up across the piney strip on another hole. He hadn't spotted her, she was pretty sure; she wasn't eager to be seen in present company. Though she'd better get used to it.

"Living right here," he said, "amongst the fairways all your life, I expect you play a pretty decent game yourself. I didn't think about that when I asked you to come along just for the ride."

"I haven't played in a long time," she said. "Never was good. I had a few lucky days. Lucky shots."

"We live for them, don't we?" He gave her a flirty sideways look. If he was sizing her up, she couldn't tell it. She was no more than an audience for his game. And she wasn't in any danger of letting herself get seduced. Her very bones recognized this man and rejected him. He supported dictators who made people disappear; he championed the jailing, shutting down, of a world-class artist like Akeem Desmond. Billy was still a bigot, he hadn't changed. Monstrous people were often charming; that was no surprise.

"One beauty of a drive can keep me playing hard for years," he said. " 'Course you have more challenging matters to think about: I imagine it would take all of a painter's wits to see how to make this old boy look good."

"Not so difficult," she said, as always. She was on edge, but managing well. Holding his scorecard a moment ago, she'd been afraid her hands would visibly shake. They hadn't. She was staying focused, on-task, by watching to catch the characteristic expressions and gestures, the details that would define him. How she'd show his energy, his famous charisma: that was going to be the trick. A hint of that quality showed on the computer video, even with the sound muted. A lot about him was just as the campaign posters had shown: his lips, meaty and damp. Hard to bring into her view of him that he had children and a wife, the vague proper-ish woman in a few news photos. You couldn't tell much about her. What sort of woman would sleep with him and do it over and over?

He'd pulled to a stop on the apron, reached back without looking and took out his putter. "Okay, missy, say a prayer for me now."

"I'll pray you won't call me missy again." Her pocketbook, which she hadn't once let go of, had the check for $50,000 in it. The first half of the money, the whole long business envelope folded twice and zipped into an inside pocket. To her surprise, he'd had an aide pass it to her first thing. Maybe the idea wasn't to check her out, instead to hook her so she couldn't back out.

"Your prayer is answered. No more missy, or sweetheart either. Come on up here and watch me sink this putt."

With deliberate slowness, she got out of the cart, sauntered up to the edge of the green. Once he'd gripped and re-gripped the putter and got his hands happily situated, he looked up and shot her a full-on smile. It startled her backward a step. Not the wattage, or the seemingly jovial intent, but his eyes, the way they narrowed, until all of the white, all of the expression was gone. Those bristly yellowish eyelashes, dry grass…and then from his eyes, only shine.

"By the time we're done," he said, "you might consider voting for me. If I drop the putt, will you consider it?"

She rolled her eyes at his gambit. She'd done it before she could stop herself. He looked smug, as if he'd scored a point by finding out what he wanted to know. He should have met her when she was a kid; with the passion she had then, she'd have plowed into him, told him exactly why she wouldn't vote for him and what he ought to do to make things right.

He took a final dry run with his putter. She dashed over to take out the flag, which she'd forgotten again. The ball rolled toward her, then sank, with its hollow thwock, into the cup. She could feel it, as if it had dropped in the pit of her stomach, sending out ripples through her body. She stood staring down at the crisp edge of the hole, for a second, until she had her bearings; then, like a good caddie, collected his ball and replaced the flag. She walked back to the cart without glancing toward him.

It was past noon by the time they rolled back to the pro shop doorway of the clubhouse. "Here you go, Colonel." Billy passed off his clubs to the man who stood waiting for golfers coming in.

She'd been preparing, as they rolled toward a stop, for dealing with the invitation to lunch, how she'd escape. No need. He shook her hand, radiated his milder, more routine smile at her, and was gone, led quickly to a car by a man in golf clothes and an ear wire, who, she now realized, had been playing in the foursome just behind them.

That abruptly, she was set back down on ordinary ground, off-balance, uncertain where she'd parked.

# 10

"Take a left," Andie said. Marian slowly, slowly turned onto the wide divided avenue lined with the towering pines, heading west out of town. "You drive like you're 90 years old. You know that?" Marian cut her a sharp look to see if she was kidding. "I told you: this is important. I have a problem."

"And we have to leave town to talk about it?"

"I don't want to run into anybody."

She felt Marian's sobered glance, then faced ahead in silence. Her hand on the door side was picking at a rip in the plastic weave of the seat cover, pulling it larger. She could start the conversation now, while they were both facing straight ahead. "It's about sex. Okay? Sex mainly."

"With?" her tone of voice careful.

"Not Otis."

"I didn't mean..."

"Yes, you did."

"Not that I have the remotest chance." Marian's laugh was rueful.

"You never know." Marian had a man or two hanging around all the time. But Otis was so much younger. And how can I promise I won't mess with him? I no longer know what I'll do. Sweat dampened her chest and upper lip. She rolled down the window, let air blow over her.

They drove through a couple of crossroads towns, gas stations, past stretches of woods. There were places she could have said "stop", but now she was delaying. To put the Mike business, the cravings, into words seemed impossible, humiliating. Fear of what she might do was eating at her constantly. Marian took a sharp turn off the road. Buzzy's Happy Hours. The windows were boarded to make the place nightclub-dark inside. "Perfect," Andie said. Her stomach sank.

The car rolled to a stop, front tires nudging the log at the end of the space. The engine switched off. She was facing the bar's blind exterior wall. Her gaze fixed on that blank wall, she said, "I'm out of control, Marian."

Marian snorted. "Out of control with sex? I've heard of worse things than that. Let's go get a beer and you tell me what's going on."

Andie got slowly out of the car, feeling wobbly, as if balancing a teetering weight on her back. She could still dodge this conversation, simply talk about something else. She could tell Marian about the intense joy that had overtaken her, three times now, in her bedroom, at the easel, on the road when she first pulled out in view of the water. Right now she'd trade all of that for knowing she had herself under reasonable control.

Inside the air was cold, the light suitably low. A shabby tinsel Christmas tree sat at one end of the long bar, in the middle of spring. They took seats at the table Andie chose, close to the door. Marian with her beach-bag-type pocketbook in her lap looked out of place in here.

The waiter arrived, a lean twentyish guy in T-shirt and jeans, the old kind that fit snug.

"I saw you checking the kid out," Marian said when he'd brought their drinks. "You looking for a youthful conquest?"

"I'm not looking for any conquests."

"We always say that, post break-up, don't we?"

"You're not doing this right, Marian. You're supposed to be in your motherly-ex-kindergarten-teacher mode, okay? Not sexy-dame."

Marian nodded, chastened, all trace of flip humor gone from her face.

Andie started into her story: Mike, the money, every self-obliterating detail. Stopping at the horse show and the lust that had followed her home. Marian's expression was difficult to read. "I tried to get myself to stop," she said, "when the boat was first going out." She paused; her breath felt hot in her lungs, her face engorged from the telling.

"I'm not sure," Marian said, picking her way carefully, "what a kindergarten teacher is supposed to say. But I'm upset by your doing anything so dangerous. The sex itself..."

"And it's not just that, Marian." She didn't want to hear what anyone normal had to say about the sex. "There's other peculiar stuff," she said, "bizarre thoughts and now and then a zap that feels electric. Like I've been taken over by weird energy."

Energy. She hadn't boiled it down to that before.

Her mother had talked about a kind of dormant energy, extra life force coiled up in the body, not the kind of thing that would show on an X-ray, or anywhere else.

"You think all this is related?" Marian said.

As a kid, she'd shut her ears when Mom got going talking about invisible forces, spirit worlds; it was scary. "I don't know if it's related or not." Thinking about it, the dangerous rush of pleasure, she found her hips were faintly rubbing, forward and back against the shaped wood seat of the chair.

Marian had sat back, was staring off into space.

"I don't suppose you've had an experience like this?" Andie said, hope nudging her. Marian shook her head. Marian, who'd had so many adventures.

The need to cry shot upward in her; she didn't know what exactly she'd wanted to happen here. Yes, she did: for Marian to be warm and kind and explain this and tell her how to fix it. To say: yes, this happens sometimes, two other friends of mine went through this same thing and it passed and they're fine.

Over at the bar, the boy was on the phone, smiling at the wall over whatever the girl on the other end was saying. In the far booth, a jowled man was drinking steadily. Dressed in all white except for the grass-green sweater draped around his shoulders. She could almost see the vaporous alcohol lifting off his heavy face.

"As far as the sex itself," Marian said, "you've been pretty solitary since you and Charlie parted," Marian said. "No chasing boys at all. You were due for some wild outbreak. Getting a divorce always hit me that way." She didn't look convinced, though, fingering the neck of her lavender top as if looking for something to straighten.

Andie made a dismissive face. Making love with Charlie, what then had seemed routine, perfunctory, now felt too tender to think about.

"I'm just trying to make sense," Marian said, after a moment; she was accustomed to handling relationship problems for everybody in the building, yet this was giving her pause. "You really felt you could not stop?"

"The person I was then wasn't capable of stopping."

"You wouldn't do it again, though." It was a question.

"How do I know? I can't trust myself."

"You're lucky it didn't end up a lot worse."

"I know." Rehashing the details, she could almost feel how it had happened, how desire had surged... Sitting here with a chaperone standing guard, it was safe to slip back into it, the filthy thrill: waiting, pants down, available for anyone to take or ignore.

The boy at the bar was still on the phone.

Marian talking: same stuff, the danger.

Through a yellow haze she could see the dark table, the puddle of condensation around the bottom of her glass. Inside her, a droning light, twisting its way upward, so quickly: all the way into her throat. She felt on the verge of retching. The live thing pulled back, shrunk to one spot, a tiny flare deep in the small of her back, then was gone.

Her hands fell to her lap. In the air before her, a splash of blue light confused her eyes for a second. Like a camera flash. She checked herself: still sitting here, all her clothes on. The man at the other table was paying her no attention, concentrated entirely on the motions of drinking, searching with his lips for the edge of that glass. The waiter, the boy... She caught his eye, he was staring at her, not trying to disguise it. A smile was starting to spread on his face.

All at once, Marian was in a rush, getting out money, on her feet, her face grim. "We're leaving," she said.

"Let me get this one, Marian. This was my idea."

"Just grab your pocketbook and come on. Walk out ahead of me."

Andie, getting up from her chair, discovered she felt almost drunk herself; but Marian had had the beer; she'd ordered only a Sprite, finished half of it.

The bar guy, phone at his ear, caught her eye, gestured with his head toward the back, the short hall to the restrooms. She felt her step pause. Marian was steering her, pushing at her elbow. She could feel what he'd do. He'd stand her against the wall back there, facing him, pull up her shirt, knowing somebody could walk in any second. She'd give him anything he wanted. He was putting down the phone, turning. He cast a look along the length of her. "Hi," she said.

Marian jerked her by the arm so hard she almost fell, would have if she hadn't been holding on to the chair.

"Jeez, Marian."

"Keep moving," Marian said, steering her out the door.

Behind them, the boy laughed. In the parking lot, Marian was right on her heels. God, it was bright out after being in that cave. She fell into the car, pulled the seatbelt across her; Marian wheeled out fast as if the road were all hers.

"You mad at me, Marian? What did I do?" She felt befuddled, as if pulled out of sleep. She sounded drunk too; she could hear herself.

"You were exuding...not just sex. It's impossible to explain. Sex and a kind of bristle. Or surge. Then you walk up to that boy...." She stopped as if there were no words awful enough, when she herself sometimes changed boyfriends every 6 weeks.

"Bristle," Andie said, picturing the white spikes of air inside an ice cube. A sack of cracked ice would be nice, to lay across her eyes.

"The boy, a kid! barely old enough to mix drinks! He noticed like you glowed in the dark."

"Nothing would have happened with you there. I was just going to say 'thanks, bye.'"

"What if I hadn't been there?" she sounded sharp, not a friend at all.

"I don't know. I wasn't planning."

"I believe that." Marian was sitting forward, hanging onto the wheel with both hands, peering up ahead; it made her look older, sitting that way.

"I'm frightened for you, Andie."

"You said I was due for a wild episode."

"Here's what we're going to do. We're going to the mental health center. That way somebody can see you immediately, while you're still in this…this state, whatever it is."

"You can just walk in? Like an emergency room?"

"I don't know. I'm guessing. We're about to find out."

"Two middle-aged ladies arrive at the county clinic," Andie said. "One is upset because the other was flirting with the waiter. Emergency! Something must be done!" The laugh that started up out of her felt like huge bubbles, wide as dessert plates. The laughing felt so good.

"You can make fun, if you want, Andie. But you're the one who had to go out of town to even tell this story."

She felt her resistance cave: so let Marian be in charge. That could be nice. All this living alone, plus being her own boss as always…those two things at once were way too much.

"You need to see somebody," Marian's voice was softened, more normal.

"Okay." If anybody as freewheeling as Marian thought she'd gone over the edge, then the situation was bad. Mostly she was starting to feel sleepy, content to be driven. Still a bit aroused, but the sensation was fading, a faint excitement sustained by the warm car seat, and quickly that feeling too was dwindling, the high evaporating.

As if she were sobering up, her regular self returning: Good God! Marian was right. She'd have gone out behind the building with that boy if Marian hadn't been there. If he hadn't been there, then the next one who walked in...

Her back felt stiff holding off panic. She closed her eyes, tight, felt the car turning. They'd pulled into a parking slot.

The silence of the engine shut off felt like water pressure in her ears. "I need to sit still a second," she said. Marian was quiet except for the jingle of her keys that seemed to clang and reverberate on and on. Andie waited; her heartbeat a pounding fist just below where her ribs joined, slowing, slowing.

She was sick, in danger. A person couldn't live with no self-control. Mike was just a taste of what could happen.

Outside the car window near the concrete steps to the building, one of the shrubs had heavy down-drooping branches: dreadlocks. At the top of the rise was a Japanese-style building, the afternoon sun harsh behind it; she could see little more than a silhouette. She wanted to go to sleep in this slanted sunlight and not wake up.

Marian was making no move to get out of the car.

"Planning your speech?" Andie said. Her voice sounded okay, no hint of her shaky state. "How to explain me to the receptionist?"

"They have to have some kind of arrangement for people in a crisis."

"Like this? Is there a drug that calms sexual urges?"

Marian, hoisting herself from the car, gave a sharp laugh: "Anti-depressants."

"Great. I could get a double benefit."

Inside, the receptionist's desk was crowded, three mother-with-young-teenager pairs. Two of the kids were trying-to-be-slutty girls and then a chubby boy. All the parents and children looked exasperated and tired. Not rich, not poor either. She'd never been to a public clinic.

These people were going to be milling around while Marian explained the problem. She could picture it: they would fall still and cut their eyes around toward her, imagining what she'd done. Her crotch tightened, as if she were trying to keep hold of a fist-sized animal using only the pressure of her thighs.

"Marian, I'm going to go sit down." She walked around the Japanese wall divider into the waiting room. Open latticework. She was her usual observing self; yet contained within her was the sly lascivious madwoman who could take over in an instant. Maybe the open lattice was for the receptionist to see through and watch you.

She'd never had a therapy session in her life or considered it. Probably she was the only person in the world who hadn't and now she wondered why. She might need a hospital. Adrenaline rushed. A hospital bed, narrow and white; her flare of alarm began to fade. It could be a relief. A few days of rest in a peaceful sunlit room, nurses in quiet-soled shoes. Soothing to imagine, but pure fantasy; it'd be noisy, with organized activities, she'd be at the mercy of officious strangers.

She picked up the nearest magazine: *Hoofbeat*. Horses. Even the mental health clinic knew it was in Pinehurst. Marian was coming around the lattice room divider, looking righteous and mollified. She felt a wave of gratitude, affection. Marian was helping after all; no longer was she alone with what she'd done. Already talking from ten feet away, she was heading toward the chairs. "I think we've got you somebody," she said. " He'll be free in just a few minutes."

Two low-slung soft chairs, a little more than arm's length apart. Hip-looking Cliff, the therapist, wore one tuft of beard on his chin, the hair so blonde it shone like a dab of mayonnaise. He had a wilted air about him; maybe the previous hour had wrung him out. She wanted to hope, but couldn't muster it.

"Were you told anything," she said, "beyond that sheet I filled out?" Her mouth had gone dry. Her eyes, the space between her eyebrows felt wary. This sitting here unsettled her worse than the first dinner with Mike.

"I was told you wished to see someone immediately. That you're engaging in dangerous behavior."

He'd been given more info than that. He was holding out.

"Sexual behavior," he added when he noted her expression.

"My friend Marian would have made sure to mention sex. I left it to her, the arranging."

"Why wouldn't you do it yourself?" He seemed genuinely puzzled.

"If I'm in need of coming here, then I'm sick and should get to be taken care of." Her tongue searched around inside her mouth, as if it needed to seem busy. "I did fill out your questionnaire."

"And the reason you give for coming here is 'lack of self-control'. What's that about?"

"Acting on weird impulses I didn't know I had." She kept her eyes steady on his.

There was something sexy about the arc of the umbrella that she couldn't define. She could feel his assessing stare. Like sitting for the art students, except his eyes weren't darting back to the sketchpad. "I started a painting. Something I'd been putting off. Hardly impulsive. I felt a surge of...of energy, really...and jumped in quickly before my nerve failed."

The pool of extra energy lying dormant in the body. Her mother had had a word for it. *Cucaracha*?

"But you're a painter."

"This was more personal." Not *cucaracha*. No, that was that perky Spanish song.

He was using a tennis trophy for a bookend; she couldn't read whether it was from the club. Tripp could call any day, she'd have to start work on Billy. "What's happened…?" she said, then stalled over where to begin, moments with Mike blurring into yellow as if his yacht had floated in paint and everywhere she looked in her memory brought forth the dog with her own face.

"I do applaud what you're doing," he said when the pause had lengthened, "coming here." She pictured him clapping as he stepped back from a spotlighted podium, blonde and neat and lean.

"Thank you." She cleared her throat of huskiness, felt her mind restore itself to order. "Why were you picked for this assignment? Why not a woman?" What had come over her with the bar guy could happen again with any man at any time.

"I had this slot free." On the shelf behind his head, the bare face of a clock was suspended in a cube of Lucite. Eleven minutes already shot. Not that she'd expected an explanation. Anyway, he was too young. "What does this cost, by the way?"

"Depends on your income. I'm not the one to talk with about that." He gave her a mildly combative smile. She remembered she was rich now; asking the price was an old habit. "Costs less than sexual recklessness," he said.

"Maybe not. I turned a pretty good profit." She'd thought to laugh but didn't. He was busying with his notes, his sketchpad-equivalent. Cash for sex, she imagined him writing. Self-destructive, self-abasing. Full of bravado. Full of shit.

"You don't have to be here," he said. "Nobody's forcing you."

"I'm aware of that."

Silence, throat-clearing, foot-shifting. She could feel his scrutiny. She imagined herself held fast to this spot, at the same time turning, like a glass case in a deli window, inside it the fat slices of cake and pie trundled in and out of sight. If she were sitting on the sofa, she could pull the afghan around her. Or he might come over and sit next to her.

"I'll just keep talking," she said, "saying something. If I stop,

I may not start again." His measuring gaze softened. She felt a faint rise of gratitude, forced it down.

"I only meant to ride down to the beach," she said, "then I wound up going off with this man on his boat, making him pay." She hesitated; noting the pause, she pushed on, keeping the talk flowing: "I like your room, by the way. You've got just the right level of cozy lamplight. Feels as if I've come in out of too-bright sun." In Costa Rica, the old hotel rooms where they'd stayed were often shaded, the ones on the ground floor with their tiny private gardens. The light that fell there felt tender, dampened. Seductive. She wouldn't have known what that meant then. Not the word, anyway. Their garden rooms were another of her memory pictures, often caressed. Her life in recent years had somehow grown un-tender. Dry.

She'd forgotten to keep talking. "I wasn't interested in him," she said. "Mike. Not at first."

"Were you using alcohol, drugs?"

"One pina colada."

He was quiet, his face blank as sand. She'd wanted help. Now here she was.

"I didn't decide. It was more like a sneeze."

He was tipping back in his chair, away from her; did he know he was doing that? Backing off that way? "Only you and Marian have heard about any of this."

"Marian and the man on the boat," he said, "and anyone he might have told."

She gave him back his same unflinching expression. With one loafered foot he was barely rocking his chair. The wave motion from the water had lingered, would not let her go. Tears welled up that didn't spill. She cleared her throat. "Have you diagnosed me yet? Slut? With over-reacting friends?"

He smiled, tight-lipped. "Let's see what we can figure out."

He started with questions, a standard list apparently. She rattled through an account of her life: the travels, an only child, art... Being a kid was the part she wanted to linger over, but he rushed her along.

Yes, she told him, she did have full memory of the recent sexual episode, no chunks of time unaccounted for. There'd never been rape or abuse. No problems with addictions. Yes, she had enjoyed sex with Mike. "In the most perverse way," she said.

"Dangerous," he said, "Not so perverse. A lot of people have these kinds of fantasies."

Maybe he was trying to seem nonjudgmental, so that she would relax and tell him more. She pictured him after the conversation, whooping it up in the break room about the lulu he'd just had dropped on him.

"Degrading stuff isn't perverse? Come on."

"It might feel relieving, to temporarily abandon yourself to someone. Plenty of people act out these desires, experiment with someone safe."

"My whole life is about independence. I'm self-employed, never married."

He nodded, sagely.

So many years of "independence". Now she wanted to be abased nearly out of existence. For so long, she'd felt tired of herself, trapped inside herself. She wanted to get loose, spread wide and borderless as clouds over the length of a mountain range, whatever it would take to be boundless. That first night alone in her room in the moonlight had for seconds taken her somewhere close to that. Or she thought it had. She didn't entirely remember.

He was watching her. "I think you might benefit from having someone look after you for a day or so."

"That's your prescription?"

He didn't answer. She waited as he fiddled with his papers. A pulse started up at her temples. "I know I'm on edge," she said, "but I'd like some kind of response. About what's going on."

"I'd look first at dissociative disorders."

"Meaning?"

"Dividing yourself into parts. Detaching from your experience."

"That's possible then? A problem with a name?" She hadn't dared hope.

"No more than a starting point. There's a therapist in town, Andie, in private practice, who has done a lot of good work with this sort of thing. Dr Rose Leon. I think the two of you might work well together. She's mainly retired. However, she sees a few people at her house, uses a hypnotic approach."

But the process of painting was hypnotic, at least after the first few minutes; and she already knew how that felt.

"You're getting rid of me," she felt sadness cross her face. "I'm too bad off for the county clinic? I thought you worked with very sick people."

"This therapist will have the most to offer you. In the meantime, what about someone to keep you company, a woman friend. I will find out if Dr Leon can see you soon. And," with a practiced flourish of his eyebrows, "we are out of time." He restacked his papers, crunched a staple into a corner.

"Just give me her number," Andie said, coming up from the low chair. "I need to think this over."

He jotted it down, and from where he was, extended a hand to shake. He wasn't going to stand. Protecting himself from her. She felt anger start to rise. She tried to decipher his expression in the quarter-second before she turned away, reaching for the doorknob to get herself out of here, before... But the door didn't open. She twisted the knob the other way, shook it.

"It needs a good yank," he said from behind her. "Here." She heard his chair scrape.

"No need to get up." He mustn't come closer. Her whole lower body swung into motion. One foot braced low on the doorjamb, she twisted and pulled, both hands. It gave, so easily. The cracking she could feel the second before she heard it. Then she was stumbling back, the lock, the doorknob unit and splintered wood in her hands.

She set it down on the nearest shelf. "Hollow door," she said, "particleboard." She'd broken down a door? She wasn't that strong, not even close.

"Andie?" his voice was careful, uneven with outrage. "Did you intend to do this?"

"I don't know. I owe you, or somebody, for the door."

"What were you thinking…?"

"I was trying to open it." Her wrist was obviously well, probably had been for days. She stepped past him into the open hallway. She'd never imagined being capable of such a thing.

"Marian!" she called out.

Around the corner from the waiting room came dear, faithful, well-meaning Marian, scurrying, feet like a propeller beneath the hem of her skirt. Andie, laughing for no reason other than her sudden pure exuberance, gestured back toward Cliff's open door: "He wants you to stay with me. He says I need a babysitter."

# 11

Still in a fog of sleep, Andie wandered into her kitchen, the room in bright morning light gauzy without her contacts. Marian at the stove: the smell of French toast tasted metallic on her tongue.

"Your birds out here start earlier than in town."

"That's not possible."

"Truly," Marian said. "You have your own microclimate. They were yoo-hooing while it was still solid dark."

"Owls." Her eyes were starting to wake up. Gradually, her mind clearing, yesterday's events coming back into focus. The spatula clanked into the sink. Almost 9 o'clock. Marian had on the same clothes she'd worn yesterday, to the bar, the clinic: the lavender top, floaty skirt, both badly rumpled. "We should stop by your house, for you to change, if you want to."

"I need to pack up," Marian said, pausing to enumerate on her fingers: "My electric toothbrush. My Grape-Nuts, fat-free half and half…"

"A day or so is all the guy was talking about." What she needed, more than being watched, was a way to know if she was back to normal. Some sign of whether it was safe to go out of the house without risk of breaking down a door, or carrying along her own sexual microclimate. She imagined herself walking around town inside a yellow haze. It would have a sharp vinegar-ish smell…

"Oh, at least a couple of days," Marian said. "Besides, it's nice to have a longer visit."

"I won't argue." In spite of herself she was starting to wake up, though not enough to do anything. "I can't believe you're cooking."

"My cooking is just what you need. It's a good start anyway." Marian set a laden plate before Andie at the table. Hot breakfast food, as if she were a growing girl; it smelled eggy, like the steam table at the dining hall, mornings at summer camp. Marian was treating this like a combo of psychosis, heartbreak and the flu.

"Your maple syrup bottle was coated in dust thick as flannel," Marian said. "I rinsed it for you. Your larder looks as if somebody set up housekeeping here years ago, and then mysteriously hit the road."

"We were mostly at Charlie's. You know that. I'm surprised I have maple syrup at all." Her house still felt unfamiliar. She missed the green tweed chair where she'd sat evenings in his living room: her spot, three feet from his, closer where the footrests angled toward each other. Close enough to smell his trademark aroma of coffee and Wint-o-Green Lifesavers, sometimes a hint of sawn wood. A clean outdoor guy smell. The thought of it made her throat hurt. When they first met, what drew her was his quiet; he'd seemed permanent, unmovable.

Marian staying here had been a good idea. She'd write the clinic guy a note and tell him. The absence of someone else in the house was probably a lot of whatever was wrong with her, not having anybody around. No company, no ballast. She didn't need a hypnotist to realize that.

At Archie's desk in his studio, Andie entered the name into the window on the monitor screen, Senator Billy Sylvester North Carolina, and hit Go. Restless, agitated, she'd left Marian at work in her own space.

"You're just tormenting yourself, reading about him," Archie said, behind her, shutting off his sander. He was grinding that wood down glass-smooth, flawless; yet he'd come to the door of his studio looking as if he'd been out hunting: three-day beard, camouflage pants, his usual sleepy-looking dishevelment.

"Sylvester: Neo-Nazi in High Office." Here was a site that would show his true colors. And a click to see videotape, hear racist words straight from the man's mouth. She hit it, leaned back. A flush was on the verge of rising in her neck and face, she could feel it.

Nothing happening, though, with the computer. Apparently some kind of download was required; she at least knew that word. "Archie, can you play film clips?"

"Sure, babe." Hunched over the workbench across the room, back half-turned, he was dovetailing two narrow panels.

"Don't get up," she said. "Just tell me what to hit."

"Much easier to come over there. How else do you think I watch my porn flicks?" Archie and porn had never crossed her mind.

He reached over her, the side of his arm brushing against her shoulder. Too soft for a guy who worked with construction tools, even his dark brown hair soft. All she wanted was to lean into him as if he were a big pillow, a featherbed. A couple of weeks ago she wouldn't have hesitated; today she needed to watch herself even with sweet, shambling Archie.

"Here you go," he said, then back to his workbench at the far side of the room.

Rising in volume, Sylvester's voice came out of the speakers: "…it is just unfortunate that some among us are little more than animals and invite themselves to be treated in that way." He gestured with his chin, exposing the underside as if daring you to attack him. "There are laws on our books…" She muted the sound, watched the suited figure. He had an intensity about him, even without sound. You had to give him that. He had charisma; if you saw him you'd remember him. With the computer, she'd robbed him of his voice. That was satisfying. Still, his presence…exuding rays that would make you glow and then come down with cancer years from now.

"Archie."

No answer. She waited until the sander stopped again.

"Archie, what would you do?"

"Take the money, just like you already have, and do the job. Same as you."

He turned to glance at her briefly. She made a wry face, went back to the keyboard, typed "whore" into the window: Mike and his yacht, Sylvester and his $100,000. Over her shoulder, she said: "He at least bases his actions on some kind of principle, however perverted." She added the word "submissive" to the slot on the screen.

The list of sites appeared: Hot Horny Housewives. Cockzilla. Spankwire. Sounded like a joke. "Mature dirty slut gets pounded..."

She clicked. Gawked at the screen: a fast-moving slide-show of huge breasts, oral sex close-ups: "Interracial gang bang..." She looked around to check on Archie: busy at his bench, back turned. This was the famous Internet porn, and she'd never before had a peek. She clicked again.

Five men. One blonde woman in a mouth-gaping swoon of pleasure; no way she could know which man was doing what, she'd dissolved into them. Andie shifted in the seat, her fingers fumbled at the keyboard. She didn't want to be caught looking at this. She hit on a page aimed at women: "...Waves of passion overtook me," it said, "as they commanded my body..."

She felt her hips doing a slow sway against the chair cushion. Probably you could find whatever you wanted, if you kept searching...and searching... She couldn't stop... Next site: a video in an upper corner of the screen, ferociously fast intercourse, the man's mind was gone, he was all instinct, quickening force tearing him free of himself... In the cabin of the boat, she'd lifted her ass; she'd waited. A tiny pulse was beating in her crotch. She leaned her chest toward the keyboard, arched her back, imagining how it would be if, at this moment... Her hand was reaching under her, playing out the fantasy just a little further, with Archie over there not knowing... Slide the skirt out from beneath her, only skin and underpants touching the molded wood of the chair, its little ridge down the middle. No one would know if she skooched the pants down a little, down around her thighs. Lifting a bit off the seat, completely bare so the air can touch… Her heartbeat loud, a squeak in her breath. He hadn't noticed, she could turn back. Her chest dipped lower, butt raised…so easy, oh God…the thrill in both nipples, ass higher than the back of the chair, skirt hiked up. All the red layers open. Now, when he turned…

"Archie," she said. The sander stopped. Sharp release of his breath…

She faced ahead, waiting, reduced to nothing but what he could see. Her heartbeat shaking her whole body.

His footsteps came toward her. With her hands she pulled open the backs of her thighs.

The chair, yanked away. His zipper, his whispered, "omigod, omigod." She could see his work boots, stepping apart to get the right height. The wet head of his penis bumped at her, sank in.

Then the smacking rhythm. His quick breath. The gap in the curtain that blocked off the front gallery jerking in and out of view. She felt herself straining, reaching…her ribs releasing, mouth swollen … hurtling outward, oh please God. But no, too soon, her insides buckled and gave her up for anything, anything….

They were done, fallen into chairs. She hadn't looked him in the face.

"Did you have that in mind," he said, "when you came in here?" He was lying in his chair, rumpled, pants hauled back up and zipped.

"I did not."

His face looked slack, his eyes assessing, the way Mike's had been when he first understood. "I didn't know such things really happened," he said.

"Something's gone wrong with me," she said. She couldn't quite think… "I clicked on some porn sites." The pictures were over there, on the screen, she could see the bright jumble, the motion. Her crotch roused, again. For a moment near the end she'd felt so close…to what? But then it was over.

"You can look at my computer any time you want." He started to smile, stopped halfway.

She'd have to go on seeing him, every day. "I don't do this," she said.

"Yeah, I know."

"I'm having a problem I don't understand."

"I know you were, like, with Charlie for years."

But it was Mike's hands she could feel, hefting her breasts, and then Archie just now behind her. "That's not it," she said, her head starting to clear; shock and upset like a train racing toward her. "My mind seemed little and far away. The feeling, the need, took over."

What had she just done? And with Archie who she'd known for years, seen every day. Archie, who seemed like a big bumbling eleven-year-old.

"We could go somewhere," he said. "For a walk. Or, maybe I'm being old-fashioned."

Never once had she had a sexual thought about him. "You probably have work to do," she said. That sounded lame. She didn't want to hurt him.

He waved away the idea.

What if it had been strait-laced Elliott? It could have been any man in the building. Any man at all. This was the way an addict must feel, pulled under by a current.

Archie was trying and failing to come up with some reassurance. There was none. For all she knew, she'd do it again in an hour. Or in a restaurant. Where was the limit? "Look," he said, "just don't worry about it." His face acknowledged how feeble that sounded.

"Right," getting to her feet.

He nodded toward the computer. She didn't look.

"I'll print you out some recent photos of Sylvester. And I'll come after you," he said, "if I find out I'm pregnant."

Walking, as if normal, down the hall, the rectangle of light ahead, out the front door of the building: keep moving.

She'd never imagined losing all reason like this, all sense of the need to stop. She'd wanted to keep going, get to whatever lay beyond and yield to it, become its meat, its human sacrifice. She came to the street, turned right toward town. How she must have looked to him from across the room... She walked faster along the weedy edge of the road. Nothing coming, nothing moving up ahead except the man at the carwash.

With the gap in the curtain that blocked the hall and whatever sounds they'd made, somebody might have noticed. She had never imagined just stripping, exposing herself. It wasn't human. The dog face, the dog dream flickered; she shut off the images. Her thin shirt was stuck to her back. It was hot, dust floating from the construction yard behind the fence. It had been hot as this one of the nights with Mike. She could feel him sliding out, finished.

She stepped over a green plastic soda bottle somebody had tossed out. Next to the Cadillac showroom the street would make the curve into the village: shade and civilization. The canopy of live oaks, magnolias, the tall pines...

Across the road, nobody going or coming at Village Printing. Or at Village Appraisers. One after another, just beyond the groomed perimeter, these servants to the town. As she had been to Mike. She stopped, bent over as if she were retrieving something, the same position, just to feel... Dirty thrill came up both arms. Quickly she stood up. Subversive desire, for sensation so intense it could dissolve any boundary, dismantle her very being.

Didn't they once do lobotomies on girls who wouldn't stop having sex? Retarded girls.

She started to run. She sprinted, pocketbook clutched at her side, keys jingling, the sweat pouring now, past the awning store, around the corner. Up ahead the trees were inviting.

Thank God, here was shade. She staggered to a stop, breathless, next to an old bungalow at the village edge, her panting like sobbing.

She wiped her eyes, her whole face, with her sleeves; looked around, a car was cruising slowly, up ahead, moving away from her. She was back in the filtered light of the village.

Maybe it was some chemical hormonal thing with an explanation. A cure.

Her childhood house only six blocks away, second left at the mailbox. Nobody home in the daytime, she could walk around to the back, to the monster wisteria vine, sit in the little cave it made, the way she used to as a kid.

She walked at an ordinary pace, in the direction of home. The cooler air felt soothing to her mind. Lucky she hadn't turned an ankle trying to run in these chunky-heel shoes. What she'd done… It wasn't as if she'd killed someone. By the time she'd known how far she was going, normal life had stopped, all rules called off, whatever she did wouldn't count or even exist.

But it did count. It did exist.

A corner, another corner, the fat hedge and here was the house, sandy-grey stone, her upstairs casement window. She'd made it. She started into the yard, as if she belonged there. But she'd long ago betrayed the girl who'd lived in the upstairs bedroom; not doing her real work because she was scared of it, wary of where her imaginings might lead her. Now she knew where they could lead.

She walked along the side of the house, trailing her fingers, cool familiar grain to the stone, toward the back.

If she didn't get control, she wouldn't be doing any painting. She'd be in a hospital. A women's prison.

Passing beneath her old window, the path she was walking, close against the outside wall, wasn't part of the familiar far-reaching view from her upstairs room. That girl in the window, her clear-eyed eager 16-year-old self, would have said no in a flash to Sylvester, would be shocked, and excited, by the sexual abandon. Would be searching intently, continuously, for the door that had opened briefly on the day of the umbrella.

# 12

"Do come in. I'm Dr Leon."

Andie had to step inside before she could fully see the woman in the dim foyer light. High cheekbones, dark hair pulled back in a ballet-teacher do. The hand she extended to Andie felt like four pencils, it was that narrow.

"Come on back into the den."

The hall opened into a bright room, a bank of windows looking onto the walled garden. A little sanctuary. She'd had to wait 2 days for this appointment, a frightening amount of time in which anything could have happened. Now she was here, her mind clamorous for the answer.

Dr Leon, probably in her seventies, was wearing a deep red dress, tailored silk. The image of an elegant and reserved older European woman. Wherever she was born, she wasn't American: she had no eagerness at all.

Andie seated herself in the corner of the sofa opposite the big wing chair. She had the impulse to sit with her back straight. "So this is Wren Cottage," she forced herself into conversational mode. "I've passed this place many times."

"I was extraordinarily fortunate when I came here to find such a house available."

"I thought I knew everything about Pinehurst." Waiting for this session, she'd held a steady level of tension, stayed mostly in sight of Marian.

"Always there are surprises. Will you take a cup of tea? I have a pot of Darjeeling just brewed."

Andie took the frail cup that was presented her. The daintiness of it reminded her of English tearooms she'd visited with her mother when she was a child. Holding this near-to-brimming *objet*, with its four gilded legs, she didn't see how she could possibly recite her squalid story. "It has been a long time," she said, "since I did precisely this."

Dr Leon, seated, waited, pleasantly expectant.

"Held such a graceful teacup, I mean."

"These belonged to my Creole great-aunt, a colorful character even for New Orleans."

"New Orleans," Andie said. "That city is Eden."

Dr Leon cast an eye toward her notepad as if to make sure all was in place, set her cup on the side table "So, Andie, tell me what brings you here this afternoon, other than Dr Brogden's suggestion." So the clinic guy had called her. "What is it you'd like us to accomplish?"

"There's been another," she paused, "incident, since I talked with him. It's urgent: I have to get control. This is two bizarre sexual episodes in barely 2 weeks. It's got to stop."

She told it all again, the horrifying Archie story as she'd poured it out to Marian on the phone. She hadn't wanted to see her face.

"These recent sexual experiences, one on the heels of the other, are uncharacteristic for you," Dr Leon said finally. "But I expect you've had a spur-of-the-moment fling at some point in your life."

"I'd been with one guy for so long. Eleven years. Once when we were briefly broken up, I had a thing for a few weeks with a friend. Before Charlie…well, I guess I was hard to please. Overly picky. Or something. I had a couple of earlier relationships that didn't turn out well."

"Eleven years is longer than many marriages. Why did it end?"

"It had dragged on and on." She didn't want to waste time on this. "We didn't exactly argue, just grumped along, together but half-ignoring each other. A lot of times I thought I'd end it. But then I didn't." Over and over she had run through what might have happened to decide him: he'd met someone, he really wanted children, he was bored... "I don't know exactly why. Or why now."

"So you dozed, or daydreamed..."

At the beginning, he *had* wanted children. She hadn't been against it, just never ready for it. She could easily picture him playing in his yard with a three-year-old, the two of them making mud pies, joined in silent absorption. She wanted to pat the heads of the two of them, in the careful fond way they were patting the mud.

No, that wasn't what she wanted, or not the only thing. She wanted to slither naked through the mud, through pond slime, dragging tits and belly, tongue and crotch hair through it. She wanted to be coated in the swarming primitive stuff...

"... And then he leaves you with a jolt. Yes?"

"Yes, something like that," dashing the mud thoughts out of her head. When she happened to drive on any of their old routes, hers and Charlie's, to the barbecue restaurant, even over to Southern Pines for a movie, she'd feel the insult repeated, that he could turn her out, that he'd been the one to decide. "He was exhausting in the last couple of years. He always waited for me to provide all the energy and excitement for both of us. At first, for a long time, I was up to it; after a while I wasn't." Still, his absence felt unnatural, as if she'd turned her car onto her road and found that someone had cut down all the trees: again and again, the jolt of dislocation. That night, he'd said, "Andie, I've got to take myself out of the picture." She'd known instantly what he meant, how absolute and huge and final it was, though they hadn't been talking about parting. "Once he left me," she said, "I found that I was very tired."

Dr Leon was watching a grey squirrel on the pine straw at the base of a shrub. It sat perched on its hind legs, balancing its white paunch. To complain about Charlie wasn't why she was here. The mud craving was why she was here. This Rose Leon was saying nothing.

"What I have to find out is what could cause me to behave the way I did with these other guys. And know I was doing it and not care. It's an emergency."

Dr Leon nodded. She looked too calm. Did she understand the gravity? The urgency?

Answering Dr Leon's questions, Andie ran through more of her history: her privileged background, the earlier boyfriends, the travels. "Too many questions too fast," Andie said, "jumping around, I can't think."

"You're doing fine. It's not necessary to think just now. Have there been other jarring occurrences? Other than the ones we've talked about and your ripping out the hardware from my colleague's door." Her eyes smiled.

"That guy was okay. I didn't seriously mean to break his lock." Charlie, his sense of order, would have been shocked. Easier to think about Charlie than her trouble.

"Any other such out-of-the-ordinary events?"

"Just the stuff I mentioned before: I'd started a new painting, a very good start, and I felt a sort of electric shock when I first looked at it. Then I injured my painting arm, took a few days off." She paused. "I've had other odd sensations, similar to the electric buzz. Flashes of light. Being suddenly forceful enough to break a door. A couple of people, knowing nothing, have told me I seemed more relaxed, outgoing." She shook her head. "I'm sure not feeling it. Though at first, up until I saw the dog, it was extra-ordinary, transcendent."

Dr Leon scratched a few sparse notes. Her first in the hour. Andie wanted to see her making notes with certainty, the woman's hand racing across the paper; she wanted to see a solution taking shape over there on that page. "One other thing: I do have an unusual and large commission."

"Are you still working on the new painting as well as the commission?"

"I'm not working on anything but my sanity."

A moment passed. No next question was forthcoming. "So let's slow down for a bit," Dr Leon said. "Let things slide. You've answered all the questions you need to." Her eyes were the kind that had a curved hollow at the top of each lid. Recessing into shadow. Dramatic. "You might want to put down the cup and let your arm relax." This must be the hypnotic part that Cliff had mentioned. Andie set the teacup on the table, fell back into the corner of the sofa.

"Yes," Rose said, "that's good. Are you comfortable?"

She nodded, didn't feel like speaking.

"Let's go back to a moment when you were at the beach on the boat…" And almost instantly she felt herself drift as if she were deep in her work, as if she were floating underwater with the capability of lighting gently almost anywhere.

A thousand a day, she'd said, sitting on that deck. She could be back there, be anywhere. Lifting herself from Archie's desk chair, bent forward, her bottom spread wide as a plate of food.

"…Into any moment of one of these times: what you felt, what your body felt, your emotions unrolling, as you breathe slowly...

"And how the air feels on your skin, what you smell, hear, as you first sense you're entering an unusual experience and you're letting yourself go with it…"

Her hips moved ever so slightly against the plush of the sofa cushion, getting more comfortable. She'd been sitting at the monitor; she'd tapped in "whore." Then the pictures: all those erections, contortions, glazed eyes, blissed-out faces. From her chair before that screen, leaning her chest forward as she pushed up. The thrill was coming back, wound through with shock.

"What you feel as you live in that moment…" The voice trailed off. She heard "sensual" and "falling away," both her hands scrambling to find the elastic top of the bikini, her fingernails combing across her skin as she pulled the panties down. "Where are you now, Andie?"

She tried to answer. The boat was rolling. They'd come out of the waterway through the inlet, onto deep ocean swells. Terrence up on the bridge driving. Mike half-reclined on a deck chair, shorts unzipped, his thighs pressed against the sides of her chest, her head moving with the slow motion of the waves, then faster, devouring him.

"Andie, what you are feeling…take notice…"

She wanted more.

A rocking chair creaked.

There was no rocking chair. Across the room, Dr Leon sat motionless, a dark-feathered staring bird.

"Tell me, Andie, about where you were. Your emotions at the time about the oral sex, if I have that right?"

"I was talking?"

"You murmured a few words that gave me that idea. You made a sharp choking sound."

"Choking?" She thought not of the sex, but of Desmond, the silenced writer. Her mouth tasted bitter, like metal. She started to speak, stopped. "Look," she said, "what do you want me to call you?"

"As you wish. Rose is fine."

She couldn't say Rose. "I was out on the boat. Doing," she tried not to hesitate, "oral sex, as you said." The tick of the clock felt tiny and hoarse as a tropical green wall lizard, grinding and grinding its insects. "Your voice is lulling." Maybe she wouldn't call her anything. "Melodious," she said.

"Your movements, Andie, during your daydream, had a rhythmic motion."

She flinched, suddenly aware of her hips. "Embarrassing."

Dr Leon nodded as if pleased.

Fury rose behind Andie's forehead and her eyes, the light too bright and swimming.

"Did you feel embarrassed about the sexual acts later when you were talking with the man, Mike?"

Andie waited, not speaking until the anger had subsided. "No. I wanted him to obliterate me. In my thoughts, I was straining toward that."

"Why obliterate?"

She hesitated. Her gaze followed a curving burgundy line of the Afghani rug that disappeared beneath the base of a chair. She didn't know how to say. "To turn over everything. Float loose." But that didn't get across the downward-spiraling thrill. To almost lose yourself: all particulars, dignity, every pretension. "Just be reduced to sensation," she said and looked up. "A primitive wet hog-wallow of sensation. Spread out so far and wide that I'm almost transparent, no line where I stop and start."

Dr Leon was writing. "And this is arousing," she said, "this feeling of expansion?"

"No, no, it's the other way around: the arousal and the sex are a way to get to the expansion."

Dr Leon waits, pen paused.

"It's like *being* sex," Andie said. "Almost. Except I don't quite get there. Hopelessly frustrating. That may be as close as I can come, to explaining. "

"That's pretty good, Andie. The submissive nature of the sex, it seems, is a way of putting your everyday self aside."

She wasn't sure what to say to that.

Dr Leon glanced at the clock. "So unless you have another immediate thought, we must quit for now."

Quit? She hadn't gotten an answer. No help at all. This was not acceptable. "What do I do?" feeling her voice move to a higher register, as she reached for her pocketbook and sought Rose's eyes. "How do I get control of myself?"

"I can't answer either question. And I'm concerned for your safety." The same squirrel was still out there, in almost the same place. She wanted to pound the window glass and scare it into motion. Dr Leon mused on. "Here's what's puzzling me," she said. "This kind of behavior doesn't usually come on suddenly..."

"What about dissociative disorders? Cliff said..."

"Not likely. That's usually the result of abuse, which isn't the case here. Also, the desire isn't what's troubling, it's your difficulty exercising any control. So," she said, rising. She seemed tired. "By the time we talk we'll have your medical report, to see if there's anything organic."

"I hope there is," Andie said. If I die, she thought, if it's a brain tumor, then at least I'll be out of all danger, I'll have had an excuse. To Dr Leon, she said: "I'm asking you: between now and then, how do I stop?

"I have no idea, Andie. Not until I know what we're stopping."

In the studio building, three slow-moving art shoppers were straggling along in front of her, moving this way and that as if their sole purpose were to block her way down the hall. From Dr Leon's house to the studio, she'd kept thinking how to handle this first time seeing Archie.

Caitlin stepped out her door, bumping one of the browsers, the feeble old guy. He'd been arduously picking his way along. "I'm so sorry," Caitlin steadied the man as she spoke. Sweet, gawky Caitlin, girlfriend of Tim, in her shirt with the swoopy, see-through sleeves. She was somebody who needed you to hold an umbrella over her, to ward off any harm; the girl was so unwary.

"My fault entirely, my dear," he said. He half-bowed to her before collecting himself to move on. Andie slipped past them quickly before she lost courage, heading toward Archie's door.

"Andie, wait," Caitlin said.

"I saw that," Andie said, her tone convincingly jaunty. "You mustn't clobber our customers." Her resolve to face Archie was already weakening; she was happy for the delay.

Caitlin had steered them out of the line of traffic, over to the wall, where she leaned her five-foot-ten frame. "Andie, I just want to say this," her voice lowered as well, "I heard."

She felt the blood rise in her face.

"I don't know how much it has gotten around," Caitlin said, "but I think anybody who gives you a hard time about it is narrow-minded."

Andie lifted a hand, trying to stop her, though Caitlin was, of course, talking about the Sylvester job.

"And I think we ought to get paid well and have no shame about it. I'm serious." She paused, smile fading. "Your face is incredibly red," she said at normal volume. "Did you get burned at the beach? Omigod, you're having a hot flash. My mother gets the same way."

"I am *not* having a hot flash."

"A hundred thousand dollars," Caitlin said, "for one picture." Her eyes were bright with excitement. "It's fabulous. I'm so glad for you."

"Thanks. That's nice to hear. Not everybody approves, you know."

Her heart was still thumping, which was ridiculous. She'd understood in a second.

Archie! Out of the corner of her eye, she saw his silhouette, big-shouldered, stepping out into the hall. She drew in her breath, glanced in that direction.

No, not Archie. It was Tim. Beautiful, easy-rolling Tim had come out of Caitlin's doorway, his smile expectant. "Hello, Andie." No hint showing of the awkward party moment, which, she now knew, could have been so much worse.

"Hi, Tim." Her voice felt wobbly.

Caitlin had watched her boyfriend's approach the proud way mothers gaze at their kids in doting moments. He put his arm around Caitlin's shoulders, at the same time seizing Andie's hand, planting a loud wet smack on the back. "Haven't seen you in days, have I?" he said. He would fear for her, if he knew. She'd barely dodged telling him and doing God knows what else.

"I guess not. You dropping by for a visit on your lunch hour?" She nodded at his tie and dress shirt. She mustn't spend a second alone with him, under any circumstances. Yet she couldn't shake the idea that he could help her.

"A little," Tim said, "and hanging with my buddy here," jostling Caitlin closer to his side.

She too had had a buddy, Charlie had been her buddy, riding with her, driving, navigating, packing mustardy sandwiches for the road, any time she had a weekend job out of town. The thought of starting over again with anyone made her feel tired. "That's good," she said, "nice for you both. So," stepping back, "gotta go. Thanks, Caitlin." Caitlin still thought Charlie was going to come back and that it would be a good thing, that all would work out well.

It wouldn't. He wasn't coming back. Her throat ached from an upward press of emotion.

# 13

Sunday morning Charlie Singer was feeding his fish in the big tank near his den window. The Bio-Pure for the keyhole cichlids, sticks of plankton for the little guys.

The fighting fish bowl was empty again, after the third try. He could not keep one of those suckers alive and they were supposed to be hardy.

"Vitamin day, boys." He dropped in the supplement and the lake trace elements. "That ought to hold you."

Ambling barefoot into the kitchen, he found half a cup of coffee standing from yesterday, punched in a minute and 15 seconds and watched through the window of the mike as the rack slowly turned.

Phone. He waited until the caller ID appeared. Foreign number. A misdial for sure, somebody wasting his money. "Hello?" The line was full of static.

"Operator, can we get a better connection?" a man's voice at the other end. Who would use an operator instead of a card? Then: "Hang up, I'll call you back."

Charlie took a sip of his coffee. It tasted oily. He picked up on the first ring.

"Much better," the man said. "Look, Charlie… This *is* Charlie Singer I've got, isn't it?"

"That's right."

"Zack Branson, Charlie."

"Sure," he put down the mug. This couldn't be good: his arms shifted into readiness. "Andie's dad. How are you, Zack?"

"Well, I want you to do me a favor, Charlie."

The voice he should have recognized first thing, hoarse, and as if he were always about to laugh, as if nothing could ever be much of a problem.

"I'm trying to catch up with her to tell her I'm coming into town. I keep missing her and her answering machine's off."

"Zack, Andie and I broke up."

Silence from the other end. Then: "Good Lord. Look, I'm sorry to hear that." Another pause. "This is just recent then, is it?"

"Three months." Recent enough that hearing her father's voice could get to him if he let it.

"Three, you say? She hasn't said a word. Not to her mother or to me."

Out the window, a bird was bouncing back and forth along the railing of the dog pen. Scruff lying there with his nose in his paws. He'd thought he was pretty much recovered, 80 per cent, and much of that before the split. "Sorry I can't help you." Charlie's finger was waiting at the disconnect, to cut Zack off before he came up with some courier errand for him to run. He was still too pissed to be carrying messages to her. She'd let him down, that was the long and the short of it. She'd cooled toward him, years ago, without saying why or good-bye.

"Zack, Marian would know how to reach her. Or Otis." She'd be with somebody by now. Or maybe not. The life that she'd like, though she'd never admit it, would be back with her folks, those three in lockstep, no room for anybody else.

"Okay, son. I guess that's that."

"Yessir." He felt a pang as Zack started to draw away, as if holding one more moment might make something different. He ought to know better about that by now. Still it was like catching sight of her. Once at a distance in the village center, he'd glimpsed her copper-colored hair, her bouncy walk, from the back.

"You still building those houses?"

"Still building them."

"I'm glad to know it. You do exceptional work."

"Yessir. Thank you."

"You take care of yourself," and Zack was gone.

He crossed his arms and waited for the memory of Andie to

fully hit and pass over, the raw edge of a hurricane.

It was baffling she hadn't told them. She couldn't be thinking they'd get back together.

It pulled at him to hear Zack's voice. Brought her back in his mind the way she'd been: she could sparkle, by God, like a carnival at night. Toward the end there was something forced about it, reflexive almost. She'd inherited that charm, though, from a master. Zack was who a lot of guys would like to be, adventurous, Hemingway or John Huston, one of those.

At least I don't have to sit through another dinner with Zack as lord-of-the-jungle, gassing on and on with Andie about lamb's eyeball stew they ate on some scrap of an island.

Zack kept his hand on the phone receiver where he'd put it back in the cradle. One way or another that boy had failed her.

He pushed papers aside, dug out the laptop to type a fax. He'd tried to buy her a computer to allow her to take part in the new century. But, no, she wasn't having any of it, she'd buy her own if she wanted one, she was a grown-up and, besides that, she "hated technology, hated progress." She was too young to think that way. The wide empty rectangle opened before him on the screen. "Andie-girl," he wrote. Any one of those kids in the studio would be able pick up a fax and read it while they waited for the drink to drop in the vending machine.

*Took a walk along the water yesterday in front of the hotel in Tel Aviv. They never tell you in Sunday school, or the newspapers either, what a beach town this little country is.*

*The business here is diamonds. "Star of wonder, star of light." I'd like to scoop you up 2 handfuls of them. You'd love the diamond-cutting shops. I'm learning a whole new field, getting into gemstones now. Every so often, you have to come up with a new thing to chase. I'm sick to death of rugs.*

*I guess if I stay with stones your mother and I will wind up back in*

*Colombia and Brazil. Emeralds!! Think about it. Doesn't the thought of green ice strike something in your heart? One of these times you'll have to meet us down in the Brazilian mountains, Minas Gerais. I'd love to show you that place. Now this is the actual truth: there's a town there with streets made out of marble.*

*I'll walk you and your mom down a street paved with white marble. Nothing too good for my girls. I keep wondering how you are. Not much word from you lately.*

*Anyhow, your old Dad hopes you are well. It has been way way too long. I'll be coming your direction soon as I can arrange it. I'll be solo this time; your mom's insisted on taking a couple of months off from traveling, she probably told you. I've got to be in New York and from there you're just a hop and a jump away. I love you, honey.*

*Dad*

He felt so dispirited he didn't even have the heart to check his stocks.

He rang Daphne at the flat. No answer. She'd been saying for weeks that something wasn't right with Andie; the phone conversations didn't feel right. But the split-up was months ago. Months! And Andie hadn't mentioned it; he felt as if she'd slapped him. She couldn't be thinking he'd feel the loss of the guy himself. Although he'd long ago resigned himself to Charlie, decent, perpetually tired-seeming, flat-footed literal, not a whole lot of pizzazz. There was a yearning about him, though, that he'd imagined a woman might like.

Daphne sat in a half-lotus on the tatami in the Buddha room, once more bringing her attention back to her breath. A long honk from the street below, quick screech of tires, then bang!

First crash of the day. A small one.

The breath coming in, cool in the top of her nostrils, cool in the dull grey, turning to reddish light behind her eyelids. So much clamor out there. Zack had said let's soundproof the place, nobody was going to redesign that trap of an intersection.

Exhaling slowly, slowly, like the sound of rolling surf. She hated the thought of workmen dragging their tarps from room to room when deep quiet was what she craved, the breath easing out, slow and measured, and even her own breathing, her swallowing, too loud. The solitude she had to have; no doubt it was turning 60, this need to get her bearings all over again. Her thoughts jumping as if she'd never meditated before. She hadn't found silence, not once, alone here for days with her calendar cleared of lunches and meetings, her soup kitchen duty; still her mind was a clatter of forks.

She watched against the screen of her closed eyelids the shifting shapes, the clouds of color, moving today like lava, flowing, then reversing its flow… She wandered inside the tangle of flashing color: now it was a forest, above her and all around her. Now the leaves, the trees, were turning ruddy gold: the rust of Andie's hair.

That beautiful auburn hair looked rumpled and dull, Andie's face downcast, turned away. And further away.

A police whistle shrieked, more angry shouts from down on the street.

Andie before her: a child no more than three, floating alone in a tiny fantastical boat on an ink-blue pond. The boat a long open seed pod, large enough to carry her, so light the surface tension was unbroken, the water bulging just before it dipped slightly downward around the sides. Her racing laughing little girl sitting still, small face sober. The boat moving as if it were being pulled…

The phone. She jolted, but let it ring. Not Andie or Zack, not their special ring. She waited. Another ring.

The waterscape was gone, the instant passed when it might have reassembled. All she could picture was that so-familiar painting hanging in the Tate, *Lady of Shallott*. The young woman, face stricken, with her long wild hair, setting out alone on dark water in a candlelit gondola, a vessel mysteriously aware of itself and its purpose. The woman…a girl, really…letting go of the tether that held the boat at the marshy edge.

Again the ring, the pause between…another ring, maddening as hiccups…and ring…and pause…and ring…and she was rocking with the rhythm of it, still rocking as the voice came on, recorded, a telemarketer. Magazines. Fortnightly. Clicking off.

In the quiet, she could hear herself swallow, see the micro-jolt to her vision that came with each heartbeat.

She could see herself, sitting cross-legged, her hands palm-up. Andie, Zack, tiny, both of them like Tom Thumb, standing, digging in their sharp little heels, one on each of her flat open palms.

Her eyes popped open. A rush of certainty: of what? Her hands lay open and loose, one on each knee.

She yanked the headband off her hair, letting the damp weight of it fall around her face. She could still locate the pointed pressure on the flat of each hand. The thought came toward her, as if from the wall above her altar: The two of them, Andie and Zack, needed to talk. Or to not talk. The way they used to sit together at night, Zack with his Scotch, Andie with her paper and colored pencils.

What I must do, she thought, is keep watch. Only that. Wrap them in prayers.

In her fax, only a few days ago, Andie had sounded fine, working on a huge job.

But with the tips of her fingers, the skin of her face, she sensed electrical storm, even though bright sun hitting the blond wood of the altar shone almost white, making her squint.

Andie dumped the plastic sacks of groceries on the counter. "Marian!" she called out. No Marian. Well, that was okay. She'd been here days on end, longer than anybody could be expected to stay

She started unloading the food: Pringles, anchovies, peanuts, grapes, the low-cal cookies, cans clanking against each other: the sound made the room feel empty. She shoved a couple of frozen dinners into the icebox. The freezer air came out in a cold cloud.

It was terrible timing, Zack coming here now. Him on the beach in Tel Aviv, walking along the water's edge among girls in bikinis and running kids. She could see it clear as anything. Him in those faded purple trunks, barrel-chested, with the thick mat of hair turned white against his year-round tan; and taking in every sight and sensation with such relish. Heading back to the hotel, he'd wrap a sarong around his waist, like some Melanesian chieftain, and think nothing of it, not a second of doubt about whether it was thought manly in Israel to wear a flowered skirt. Telling him not to come would only bring him sooner.

Nothing could stop him once he got it in his head. She dropped down into a kitchen chair. The shim had come out from under the corner of the table and it teetered as she leaned her head in her hands.

Then there was the matter of her Charlie news. From one fax to the next, she'd delayed telling them. Being left, dropped cold, made her look like a failure in the most fundamental way. But that omission was small compared to what she'd be hiding now.

What if she couldn't hide it?

No medical excuse either, that much was clear now. Her doctor would have called already if the physical had shown brain tumors, anything amiss.

She could leave town, pretend she'd never received Zack's message.

Not possible. She couldn't do that to him.

He'd never in her life said one word to her about sex. So old-fashioned that way. And all the while flirting with every living female, including her. She tipped the table back and forth, rocked it faster.

At the front of the chapel, the sexton was pushing a vacuum. He hadn't seen her slide into a back pew. With the place near empty, you could smell the wood, the musty hymnbooks. She wanted to take a hymnal in both hands, whap it against the top of the pew ahead: raise the dust and demand an answer. Two shrinks, her doctor and Marian: none of them could explain. She was running out of places to look. She'd stayed out of trouble for days now, but waked every morning with clenched teeth, with pain in her jaws and temples, scared to throw back the covers and put her feet on the floor.

Pressed close at the aisle end of a pew, she wasn't sure what to do but look around. She'd sat here a lot of Sunday mornings as a child; her mother, pagan though she was, had still insisted on Sunday school. She'd balked: it was boring. Her resistance finally had won out.

So now she was flung back here again, panicked, beseeching.

In the chancel, the vacuum made its hollow roar with the shrill note on top. If the janitor would get finished and leave, she could go to the front and light the candles. She craved the weight of a hush. Empty, the sanctuary was an ordinary room, all the life gone out of it. Sitting by herself in this flattened air wasn't going to help.

The guy up front took a step away from her with each rake of the vacuum wand. On the aisle carpet near her, smooth sweeps were fresh; he was almost done. Under the khaki work shirt, his wide-spaced shoulder blades moved together and apart. She wanted to slip up behind him and put her hands under his shirt, up onto those warm plateaus of muscle and bone, feel them shifting.

Her legs trembled, a rush of energy running through her, waking every membrane. She slid forward on the pew. She had to leave. If she stood, she might head toward him. She sat motionless, eyes locked on the pew rail ahead; so she couldn't see him.

The rumble of the vacuum died.

Her breath came quicker in the silence; where was he? A door creaked open at the side, the wheels of the cleaner bumped off the carpet and onto the tile of a hallway. Door closed behind him.

Gone.

She slumped against the wooden back. Saved.

But no place was safe. She'd turned into some kind of freak. You couldn't live like this.

She let her head loll back, stared up at the dark beams of the ceiling.

A friend of Marian's knew someone who'd gone through an exorcism, in some swampy-bayou part of Louisiana. A horrible ordeal, three days with no sleep, a shouted interrogation, on and on and finally "the voice of the devil" had left the girl; she was young, 13, and different forever after.

Marian was parked outside and waiting, on duty again, giving her the privacy she'd thought she needed in here. Which meant she'd had no bodyguard just now when she was in danger. Marian kept showing up for duty. For the company, she said. But that hadn't stopped her with Archie. So what good was it doing? Other than it was nice to have her around.

Sliding forward onto the kneeling bench, Andie looked to be sure no one else was here. Eyes closed, she began to pray, saying the words in her mind: Please fix whatever is wrong, so I can count on myself, not live in fear.

The words sounded wrong. Too flat.

She tried again: Help me! I'm in trouble.

A loose hair tickled her face, moved by a barely perceptible draft.

God, I'm here, Andie, daughter of Daphne and Zack, 38 years old…

Single, a painter….

Begetter of no one…

The biblical rhythm was comforting.

And in Jesus Christ, his only son our Lord. The murmur of it seemed to swell up under her: Maker of Heaven and Earth...Father, Son and Holy Ghost. A hesitation in her throat stopped thought of the words, then released her again.

Yea, though I walk through the valley of the shadow...

Elliott went to Quaker meetings, he would pray for her.

Leadeth me beside the still waters...

She was on the verge of sneezing, the singsong broken. Every slanted shaft of window light was full of dust. Her eyes had come open.

The fragments of scripture, so familiar, floated.

Hallowed be thy name.

Restoreth my soul.

The sneeze had retreated.

The trouble might already be finished, might have finished yesterday or the day before, no more episodes, no more electric shocks like little seizures; maybe the thing with the janitor had been normal interest.

It hadn't felt normal.

How was she going to deal with any client, much less Billy Sylvester tomorrow afternoon? She wasn't safe left alone with his driver... Or did it even matter whether she was alone with a man? It could happen in public, in front of people. Jesus! She rose quickly and headed out of the church, praying as she walked:

Please, I need this ordeal to be over. The prayer was taking her over: God, I need a sign, like Noah, watching and praying for dry land, wanting a dove with an olive leaf in its beak.

She put a hand on the twisted iron handle to the outer door. What the poor man, Noah, must have felt, staring out across endless ocean, the deck under his feet trembling from the force of the pent-up wild animals.

# 14

Lots of fat new tubes of paint. She laid them in her traveling case with the half-used crumpled ones, tucking the luscious pristine ones in gently, so as not to dent their glossy white sides. She'd bought them to cheer herself up.

Today was the day: off to Raleigh to paint the senator. The first sitting tended to be the hardest; soon it would be over. She'd given the umbrella a glance on the way in, then packed with her back to it.

Otis knew she was going. Marian, busily at work down the hall, didn't have to be burdened with this information; neither did Elliott, whose disapproval she didn't need.

She'd loaded up both arms, with the case, the folding easel, before she turned. One more glance at the painting. Whether she could bring herself to look was a test of how well she'd gotten herself pulled together.

From ten feet back, she took it in whole: yellow arcs, concave and full of light, rising and falling. She hadn't touched a brush to the canvas since she'd swiped on the crossed circle: the yellow-on-yellow, barely-visible message to herself that said Don't Paint. The work was just as rough as she remembered; though the image had integrity, an organic, inevitable feel, the way any life form did.

Doing this much had been fairly easy. If blanking out your mind and falling into feverish sleep could be considered easy. She doubted now if she'd ever have the courage to fall into that painting trance again.

She wouldn't dare touch this piece in any other state, never mind that the composition was absurdly simple, too simple: a crescent hanging, a sharp downward sliver of moon or sun, giving off perverse light.

Three hours later, Andie, seated in the brass-nailed leather armchair, made quick sketches, mainly to give her hands something to do. The senator, tipped back behind his desk, was on the phone. She shouldn't have taken this job. What was she doing sitting here in this room with him? It was an endorsement. Elliott and Marian were right.

She flipped a page of her pad, started another rough drawing. Sun from the floor-to-ceiling window was hitting his right side; the two halves of his face, one more brightly lit, looked slightly and peculiarly different from each other: it was the way his blunt features cast shadows. He had on a patronizing smile for the person on the line.

"Arguably," he said to the caller, "but you and I are not going to take the time to argue." He was looking at her now, but she resisted meeting his eyes. She maintained her air of studying the situation professionally. She'd had other tough assignments, creepy customers, too-friendly ones. She'd never foundered.

He leaned forward, elbows on his desk, fast on his way to signing off. Her stomach tightened. "Nossir," he said, "that's what I am telling you. The train is on the track and the rails are bounteously greased."

She could hear the pleading tone in the unintelligible voice in the receiver.

Billy licked his lips, jerked on the knot of his tie. "Now, sir, I'm going to excuse myself. I have another loyal constituent before me awaiting my attention." Pause. "Well, maybe that's something we can help you with. Best to Samantha and the girls." He put down the phone.

"I usually use a speakerphone," he said, "to keep from getting a derned crick in my neck. I felt this gentleman would like his dignity spared."

"No doubt," she said. "And good morning to you, Senator."

He made a token rise from his seat in greeting. "And the same to you, ma'am." He gave her a purposely devilish grin and leaned back in his chair. The lower buttons of his shirt pulled.

"And you remember I told you to call me Billy."

"About this portrait," she said. He was not going to charm her into forgetting who he was.

"Looks like you've got the thing well underway." He nodded toward the sketchpad in her lap, unfazed by her unresponsiveness.

"Capturing a few gestures, that's all." She dreaded having to move from where she sat, to start to work with positions for him. Her chair seemed almost a safe harbor. She imagined the yellow canopy of umbrella over her, protecting her.

"I got the pages yesterday," she said, "spelling out your specifications."

"That was supposed to have gone to you a week ago. I'll have somebody's head on a stick."

"It arrived soon enough." She heard a hint of sarcasm emerge in her tone, surprised to find herself so bold.

"Don't people usually have some idea how they want their picture to look?"

"Sure," she smiled to defuse any combativeness, "though that's a lot different from having an image consultant's views on message management." She forced herself out of the chair without having planned her next move. "Not that any of that's a problem," she said. "People sometimes give me a snapshot to copy, rather than taking time to sit or trying to force the kids to hold still."

Her automatic professional demeanour had mostly taken over. "Let's have you roll your chair a bit to the right and back. I'm told we'll need to get the state and US flags in, if you don't mind." She moved the tall flag stand; she was stepping behind his desk…it had to be done…then moving back to have a look. The brass eagle at the top of the flagstaff behind him was nice, with spots of yellow gleam; the drape of the flag was good too, fat folds heavy and rich. Enough room behind his desk to pull in a small car, the office was spacious.

"I like room to turn around in," he said, as if in explanation. He was awfully good at reading expressions. Not surprising, given his political skill. He seemed uneasy with her tromping freely on his turf. Which helped her relax a little more.

Last night, she'd decided she would avoid any of the usual adjusting of the subject, no lifting of an arm or chin. No contact. She'd tell him from a distance what to do. She looked again at the composition. Under her breath: "That's not bad."

"You going to need to paint same time every day, to get the same light? And what if the weather changes, and we have a grey bluster coming out of the northeast instead of this sweet ray of sunshine I'm basking in today?"

"We can work around any of that."

"I didn't see you bringing an easel in here." He probably wasn't capable of sitting quietly. But then a silence in this room could be even more unsettling.

"I don't need it today." She was quickly drawing, the pad balanced along her left forearm. "First, I'm going to put together some sketches to show you. You and your committee."

"Used to be I didn't have a committee,"

"Hold it there just another second, let me get this." Staying automatic was going to carry her through.

"Sorry. Sorry. I don't mean to interfere with Ms. Rembrandt."

Her pencil slowed.

"This image thing," he said, "I always did just fine without one."

"I'd say you've had a pretty definite image from the start." She motioned him to be at ease, as she moved around the room, searching for the view that would tell her she was getting warm, closing in on the arrangement that would click him into place.

"I reckon I am pretty definite. Morality is not a relative thing, you know. Times may change, a lot of things may change; however, your friend Billy stands where he always stood." He laughed to himself, glanced down at his own extended leg, the plain preacher shoe rubbed to a high polish. Probably he got a shine in airports, in one of those tall chairs, a jovial black man whipping a rag back and forth over his instep.

Before this job was over, she'd have to speak: say how she opposed him and all the atrocities he'd supported. The whole hateful history behind his easy charm. He was probably expecting it.

"Remind me how long we're going to be here today."

"I'm going to need another fifteen or so minutes, hard to say. I can come back if you need to stop."

"I expect we'd better do that."

He had relaxed into a different position. A much better one, unposed: the way his legs fell apart from each other, his face complacent, showing the hint of a dare. Dazzling! this glimpse of him. She memorized it: the leg position, the set of his mouth. This was the one, the defining image: his too-smooth unsettling ease with power. He seemed unaware of what he'd shown.

He said, "You're not making the commute all the way down to Pinehurst, are you?" She felt a tug of resistance to saying where she was sleeping. Which was silly. As if being touchy and disagreeable would somehow exonerate her for doing the work. "It's not that far," she said. "The assistant in your outermost office found some closet space for my supplies. If I decide to leave anything."

"You drive carefully, then."

Even his show of concern grated, never mind that it shouldn't.

"Aren't we paying you enough to put up with a little of my foolishness?" He smiled with a trace of that gleam she'd seen on the golf course, clearly proud to have noticed her grain of irritation, even more so to have caused it.

"All right then," he said, before she'd pulled together a reply. He gave her a slow thoughtful look, though he had claimed to be out of time. "Let me show you something," he said. He slid open his top desk drawer, which rolled without a sound. "Look-a-here." She was going to have to walk over there next to him to inspect this item, whatever it was. She stepped closer. He was turning in his hands: what? A church key, bamboo-handled, the wood varnished shiny as his shoes. "I keep this here," he said. "Not that I was ever a drinker myself. Not much of one." He grabbed the tab-top can of iced tea that sat open on his desk, punched a second hole. "See," he said, "how easy, cutting through that soft metal skin like tearing wet paper. What I'm saying: It's just that easy and convenient to get into trouble, any kind."

That was one thing she already knew. She stepped back, put three feet between her and the circle of his heat. "I assume you're not suggesting you want a church key in the picture."

"No, that wouldn't be too smart, would it?" He dropped it back into the drawer, which rolled shut. "But you make sure you show in this picture a man who believes in ideals, who does not walk close to the edge."

"I'll keep that in mind. Where'd you get it? The can opener."

"Saigon. Congressional delegation." He stood, offered her his hand. They shook; the flesh of his palm had the firmness of tight upholstery. She smiled, half in relief at leaving.

"I apologize for my old-fashioned sexist over-protectiveness," he said. "It's hard to change old ways."

"Maybe it's too late," she said.

He laughed with genuine warmth. "I want you to tell that to my image people. Those boys and girls have got no better sense than to argue with success."

Early evening by the time she got back to the studio. Turning onto the hall, she saw Otis locking his door. Time for him to clock in as bartender. He'd already changed to the white shirt, black vest and pants they made him wear. He didn't look up; she walked louder, purposefully, not a browser. He still didn't turn. She sidled up behind him.

"Otis," she said, in a stage whisper from behind, "Since when does locking the door require such concentration?" The back of her hand trailed across his butt, the two hard rounded forms, neatly cleft, as she came around to his other side.

He turned, half-smile uncertain on his face. Seeing it, she felt her heart go to beating fast in the base of her throat, pounding under her collarbone. What had she just done?

"Since when do you grope my ass?"

Her hand had acted on its own. Not a moment to stop it.

"I wasn't thinking." Her gaze fixed on his keys dangling from the lock on the door. A hot chemical of bodily alarm was rushing through her; I'll have to tell him: that I'm a risk. Elliott too.

He lifted a hand and pulled the door key out. "No complaints," he said, "I was just curious, is all." He nodded at the door. "This lock has been giving me trouble."

Otis had gone to get coffee refills at the canister behind the bar, no doubt buying time while he thought of what to say to her, now that he'd heard her story. The neon beer signs cast a blue tint on his white shirtsleeves, the vest soft as black velvet in the dim light. She watched his slow saunter back to the booth. His break had already gone on for more than 15 minutes. He glanced out around the room, didn't look at her as he put the heavy mug down in front of her. He slid back into his seat on the other side.

"I think I'm recovered now," he said. "From the shock."

She searched his face for signs of disapproval. "You're not recovered at all," she said. Three sentences into her story, by the time she'd gotten to the thousand dollars, his face had flashed alarm, then turned watchful and masked. "Your knowing will make you a safety zone," she said. Her stomach felt full of turning weight. "That's what I want to count on. I need a team of guardians, a monitoring committee. Not just Marian and me."

"It's good to know I'm on your shortlist," he said. "Of people to inform."

Surely he knew that. He was one of her closest people. Apparently he didn't. The thought made her heart sink another notch.

"It's a pre-emptive move," she said. "You're the obvious choice of somebody I'd come on to." The backhanded touch in the hall, it hadn't gone further. She'd managed to stop there. "I don't want to mess up how we're friends," she said. She felt herself leaning closer across the table, as if this were a date.

"But Archie..." he said into his coffee with disbelief and something like indignation. If anything, he seemed protective of Archie.

"I don't know," she said. "I guess he either got lucky or unlucky."

Otis started to speak. Didn't. She shouldn't have said it was Archie, hadn't meant to. Now, with Otis knowing, she'd set up a permanent tension in the group, an additional one.

She was tracking his every facial move, to see how badly her stock had sunk. Already it was clear he wasn't going to have any solutions, simple or otherwise. How could he?

"You do know, I hope," he said, "that this kind of shit isn't good for you. You're not as easy-come-easy-go as you pretend. Nobody's fooled."

"I see. I don't remember making any claims along those lines. And, yes, I know it's not good for me. Why do you think we're talking?" She put her head in her hands, raised it again. "Sorry," she said. "I don't mean to be that way."

"Damned if I know what to tell you," he said. He adjusted his hammered-silver belt buckle, his standard move when anything unsettled him.

"Just keep an eye out, Otis. If you see me edging toward any kind of trouble, steer me out of it, if you can. And pay attention to what led up to it, any kind of trigger." In the bar, Marian had seen her while she was dangerous: wet electricity inside her and lust for the boy-waiter, all at once. Desire and the strange sensations were all wound around each other. The burst of umbrella-painting too. Her thoughts kept coming back to the mysterious energy pool. She knew only that some religion or other believed in it.

"One time I was about sixteen," he said, "I got between my big sister and a boy I knew wasn't any good," he shook his head, laughed. "I paid for that a long time."

"You have a wonderful laugh, Otis. I know I've said that several thousand times."

He threw her a sharp glance, obviously checking her intention.

She held up both hands, as if to show she was unarmed. He could easily view the whole conversation as a come-on, a bit of foreplay. Which was not what she meant, not that she was aware of.

"Okay," he said. "Sorry."

He seemed to be easing back to normal, with an added assessing quality to his gaze, as if he were watching the needle on a scale, waiting to see where it stopped.

# 15

She sat with her case of drawings in Billy's outer office. He was in no rush to see her; she'd been waiting almost 20 minutes. The assistant at the desk was a young black guy; wouldn't you know he'd be black? A racist senator's most important accessory: Shawan Dupree, her partner in crime, looked crisp, well-starched, busy-busy at the computer. After asking her to be seated, he hadn't cast another glance in her direction.

Surprising that the senator didn't have more phone calls. Maybe they were all cut off at the pass, somewhere down the hall.

A beep came from some unseen appliance.

"He's ready," Shawan said without getting up. "You may go in."

This time Billy came out from around the desk to greet her. He was more unnerving when he was on his best behavior, his attentiveness inescapable.

He glanced at her carrying case. "What we got?"

"Rough sketches. Different angles and positions. Just to show you some layouts."

"That means I won't know if you've properly captured my beauty."

"Right," as she glanced around the room. How to display these without pulling up a chair behind his desk…?

"You have a conference room empty? So we can spread these out?"

"We do indeed. Suitably serious for the occasion."

By the time they walked into the room, another well-starched young man, this one white, was setting out milk and sugar for coffee.

"Real milk," she said. "Other boardrooms use the powdered stuff."

"Real cream. Do you know what the press would do to me if

I got within a mile of white powder?" He looked on the verge of a wink. "You know, news reporters are the only people who talk to me the way you do."

"How's that?"

"Uppity. Making a real point of being unimpressed."

"I doubt if you talk to them," she said, "the cheeky way you do with me."

He laughed. "But I do."

Seated, they both loosely gripped the arms of their captain's chairs. Her drawings were laid out for his inspection. "So are you objecting to my manner?" she said. "I can be formal, obsequious, whatever is required."

"See, that's exactly what I mean." He put on a pair of glasses, rimless, that she hadn't seen. They were almost endearing, as if he were wearing flannel pajamas, instead of that maybe-Armani suit. "I'm not objecting. You be as sassy as you want to. I find it appealing."

He was studying each sketch as if it were a potential investment. He was certainly good at charm, at hiding his true nature.

"Now you know that I'm not going to be allowed to make this decision all by myself. We've been over that."

"I understand."

"But just shooting from the hip here, I like this one where I'm sitting with both feet planted on the floor, without the desk being such a barrier."

The dangerously honest one, with knees slightly akimbo. "It's unusual," she said. If he were looking at more than an outline here, if he saw the facial expression inextricably linked with that pose, he'd think twice.

That look: smiling, calculating, disturbingly mixed, self-possessed. No way, though, that she was going to do anything that would endanger the second payment. Or drag the project out. She mustn't let herself stay in this situation a moment too long, him with his oily charm and his monstrous history, far worse in effect than any one lynch mob.

Elliott came to his apartment door in running shorts and a stretched-out undershirt that hung on his skinny frame. "Come on in," he said. "But don't get close. I'm sweaty. Came home for a lunch-time run." Elvis, his goopy-eyed old hound, didn't bother to bark.

"I can't," she said. Taking precautions was now almost automatic. "You come out and talk a minute at the picnic table." She gestured behind her to the sun-blasted play area near the parking lot.

He peered out over her shoulder. "I never saw anybody sit there. Is this some kind of special historic occasion?"

She hesitated. "I'd rather not see it that way." He clicked the leash onto the dog's collar.

"I'll get to the point," she said, before they were fully settled on the benches. Her voice had the hint of a shake. He would never see her the same way again. "Before I lose my nerve. I'm having a problem. I just want you to be warned, to be sure I don't…I mean, so nothing interferes with our being buddies."

He propped his forearms against the edge of the table, cleared his throat, as if he were the one who had to speak. She focused on his sharp Adam's apple to get the story started without having to look him in the eye.

She made the telling as quick and general as she could.

He watched her, his long face canted to one side. She couldn't tell what he was thinking and he didn't interrupt.

"Say something," she said finally, when she'd told him as much as she was going to.

He cleared his throat again, the Adam's apple, up and down, up and down. "I'm surprised," he said, "that you feel you can't control it."

"But not that I did these things? You think I would do this on purpose?"

"No. Definitely not. But, Andie, what about the nude modeling, for my class? I was floored…."

"I was already crazy by then, or on my way."

He nodded. They sat in silence, each of them making restless moves, as if starting to speak and then stopping. Elvis was nosing at something in the grass.

"Elliott?"

"What?"

"You still go to those Quaker meetings, right?"

He nodded.

Did she dare risk a long ride alone with him? If she seduced him, he'd wind up feeling horrible: he was so scrupulous, and devoted to Belinda.

"Why do you ask?" he said.

"I was just thinking…" Sitting in a silent meeting she might find out what was going on inside her.

He waited. But she needed him to do the asking. She'd feel less at fault. He knew perfectly well what she wanted, yet sat there impassive.

"Take me with you," she said. "I need to go." She'd already spent a dangerous half-hour in a church, but this was different.

"Sure," he said. "You'll like it. It gives your mind a break."

A break. She caught a breath that threatened to turn into a sob. "I'm so tired, Elliott, from keeping watch on myself." She yearned to press her face against his damp T-shirt, his chest, and feel his hand lightly stroking her hair.

# 16

The den had a good feel to it, all the pillows and throws, brocade, tassels, velvet, so soft and sensual, the kind of atmosphere she associated with grown-up secrets. Half-reclining in the corner of the sofa, catching just enough drowsying warmth from the sun, Andie wanted to let her eyes close, slip away from the upcoming conversation, let Dr Leon solve the problem without her.

She was still on the phone, taking the call around the corner in the kitchen. "Unfinished business," she'd said, hurriedly pointing Andie toward the entrance to the den. As if it were likely she'd forget how to find her way.

Rose didn't sound close to signing off. The words were muffled. Sitting here uneasy was much the same as waiting for Billy, but in a house of velvet pillows.

At home, her decorating theme was dusty boards, except for the kitchen's starting-to-curl linoleum. Otis had always said she was peculiar not to have any of her work on her walls.

She could hang her two rugs, the gift from her parents' Morocco trip she'd missed senior year. The big one on the living room floor was a furious firestorm of color, red melting toward yellow under the black geometric pattern of diamonds and the stick figures that supposedly had conjuring power. When she'd asked Zack where they'd bought the carpets, he'd told her an *Arabian Nights*-type tale about a tribal village in the Middle Atlas Mountains. He and Mom had gone there in a Jeep, rattling along behind a rug trader who'd led the way on his camel. So easy to slip back into that world and the languorous feeling it gave her. The way she imagined the feel of opium, which she'd once had a whiff of: sweet, floral, numbing, mild. But this nostalgia was worse than a drug; it was available day and night, free and addictive. Had she no other inner resource? She had hopes for the Quaker meeting, but would probably daydream there as well.

"Finally," Rose said from the doorway. "I do apologize." Crossing the roon, she dabbed a tissue to her forehead: the phone call must have been personal.

"You're not late," Andie said. "I think I was early." Rose smiled like a mother whose child has surprised her with politeness. By the time Rose was settled in the chair, she was composed, focused.

"Quick change of gears."

A slight nod. She waited for Andie to begin.

"A scary episode to report. I groped the butt of a guy who's a friend."

Rose lifted her eyebrows, made a note. She seemed a little cool, more detached and clinical than before, which was disappointing. Maybe she was still trying to recover from the phone call.

"And you stopped there?" Rose said.

"Yes."

"That seems to be progress."

"Didn't feel so to me."

"Have you had other times this week when you've felt out of control?"

"I don't think so. No."

"Life has seemed normal then, other than the one gesture of touching your friend."

"As if that were nothing! It wasn't the kind of gesture people usually make, not like that."

"The previous week you managed to avoid anything inappropriate with the church sexton."

"Do you hear how that sounds?" Andie said, her voice rising. "Ludicrous! To consider that an accomplishment?"

Rose let the pen fall loose between her fingers. "Andie, what if you made a conscious decision to take some brave step? Instead of blindly leaping into trouble, choose to make a move on behalf of something you're passionate about."

"Why? How's that going to help?"

"It might channel some of this energy you have."

That word again. But Rose was a medical doctor and probably not a big believer in energy pools. She let her head fall back against the rail of the sofa, stared up at the ceiling. Over the center of the room, the light fixture was made of short loops of crystals, held fast in the center, a little upside-down umbrella. Thinking of the yellow canvas, she felt no passion, only gut-queasy fear.

"I'm not passionate about anything but stopping these episodes. When I get home at night and climb into bed, when I know I've made it through the day, I'm so relieved I could weep. Up until then I don't have a moment of safety." She imagined a flash of sympathy from Rose but didn't lift her head to see. "Anyway, I'm shaky these days," she said. "I can't risk strong feelings."

"When did you last feel passion, of any sort?"

She saw again the dried-up old woman in the hut in Guayaquil, the one she'd promised herself she'd never be. She lifted her head. "I loved Charlie."

"I believe that."

Saying it like that, so simply…I loved him…without qualifying or explaining, gave her a bruised feeling in her chest. She forced herself back to the question: passion. As a kid, she'd been in a lather about everything, all through her school years. For a while, she'd been a maniac about gymnastics, even after she'd cracked three ribs falling across the balance beam.

"I know I was excited about work, the first couple of years after college." Unbearable to think she'd been sinking since that far back. The only passions she felt now were for past times. She should tell Rose that Zack was coming.

"The umbrella project," she said, "I got to the studio just past sunrise that morning, so excited my hands were on the verge of trembling."

A nod. "And after you had begun?"

"Urgency, that's all I remember, the need to hurry. The time spent working was a blur, of no particular length. Then something like inner fireworks." And she'd insanely thought something almost angelic had touched her. "That rush of beginning," she threw out her hands, "that was the whole show. I'm a failure in the passion department. It's hard to get it right: either it's too much to hit anybody with or it shuts down completely." Her arms dropped at her sides, she stared out at the stone wall along the back of the yard. "What is it you're wanting me to come up with?"

"You already know. As I said before: channel the energy. Throw yourself into painting the umbrella. I don't know why this canvas is so important, but it is."

Outside the window, the pattern of dark seams in the garden wall seemed to float loose, hovering inches in front of the stone, an irregular black grid like the overlay in her carpets at home. She was drifting away, as if Rose had used her lulling voice. Under her fingers she felt again the stone as she walked along the side of her old house, toward the back yard. The young Andie in the upstairs bedroom would say the cause of this whole implosion, the self-abasement, electric shocks, the furious painting, it had to be one thing, one force.

How would she know?

By studying the timing and sequence of what she'd felt and done, by taking a long look the way a painter does: seeing what's there, rather than what's expected.

She pulled her gaze away from the window. Rose was watching her. The hour was over, and more. Her body felt like a sack of heavy weights as she leaned to collect her pocketbook. Her check was already written.

Rose wanted her to paint with passion. She pushed herself to standing, made a promise to herself. "I'll go to my studio," she said, "make a stab at working."

She stood in front of the canvas; then paced before it as if she were a tiger in a cage walking back and forth, her gaze fixed on an unmoving target. For the last 10 minutes she'd been sitting cross-legged on the floor in front of it, straight-backed as a yogi, seeing and not seeing the livid yellow shape. Noticing, then losing sight of, the crossed circle she'd made to warn herself off.

Rose's parting shot: Sit with it, whether or not you get anything done. The tactic hadn't worked. Half an hour she'd stared at it and what had changed? The fear felt more diffuse, more amorphous.

She'd at least squeezed paint onto a plate. That showed good intent.

A knock at the doorjamb. Otis. He wended his way back to where she sat, pulled up a chair beside her spot on the floor. American men, almost all of them too stiff to sit cross-legged.

"What?" she said. "You never come in. You talk from the doorway." He didn't smile. Something was wrong.

"Caitlin's boyfriend," he said. "Tim."

"Yes?"

"Killed last night," his voice turning thick, "in a motorcycle accident."

Killed?

Tim?

Tim wasn't dead. He was too robust.

But the news began to move into her mind, pushing everything else into the distance. Four days ago in the hall, he was kissing her hand, delighted with himself and everybody else. So warm and physical, unhesitating.

"Ten o'clock," Otis said, "a few minutes after. A drunk driver hit him head-on."

She saw him flying. Tears welled up.

"Fractured his skull," Otis said. She pushed horrifying images, his mangled body, out of her mind. Otis pressed his lips together, as if he'd said too much.

So many nights they'd all played volleyball in the back yard there. Tim, bare-chested, heavy-muscled, jumping with his legs flung out like a cheerleader. All the times he'd come to the building wearing those beat-up boots with the buckles hanging, carrying his helmet, flushed to his eyes from the wind. "Caitlin must be devastated."

Otis bowed his head, made a sound, maybe agreement. "They'd been together," he said, "since ninth grade."

Tim, so hyper-alive, you could almost see his heartbeat. Tim was *gone*? She wanted him here, with all his pats and hugs, coming around a corner, saying: Hey there, Ms. Andalusia. She wanted him back, with his easy air of knowing.

To Otis: "What can we do?"

"Archie talked with her, he said no flowers."

She hadn't meant flowers, she didn't know what she'd meant.

Otis got up slowly from the chair.

She put her face in her hands. The full weight of the news was starting to rush toward her, a tall wave.

Otis leaned, patted her shoulder. "I'm sorry, Andie," he said. She didn't look up. His hand touched once more, brushing across her hair.

He wandered out, patting at counters and cabinets as he walked. In a moment she heard him talking to someone in the hall, their voices too quiet to be understood. She opened her mouth to let out the cry, but what came was no more than a squeak.

At the turn-off onto her long dirt driveway, Andie looked hard into the shadows to the right of her house. Just outside the reach of the porch light, a car was parked, she was sure of it. She couldn't handle company tonight, unless it was somebody who knew Tim.

While she watched, the car's interior lit. Zack. A smile relaxed her whole face. It was him, getting out, the door still open, only his middle lighted by the car's insides.

She pulled in on the other side of the driveway, hopped out. Behind her, his door slammed and the light turned off. His footsteps on the grass rustled toward her. In the dark with the moon behind, she'd recognize his big head if she knew nothing else.

"Hello, my girl," he said.

"Hello, Zack."

She could barely see his face. He held out his arms. He smelled exactly the same. Cigarettes, a hint of burlap or sawdust, the faint scent of alcohol.

He rocked her, slightly, side to side. She put her face against his shoulder, rested there a moment, then forced herself to lift her head. "Where have you come from?"

"New York. Tonight." When they stood apart, she could see half his face clearly, his head tipped back, eyelids lowered, mouth held in the perusing way that said he was concentrating on nothing in the world but you.

"You got here quicker than I thought."

"I needed to see you." They were crossing the porch. His heavy footsteps on the wood sounded amplified.

"Come on in." She reached in and flipped on the living room light. He was wearing the kind of shirt a photographer or trout fisherman might wear, his Ray-Bans showing over the top of one of the many pockets. "No, wait, instead go get your bag out of the car and I'll put on the coffee. You've eaten? If you haven't, we can go to the village, the Holly Inn maybe."

"Lord, I haven't eaten there in a while."

"You've left the town behind."

"I never would do such a thing. Anyway, don't worry about feeding me. I had a heartbreakingly good old American steak only a couple of hours ago. And I've booked a room. You don't need to haul out the mildewed quilts on my account."

"Nice, Dad."

"I know I'm in trouble when I'm addressed formally."

"What kind of visit would that be with you staying in the hotel? You already have a bed reserved."

From the doorway, he cast an assessing look at her sofa, with its slight inward tilt of the seat. "I'd consider it an honor," he said. His eyes looked gentle with fatigue, older. Eight or 9 months since the last get-together. It was strange to have him here by himself.

"So go get your stuff. Let's don't stand here all night." She headed toward the kitchen. Was there anything besides decaf? He wouldn't want any "gutted coffee", as he called it. Maybe she had an old bag of beans in the freezer. Making this small effort, she felt brisk, motherly, competent, as well as pleased to have him here in the house. They could sit at the table where the light was warmer and didn't take all the color out of everything. She probably looked older herself; it hadn't been an easy year.

Ten minutes later, with his gear stowed, his same old shaving dish plunked down on the sink, he took a seat in the kitchen with such an air of arrival. This was going to be fine, a few days of good distraction, when she didn't talk or think about herself or her trouble.

"So catch me up on the news," he said. "How are things?"

She made a semi-shrug, took a sip of coffee. "Okay," she said. "Not bad. *Pas si mal*."

"In French, correct me if I'm wrong, 'not so bad' means 'pretty good'." He lifted his eyebrows in an open question. "Things are pretty good?"

"I have a big commission." Billy was by far the easiest piece of news.

"Your mom said she'd heard from you about a burdensome big job you might take."

She laid it out for him without hesitation: the money, the shame, conflict, the slippery seductiveness of the guy.

A bitter look crossed his face. "Mother of God," he said,

shaking his head. "That sets me on my ear. Honey, I hope you still know that if money's the issue, I'm willing to be a patron of the arts."

"I know. Thanks. I have to be an adult, though. It's required."

He turned a bit to the side to give his legs more room, laughed the way he did when he was about to philosophize. "I'm not sure it's required. There are parts of the whole adult business that seem to me optional and maybe not wise." His watch was turned on his wide wrist, the complicated face on the inside.

"You're in a good position to say that. You've married, raised a child, made a bunch of money in a risky business. I haven't done any of those."

"Neither has the Dalai Lama, or two or three others for that matter."

"The D.L. has at least gone to the top of his field."

He gave the comment a perfunctory smile, rubbed the whiskers on the underside of his chin. "Darling, what's with you and Charlie?" He lifted his mug to his lips, hiding behind it, looking at her. The coffee was still steaming.

"Hard to say." She wasn't surprised he knew. He always had early word on foreign revolutions.

"Must be. Since you haven't gotten around to telling your old ma and pa." He paused. "You can be in communication and still be an adult."

"I know that!"

He made a mock-startled face. She'd snapped at him.

"I don't mean to intrude on you," he said. "We won't talk about it. I guess if you'd wanted to tell me, you already would have."

She slumped back in her chair. "We broke up. It was Charlie's idea, but I was fine with it. We'd died on the vine."

He made one deep nod of acknowledgement. Emotion gathered in her throat.

"Tell me how many years was it you two were together?" It

gave her a quick twist of pain: the way he said "you two".

"Eleven." She was tired of saying eleven.

"Long time. You're going through a divorce."

She took a napkin out of the basket in the middle of the table, and a pen that turned out to be felt-tip, drew his nose. "I suppose. Makes it worse to think of it that way." The ink spread out on the napkin until the line itself was a quarter-inch wide. A line from a Roualt. He watched what she was doing. The sharp sadness was easing.

"Why haven't you let us know? I can't imagine why you wouldn't." He looked boyishly befuddled, which hurt to see. She turned back to her cartoon of him: craggy-looking, a hint of De Gaulle. He'd like it whenever he turned it around to face him. "Why should I advertise my defeats?" she said. "It's embarrassing." She forced a laugh. "I'm devalued currency."

"Devalued! Don't say such stuff about my girl. Besides, there's no such thing as embarrassing when you're talking to people who love you."

"You're wrong about that. It's doubly important, to amount to something."

"Doubly, hell! It's not a mathematical situation. You are the gold of infinite value. That's the inalterable truth. What did you think? That Daphne and I were going to go through the rest of our lives believing you were still with that sorry bastard?"

"He's not a bad guy, Dad. He made the gut move I should have made long ago."

"He didn't make you happy, he's a bastard. That simple." He cut her a sharp glance: "Unless the two of you get back together?"

"Not going to happen. I was going to tell y'all, of course, at some point. Probably whenever I met somebody else."

Tim. For minutes she'd forgotten. "We had bad news at the studio today. A death in the family. You remember Caitlin? Winston and Millie Evers' daughter. You met her when she was a teenager."

His face altered in alarm. "That real sweet girl? The tall one? My God, don't tell me."

"Not her. Her boyfriend, killed in a motorcycle accident." Zack winced, shook his head. "She likely wishes it was the other way," she said. "I'll need to go see her tomorrow."

"You go ahead with whatever's on your docket. I don't mean to get in your way. I have a few things I need to check on here. I'm sorry about those two kids, though, your friends."

"Yeah. Me too."

"Do you ever ride down our old street?"

"Sometimes."

"I may go by there tomorrow, see how those peach trees did."

"They've done well. Been bearing fruit for years. I don't know whether it's edible. I think peaches need to have the right kind of tree nearby, to cross-pollinate."

"I'll trust you on that one."

"You look tired," she said. "I suppose you came straight from Tel Aviv with no layover."

"Except for riding into the city for dinner. I was eager to see you."

"So what do you think? Do I seem like I'm doing okay?"

He gave her a studying look.

"By now, you should already know," she said.

"You're not so far off the mark," he said, "of your usual self. But roiled up in a way I don't remember seeing."

She looked away, at a cabinet door ajar.

"You working too hard?"

"Don't interrogate me," she said in a warning singsong.

He held up his hands in surrender. "Sorry. Sorry."

They slipped into silence, after a moment, comfortably, as with someone you live with.

"We had it easy, your mother and I, when you were a teenager. None of that touchy adolescent stuff. I suppose you're due a chance to be testy and secretive and have folks walking on eggshells."

She smiled; it was as good an interpretation as any. She put the napkin portrait and pen away; he didn't notice, his ruminative gaze fixed high on the wall as he sat thinking and smoking. She and Charlie had sat this way so many nights. They'd kept that ability to the end: a companionable feeling, a vital trace element she was currently without. "It's nice to have you here." In truth, it was more than nice; and it was better, more honest, their ease with each other, than she remembered with Charlie. "Stay as long as you can."

"Couple of nights."

"Stay a couple of weeks. I'm serious." He could be her guardian, instead of Otis or Elliott. He wouldn't know he was doing it. Perfectly appropriate that her father would keep her from harm. The thought gave her a feeling of lightness. both serene and exhilarating.

"We'll see," he said, getting to his feet. "I'm going to hit the sack, get a solid night of good old American sleep. You ought to do the same thing."

She looked at the clock. It was only 9. Underneath the buzz of excitement, her mind and her bones, even her face, felt tired.

# 17

She stood for a moment outside Archie's door, then knocked… once, twice…on the glass front wall. They had to talk, get normal, if that was possible, before crossing paths at Caitlin's. She'd put this off far too long.

He was in there, back behind the divider; she could hear him. The computer was in its same place: she glimpsed the side of the monitor there where the doorway curtain gapped. No one had caught sight of them on the other side of that curtain; if anyone had, word would have gotten around. Marian or Otis would have let her know.

Maybe the radio kept him from hearing her knock.

"Archie," she called out.

Footsteps, and he came into view, big and heavy-headed, awkward. His face, when he saw her, registered a fast sequence of emotions: hope, lust, anger. "You," he said. His expression settled into grudging affection. "Come to visit your neighbor, have you?" He motioned her in. His dark hair held its usual sprinkle of sawdust. She felt a twinge of rueful affection.

"No, come out. Please."

"Being alone with me is too dangerous?" he said, stepping into the hall. "You might get swept away?" His face changed. "Andie, what were you thinking?"

She glanced down the hall, to get control of her breath, the volatile mix of feelings: crushing embarrassment, angry self-defense. What she'd done…it wasn't as if she'd attacked him with a knife.

"Alright," he said after a moment. "Let's walk." Side by side at a little distance, they headed out, then down the stairs, Archie behind her, onto the street. Sunlight on the top of her head felt consoling, made her want to weep. They were setting off in the same direction she had taken after leaving his studio that day.

"What I thought…" Everything she'd planned to say was

jammed together up high in her throat. She let the sentence drop. "I don't know." The splotch of sun on a slow-approaching car held her attention, steadied her. Archie, ambling, loose-limbed, was seeing nothing; she could tell from his straight-ahead stare. "There's no explanation," she said after minutes had passed. "But I thought it would be better if..." She'd trailed off. He wasn't making this any easier. "Also, I wondered..."

He put his hand solid on the back of her neck, gave her a gentle shake, the way he did with people; she yanked herself away.

His outreached arm still hung in the air. "O-kay," he said, with exaggerated tolerance.

She hadn't meant to do that, wanted to take it back. "Archie, look, I'm sorry. All of it." She hated having hurt his feelings.

"Well, that's too bad. I'm not."

"We just need to start over. I couldn't avoid you forever. I mean, I wouldn't want to."

"Hah. You were doing a good job of it."

"You'd have done the same thing. You probably have," she searched for words, "kept your distance from some woman who..." She faltered when she saw where that was leading.

"Hah."

"I didn't want to try to have this conversation in the crowd at Tim's funeral."

"Tim." He shook his head. "Good guy."

She felt sadness like water risen to the level of her bottom ribs. In the set of Archie's profile, she could see his bewilderment.

"Tim wasn't reckless," he said. "At the same time, he didn't think ahead. Didn't have a grain of ambition, not that I could see."

She opened her mouth to protest: he'd been young.

"So you come knock on my door," he said, "to get over the hurdle of speaking to me."

"Yeah."

"It's pretty obvious I shouldn't consider asking you for a date."

She looked away.

"That's what I thought."

"I'm not in a dating frame of mind, Archie. I'm trying to figure out what's going on."

"How do you do that?"

"Doctors. Both kinds."

"Have you learned anything from your research so far?"

"No. But I've stayed…" What? Clean? He knew what she meant.

Another long silence. He was working around to saying something. She waited. "Are there people going around having sex like that all the time," he said, "just dropping their pants, and I never knew it? It wouldn't surprise me if I were in the dark."

She had to laugh. "Not quite so abruptly, I don't think." It was going better, for moments, than she'd dared to hope. "Not at my advanced age, anyway."

"You probably would know."

"Maybe you didn't mean that the way it sounded." She didn't look at him. And he made no response.

They were approaching the curve of the road that led into the village proper. "We can turn around now," he said. "You've accomplished your mission and re-established contact. I promise I won't point any fingers at you in public."

"You could have said no."

"No, I could not. Anyway, you wouldn't have been happy with that either."

She imagined the rejection scenario. "That's true."

At least they were talking; and sex wasn't, at this moment, in the air. Maybe they would come through this better friends, the more complicated way she'd gotten to be lately with Otis, Marian, Elliott. Being in trouble apparently made her more sociable, or less glib.

The studio was just ahead. They'd picked up speed coming back. "On my computer," Archie said, "I checked the sites you visited."

Her eyes closed for the space of a step, a breath.

"Raunchy stuff," he said. "Did you know about those sites before?"

"First time."

"Sizzling. Although, if I were a woman, I wouldn't much see the appeal."

"Not a topic I feel like discussing."

"I didn't say a word to anybody. Like I said, I wouldn't."

"I did."

"Marian, you mean."

"And Otis and Elliott."

"Oh, man." He put both hands to his head, gave a raucous laugh. "They can drive themselves crazy wondering what it is about me."

"With Elliott, I didn't get into names."

"Just as well," he said, with something like smugness.

She shouldn't have told Otis either; that hadn't been necessary.

"We're back to home base," he said as they came around the side of the building to the back lot. She started toward her car, expecting him to head for the studio door.

"Andie, why don't you ride with me over to Caitlin's? We're both going. It's crazy to take two cars."

She felt a trace of a change in his tone, indecipherable. She'd already imagined ahead, her galloping to her own car, conversation concluded, sealing off the world to relax in that sun-warmed space. "I better take my own. My father's visiting and I'll need to go straight home."

The scene running fast in her mind: him pulling off the road, attempting a rough grapple. That was the change of tone she'd heard. He was strong; she knew that much.

"I only meant a ride," he said. "Caitlin's the main thing right now."

Andie had her keys out of her pocketbook, in her hand.

"Although," he said across the hot roofs of the cars, "it might surprise you to know that I was a pretty good actor in school."

"Actor?"

"I was in a couple of plays."

She could already be inside with the door shut by now, if she'd just move. She stood examining her car key.

"What I'm saying," his gaze, she saw in a quick glance, was dull-eyed, his lips parted, "if you want rough, like on the websites, I can do rough, or whatever," his confidence was fast eroding. "You wouldn't have to know it was me."

She stepped into the car. Her heart was pounding upward and outward from her chest.

At the edge of her vision, he was getting into his truck, still talking, his lips moving. She couldn't hear him. None of what she'd said had registered with him. Of course it wouldn't, compared to the impact of what she'd done.

By the time she was out of sight of him, his last words were repeating in her head: you wouldn't know it was me. The sadness of that could almost blot out everything else.

Caitlin's front door was open: older people Andie didn't recognize standing out on the steps, vague figures behind in the dim space of the doorway. Caitlin and Tim had lived here over a year. The door to the shed where he'd kept his motorcycle was closed.

A departing couple hurried across the rutted gravel driveway, down the embankment toward the cars, the woman's high heel catching, the man steadying her by the elbow. Both of them looked grey-faced and drawn.

She didn't want to go in.

Caitlin couldn't want to see a crowd of people.

No sign of Archie's truck.

She got out of the car. Needn't stay long. The steps to the box of a house were clear of traffic. She tapped lightly on the front door that stood ajar, then pushed on in. The smell of chilled carnations filled the foyer, a murmur of voices drifting from the living room.

There sitting in the worn armchair next to the shelf of CDs was Caitlin, red-nosed and pale.

Andie headed for the other end of the room, before Caitlin could spot her. She wasn't ready.

A table held trays of food people had brought. She picked up a brownie; it was something to do. She looked around for a napkin. The crowd was full of familiar voices. She kept her eyes focused on a half-distance, not landing on anyone. Just speak to Caitlin, then go. No anguished conversations about Tim, about the camping trip she'd heard they had planned, the ground he'd tilled Saturday for a vegetable garden.

A scraggly boy in ear cuffs wandered past. Bikers seemed to have such loyalty to each other. Things weren't square with Archie, probably never would be. He was a fire she had poked at and flame was leaping out in unexpected directions.

She heard Otis's voice somewhere in the room. But the presence she most felt, if she let her mind stop, was Tim. His personality permeated everything, twining into the fabric of clothes and chairs. All that tremendous buzz of life he'd had, now uncontained. She pictured heat rising off the fire pit outside, making the air shimmer, disappearing into sky; dizzied, she reached and caught the edge of the table and got her balance, the hushed talk of visitors continuing all around her. A loaf of dense homemade bread had slid half off its cutting board from the force of her grab at the table. She pushed it back into place.

Okay, do it: go over there and face Caitlin, her pain, full on. She felt shallow and trivial in front of such a loss, but 5 more minutes standing here wouldn't change that. She worked her way around the edge of the group, quicker than she wanted, to reach the side of that central chair.

"Andie," Caitlin said, as Andie leaned to hug her.

"I'm so sorry, Kay."

She looked fourteen, bedraggled, her very hair sad.

Caitlin's wet eyes filled. "Thanks." She patted the fat arm of her chair. "Sit here," she said.

Andie perched, half on and half off. "Are Tim's parents here?" Andie asked as a caller turned away. Pointless question. She was too old not to know what to say, to have nothing to offer.

"Gone to the funeral home."

"How is it with them?"

"Bad."

Andie sat silent and unnoticed as the next person came to say, "Darling, I'm so sorry," and the next with, "You know we lost our Joey."

From the window at Caitlin's side, you could see the stone dry wall of the fire pit, which Tim had built. She remembered one all-night party, people milling in the dark and the firelight, someone nobody knew playing an antique stringed box of an instrument. If Charlie had died, she'd have been expected to sit like this, and probably would have, sincerely grieving. She might never have known the real demise, or admitted it anyway.

Archie's voice, from the foyer. She recognized his slow gait on the wood floor, coming into this room. She saw she was picking at the upholstery on the top of the chair back, and stopped.

"I don't know," Caitlin was saying to a twentyish woman who looked like her, the same long hair and legs. "Jen and Ellie are staying with me a few days. My parents want me at their house, but I can't leave here."

Marian could take a turn staying. I could take a turn too, she thought, but Zack's here. And I'm really not in her innermost circle. All true, but she was making excuses, which weren't needed anyway.

Caitlin would move, maybe into town, or another city for a

new start. She wasn't going to want to live out here, isolated, without him. Her parents were in the living room somewhere, the mother closer to Andie's age. Otis was working his way forward. Otis would know what to say and do, no need to think about it. Caitlin, catching sight of him, sprang up out of the chair into his arms. Andie looked away, at the puff of stuffing that was coming out of the chair upholstery in one spot.

The sack-like cushion sloped to one side, worn and inviting. Andie let herself slide down into the seat. Still warm. Caitlin and Otis had drifted a little distance away. Sitting here, she had Caitlin's view of the edge of the woods, and of one end of the raw garden plot. Bare dirt. She pulled her gaze away. As if, in breaking open the ground there, he'd been digging his own grave.

A feather-light touch grazed her shoulder; she turned back to the room. The face hovering near hers was straining with sympathy. The woman was old: her skin powdered and soft. "Darling," she said; her eyes held the plaintive, searching look old people get.

"Darling, you don't know me. I'm a friend of Tim's grandmother. I want to tell you how sorry…"

"No, ma'am!" Andie pulled herself to the front of the seat.

"Those of us who lost someone in the War... And when you're young," she was saying. "And have such a grief…" Andie felt her body give up before she decided: let her say her piece.

"Pray to the Lord…" she was going on, "there's nothing else."

I've prayed, Andie thought.

"...Rest in His gentle arms...."

Andie sat limp as the sympathy poured into her ear. A needling feel at the back of her eyes, then tears started down her face. She fought back the sob, stared hard at the rug. Better if she had died before she got so crazed and lost, not Tim. The woman still murmuring, absently dabbing at Andie's damp cheek, the tissue smelling of chewing gum. This was wrong, disrespectful to

Caitlin.

Andie pushed up to standing. Couldn't someone help steer her out of here? A few steps, zigzag, and she'd be out in the foyer. "Please excuse me," Andie said, squeezing past.

"I certainly do understand…" the woman still talking.

Pocketbook slung over her shoulder, Andie bolted through the entranceway, seeing no one, then straight out the front door into light and fresh air. Rafts of misery, wide flat clouds, were passing through her.

The threesome coming up the front steps, expressions sober, stepped back to let her hurry past.

# 18

Her studio door was standing open, probably Mayrelle, making her rounds, changing a lightbulb. Andie gave her face another wipe, headed in.

Zack! She stopped. He stood staring at the umbrella. "How did you get in here?"

"Your custodian is a sweetheart." He glanced back at the canvas, then sharply at her. Her eyes would still be red and puffy. "Honey, I'm sorry. Did you tell Caitlin I was sad for her?"

"I forgot."

He'd taken a step closer, eyes warm with sympathy. There ought to be more than one Zack in the world. But at some point, there would be no Zack. What then?

"I look like shit," she said. She threw her pocketbook onto a chair, took a seat.

"You're upset, you look fine. You sure must have been feeling like an angel when you painted this umbrella." As he glanced across it, she had the sense, though it wasn't true, that the yellow reflected on his face.

"It's not finished and you're not supposed to be barging in here looking at it."

He turned, eyebrows raised, expression somber. She'd meant to sound jokey. "I apologize," he said. He came around the painting to face her. "I wasn't thinking. The place seems public with all this glass, and people in the halls."

"It's okay. Anyway, I'm not likely to finish it."

He frowned. "How's that?" He started to sit down too, but changed his mind. She motioned him toward a chair where the canvas would be visible only from the back.

"The day I did this much, it was one of those flukey moments. Nothing I could sustain. Plus, there's the senator, a college job, some smaller stuff, maybe a mural; I think I can get more time on the school project if I need to."

"I won't compound my error by trying to give you advice." He glanced at the upright back of the easel.

"If you want to offer advice," she said, "tell me what's wrong with me. I've been out of sorts for weeks." Of course he couldn't tell her anything; asking was simply a backhanded way to get to complain.

"I don't like that a bit," he said, his voice uncommonly sober. Her throat locked. She made a dismissive face until she'd gotten a grip.

"Hormones probably. I don't have any diseases." She felt soft with gratitude that he hadn't jumped to the Charlie conclusion.

"You're sure?"

She nodded. "Yes."

"Not quite yourself," he said, as if reminding her.

"Odd sensations, impulses."

She saw him consider whether he wanted details. "You're being careful, I trust. In every way."

"Yeah, of course." She wasn't exactly sure what he was referring to; she was still on the pill, if that was what he meant. No condom with Archie, nothing to do about that now.

His eyes, the half-circles below, looked sagged, more than before, fatigue and age she hadn't noticed when she'd walked in. She put her head in her hands. "Pop, I'm just a mess right now. In a bad mood." She heard his footsteps toward her where she sat, felt his hand on her hair; her shoulder rested against the side of his leg.

After a moment she made herself pull away, shaded her eyes for a moment against the window light, until they were adjusted again. The moment had been longer than it had seemed.

She saw him take note that she wasn't crying. She got to her feet.

"How bad are these moods, on a scale of 1 to 6.75?"

Their old joke. She felt her forehead relax.

"Hard to say. I'm feeling better, just from mentioning it." He cast her an assessing glance. "What are you up to this afternoon?" she said, needing as always to end the tender moment.

"Going to look at a piece of land." He kept the same sober tone, watching her carefully; she'd seen him look at rug traders just this way.

"Land? Are you kidding? What for?" They couldn't be thinking of moving back; if they lived here, she might as well give up on adult life. She'd instantly be over-involved with both of them.

"I'm not sure. A fellow downtown told me about it. I thought I'd go have a look. It's an old stand of timber and a creek. Ride out there with me. It's a gorgeous day. A few minutes with Mother Nature would do us both good."

Zack's rental car smelled of pipe tobacco. "I thought you were a twice-a-year smoker these days." He pulled out from the no-shouldered lane onto the highway.

"This is one of those days. Yesterday was too. I'm through for the year."

"It's only May, Pop, a long time until January."

"I measure by the fiscal year starting in July."

"Seriously, do you make New Year's resolutions? Or some kind of resolve to do more of this or less of that?"

He lifted the weight of his upper body in a great thoughtful sigh. "I suppose I'm one who ought to."

"I'm not saying that. Do you keep track in your mind of things like how many drinks you've had, how many you allow yourself, how much money you've spent? That sort of thing."

"Are you thinking I drink too much?"

"No." They were passing the mental health center, hidden in the trees off to the right, an outparcel of the huge hospital. She thought of lanky blonde Cliff sitting in there with his legal pad. Elliott's Quaker meeting probably wouldn't solve anything either. "I'm wondering how you keep from drinking too much."

"I quit when I've had enough."

"Is that when you're starting to feel a certain way?"

"I never thought about it. I suppose along the way I developed some automatic monitor, so I don't have to be keeping count."

"That sounds like a good arrangement."

"Is alcohol giving you trouble?"

"No, I'm still maxing out at two glasses of wine. Same as always."

"So what got us going on this? I'll bet there are some drugs around that studio."

"Nobody there can afford drugs. Not enough to do any harm."

"People often manage to work around that." He put both hands on the steering wheel. They were beyond the edge-of-town traffic.

"Anyway," she said, "it's interesting to me, the whole idea of self control. I don't know how anybody does it. For example," and this would throw him off onto safer ground, "how does anybody get themselves to work, to finish a painting? Unless a customer is waiting for it, and then it's hard to start before the last minute."

"Used to be hard to get you to put your drawing pencil down long enough to hold a fork."

"Doodling," she said.

"Maybe you ought to look back at some of what you call doodling. You sure aren't doing yourself any good talking down your own work."

"That's true. Still, I want to know what switches you can throw to stop going one way and start going another."

"Your mother stopped smoking that way, as if she'd thrown a switch."

"That's right, she did. I should ask her how she managed that and did it in just one try. I can imagine a smoker lighting up without knowing she's doing it."

"You've always been disciplined, though, Andie. Knowing exactly what you wanted and then getting on with it. That can be an intimidating quality in a child."

She had to laugh. "I remember how you were always quaking with fright. I love the idea, though." She tried to picture him. No, she didn't like the thought: Zack uneasy. When he was scared for his business and then when Gram was dying, his fear and grief were big and robust, nothing timid.

The sound of the tires changed. He was turning onto a dirt driveway that ended maybe fifty yards ahead. "You were right about trees," she said. This was a turn-off you'd pass even if you were looking for a place to turn around. She slid her window down. He switched off the car. The quiet had a weight to it, as if it were summer and the air heavy. The place would make a good lovers' lane. Zack was already out of the car, taking in 180 degrees of the view at once. Nice woods, not much underbrush; instead the spacious feel of old pine forest. She got out slowly, to see what it was he wanted her to see.

Zack was trying to find where the property lines were located. "Jimmy said the highway exposure was about a quarter of a mile," he said. "I'm not seeing the marker."

"There." Andie pointed to a bit of plastic ribbon half-buried in clay dust. "Who knows where it's supposed to be attached," she said.

"Well, we can figure we're pretty close." He was starting toward what she saw was the mouth of a path into the woods, an orange blaze across a pine trunk. They stepped into dimmer, almost chilly light. The path, like all the rest of the forest floor, was brown pine needles, a soft layer on ground that felt more sand than clay.

"We're heading for the stream?" she said.

"Yeah, I'd like to get a look."

"Are you getting inspired about what you might do with this

land?"

"Now that I see it, I don't think a soul ought to touch it."

"Pretty nice," she said. The sense of hush extended far above her. She looked up. Wind was gusting high above, the tops of a few trees twisting slightly back and forth, as if from the waist, branches pushing upward into the canopy: the umbrella, from underneath. I could set my easel up here. Zack was moving on; she didn't want to lose sight of him behind a trunk and then more trunks. On these pine needles there wasn't a sound. She could stay in here and work until the piece was finished or ruined. At the moment, though, it felt unimportant, either way. The presence of Zack trumped her work.

She walked, but slowly. The air, the smell of bruised green pine needles, felt cleansing. With this much space a nasty odor, anything toxic, would float loose and disperse. Again, her recurring craving: to escape her repetitive little mind, to disperse through the air in a place this large and fresh and alive.

Some of the peculiar sensations had felt like something in her struggling to get out. What was supposed to have come out of her that hadn't was her own painting, her real work.

Zack was calling for her from far ahead. Must have found the creek. He was always discovering something whether he had any use for it or not. He wasn't going to buy this piece of land.

The path went straight up and over a knoll. There, five feet below, was Zack already on the other side of the little pool in the stream; he was poking at something in the water with a stick, as any nine-year-old would be. She felt a tiny ping of love for him, a light-burst off the water.

She wanted to go and put her arms around him.

I'm scared to risk it.

To have such a fear, and this her own father... She couldn't follow that thought where it led. Saw only an explosion of feeling, a flying-apart...

"This place is absolutely sylvan," she said. She made herself look around. The water was clear, with about as much trickle as the fountain in the studio gallery downstairs. Ferns clumped all along the far bank. Her heart was settling down.

Zack looked up to where she stood on the rise, holding back the scrappy pine that had half-blocked her view. "You look like the woodland Faerie Queen," he said, "come forth to be sure that not a leaf in your queendom is disturbed."

"That's me." She picked her way down to the edge.

"Now that I think about it, though, you were never any great fan of the Romantic painters. I remember you standing up in the audience at a panel discussion at the North Carolina Art Museum...you couldn't have been more than fourteen...informing the renowned experts that the pre-Raphaelites were liars. You gave those fellows something to think about. Daphne said my chest literally swelled with pride."

"I was awful. No doubt showing off for you guys."

"You were marvelous. Still are." He leaned down, put a hand in the creek. "The water's surprisingly cold. I'll have to stop by the county mapping folks' office, see what they can tell me about the source."

"I'm surprised we're not hiking to the headwaters right now." She was stepping carefully across the stream on the pieces of fallen tree trunk.

He laughed, big.

"Did you hear that, Zack?" both feet on the bank. "You echoed."

"That's the land calling out to us. Saying we passed inspection and it's okay to put down a deposit."

"You're not serious. About the deposit."

"No, you're right. I'm leaving Saturday night, by the way; I can't remember if I said that."

"You didn't. Not exactly." Her breath cramped in disappointment, let loose in a rush of relief. "Where are you going?

"London. Home. I don't like being away from Daphne this

long." She pictured the two of them wrapped together in one of their long kisses in the foyer. She was forever walking in on them, had assumed everyone's parents behaved the way they did, the very air around them altered by their passion.

"I know," she said. Maybe the kind of sex she'd done, the self-abasement, was a penance, punishment for her yen toward Zack. Difficult to even think words of desire in relation to him. Instead a euphemism like "yen". As if someone…her mother?…might be listening. She had never let herself imagine…her mind veered off from naming what she wouldn't imagine.

"I'll be glad," he said, "when she's ready to spend more time in the world of ordinary travel again, planes and trains instead of these inner jaunts. It's no wonder you turned out to be an artist." He tossed the stick behind him up the bank. The water he'd stirred up was clear again. "And I'm estimating," he said, "that if you're going to let me in on what's going on, it won't take you longer than these few more days to get around to it."

"I see."

He leveled his eyes at her. She wanted to look away.

"I'm just in a sticky place emotionally, Pop. Temporarily." She produced a small smile. She longed to ask him about the force, the bodily electricity, what he knew of it; but what would she be admitting to with the question?

Even the subject felt dangerous. She'd managed to get herself into the one kind of trouble she couldn't tell them about.

"I probably ought to mention," he said, "that I talked a minute with that old Charlie. By chance, I passed one of his Chas. Singer Construction signs, saw his truck and stopped."

A hot rush of anger pressed against the backs of her eyes. "You tracked Charlie down? First, you're in my studio. Then this? What's next in your research?"

"He was my son-in-law over 10 years. I'll stop and say my good-bye to the man if I want to."

"You never liked him. You made a point of upstaging him

every time the two of you were together. And now you go visiting him? You were scouting for information about me."

"I liked him well enough, and I didn't ask him a damn thing. I told him I'd seen his sign from the road. It didn't feel right to come to town and not speak to him. Told him I was sorry and wished him well. Is that too much interference in your private affairs? You're acting like a teenager. You didn't do that when you *were* one."

Second time he had mentioned that. And, no, she hadn't acted like a teenager back then, instead more like a three-year-old, still wanting at eighteen to go places with Mom and Dad. He was studying her face. Her hands pushed down in her pockets were fists. She loosened them. He said, "I'm getting the idea what's eating you. I think it's probably the obvious: the break-up."

She made a noncommittal motion of her head. If she was grieving, the loss wasn't new, and it wasn't mainly about Charlie, or Tim.

"It's understandable," he said. She was moving them to the log crossing. Neither of them, she noticed, reached to hold onto a branch for support.

He stepped off the log onto the narrow path behind her. Up the little hill again, heading back. All her fire was gone; she felt wrung out.

"I'll stop nosing into what's none of my business," he said.

"I over-reacted," she said. "Sorry."

Fatigue fell heavier; she felt it on the back of her neck. There wasn't going to be any relief, anything Zack could do. At least, she consoled herself, she'd managed so far to seem fairly normal.

# 19

Billy, a bit rumpled, shirtsleeves rolled, caught sight of her approaching as he was coming out his office door. "Hello there, Andie. I was just getting set to spiff up for this occasion." He motioned around his office full of bright yellow morning light, the shade she thought of as the color of May. "Make yourself to home," he said in his fake down-home mode. "I'll be back with my tie knotted and my hair slicked down."

Without him, the room felt enormous and high-ceilinged as a courtroom. Already he'd somehow spun her in a circle. Without noting what she was doing, she'd begun setting up. At last to sink into the process of laying down the paint. Once that was begun the project was near finished and she'd be safely rid of him.

She set out the same old chipped mixing plate. He'd been plenty decent to her, and certainly entertaining, though that was hardly the point. In one sense, there was no reason to rush. When this was over, she'd be just as much a turncoat as now. Not only that, the whole thing would go public: I'll be branded forever as the collaborator I am.

But she did want the other $50,000, and to be out of here, finished with this, with all its dangers, visible and invisible. She pictured herself in a small fragile boat, jagged-edge rocks just below the water's smooth surface.

Here he comes; and he's whistling, for God's sake, "Old MacDonald." The room was already starting to fill up with him.

"Do I pass inspection?" he said. He had on a blue suit, flag-striped tie. And a yellow pocket square?

"You look fine. You surprise me with the yellow, though."

"A man doesn't like to be predictable. It makes him vulnerable. People can catch up with you if they know where you're going."

"Vulnerable is not a word I would associate with you."

"You ever sit to have your portrait painted?" he said.

"No. Yes, what am I thinking? Of course I have."

"Then you know what I mean."

"I guess I do." The memory of the nude modeling felt tender, but long ago, an old bruise. "Let's get you situated now." She checked the layout she'd sketched onto the canvas: the one with the dangerous face. He'd insisted, though he hadn't seen the expression when he chose the sketch.

Adjusting himself, settling the position of his head, he did look ill at ease. His face was taking on a bit of that look she'd seen and seized on. A shadow of it. Something about the position provoked that expression. Whether it came forth or not, she had it memorized: power, pleasure, the unnameable shine in his eyes she'd seen on the putting green, and, yes, something like fragility.

"Okay," she said. "All set." She was already at work: the plane was in the air, had leveled off. They could both relax.

"Am I allowed to talk?"

"Sure. Tell me the story of your life. No, tell me how you got your confidence. It must have taken a lot when you were first getting started. Not just to run for office, but to wield power once you got it."

"That's a question up to my expectations of you," he said. "The answer's real simple. It was in my chromosomes. One thing that I never had to worry about."

"You're fortunate."

"I have some other chromosomes I could do without." He drew in a breath, full of intention. "You know," he said, "people are over-sensitive about genetics. It's plain as day that your different races have certain inborn proclivities. Greater intelligence here, better basketball there."

Her brush had stopped, her gaze fixed on the canvas. Slowly, she brought herself to look at him: a trace of amusement twitching the muscles of his face. He dared to smile.

"You're baiting me, Senator." She forced the brush into

motion.

He tilted back in his chair. "Now you have to admit..."

"Sit still, please."

"Yes, ma'am," he said, precisely restoring his pose. He kept silent for maybe half a minute. "I'm surprised," he said, "that you wouldn't want to grab hold of the opportunity to set me straight. That way you could justify to yourself that you're working for me."

Her lips pressed shut. The paintbrush whispered. She turned a clinical gaze on the light on the side of his neck and on the hard matte surface of his shirt collar, which was tight, the edge of it raising a slight ripple in his flesh. She dabbed in that chafed red ridge.

"Probably I shouldn't be getting myself agitated in pointless debate either," he said, "my doctor's been on my back lately."

"You'd follow a doctor's advice?"

"Look over there," he said.

She looked, in spite of herself, at the pile of books and papers. And she'd let his racist comment pass, when she should have taken him on. Never mind that he was playing with her, he'd handed her the perfect opening and she hadn't said a word.

"See at the bottom of that stack of files?" he said. "Orange? You can just barely read the title."

She could see it fine. "*Idiot's Guide to Meditation*."

"That's the one. Janice, my doctor, gave it to me yesterday. The woman's completely lacking in PR sense. Imagine giving your customer something that calls him an 'idiot'."

Andie snapped off the impulse to say something pointlessly rude.

"This medical lady," he continued, imperturbable, "wants me to use mind over matter to lower my blood pressure. I'll flip through the book, I suppose. I have no intention of sitting cross-legged for any purpose. If I'm going to do nothing, I'm going to be snoring while I do it."

"I'm surprised you'd go to a mind-over-matter type doctor."

"You sell me short, my dear. I'm open-minded, especially when it comes to alternatives to sawing my chest open. And since we're right here at the start of a new millennium…" He stopped. "By the way," he said in a new and measured tone, "if I read one inkling in the newspaper about my health being anything but perfect, I'm coming to find you. I stuck that book under there so it wouldn't be the first thing anybody'd see when they walked in."

"Anybody who thought about it would assume you have high blood pressure," she said. "You're the type."

"The type, is it? I thought you didn't go in for sorting people into categories," he said with a smug grin. He gave her not one instant to answer. "Do you do any of this meditating or whatever kind of New Age stuff, so you can stay calm when you have to work with SOBs?"

"No, I'm fairly feet-on-the-ground. No crystals or faith-healing. The Hindus, though, have a goddess of the arts. I like that. Artists could use divine protection."

"What does she look like? Venus on the half-shell?"

"A fierce-eyed woman riding a bird."

"That's you," he said, "to a T."

"I have one of those Saraswati figurines in a closet somewhere." She could be as cool and unflappable as he was, chatting along about whatever. "She's holding a *veena*, a stringed instrument. I bought her in Benares as a teenager. My father was working there, an importer."

She sensed a change, glanced up. His gaze was focused at a spot in space, completely elsewhere, the smarmy persona gone, his lower lip softer, yet belligerent, as if he had something to defend. She grabbed a smaller brush to catch the effect, lightened a spot on the canvas, just below the line where his lips met. Nice! This touch was worth the drive from Pinehurst. You could see the scrappy combativeness, as well as a shadowy uncertainty.

He cleared his throat and shifted. The peculiar layered expression was gone. He flipped his wrist to check his watch, but didn't look at it. "Okay," he said, still distracted, sliding forward in his chair. His legs had already broken camp. "You got enough for today, sweetie?"

She stepped back from the canvas. Already? They'd been at it what? Fifteen minutes? "Okay," she said. "Sure. We've made some progress." She put down her brush, glanced at his face, saw no explanation.

He gave her a backward wave as he went out the door. She wiped her hands. The tendons or whatever-they-were in her neck felt tight as bridge cables. He'd probably known all along he had only a few minutes and let her come anyway, jerking her around just to flex his muscles, show he could.

She dropped down into the leather wing chair, checked her hands and wrists for dabs of wet paint. He owed her time to sit here and recover.

In front of her sat the stack of files he'd piled on top of the orange book on meditation. She slid the big paperback out from beneath the heap, waited to be sure the mass of papers was steady again. Her mother's spiritual library was abstract to the point of inanity. No credible how-to or why, instead a lot of talk about transpersonal psychology, and piles of antique books from those tiny dark-wood Paris bookshops that were each about the size of an armoire. She'd only glanced at that collection, back in a different lifetime. Pre-crisis. Too bad she couldn't ask her mother about any of this. She didn't want to deal with the follow-up questions. More important, she had to find her way to the bottom of it herself. Her very existence seemed to hang on doing that.

She opened in the middle: "Fasting Meditation", "The Physiology of Breathing". Self-contained smoothie-drinking Elliott had books of this sort, and Caitlin, who was now in the worst kind of crisis. Andie turned a chunk of pages: "How many sheaths of existence does a body have?" Billy was going to make hay with this: the "subtle body" or astral body, the *chakras*: even she knew about the string of psychic energy centers up the spine. In fact, she'd overheard a fair amount about this kind of thing, simply never put any stock in it, for herself anyway. There was no end to the strange things her mother believed.

She paged on. Relax, it said, breathe deeply, breathe slowly. Familiar territory. She focused attention on slowing her breath, turned another page.

"Coiled energy," caught her attention: "...a sleeping snake called *kundalini...*" She sat back as if pushed.

*This* was the word she remembered!

She scrambled to find her place on the page: *kundalini* "when awakened, is said to travel up through the *chakras* to the crown of the head."

A snake. Waiting in the most intimate of all places, at the base of the spine. Horrifying. She felt sweat rise from her scalp, her pulse beating hard in the sides of her neck. Mom had talked about energy but never a snake. She'd have remembered that.

And her strange sensations: they certainly weren't sinuous, more a Roman candle hurtling upwards.

She searched again for the little box of information. It didn't say anything about a connection with sex, instead *kundalini* was "the energy of self-actualization". Had she simply been becoming herself? Showing her true nature? The most awful possibility of all and it hadn't occurred to her. The top chakra was, of course, the spiritual one, whatever that meant.

She flipped to the index. Her hands paused. Billy was coming down the hall, she heard his feet on the linoleum tile; he'd be in the foyer in a second. She cast a wild glance around for some excuse. She was supposed to be packing. Too late to move.

"I took a break," she said, as he walked back in, "made myself at home with your new book," lifting it to show him.

He glanced at the cover, grinned. "I knew that, of course. I keep cameras in here to be sure nothing un-American goes on while I'm out."

"You're kidding."

"Yeah, I'm kidding," he said. "You think I would do that?"

Turning onto her other side, Andie realized she was awake. Not just surfacing for seconds, instead completely alert.

Across the hall in the living room, Zack snuffled, drew in a good-sized snore. Like the poem she'd written for homework in ninth grade: "Sounds have shapes/Snores float to the floor/As pinecones…." That was as much of it as she could remember. He'd be sleeping on his back with an arm flung out. So familiar, as if there were an old groove in her brain that the sound of his snoring fitted perfectly.

She imagined going in there and lying beside him, tucked under one arm, the way she'd often flopped down next to him on the daybed in the den when she was small. To be snuggled in that warmth, barely stirring. She couldn't imagine a greater feeling of comfort.

Or anything more reckless.

As a child you were allowed to cuddle with any and all. As if children weren't sexual. Riding a fiberglass horse on a merry-go-round had sometimes made her face hot, her stomach quiver.

From across the hall, through the door, another big pinecone rolled across the air. It was going to be impossible to get back to sleep. If she got up and walked around… Best not.

Until now, she'd felt safe from herself in her own house. But that was when she was alone. She pulled the covers up tight against her throat, under her chin, held them across herself like a cloth restraint.

The dark in the room was absolute, her window shade tight-fitted against the glow of the security light outside. Lying completely still, she felt disembodied, without physical sensations or desire. She was nothing but awareness, free-floating and in no danger, as long as she lay motionless. As long as she was paralyzed.

This was what her life had come to: paralysis. Stillness took a deeper hold on her. Tears slid from the wet outer corners of her eyes. She felt in her chest, at the base of her throat, a stir of anger, pushed it down, fearing it would make her move.

When she woke again, she heard morning traffic sounds from out on the road and Zack knocking a pot against a burner in the kitchen. She'd been dreaming. Mom, in her purple yoga tights, calm and mild, had been reaching to give her something, or show it to her: a small object held cupped in her palms, the air around her hands alive and shining, as if she were protecting a glow-worm, careful not to disturb it. The thing was the size of a compact, snapped shut: hidden inside, the mirror and foundation. She squinted into her memory, trying to see before it was gone. She'd glimpsed the shape: round, or almost round, a spiral compressed.

To have let it slip away... She moaned into the mattress...nothing left except the dream fragment. What her mother had held out to her was somehow the essence... She hungered to have it in her hands. She should have seized it, but her courage had failed her.

Mid-morning, still agitated from the night, she stopped trying to work. She kept picturing the round shining object from the dream. She picked up a sketch pad, drew a circle. A spiral. A circle around a spiral. What might *kundalini* look like? There would certainly be images, some sort of representation.

She grabbed her phone, dialed sometime-assistant Lexie, now in Boston, a good safe distance. Voicemail picked up: "Leave a message," the voice young and weary, "probably I'm at the library. Will call back if my dissertation doesn't kill me."

"Lexie, this is Andie. Once again, I need a tiny bit of research assistance if you can take a break. Send me some images that illustrate the idea of *kundalini*," she spelled the word, "and...," she hesitated: Do I want her to do any more digging? "And, okay, any information you find in time to make Fedex today. Then bill me a rush charge, a big one. A thousand thankyous. " Lexie would of course assume that, as always, the pictures were background for a job. She wouldn't have time to dig up too much.

By noon the next day, Andie was ripping into the cardboard envelope. She pulled out the few sheets, printouts from websites. Lexie didn't exactly go overboard on this assignment.

She spread pages out across her table. The outline of a figure seated in lotus pose; the body so covered with diagrams and images that it looked like a disastrous tattoo job.

A second picture underneath. Her heart gave a lurch. A close-up of what appeared to be an amulet. A burnished gold spiral within a circle, a perfect tight coil. So close to what she'd seen in the dream. She held the page aloft, in triumph.

Then the last of a page of text caught her eye: the word "dangers". The quote was from Jung, his intro to *The Tibetan book of the Dead*; her eyes quickly scanned. "*One often hears and reads about the dangers of Yoga, particularly of the ill-reputed Kundalini Yoga. The deliberately induced psychotic state*," she drew in a sharp breath, "*which in certain unstable individuals might easily lead to a real psychosis, is a danger that needs to be taken very seriously indeed.*" Psychotic! My God! Mouth dry, face hot, she read on: "*These things really are dangerous and ought not to be meddled with in our typically Western way. It is a meddling with Fate, which strikes at the very roots of human existence and can let loose a flood of sufferings of which no sane person ever dreamed.*"

But I didn't meddle. I didn't ask for any of this. Rose never said anything about psychotic. She would have said...

She scraped the pages into a ragged sheaf, pushed them into a file drawer and slammed it shut.

Late Saturday afternoon at the soda shop: this, of all the restaurants in the village, was where they'd landed for their farewell dinner. The place was crowded. "Pinehurst goes to bed early, Pop. Most of the parties are in the afternoon. You remember."

"I'll need to eat again before I leave Atlanta."

"You won't mind that."

"With this many people hungry," he said, looking around, "the hotel dining room ought not to make us wait until a proper dinner hour. Here I am in coat and tie. Somebody should take a photograph." She too had been ready for the white damask and table settings of that grander, quieter room. Here instead, at this old-fashioned soda-shop booth, would be his last and most subtle effort of the visit to discover something wrong he could fix. While she'd be angling to covertly get his help without appearing even to herself as if she needed any or hinting at what was going on.

"If you'd like a formal portrait in your finery," she said, "I can arrange that."

"As I recall, I sat for my portrait a time or two while you were coming up."

The wait arrived at the table: a girl with a long, thin-featured face, an outmoded quiet beauty. "What can I get y'all to drink?"

Water. A Philly cheese steak for Zack with tomato tortellini soup; for Andie a bowl of ice cream. "With a lot of walnuts on top," she said, "the ones that come in syrup." Zack handed over the menus, startled the girl with his split-second of full-on eye contact. That warmth always surprised people the first time.

From where she was sitting she could see out the screened-door onto the brick sidewalk. A sweet little breeze was making its way into the room. The perfect tendril of spring.

"That's all you want?" Zack said when the waitress was long gone.

"It's what I've been wanting all day and didn't know it until I saw the list of flavors on the wall."

"Did you work on Sylvester this afternoon?"

"Yes, in the studio. I don't need him in front of me at this point." Once she'd crammed Lexie's notes into a file, she'd thrown herself into work: anything to escape.

"I have some difficulty imagining the two of you in the same room. You know he supported Franco," Zack said. "Old Billy started early on his life of crime."

"I did read that."

"The man has stuck close to his convictions. From Argentina to Rangoon. Sea to shining sea." He winked. "I'm not trying to make you feel bad, honey. Should I not be talking like this? You made the right choice, to take the job."

His style of teasing, she realized, wasn't so different from Billy's. "It's okay," she said. "I've desensitized."

He gave her an assessing second glance. "You're in unusually perky spirits," he said. "Happiest I've seen you since I've been here."

More giddy than happy, but I won't argue. "Your company," she said. 'You've succeeded in cheering me up. Seriously, I'm glad you came."

"I don't feel satisfied of that myself, my cheering you, I mean. I notice it's when I'm an hour from leaving that you're feeling chipper."

She started to protest; he waved it away. There was relief in knowing she wasn't going to accidentally make the slightest suggestive motion toward him. She'd like to think such a thing impossible; it surely was. But she couldn't count on anything.

The soup and ice cream had arrived. Vanilla and the dark gold of the walnut syrup. "Milk and honey," Zack said, as she took a moment to admire it before plunging in. The group of women seated one table away was laughing, rambunctious in their delight at taking a break from their children, their husbands. All these weeks she'd been avoiding lunches with the studio gang. Another gust of laughter. The absence of her buddies, the whole clump of them, ached like a sprain. Surely it was safe to be with them in a group. The women too were eating ice cream, most of them pretty large in their knit pants. They'd probably come to the village from one of the nearby towns, a voyage to another richer culture, or a different one anyway.

"In your travels," she said to Zack. His face turned watchful at her semi-formal opener, "did you ever come across a belief in something called *kundalini*?" She couldn't leave the subject alone."Maybe I'm not pronouncing it right; I don't know how else you'd say it."

"Close enough, I'm sure."

"You've heard of it?"

"In passing. It's more talked about than experienced, I expect. A powerful metaphor at the least."

"A sleeping snake," she said.

"The sleeping Goddess," he said. "At the base of the spine. Why do you ask?"

She had an answer ready for the dangerous question. "I picked up a book on meditation. In Billy's office." The book had said it could travel up through the *chakras*, which pretty much matched the sensations she'd felt. Sexy territory: the base of the spine.

"Good God. I wouldn't suspect Billy of anything but premeditation."

"His doctor forced it on him."

"She must be good-looking."

Andie felt her scalp tighten. She couldn't be wanting to defend Billy, not that picking an attractive doctor would need a defense. "His heart condition made him at least take the book, if not— Oh, no!" She lifted her hands toward her face. "What have I done? I swore not to speak of his health to anyone. That is entirely in confidence. Promise me." She looked around. No one else in earshot of her voice.

"Absolutely." He pushed his empty soup bowl aside, leaned

on his crossed arms, which brought him a foot closer to her.

"Unless you want his people coming after me," she said, leaning toward him as well. "I'd be out a lot of money for a start."

"I'll never speak of it. Although anybody could look at him and see he's about to explode. Anyway, I don't think I've told a secret in my life."

"That's a nice thing to know about yourself."

He made the kind of diffident shrug that signifies importance. "Did I ever break any promise to you?"

"No. I'd remember if you had. But that's different from secrets. You must have told something you shouldn't have as a kid."

"Never did. It was a point of honor with me."

"You should have been a spy, Zack. You're in just the right business for it."

His face stopped, eyes searching one way, then another.

Andie drew back, puzzled. "A spy… Zack, I was joking."

He shifted his weight on the seat of the booth.

"Pop, what's going on?"

He rubbed at his lower lip. His motion, the unfolding of his arms, was too deliberate. He was wavering about whether to answer.

Long silence. He still wasn't looking at her. "Zack, tell me."

"You were 4 years old," he said, "when we went through all that."

"All what?"

"I was suspected, your mother and I both, of being on the wrong side." She must have looked confused. "Of carrying information," he said. "Spying."

Her gaze darted around the room, pausing at every set of heads.

"The early 70s," he said. "A time I won't forget."

"Spying?"

"I was in and out of Eastern Bloc countries for a couple of

years, buying beads in Czechoslovakia, et cetera. They, someone in our non-intelligence, thought I was selling information to the Communists. As if I had personally paved the way for the Red tanks to roll into Prague."

"That's preposterous."

"I *had* no such information. And what they did to us, it was a terrible, sinister business."

On his face, an expression she'd never seen: wary, hyper-alert. As if at this moment he was hunted.

"We were followed, the phone tapped, we were interrogated. Your mother would have someone trailing her in the grocery store. We never could see the dimensions of what was coming at us. It was an assault; I had nightmares about the execution of the Rosenbergs. Julius and Ethel, they left two little boys, 6 and 10." A wave of emotion altered his face. "Here I was, unable to protect my wife and my daughter."

"Good God, Dad."

"For a while, I kept a copy of the letter the Rosenbergs wrote to their boys the day they were executed. Then Daphne discovered it and told me having it around was crazy, dangerous: get rid of it. Apparently they, or at least he was guilty."

Four years old, she'd have been at the living room window, screaming: No! hurling herself against the glass toward the police car taking them away.

"There never did come one clear moment when I could say: it's over. We're safe."

Andie touched the spoon she'd left in the ice cream, put her hand down. She fought back the fear that threatened to balloon: they could have been taken away from her. But justice had prevailed, she told herself, and long ago. That didn't diminish the shock.

"You didn't tell me," her voice threatened to crack. "I thought we were the three musketeers." All this time she'd been in the dark. She didn't want to ask questions; what she already knew altered the shape of everything.

"You were young. Then it became history, no need to plow back through it." She waited. "I wanted you to feel safe in the world," he said. "At least with me. For as long as possible."

"But all those years I thought I was right there with you. I mean, as much as a kid could be." She looked at the saltshaker, and beyond to the yellow daisies painted on the frame of the screen door.

"Better if I hadn't spoken of it."

She shook her head. The rest of the room seemed to have drawn away from them, people at other tables moving their mouths, making their gestures in silence. Nothing reached her but a bland white static. Was there a time when she'd guessed that something might be wrong? If there was, she didn't remember.

The wait appeared, plate in hand, smile aimed at Zack, touching the corner of his shoulder. "Your Philly steak sandwich," she said, her voice crashing through, letting in the rest of the sound of the room. "Did you not like your ice cream?" she turned, face sympathetic, to Andie.

"No. Yes. It was fine." There was still an unmelted lump at the center, all the ridgy ice cream texture smoothed slick. It was logical that they'd have had secrets; they'd been the adults, they were the couple.

"Bring her another dish," Zack said. "Same kind, Andie?"

Andie shook her head no; the girl hesitated, moved on.

"I threw you for a loop," he said.

All that time, kindergarten, her first years of elementary school, they'd walked, the three of them, so close to a precipice and she hadn't known. "I'm wondering what else I don't know."

"I could say the same thing about you."

He ate half his sandwich as she piddled with her bowl of milk soup. Her stomach felt as if she were in free fall.

When Zack gave up on his dinner, they stepped out into the

dampish dusk air. "Time for me to hit the road to the launch pad," he said. "So I can get my shoes X-rayed."

"Right," her fists shifted in the pockets of her skirt. "It may seem I'm mad at you," she said. "But it's that I'm stunned. I thought I was more in on things than I was. It was always the three of us. Back then." The news was filtering through her still, collecting here and there, at the bottom of her lungs, the ventricles of her heart; she didn't know what to do with it, with herself. "At least if they took you guys, they should have let me come too. We were a unit."

He kissed her forehead. She pushed her hands harder against the pocket seams. He hugged her; she couldn't get her arms free.

Their two cars sat side by side. He walked around to hold her door for her while she got in. Then as he got to his own door, she lowered her window. "I hate it that they hounded you." Of course he wasn't invincible, had never been; she'd always known that.

"Over and done with," he said. "No lasting harm."

# 20

Elliott was driving with one elbow in the open window, the other arm draped over the top of the wheel, heading into Chapel Hill for the Quaker meeting. Too quiet, he seemed preoccupied. Of course he wasn't going to say a word to her about how her confession had affected him, not Elliott. His response was pretty clear, though: his mouth set hard, the thick sandy eyebrows lowered. His mood would help her stay out of trouble.

It was a jolt to be with him, such a solemn stick of a boy, after Zack's warmth and charm. The contrast was severe, which really wasn't fair to a guy, especially Elliott, who was so young and shy.

"Here it is," he said and spun them off the road, barely slowing to make the turn.

"For such a serious fellow, you're a devil-may-care driver."

"I got us here," he said. "I've never had a wreck or a ticket in my life."

The parking lot at the Quaker house was crowded. People getting out of their cars, most of them, had skipped the church finery, looked dressed for a quick run to the store for dishwasher detergent. She'd fit in fine. Or at least imagine she did, until someone told her there was a big secret she wasn't in on, an inner sanctum she'd never enter.

Over the last week, she'd built up expectations for this meeting: sitting in a silent room she'd feel the doors inside her quietly closing against all demons, against every troublesome thought. That hope had gotten her through a depressed few days since Zack left, since she'd glanced at that alarmist material Lexie had sent. She was a little ashamed of the sinking spell. Of course they wouldn't have told her they were being chased. It was childish and petulant, her upset at being left out. Anyway, she must have sensed back then that something was awry. Kids were like that, taking in everything: noticing without noticing, remembering without remembering.

Sun glinted on flecks of mica in the gravel parking lot. Elliott, ambling beside her, seemed tall and, in his stiff way, calm. "Tell me how to behave," she said.

"Walk in, sit down, be quiet. During the meditation people stand and say something if they feel moved. This being your first time, you probably don't want to be the first one to get up."

"Are you worried I'll embarrass you, Elliott?"

He turned half away; still she caught a glimpse of his shy sunburst of a smile. "You have a magnificent smile, Elliott. Radiantly transformative. As you've heard me say before." She'd said almost the same thing to Otis, that night in the bar, about his laugh; here it was again with the same faint sexual tinge. But that was normal; she wouldn't want to lose it. They were climbing the steps, up on the porch, greeted and welcomed by one and then another. The foyer was full of people yakking. The smell of fruit tea floated from a doorway that led into what looked to be a book-stuffed family den. Her worry about interrupting a cosmic silence was clearly off base. Elliott was steering her into the door of a big room that did indeed look like a courtroom; she'd been right about that much. They took a seat on one of the rear pews that lined the walls and faced an open center. Andie leaned back. Nothing to do but sit, in company. Elliott, beside her, had relaxed too. She could feel the shift, though his arm, close, wasn't touching.

Her eyes had drifted shut. She'd effortlessly fallen still. No desire to fidget. This would at least give her a break from herself; she could think, and she wasn't going to do anything dreadful in a crowd of silent strangers with Elliott at her side.

Someone, a man, was thudding his way to a seat, adding a bass beat to the quiet slidings and thumps of the feet of the seated. Now a woman with a hesitant voice was making a business announcement. Apparently the quiet part of the meeting hadn't officially started. Andie didn't move or open her eyes; this driftiness felt like the quiet burble of the New Age CD Caitlin had given her, like church organ music, the bass notes. Tim would hate a funeral, everything about it. Unless maybe there was one of those New Orleans parades, old black jazz trombonists playing a wild march for his last ride. She couldn't imagine sitting at a dark-suit funeral for Tim. But the memorial service was going to be at a church.

Elliott made a throat noise as if he'd thought to clear his throat and then decided not. From the sound of it, a child was coloring, down near the end of the pew. You wouldn't tell a kid that age that her parents were in danger. No one would. And why bring it up then a few years later? She could hear the light rub, small and deliberate, of the hand against rough paper; the primal smell of crayon, thick as pheromones. What if she did the umbrella in crayon? A practice finishing of it. The changes had begun on the day of the umbrella; she kept coming back to that. She'd felt nothing like any of it before.

Energy rising: that did describe it. Thinking of it, a chill crossed her upper back. In her mind, she tried out the lascivious-sounding word: *kundalini*. Even saying it silently was arousing, a perverse invocation; it was meddling in psychosis.

Forcing her mind back to her breath: think of nothing else, as Elliott had said to do. The movement of air going out bent her over slightly; coming in, it lifted her top half.

Sun hit the back of her hair from the window directly behind her. Yet it was cool in the room. No doubt to keep people from going to sleep.

Elliott was probably doing someone's tax returns in his head, or deep in a sexual fantasy after telling her to think only of her breathing. Maybe he was flooded with images of Tim; they still had the service up ahead of them. Impossible to predict how someone familiar can alter in a serious moment. In Israel, that English boy, Benjie, who'd gone with her to see the Wailing Wall. Seventeen and arrogant. In the dining room the night before, he'd been wearied and bored by the broiled fish and the word of fresh violence at the Lebanese border. Yet at the wall, he, like millions of others before, had stuffed his prayer, written on a scrap of the jacket of his plane ticket, into a crack between stones. He'd touched his forehead to the gritty wall, held there for a moment. When he turned around he was quiet for minutes before he started complaining again, launching into Jerusalem's "travesty" of a public transport system, as if he knew something about it. She'd thought about that boy a lot: the two halves of him, one jaded, sardonic, one wistful and tender.

Back to the breath, so hard to stay focused, her stomach moving out and in. The singer's way of breathing, much better than chest breathing. An experiment: she fixed her attention on her forehead, as the English boy had, on what her mother would say was the "third eye" in the center. Her eyeballs felt slightly crossed.

Thinking about the spot made it seem something was touching there. A crawling sensation. Like a finger circling on the skin, touching only the tips of the tiny hairs. A foot shifted against the floor nearby, a rubber-sole squeak.

In the darkness behind her eyelids, she could see a turning circle, a pale blue-white. The shape seemed to hover in front of her, luminous, a thin slice of moon. Still she felt the motion on her forehead. She strained to see better, make sense of it. But the image faded out.

Her thoughts fell apart into eddies she couldn't hold onto. She tried to reconstruct what she'd seen; but the light wouldn't hold its shape, breaking up into half-imagined yellow-white streaks, ruffle-edged jet streams darting and vanishing. Her voice in her head shouted sharp commands: Turning circle! Come back!

But she'd lost it.

Around her, people were stretching, starting to talk. There must have been some signal she didn't hear. Her mouth had a waking-up feel, as if her face had been set long in one position. Twenty minutes had passed; felt like less than five.

"Now," the man was saying, "we'll invite our visitors...."

First to stand: a young black man in a red T-shirt who said he was in town visiting an old professor friend of his. His story, the feeling in his voice, brought her back to regular wakefulness.

Elliott looked worried; she shook her head to show him she was sitting tight, saying nothing. Two early-teenage girls, sisters, were thrust to standing by their grandmother. They said their names, their grandparents' names, and sat down.

Then the old man seated just down the pew. He steadied himself, both hands on the head of his walking stick, getting into solid position. Clearly he meant to deliver a sermon. He introduced himself, Andie missed his name for listening to his accent. Scottish. Lovely. "I wairn ye," he said to the group. "I speak a mixter-maxter of Scots and England's English. My Chapel Hill daughter here, she gives me cheek aboot it." Interest had rustled across the room. People had hushed. "I come from a Quaker meeting 350 years auld. It's the gaithrin for aa my kin, for generations."

His grandfather was known, he said, for his bowler hat; he'd arrive at meeting, take his seat, but keep his hat on. Then would come a moment when he'd take off that old topper and set it on his knee. "It was a grand comfort to those gaithered. The auld man, ye see, wad doff that hat only, *only!* whan The Almichtie was thare i the room."

Laughter erupted, and clapping. What a delight, the old guy. A charmer. She imagined sailing around the room with him, to accordion music, of all things, dancing a jaunty polka.

But he hadn't stopped talking: His grandfather, Mr Dinwiddie, he said, would have tossed his hat had he been here today. "I know ye felt it, how the great an fearsome Almichtie was wi us in this oor. An I thank ye an I'll take my seat." The man lowered himself, with his aging daughter's help, back into the pew.

God with us in this hour? Maybe the others had felt God.

She'd seen only a turning circle, the mere hint of a spiral. Then her mind or her courage again had failed her.

# 21

Stepping out of the elevator, she could hear Billy's voice. In the middle of the hallway, he stood talking to a tall thin twenty-something, ash-blonde, sweetly giraffe-like as she shifted her weight. The girl was listening so hard she stood curved over toward him, a question mark. He caught sight of her approaching. A sharp glint surfaced in the warmth of his gaze.

"Hello there, Andie," taking her by the elbow. The appointment had perhaps slipped his mind. The young woman with her clipboard was eager to disappear down the hall, but Billy announced their names one to the other as the threesome pulled apart. "Alison," he said, as she was already walking away, "You get back to me today. Don't let me leave here without talking to you."

"Right," Alison said from behind them.

Right, *sir*, Andie thought, if she's as nervous as she appears to be. There couldn't be anything going on there, not in the office. Not Billy. Other than his flirting. She'd like to think too that he'd choose someone who didn't give off the feel of high school. Billy still had her by the elbow, the two of them heading for his reception office door. He was staring ahead, smile steady, his hand hot where it gripped her arm.

"So," he said, as they stepped into his office suite, "go ahead and get yourself situated." He headed out again, but not in the direction of his private powder room.

She unscrewed the first tube, the oil smell escaping. The room felt creepy without him, as if he'd taken his charm with him and left a cold residue; she had the impulse to turn and be sure no one, no camera, was behind her. Still jangled. The meditation with the Quakers, which had first felt so serene, had increasingly agitated her since: the turning circle of pale blue light, her inability to hold on to it, seemed a sort of cool warning.

When he walked in again, he was adjusting his yellow pocket

hanky. "You know I can't possibly get the folds exactly the same as they were last time," he said, settling back into his chair. "Knot of the tie, either."

"Or your facial expression or anything else," she said as they settled and began. The tone of her voice sounded like the one her dentist used while he was working: safely preoccupied.

"I could probably hold the expression," he said. "I'd miss the conversation though, sitting mute. I don't see how you can paint a face that's in motion."

"I could finish it without you."

"I don't like that idea."

"I know you don't."

He let a silence settle. She was the one to break it. "I see you hid that Idiot meditation book from me." Though if she wanted to do research on meditation, on the snake, the *kundalini,* there were plenty of books. She'd forced herself to look at the rest of what Lexie sent – nothing more there than what she'd seen. She understood now how somebody could find a suspicious lump and put off having it checked. As if the problem wouldn't be fully real as long as that action wasn't taken. Anyway, you couldn't fix anything with pop psychology or a Google search.

"I carried the Idiot book home," he said. "It wasn't going to do me any good here."

"People take meditation breaks at work. Folks in my studio do it all the time." She didn't like the feel of this room when the banter stopped.

He laughed. Laughed once more as if he hadn't already. "Maybe I'll take up sitting in a lotus position on my desk. Whatever anybody comes in asking for, I'll just tell them something enigmatic, keep my eyes closed until they leave."

"I had imagined you liked receiving supplicants." His eyelids lowered, corners of his mouth twitched up into a hint of a smile.

That man on the phone her first day in here, he'd been begging for something; she'd heard his wheedling tone from across the room. Billy had been sitting here year after year smugly dispensing or not dispensing favors, effortlessly conniving and conspiring.

Wait a minute! Her heart picked up speed. Billy would have been in office when her parents were persecuted. She quickly did the math; of course he was! And wasn't it the moment she'd mentioned Zack last time that Billy's face had altered, that he shut the session down?

Her whole system accelerated, heartbeat loud enough that she could hear it, the room lighter, then darker with each hit of her pulse. Billy knew about the witch-hunt of her parents. Of course he did. He'd have stayed in touch with any such investigation in his district. Not that he'd have been directly involved, but he had to have known.

Her hand kept working.

He had recognized Zack's name; she was sure of it.

But there was nothing she could do. Quit this job? Accuse him? She couldn't hit him with it and cause her parents even the slightest risk of more trouble.

"That playwright," she said.

"What's that you're saying?" as if he hadn't heard her.

"You know. The one who's in jail."

"Desmond," he said. "Detained for investigation. You're thinking to make me a speech about that matter?"

"He hasn't done anything except stage a play." She strained to keep her voice appropriate, conversational.

She wanted to scream the names of her parents in his face, make him own up. He could have stopped that torment of them. He had influence, more than anyone else in his right-wing invading witch-hunting camp; he'd been a force long before he took office.

"That man, Desmond, has extremely questionable connections," Billy said. "His play…I was there, it was full of hate, and not just the car-bombing part. The man walked out front at the end."

She pictured the playwright from the news: narrow-shouldered, his skin a ruddy shade of dark. It wasn't that she cared about him, or his work, particularly. But he had the right to speak.

"He stepped up to the edge of the stage," Billy said, "stared us in the eye, those of us in the first rows, before he looked up into the balconies, said, 'Ladies and gentlemen. Your plans are at an end. A great shift has begun, making mountains where there were oceans,' and on with that malarkey. He pretty quick made it perfectly clear what he meant, overthrowing America. I don't need to hear that kind of thinking flung in my face in my own country."

"I don't like that either," she said and looked up to meet his eyes. She half wanted him to call her bluff, say I know who you're talking about really. "But you can't have him hauled away."

"Don't give me all the credit. Anyway, you know you're not going to change me. You're just speaking up so you can tell your artistic friends what you did. Well, you've met your social obligation," he said, "and I congratulate you on your big bold move." His eyes were cold but for a bright spark.

"I'd think you'd be used to hearing dissenting opinions," she said, "and not being bothered by them."

The silence seemed to rise from the floor under her feet, pressing beneath her diaphragm. She'd gone too far, antagonized him without doing anyone any good.

But he smiled. "I don't mind a good discussion," he said; his playful tone returned as smooth as if there had never been a ruffle. "I welcome the views of all my constituents. And you, darling, whether you like it or not, are one of them."

Andie shuffled a pack of cards, whiffled them into a bridge. Then carefully, precisely setting down each card, she dealt herself a hand of solitaire. Pitiful Andie, home playing cards alone. To have thought of it in the state she was in was a stroke of genius. Rearranging her closet, pants together, shirts together, skirts together, then grouping within each category by color, hadn't satisfied her craving for order.

This afternoon Billy had upset her in a way that wouldn't settle. There was nothing she could do to fix what had happened to her parents. Her skin felt restless, itchy. She wanted more items to sort and put into proper piles. She moved a red six over to a row of cards that ended with a black seven, made the card snap against the table. There! Wasn't that satisfying?

When Mike had shuffled, the cards looked for a moment like paper he was balling up in his big hands. Almost 6 weeks since then. She'd half-expected to hear from him by now. He could have showed up at her door, still could, tonight or some night a year from now. Home wasn't safer than anywhere else, though she was still able, on and off, to pretend that it was.

Her mind did a spin at the fact that she'd had to watch herself with Zack, not run the flat of her hand over the outer edge of the hair on his forearm, as she had for a fraction of a second had an impulse to do.

She put the Jack down on the Queen. The cards had a nice sliding sound. Cards, oddly, were objects that seemed to feel sure of themselves. Each with the same thickness and finish, the same slap. Like money, but smoother, more resilient. She studied the long rows of cards in sequence. She wasn't going to win this game.

Billy's history proved he was dangerous; evidence of that ought to show on him more. In the portrait, she'd captured a bit of it. Mostly, though, what she saw, looking at him, was confidence, the sly warmth, a gaze that was both calculating and admiring. She'd liked that look. Hadn't felt bad about liking it either. Not until the thought of her parents had crossed her mind.

She dealt another fast hand; it would be easy to play this

game over and over. The craving felt soothed, not gone. She could play until the sky started to lighten outside.

Four kings showing. What were the odds of these four turning up? She named them: Zack, Billy, Mike and who? Not Archie. Not Charlie, though he came close. Otis? Yes. All four with a kind of heft to them. Their footsteps sank in heavy. So what? Did that tell you anything about them? The book she'd bought this afternoon in Raleigh, on Eastern religions, said it did, and set out personality types based on such details. Apparently she was somehow like a bird, an earthy bird, which strained credibility. Standing in the store, appropriately called Quail Ridge, she'd found herself: part *vata*, the sort of person who is airy, light, dry, quick, always in motion, and part some other type that had to do with being heavier, slower, juicier.

She'd finally made herself go hunting for such a book, buy it, glance at it. But that burst of courage was gone. She hadn't looked again, hadn't read about the sleeping snake. She was too suggestible; no need to give her imagination any bad ideas. The topic, though, was at least mentioned on one page; she'd had a look at the index. One more hour or day of ignorance wouldn't hurt. It wasn't as if facts about religion could have stopped her from exposing herself to Archie, from going off with Mike. Nothing was going to do any good. Plus, she felt a physical resistance, from deep inside her, to moving too fast. Or maybe she was simply making excuses out of fear.

Still dark when she woke. The rough weave of fabric at her fingertips. Chair arms. She found she was sitting up. Still in the big chair in the living room, cards in a stack in front of her. She could see their neat white edges in the dark. She'd had in mind to close her eyes for a moment, between games. To put away all thoughts.

Nothing moved in the room but the slow blink of her eyes. Her body felt no need to stir. She was a sleek quiet animal: she could sit here and wait. Skin smooth and cool. The darkness holding her was as tangible as water.

Now, she thought, this is the time: Snake, make your move.

She let her eyes close. Twitch open again. She made her mind blank.

Inside her back she felt only breath, nothing more, slow, almost even, following the way the shape of the chair curved her spine. Come on! Now! A hard shudder pushed the air out of her. She let it pass, fell still again.

The way to do it was without thought, without bullying or any kind of force. She'd learned that much. But the impulse to work harder at it was difficult to resist.

With her eyes closed, she watched the darkness. The darting white lines, as usual, taking on some depth, shape. The umbrella, all ribs and spokes, with the canopy gone. A complicated scene already fading as she rushed to see it all. The studio, a stream of people walking from the front door across the street to the laundromat, the group silent and solemn in bright sun, everyone carrying a naked umbrella, metal skeletons that offered no protection. In the midst of them, like soldiers, they carried Tim's body on a stretcher. Where was Caitlin? Then the picture was gone.

She let her head fall back, from where she'd craned it forward, trying to see.

Ask to see and you don't see.

Inside her body was quiet. No electricity.

She felt righteous: I was here.

And angry: You didn't come. Don't blame me.

Maybe taking this tack was the answer: Welcome the sex and insanity. Invite it. Then whatever it was would stay away.

But what a fantasy movie she'd just seen! If Mom were here right now, she'd open a cold bottle of Vouvray, they'd prop up their feet and study the images as if they were a painting: Tim's body, the skeleton umbrellas. Mom would know about serpent power, too much. Zack might well mention it to her. Oh please not. If my mother becomes my shrink, I'll never get loose, never be an adult. I have to do this myself.

# 22

Andie settled deeper into her usual spot in the corner of Rose's den sofa. In every pause in this room she heard the same scritch-scratching clock. Too many sessions here with no progress.

Rose took a sip of her tea. Andie picked up hers. The steam condensed, a warm-then-cool layer of dew on her face. The vapor of their two cups drifted like faint candle smoke between them, making the resolutely silent Rose seem more than ever a gypsy fortuneteller.

She'd planned for this hour to be efficient, for Rose to offer whatever practical ideas she could and to be conclusive. Fish or cut bait. But Rose, as usual, seemed set on meandering through the hour. "Here's what I want to know: do you see me as psychotic? Or on the verge...?"

No change in Rose's steady gaze. Not a blink. Or a sound.

"A simple straight answer," Andie said, "is too complicated an assignment?"

Rose laughed. "No, you're not psychotic."

"That's good to know." She said it lightly, but felt weak with relief.

"But the brittle humor and your feistiness have been much in evidence here," Rose said. "I think that's likely true in the rest of your life."

"Wrapping a moat around the castle," Andie said. "It's a reflex."

"It's a handicap."

"You're right. It's how I've mucked up everything. Work and love. It's why I'm alone."

"Then there's your opposite style of defense: total impossibly-sincere capitulation."

"You're hard to please." She didn't feel like arguing. "Look, I'm sure you're right, but you're fixing the wrong problem. I don't have time for chatting about small stuff like my personal style, or relationships. I have to get a grip on myself. Quickly."

No comment from across the room.

Rose isn't going to fix anything anyway. I have to be the one to do it, if it's going happen. Everyone knows that much about therapy. The clock did its click-and-rasp. Andie's vision blurred, but tears didn't spill. She pinched the inner corners of her eyes, blotting the excess. Rose's face had softened. "What would be the worst that could happen," Rose said, "if there were no moat?"

"Having sex accidentally. With the wrong man." She braced herself for the set of comments she could already see coming.

"Which is what has already happened."

"Yes."

"You've developed a habit," Rose said, "of keeping people at a distance, in part to keep from falling into the wrong bed. And yet?"

"I'm to fill in the blank, right? Okay: the moat it isn't working." She let her head fall back, examined the familiar light fixture. "So I'm in need of a better line of defense."

"I believe you know that's not what I'm suggesting."

"Yeah, I do know." Her voice sounded tired in her ears. She didn't have the strength or will for sparring.

"Rose, have you ever heard of *kundalini*?"

"I've come across the word, back in New Orleans, in advertising for a yoga class or some such."

"Dormant life force," Andie said, "coiled at the base of the spine, or so I read. It can get roused through spiritual practices, yoga or meditation, or while you're deep into doing some kind of art." The word "art" hurtled across the space, as if Rose had forced her to paint. "Then it can make you feel electrocuted, or as if you have malaria, or your brain is burning." She paused, having exhausted the knowledge she'd found in her one book when she finally made herself look at it.

She was still taken aback by what she'd learned. How could anything so explosive come out of sitting quietly and meditating?

It seemed wrong that it could happen suddenly, whether you wanted it or not, simply because painting put you into a sort of trance. She'd brought that information here, held at arm's-length, not letting it touch her. Yet now it seemed to wash over her.

"It's your feeling that this has happened to you?" Rose looked slightly discomfited. "You're describing it as a religious experience, a manner of spiritual awakening."

"For an hour or so, I thought something like that was happening. It certainly hasn't turned out that way." Again came the voice of her 16-year-old self, conjured when she stood beneath her childhood bedroom window: The explosion of sex and painting, the young Andie had said, it's all one force. "I guess I don't know," she looked again at Rose. "Certainly something strange has happened."

It was incomprehensible that people meditated and did yoga because they *wanted*, were actually *seeking*, this experience. Though she'd read the few lines on how differently it hit different people, everything from itchy skin to psychosis to feeling generous and at one with the universe.

"This past week," Rose said, "have you had more sensations, or thoughts, that seem part of the sexual trouble?"

"Not that I've noticed."

"What has been happening in your life in these recent days?"

She sucked in a breath. "It's not what I'm here to talk about, but a friend was killed. Tim. The boyfriend of one of the studio artists. The service is this afternoon. I've been forcing myself not to think of it."

Rose's eyebrows lifted. "I'm sorry. Were you close to him?"

"Yes and no. He was important. I had a 'thing' about him. But he was Caitlin's boyfriend. I couldn't get too close."

"You couldn't? Even before these sexual episodes?"

"Right."

"So you've always made sure not to step out of bounds."

"I told you the first day: I was embarrassingly conservative that way. Especially for a young artsy type."

"How was Tim important, Andie?"

"He stood out, the way he treated everybody, as if saying hello to you was just the greatest thing. He acted like walking down the hall was a delight: he seemed happy, at ease. Part of a happy couple. Plus, I had a feeling he could help me deal with this."

"Help how?"

"I have no idea. Doesn't make sense. Too late now anyway."

"So this week, you've been spending time with…Caitlin, is it?"

"I'm not someone you'd choose when you need comfort. That's the other thing about Tim, wherever he was, his body always seemed to know what to do. I've never been like that, except for painting." She hesitated. "I couldn't stay with Caitlin right now, anyway; my father has been in town." Adrenaline threw sparks inside her chest at the mention. She wasn't dragging Zack into this discussion. She sat forward, body on alert.

"I'd like to meet your father," Rose said. "He'll come in with you before he leaves?"

"He left already." She heard the warning chill in her voice.

"I gather you wouldn't want him to come."

"Indeed I certainly wouldn't talk about these sex episodes in front of my father. And I don't think your meeting my relatives is going to tell you anything. Plus, my time with him was limited."

"Your opposition to the idea is certainly striking. It has occurred to me before that you idealize your parents."

Anger popped. Andie pushed up to her feet. "No doubt I do. But neither have I found anyone else who comes as close to ideal. To my ideal, anyway." She seized the strap of her pocketbook, digging for the check that was already written. "And I have to tell you, Rose: it's time for me to stop coming. We've run out of subjects to talk about that have anything to do with the problem."

The heat in her face and head made her feel top-heavy, as if she might topple. Anyway, it was the threesome that was the main thing, not just him.

"Andie, the mere mention of your father coming here makes you decide to leave?"

Andie placed the check on the coffee table with a thump of her fingers, steadying herself as she did so. "Maybe I don't feel like sharing him," she said. "I'm not a very good sharer. An only child, you know."

In the doorway, she turned. "I never said my childhood was perfect. For one thing, I didn't learn to deal with other kids. But my growing up was better than anybody else's I knew, and a lot better than anything since."

"I believe it," Rose said, "and such good fortune can present its own complications. The door here is always open."

Andie nodded her farewell, headed down the hall to the door while she still had any composure.

Out in front of Rose's house, Andie sat in her car, collecting herself. Crap! She hadn't meant to leave that way. There'd been no need to be huffy and semi-rude. She felt a little silly and in the wrong for making such a scene.

She let out a long breath. The car seat...she'd left the windows just cracked...was pleasantly hot, exactly the toasty-but-not-sweaty temperature that felt most comforting.

The church for Tim's service wasn't far from here. She dreaded it. Less than an hour from now; not enough time to go home or to get anything done in the studio. She put it out of her mind.

The May air felt lovely. Probably 72 degrees, the fruit trees past blooming, last days of spring. Sitting here, window now open, was smoothing the ragged feelings. The knot in her throat had eased.

As her eyes shut, she could feel, just barely grasp the sensation of heat in her sacral bone. A little space heater there. Was it the car seat? Not actual warmth, though, so much as a fine vibration. She held still, mind and body, let her attention settle around the tiny chirring.

It was arousing. How could it not be, located where it was? The fine tremor fanned outward in diminishing circles from its epicenter; she could feel the sensation, though so faintly, all through her crotch and hips. As if a purring cat were lying across her lap. She'd noticed a hint of this as she first sat on the back of the boat at the dock with Mike. It was subtle enough, though, that without knowing to pay attention, she could have missed it.

Movement at her side. She snapped into alert. Rose. Leaning to peer in, her beakish face so close. "I hesitated to disturb you," Rose said, "but you left your sunglasses," handing them through the window.

"Thanks. I don't know how I got as far as the car without them."

"The shade," Rose said, gesturing back at the yard, "it's all these trees."

"Yes, we live in an enchanted pine forest," Andie said, "where princesses sleep. I, for one, have been asleep in these woods for decades," she smiled, an effort at conciliatory. "Still, a person needs her glasses."

"Andie," Rose said.

"Yes?"

But Rose had stepped back from her, staring. "You look radiant," she said. "Quite literally."

"Thanks."

Rose was still assessing, a look of sharp new interest on her face. She started to speak, stopped herself.

In the daylight, Andie could see Rose's make-up, how skillfully applied. Odd to see her in full light when she seemed rooted in a dim interior world, some liminal zone. Andie gave her a little wave, turned the key in the ignition far enough for the radio to come on. Rose continued to appraise her with a puzzled expression. Time to get moving. They hadn't said good-bye, she and Rose, not out loud in words, anyway. This was her last session; or maybe it wasn't, since she'd "accidentally" left her sunglasses behind.

Outside the church, a row of motorcycles lined a stretch of the road. Not the police-bike type, instead brightly colored as hard candies. They looked festive, with their gleaming chrome. The studio gang, those who were coming together, had already arrived. Tim should be sitting there, part of that gang, or with his biker buddies; everyone would want to claim him.

Stepping up to the arched open door, she heard the organ hit a ponderous note. This was a mistake to come here alone, as bad as it would have been jammed in next to Archie in Otis's van. She should have asked Marian to meet her. This was exactly the kind of traditional funeral, smelling of carnations, that she hadn't been able to imagine for Tim.

She took a seat, sliding to the middle of the last pew. Having signed the guest book, she could probably skip out and no one would know. The mudslide of sadness that had engulfed her in Caitlin's chair; that wasn't going to happen again. It wasn't fair to Caitlin or Tim. Though she ought to have at least felt some relief afterward from the crying, some sweeping away of clutter.

She was a bit early. The place was filling quickly. The bikers had apparently been waiting at the door. She could see the tousled and spiky heads, a row of guys in their twenties up near the front. A show of solidarity. Maybe they were pallbearers, honorary. That bright silver box on the table in front of the altar could only be ashes.

Otis's voice rose out of the field of heads in front of her. She lifted up in her seat. There they were: Archie and Marian, side by side; Otis, down the row. All she wanted to do was sneak back to the studio and paint...didn't matter what...with the whole building quiet, empty. A grand silence, the way it had been in the woods, with room for bad thoughts and memories to get lost in.

With room for her own sense of Tim. Now of all times she wanted to work, while she was alive and had the chance.

Here they came, the family filing into the sanctuary. All stood for the somber procession. Caitlin leaning on a boy no more than eighteen who had to be her brother, Sam. Tim's parents were holding each other up. She couldn't look. Along the rows, people were getting out their tissues, one old man vigorously blowing his nose.

The congregation settled, quieted. She sank back down to the pew. Now just to ride it out. Skate over what was going on here. It wasn't right that people disappeared, were taken, leaving so much damage.

The minister spoke, his voice sonorous and impersonal. He took his seat again, the organist played. Then a tall lean young guy, wide-shouldered, walked to the front: one of the bikers, come forward to talk about Tim. This would either be embarrassing or heartbreaking. Andie felt her senses and mind retract, gather with the knot in her throat.

The boy said he and Tim had ridden together. He seemed extraordinarily beautiful, standing there with unaffected dignity. "I read this story one time," he said, "about a holy man who sat under a tree in a village in India." Mercifully he launched into a complicated, not-very-personal tale that Andie was able to let slide past. From across the crowd came audible crying, here and there. Her own eyes were damp, nose drippy; she felt again for the wet wad of tissue. The boy sat down. No one got up to continue. Was it over? Around her the light seemed dim, the colors of hair and clothing dusted gray. She looked far ahead toward where the family sat; she could see little more than their outlines, they seemed engulfed in air so heavy it was impenetrable. Smoky currents moved within the near dark. She didn't want to see their faces, not Caitlin's, the parents', the grandmother's. The almost-hum inside her felt larger, more generalized, as it had been since she'd driven away from Rose's house, the sensation so slight she could easily question its presence.

Now the organ moaning its dirge. Her eyelids and the corners of her mouth felt weighted and pulled downward by the grey air. The family was filing out through a side door, sparing everyone the head-on sight of them, the father muffling cough-like sobs with the side of his fist.

Andie stood and slipped out the back door. One solemn man in a suit stood in the lobby, hands clasped before him. He nodded respectfully, did not look at her long. Outdoors, on the steps, she took in everything at once, the wide green front yard and heavy-barked pine-tree trunks, a dull shine on the parked cars, all color and light dimmed. She looked back at the man behind in the lobby, standing in profile. The white of his shirt and his face she saw through a fine haze of ash. This was what it would be to see sadness, the great mass of it. She walked quickly toward her car, before the wave of people coming out the door could surround her.

Without stopping at the studio or at a drive-through for a bag of late lunch, she headed from the church parking lot toward Chapel Hill. The university. Her old campus. She was on her own now, no Rose or Zack or Marian to read over her shoulder. Only the thought of Tim to remind her not to delay, not to let anything important wait. She was going to find this strange inner creature, whatever there was to know about it, at the source, in scriptures. Not in some bold-faced-for-idiots paragraph—no second-hand analysis. Instead the real, no doubt incomprehensible, root. The word *kundalini* after all was Sanskrit, sacred language of Hindus.

If she went online on somebody's computer, not Archie's, she would surely find lots of flaky people who talked about *kundalini*. What could be flakier? She'd always meant to be one artist who was clear-headed and rational, but that was over: she'd never be able to see herself that way again.

A few minutes out of town, flipping down the sun visor, she realized she'd left the grey haze behind: the day was bright. Her spirits lifted as if adjusting to the information about the light.

It was nearly dinner hour by the time she was searching the campus for parking.

Charging across the brickyard to the library, she felt nineteen again, a student with paint in the cracks of her fingers, racing to find a book of color plates she immediately had to see. Rose was right about one thing: she hadn't felt a rush of interest in a long time. Utterly fearless interest, too. She was ready to face whatever she found.

The dusk air had drizzle in it; what had happened to the sun? She dashed into the library, prepared to be in the wrong place, to find that no such books existed, that she'd need to go to India and the search would take years.

Up a flight or two, with a call number on a scrap of paper, she looped through two aisles, then walked straight to the right shelf. A bright orange book there caught her eye, the color of Eastern monks' robes. Reaching to take it down, she had the sensation across the back of her shoulders that someone was watching.

She turned; the long aisle was empty. Checking the other direction where she'd just come, she jumped. A gaunt-faced man leaned against the bookcase, looking at her from four feet away. "You startled me," she said, "I didn't hear you," trying to make her tone sound normal. He had on a dirty railroad cap.

"Sorry," he said, in a soft voice. "I sure didn't mean to do that." He was carrying no books or papers. "I came in here to use the john," the man said. "Then I saw you."

"Me?" Her voice, she could hardly hear it.

"I don't mean harm to you." He took a step forward. The closest other person she could hear was several aisles away. "I could tell looking, you wanted to meet a man. Not one of these college boys."

"No," she said, backing. He was coming forward; reached and touched the side of her neck with the tips of his fingers. She felt instant gaping arousal.

"No," ducking away from his hand. With one arm, she reached behind the nearest shelf and swept it clean, heavy hardbacks hitting him in the chest and stomach, throwing for a second a wall between them. She turned and ran, came to the end of the row, swung around into the next aisle, heading back for the main desk, bright-lit, crowded. Running, books still gripped in one hand, elbows jutted out like a kid, she meant to yell but couldn't.

Then she was standing before the counter, breathless. "There's a guy back there," she said, to a boy loading heavy volumes onto a cart behind the desk. "He's…" What was he? "Dangerous," she said.

The boy spoke to an older woman who picked up a phone. Calling security.

But that's not true! I'm the one who's dangerous. "Wait. Don't call. It wasn't him."

The woman gave her a patronizing look of sympathy, continuing to push the numbers, as if the victims always tried to recant.

"I'm leaving. I don't want to be here." If she'd hesitated one moment, what she might have done... Right there in the stacks, or outside on the grass like the dogs that used to wander the campus.

A uniformed guard rounded the corner from the stairs. The student said, "I'll walk you out."

The way he led her was through administrative offices, not the public route. In moments they were outside on the courtyard, warm night air hitting her face. "Where's your car?" She pointed. They headed around a building toward the lot.

This boy beside her had a limp; she hadn't looked at him until they'd come out here into the dark. He was lanky, long-armed in his white short sleeves. She felt herself pulse again with the craving that for minutes had gone into hiding.

She and the boy were alone on the walkway, no one near; the

only people were moving silhouettes off at a distance. Her elbow brushed against his arm. She drew in her breath, walked faster. They were almost at the parking lot. She focused her whole mind on her car: getting there, closing the door behind her and shutting him out. Now she could see: the top curve of the steering wheel, her jacket over the seat. Almost there, keeping to the far edge of the sidewalk, away from him, but still inside the lighted path. She leaned, grabbed the door handle, jumped in, thanked him through the half-opened window. What about her contact info, he said, in case they needed it? She buckled her seatbelt, shook her head no. "I'm the problem," she told him, "not that man." The car was rolling. She backed out; from the corner of her eye, she could see the boy still watching her.

Pulling to a stop at the first light, she checked to make sure her doors were locked: in her lap, she discovered, was the orange book she'd reached for and one that had sat next to it. She tossed them onto the other seat.

She'd escaped twice, in only a few minutes. Hadn't had sex on the public quad. But the man in the stacks, she thought, chose me. One glimpse and he knew. The thought made her stomach roll.

At home hours later, showered and clean in her summer robe, she felt closer to calm, able to think. She needed to know: What had he sensed to make him choose her? Was it the way she looked at men? An actual smell?

Worse than attracting him was her excitement. She felt again his fingers on her neck. Then the boy, a precarious moment out in public. She was still in danger and even less discriminating, quicker to ignite than before. There was going to be no end to this free fall. She was going to turn into a joke, then a hospital patient in restraints. Her breath grew audible, then slowly, with effort, calm again.

For the moment she was safely alone inside her house.

The two books sat on the kitchen table. She picked them up,

took them with her into the bathroom, settled herself on the toilet.

The top book, by Swami Muktananda, *Play of Consciousness*. She tried to make her mind focus. In the photo, the swami was about forty or so, with a neat beard and a red dot on his forehead, gazing at her with a half-smile. The warmth in his eyes seemed fond, seductive, amused. The subtitle billed it as "A Spiritual Autobiography". The man's expression on the cover said he'd be the one to start a slightly combative conversation with you at a party, just to get something going. Not scripture at all, but she hadn't had a lot of time in the stacks for research. She flipped through pages. Knowing: that was the kind of look he had…

She came to a stop at the chapter on "Dissolution of Desire." But Rose thought she was already too detached, not passionate enough; and she was right. You couldn't call these sexual surges passion.

She turned back to the beginning of the book: "The Necessity of Meditation for Happiness in the World". But the process of painting was meditative and that hadn't solved her problem. Apparently, it had started it.

The guru/author proceeded to chide the reader for being taken up with worldly matters: "You search for savor in various foods, in tea, coffee, Coca-Cola, puddings…You look for enjoyment in the latest perfumes."

Pretty decadent. Careful with those puddings. Her face made a slight motion toward a smile; the grain of normality in that response gave her a twinge of hope for herself.

"You will find," she read, "that at the place where the nose meets the eyebrows, there is incomparable fragrance." The third eye, that's what that meant, the location of his daub of red.

She turned to the index, to the Ks. At this point, she wasn't going to learn anything more awful about herself and her situation than she already knew. She saw the word: *kundalini*, with a 2-inch-long list of page citations: "nature of…" "praise of…" "effects of Kundalini awakening on daily life…"

Her stomach tensed to a hard ball, she flipped to one of the pages.

"'One day,'" she read, "'...I was meditating in my hut at Suki, and in meditation I was seeing the red light. I was happy. Then in the middle of my meditation...I could think of nothing but sex!"

She closed the book, the stripes of the shower curtain in front of her wavered as if from heat. If she read on, then what? What was the danger? She saw herself trapped in the back of a car careening toward border guards with rifles.

She opened to where she'd held her place.

"'My whole body boiled with lust, and I cannot describe the agony of my sexual organ. I tried to explain it to myself in some way, but I couldn't.'"

The sides of the toilet seat were framing her bare genitals. She shifted on the seat and felt the pull. Like her, he'd tried to explain it to himself and he couldn't; he too knew that what he felt wasn't ordinary desire. She wasn't the only one this had happened to. The *kundalini* had done this to him too. She got to her feet, shaky, letting the book drop to the floor, pulling the robe tighter around her.

She turned as if going back into the bedroom. Turned again. Picked up the book, scanned pages, read standing: "I began to feel afraid of all women... I was afraid that I might indulge in wanton behavior."

Her eye raced down the page: his retreat to a solitary hut...his fasting...his striving for "spiritual realization." Then: "...lust destroyed forever."

Destroyed?

"...Sexual desire becomes very strong, but this happens so that the flow of sexual fluid may be turned upward and the *sadhaka*'s lust destroyed forever."

She stared through the doorway, across her bedroom, to the

open night window. Her face felt rigid with fury. No part of her was going to be destroyed. She tossed the book; it hit the side of the bathtub and fell to the floor.

# 23

Billy's jutting chin emphasized his jowls. "I don't know how you can think you're through with me posing," he said. "I haven't seen the damn picture. Much as we're paying you, you've hardly been here, and now to say you're finished…"

"Not finished," she said, dabbing deeper shadow along a crease, "but nearly done with the research part."

"You really think you've got me," he said, "then I'm going to come over there and look." He was on his feet, crossing the space to stand in front of her before she could open her mouth. He stood now on her side of the easel. But, facing her, he still hadn't looked. He was waiting for permission, with the sexy smirk of one who knows he doesn't need to ask.

"Remember," she said as she moved out of the way to let him circle around to face the canvas, "the portrait isn't done. A lot is still rough."

He was looking, not listening, and whispering to himself. She couldn't hear the tone, or see more than a quarter profile. His ear, though, was red, and the side of his neck. She stepped closer again, beside him, to look at it with him and see what he was seeing. In the portrait, he sat at his desk, his swivel chair turned sideways to face the viewer with no furniture blocking the way. One arm lay at ease along the blotter, his legs akimbo, feet planted. The set of his head on his neck was enough to tell the story, his bullish charm and his ease with power. The pride inside her chest felt like a string of tiny jingling bells.

He studied on, his eyes roving and stopping, making the same trip again. It was the face that was holding him. No, it seemed to be the arrangement of the legs. Beside her, his shoulder and arm packed into that suit jacket seemed to give off a sweetish smell. She was certain she could feel his heat, as if he were sunburned, bare-skinned, a mere half-inch away. She moved so that one breast brushed his arm. Excitement, over the work, the quality of it, his nearness, making her giddy. He didn't seem to notice her. He stood and stared at the canvas but she could tell nothing, his face vacant as if he were doing math in his head. Her nipple had a nice sore feeling, alive and sensitive. She could dispense with her brushes, with fingers even, and paint with that nipple, dip it into a puddle of color, the cool of the oils pulling the flesh to a point. Then she'd touch it to the canvas, holding the breast with her hand or drawing with only the motion of her body, breasts, belly, hair…

Billy had walked away; his back turned to her still, he'd stopped in front of a window. When he turned, she could barely see him, the sunlight at his back. His face, as much as she could see, still blank.

"Andie, I'll need you to leave this here, so I can show it to the committee." His voice was flat. He hated it and he wasn't going to tell her face to face.

"I can't do that." Her throat was tight now with panic; she'd stood here indulging fantasies and putting herself in danger: was she mad? "Not without a lot more work," she said. "This still needs a lot of filling-in," she tried to speak slowly, low-pitched, with confidence. "It'll be a different situation when I'm done." She wanted to look down, make sure her breast wasn't exposed. By the time he'd left her side, her hips had been faintly circling. Had he crossed the room to get away from her? If he hadn't moved, she might have gone further. She would have.

He was watching her. He'd come a few steps toward her and she could see him, his mouth fixed in a smile, eyes abnormally still, an expression of his she hadn't seen.

"What kind of filling-in?"

"More work on the face. The most important part. You, the committee, none of you should judge it now. Those people will come up with all kinds of odd ideas that won't have anything to do with getting it right."

"You're right about that part," he said.

"Let a committee loose on an unfinished painting," she said, "and it'll be a certain disaster."

He was thinking. Maybe more than the painting had catapulted him across the room away from her. But she'd barely brushed fabric to fabric. He walked over behind his desk, the line of his mouth still set, checked his calendar. "How about you be here with the finished canvas Thursday at three o'clock."

"Sure." Her heart was beating like a pigeon's, sweat at her hairline. A disaster avoided. Two disasters.

"Okay then," he said.

He sat down at his chair, picked up his phone: "Calls, Shawan?"

She hesitated a moment once she was packed up to go; this was foolish: she should dash out of here. He put his hand over the receiver, impersonal, lifted his eyebrows at her waiting.

"Will the committee be here Thursday?" she said.

"No." He shook his head. "Just you and me."

From Billy's office, she drove straight home, hot-faced, hot and dry inside her skull. Her research had done her no good; she was in more danger than ever. And with Billy! She walked in the front door, locked it behind her. Then through her bedroom to the closet.

She bent her knees, backed in, parting the heavy curtain of clothes. Dropping to the floor, she crouched in the smell of dust, squatting on top of shoes. Pushing her fingers under the bottom edge of the door, she pulled the door shut, scraping skin off.

In the narrow space in the dark, she had enough room to rock, forward, backward. She'd rubbed against him. Billy Sylvester. And would have gone farther… There was no limit to what she might do. She banged her whole weight against the back wall.

She'd die in here. Suffocate in the dust.

What if death wasn't the end and she'd never escape? Something fell across her head, over her face. She grabbed at it.

Wool she'd forgotten to store. Her pea coat. She gripped the coat, held it against her with both arms. Her ribs hurt, and her scalp... She hit the wall with the side of her head, saw quick flecks of light, stars. She knocked her head again. It felt good. Again. More spangles of light, and this way she could control them, make them show up and go away and show up... A drop of liquid, blood, was moving through her hair, down the side of her head, feeling its way like an insect. She hit it with the heel of her hand, spread it so the tickle would stop. Her skull felt sore.

If someone came in, they'd put her in a helmet, a straitjacket. No one must find me. I'll be quiet.

Crouched still, she felt her knees burn cold, couldn't feel her lower legs at all. Tiredness was creeping over the rest of her. She slumped her weight against the wall.

Half-dreaming, half-dozing. This was safe, this was where she would stay.

She wasn't sure what had waked her. A rattle, maybe, inside the furnace duct close to her ear. She tried to get up, moved barely an inch; her back was locked into a curve. She remembered: her closet. Her head ached, her face felt smeared with dry paste. If she managed to stand...but her legs couldn't. The hems of all her clothes hung just over her head. She let her weight fall sideways against the closet door. The door swung open, letting her roll out onto the floor.

The room was dark. It was night. Two o'clock this afternoon was when she'd crawled in there. Jabbing pains, thousands of them, were flashing in both legs as they fell loose on the throw rug.

After the first hour, she must have slept. She had to have moved in her sleep or her legs would be dead. She lay still on her side, knees bent. This was as far as she could go tonight. She imagined herself curled up under a dark umbrella, her body wound around its post. She'd rest here until morning.

# 24

Marian sat silent in her big armchair in her studio, Andie paced, though her head still hurt. "I have to get through with him. Be done," Andie said. "Obviously, he's unhappy with the portrait. He stood there telling me he wanted his committee to see it. An excuse is all that was." She wanted to talk about the closet, but not about what she'd done with Billy that had driven her there.

"He could have outright rejected it," Marian said, "and asked for his money back. He wouldn't pussyfoot around. I agree with Otis" who'd needed no more than ten seconds to voice his opinion in passing. "I don't doubt Billy's ruthlessness."

"I'm not going to go back and take the guts out of it." Her head felt hollow and cottony, like some sort of hangover.

"Where's the picture now?"

"In my car."

"Bring it up here. I want to see if he's got anything to gripe about."

"You think it's that simple, do you?" No need to get sharp; Marian was trying to help. She headed for the door, joggling her brain with each step. She was too depleted to feel bad any way but physically and too antsy to sleep.

When she'd hauled the canvas upstairs, careful to avoid traffic in the hall, she set it on Marian's counter, leaned against the hanging cabinets. She didn't let her own eyes focus. Not until she had to would she see his face again. She'd figure out, too, how to avoid being alone with him. With any man, for the time being.

"I'll be in my studio," she said to Marian. "I'll give you time to arrive at your judgment without my interference."

Back in her space, she picked up her phone. To call who? She wanted to talk to her mother, but she'd wind up telling her too much. Mom would guess too much of whatever wasn't said. Or maybe, for once, she'd have nothing to offer; then where to turn? The answering machine was blinking. She hit the button.

"Andie, Tripp," the machine said. "Give me a call this morning, will you?" She reached for the Rolodex. Get this over with. Tripp hadn't felt the need to leave his number, and she hadn't been able to stand the idea of putting him on her on speed dial.

He picked up on the first ring. "Andie, my good friend," his voice all bright and friendly. Her heart sank lower. "What's up, Tripp? You sound concerned."

"I know we're going to be fine," he said. "Just a thought I'd like to make sure to pass on: the senator, you know, needs to convey his full dignity, his stature. Those qualities have to come across."

"That's not coming across?"

Marian was sailing into the room, talking; Andie, with the full length of her free arm, waved her out.

"I haven't seen it, you recall. I'm just aware of the lasting importance of this picture, this enduring memorial."

"Of course," Andie said. "I understand."

"He's the furthest thing from a vain man." Pause. Andie let the quiet continue. "It's only that I sense," Tripp went on, "that he's looking for a more serious, authoritative look."

Another pause.

"Think of the George Washington faces, Andie, not the features, but the bearing, the gravitas. Of course Billy didn't use that example. I'm just saying."

"He isn't impressed, I gather."

"He's impressed, definitely. As I mentioned to you at the start, he has a good eye. I think he was quite affected by what you've done."

"Affected."

"Yes, he made some noises about keeping it, as is, for his own collection."

Which would mean his fireplace, his trashcan. It would never be seen again. She felt anger massing, a deep shifting of weight as she began to take in the threat. Billy Sylvester wasn't going to get the chance to throw her work away.

Footsteps at the door: Marian again. She waved her off.

"I think I've talked him out of that," Tripp said. "We want this picture for more important work than decorating his back room. We need it to carry on all he stands for. To be a flag for the troops."

Not until Tripp signed off, the receiver at a safe distance, did the full rush of upset come over her. Now she was caught in their tangle, their tentacles all over her. And George Washington. Dear God.

Ordinarily the Washington comment would be little more than a funny item to report with an eye roll to the others at lunch. But her painting was in danger, the canvas itself, not to mention the final $50,000 payment. Elliott would tell her to give them their money back and get out. Then do what with the portrait? Every alternative shot out more questions.

Nothing was going to happen to this picture, that was the sure thing. The thought of wrecking it, installing on him a blander face… She groaned out loud.

Marian stood in the doorway, solemn and calm. "I've been sitting looking," she said, "at that portrait for the last 20 minutes. A picture of Billy Sylvester is something I never thought I'd want to stare at."

She cast Marian a second glance; her eyelids felt weighed down.

"Andie, it's better than terrific. Don't tell me you don't know that. Darling, this one's the real thing."

"He wants it changed." Her next breath brought her near to crying.

"Of course he does. You've nailed his soul."

"He wants more of a George Washington look."

Marian laughed, gave Andie's shoulder a pat as she crossed to a seat. "I want more of an Angelina look."

"This is serious, Marian. You'd know it if you worked for hire. I can't blow off any customer. Much less this one."

"There's a way around this," Marian said. "I'm confident of that. Just because of the portrait. The pure force of it."

"That's the problem."

"At worst, you can give his money back and keep the picture."

"I thought of that."

"I'm serious. It's museum-quality. It's going to put you out in the world in a whole different way."

"No museum that would want this is going to pay me close to what he's spending."

"You don't know that. And you're being defeatist and negative. If you don't believe me, get a second opinion, somebody with more impressive credentials who might be able to convince you."

Andie cast a sharp look over at Marian, who had pulled herself up too straight-backed. "I don't need another opinion, Marian. I trust your take on it, and my own. I also think Billy may have arrived at the same view. That doesn't help my situation. One way or another he wants it destroyed."

Marian nodded concession.

"I could take a picture of it," Andie said. "As it is now, before the surgery."

Marian shook her head. "I don't think we can settle for a souvenir."

"I have a deadline. I have to be back in his office with this next Thursday. Just the two of us, he said. No committee." She could feel in her nipple that moment of contact.

From downstairs, the banging of Justin's hammering. "Suppose," Marian said, "that you took someone with you. A hotshot expert to plead your case."

Andie nodded. Though Billy wouldn't be persuaded by anyone.

A slow cloud was coming over Marian's face. "Andie, this may seem silly, but I think the canvas needs to be locked up tight somewhere." She paused. "I'm serious."

"I want to laugh," Andie said, "but it's not totally far-fetched. I wouldn't put it past Tripp to arrange to have it 'collected'. In the most innocent and 'helpful' manner."

She got to her feet, as did Marian, both of them heading for Marian's studio where the painting sat and the door stood wide open.

"They can claim it's their property, after all," Andie said, as they headed down the hall. "Legally it is. I barely got it out of Billy's office yesterday."

Elliott, again in sweaty running clothes, opened his apartment door, stepped out onto the landing, as she came to the top of the stairwell with the crated and fully hidden canvas. She'd nailed together a housing around it, though it wasn't fully dry. Marian, winded from the climb, was breathing audibly behind her.

"Good timing," he said, his eyes following the unwieldy box in the door. "I was just about to get into the shower." He took one end of the crate. "Let's put it in here," he said. He'd opened the tall cabinet at the dining room end of the apartment. She lifted, fitted it into a space he made behind his cherished collection of car prints, in with a series of vintage Chryslers.

"It's more than decent of you to do this, Elliott, harboring my stolen goods."

"No problem," Elliott said, locking the wardrobe. "The way I see it: I'm keeping the guy from getting hold of what he wants."

"I wish you'd had a look at it," Marian said, "before she boarded it up."

Elliott gave her a skeptical glance.

"You'd be impressed."

"You think?"

"I'm sure."

"Go take your shower, Elliott," Andie said. "It'll be here a few days at most. Until I've decided what to do."

By late afternoon: two calls from Tripp. She didn't call him back.

Then bed around midnight, after going out for a run in the dark: from the house to the road and back, five long laps, avoiding the highway traffic. The exercise hadn't calmed or relaxed her. Neither had the hot bath and washing her hair.

Now the sheets were trying to bind her up in tangles. Even as she tried to settle in, the planes of Billy's face took shape in her mind, vivid as if the canvas hung in the air in the room, but larger, the image of his face alone. In the darkness, his face was everywhere. She sat up, got out of bed. Then stood, without direction in mind: not wanting water or bathroom. Snapping on a light, she padded into the kitchen. The thought of food: unsettling. She wandered out through the other side of the kitchen, across the big room, down the hall back to the bedroom, made the same circuit again, like her run earlier, a loop.

Tripp would call tomorrow if he didn't hear from her. He wouldn't stop. He'd call here at the house too, and act as smooth and gracious as if this was his first casual effort to reach her.

So she'd leave town, go somewhere he couldn't find her. She'd go to New Orleans! Of course. Perfect! A labyrinth of wrong turns. And full of the occult: certainly the right place to find people who knew about dangerous energy. She had felt a sort of subterranean hum there even in daylight, there as a teenager with her parents so long ago. They'd wandered among the blinding-white mausoleums piled close against each other along narrow paths; and that feeling, of unseen presence, had followed her out past the cemetery wall and back into the city of the living, where it only grew stronger.

That evening she'd set off exploring alone, chased the mystery block after block. Then a cross street lured her with its feel of a welcoming party but soon dwindled into a different sort of neighborhood, a bombed-out hell that closed behind her. By the time she'd recognized the change, she was lost, out of the path of taxis or anything that looked safe. She walked and walked, staying at the street's edge, as far as possible from the boarded-up doorways and deepest shadows, the knots of murmuring voices that quieted as she neared. The scrape and hiss of a struck match where she'd seen no one shot fear through her, then a sharp cry from the mouth of an alley, a scramble of feet on gravel. A car nudged up behind her at the street's edge. She could feel afresh even now her alarm as she'd turned to look behind her. A cop car: a pair of police, they'd been out looking for her. Her parents had called them an hour earlier.

Still, New Orleans was where she needed to go. Billy could wait…he'd have to…while she had a chance to hide out and search and think.

# 25

Shortly before 7 a.m. Andie sat in the stairwell at Elliott's apartment building, watching the minutes tick past. No answer to her thumpings against the Army-green metal door. He'd be at his girlfriend's, but he always came back by the apartment to dress for his job. She knew his regular paths, as if he were a sixth-grader and she his mother. But she'd returned for the painting sooner than either of them had expected.

The air felt mild and accommodating, the light tentative. Her own engines were surging; she'd be out of town in minutes before anything could stop her. Elliott would be here soon; except for his teaching times, he had to be at his office by 8.

Everyone in the complex seemed to be up and rushing around, full of agitation. Doors opening and closing inside the building, out in the parking lot. Do this, do that, hurry up. Each family a little hurricane spinning separate from the others. But no breakfast smells. In a warmer poorer country, windows would be open, doors open, everywhere dogs and chickens and three-year-olds coming and going. She was going somewhere like that today, where life felt looser and freer.

She stood up, walked back over to the door. Not a sound from inside.

To fly, she'd have to check the portrait as baggage, which meant letting it out of her sight. She picked at a dry streak of paint on her hand, until the place where it had been was scraped red. Some uniformed person would set the crated canvas on a moving conveyor belt that rolled it away from her.

Getting out of town in the car would be better. No, that felt wrong. She needed to be airborne to feel safely out of reach. She needed to touch down in New Orleans today, before she changed her mind.

Footsteps on the sidewalk, Elliott coming toward the stairs, was stopping to check his mailbox just below in the breezeway, pulling out rolled-up catalogues. She felt her layer of calm growing thin, at the same time she wanted to reach down and lay some kind of benediction on his unsuspecting curls. That impulse was the kind you were *supposed* to get after a religious experience, certainly not the lust for abasement, obliteration, the need to dissolve, that had seized her.

"Elliott, hurry." Her voice sounded amplified and hollow in the empty stairway.

"Hi," he said, coming up the steps toward her. He didn't look surprised. "I guess I know what you've come for." His face shadowed with second-day stubble, he looked dissolute almost. Attractively so.

"Come on in," he said, tossing keys onto the counter. She stood stiff in the middle of his cramped living room, wasting no time with sitting down. On the floor were weeks' worth of unread *Financial Times* and his *Foreign Policy* magazines. Elliott was one artist at no risk of being flaky. He searched in the bathroom, came back with a smaller key to the big wardrobe, but then couldn't make it turn in the lock. "For chrissake, it's the wrong one," she said, as he kept trying.

So he'd lost the key. She would cut the wardrobe open with a saw. He came back with a second key, handed it to her.

"Try this," he said. "I've got to make a call. I'll help you out with it in a moment."

As she opened the tall cupboard, her mind fluttered: the painting might be missing. Here it was; the packaging made it larger than anything else in the dark cabinet. Three feet by 4 feet, roughly, for the canvas, not counting the boards protecting it.

She wrested the big rectangle out. With her hands on the splintery wood of the crate, she felt a chest-swelling certainty: it was her painting, she was doing the right thing taking it. These guys, whatever they had in mind, or were capable of, they didn't mean well by this portrait. The heady sensation of focused power traveled through her body, making her stand up straight. That power in Billy was part of what showed in the picture, though you couldn't pin it on any detail. To have that showing was what he didn't like.

The same potent feeling rose from the taut shape of the umbrella, too, its spokes and turning circle somehow an image of the power itself. A portrait of a *chakra*, that painting, or a wheeling galaxy, a sort of mandala even. She was starting to speak her mother's language. And she was learning it on her own.

In the car, heading for the airport, she had the impulse to reach into the back and pat the wood frame, not to be sure it was there, instead to reassure it, help it stay calm. I'm simply a parent, she thought, getting my child to safety, though Billy might call it kidnapping.

The ride to RDU felt endlessly long. She had the feeling she'd passed the same Mobil station three times, that without knowing it, she'd chickened out. She was riding in circles and would miss her flight.

Arriving at the airport exit finally, with some relief, she pulled into a park-by-the-day lot. In the terminal she might well run into someone she knew. As long as it wasn't Tripp. Or Billy on his way to Washington; it was a day he usually commuted.

Inside the terminal, she hoisted the flat crate onto a rented cart. She'd flown maybe two times in the last five years. As a small child, she wouldn't have believed it was possible to travel this little. Driving to places between Atlanta and Washington the way she did for jobs didn't count. Being at this old familiar airport was a homecoming, the excitement of the adventure starting to mount.

Her eyes raced down the list of departure times up on the display. Her plane was on time. A hard bump: someone passing behind her, running up her heel with a cart. She grabbed for the painting.

"Sorry, sorry," he said, "I wasn't looking." The man had two small children riding the top of his luggage cart, as if he were grocery shopping. He hadn't touched the crate. Her heart, though, was beating fast. Time to get out of here, on to New Orleans. An Eden, she'd told Rose, though that was leaving out the seediness, which was part of what she needed.

Her flight was leaving in 48 minutes.

She bought the ticket, exorbitant, and placed the crated portrait on the scale. "Where will it go," she said to the man in his navy jacket, "where in the plane?"

He gave her a second glance. "In the belly, the freight hold just beneath the passenger cabin." She watched as the flat box she'd marked 'Fragile...Fragile... Special Handling' rode away from her on the moving belt, disappeared through the tunnel door.

Gulf coast summer heat hit her as she walked out onto the pavement, then into the edge of the street. She took a deep gulp of humid Louisiana air, thick as pudding almost. She'd arrived, stepped across a border into this anonymous crowd, on a sidewalk of the New Orleans airport, where she slowed for a moment to plant herself. She was here. Away from the tight space of Pinehurst. The sweltering breeze melted any jangled thought or misgiving before it could arise. A couple of cars honked as she slowly pushed the cart along the edge of the curb. Fuck 'em, they had plenty of room to pass; but the feeling that rose with the thought was friendly. She was here in this delicious old town, rich like fertile dirt, with her newly felt strength and her dangerous picture. And she could easily afford to enjoy it.

In the taxi, she sat with the portrait propped on the tops of her feet. Lying on its side, its length almost crossed the backseat floor. "Windsor Court, please," she said to the driver with his neck craned back to hear her. At the name of the hotel his shoulders twitched to alertness. "Yes'm."

The three of them had stayed there a few nights when she was maybe eighteen. The hotel was brand-new then and, as it happened, that had been their last trip of her "childhood". A customer of Zack's had paid for the suite. Maybe she'd take the two of them, her parents, there for a couple of nights as a Christmas present when all this was resolved. By Christmas, it better be.

On either side of the throughway the land lay low, faintly concave, famously dipping below sea level. The roofs of the low-lying warehouses rushed past, and the tall billboards. Breeze poured hot into the open windows. They were entering the city now, the driver pointing out the sights, telling her where she should have dinner. His accent was Haitian. Into the center city: iconic New Orleans, as always. Sitting up on the seat like a kid, to see better, she felt exhilaration take her over. She'd chosen the right flight; in the heart of this city, the outside world vanished: she was now far...far!...outside of Billy Sylvester's district. Let him try to find her; she couldn't picture Tripp playing detective. The thought made her smile. She didn't care if Billy sent the nation's top cop to look for her, or President Bush himself. This was the place to get lost in, to be as unbounded as anyone could be: a geographic time-out.

A few slow blocks, and then they made a sharp turn through a gate into the walled-garden entrance to the hotel. It was as she remembered, a quiet fountain, a brick drive, the waiting doormen, discreet and low-key nice.

One of the young men, first bending to greet her as if she were a head of state, carried the crate in and, as if he could read her mind, set it next to her at one of the reception tables. This painting wasn't leaving her side until she'd figured out how to keep it permanently safe. It was going straight up in the elevator to her room. She looked around, felt time slowing with each breath. Staff moving quietly about, the light subdued, the furniture seriously good, carpets absorbing any objectionable sound, softening the voices of the group of guests passing who looked to be a rich rock band on good behavior. And then the treasurehouse of art on the walls. This hotel lobby had the feel of her growing-up years, life's edges softened as much as was humanly possible.

"Welcome, Ms. Branson." Seated at the table with her, the woman preparing to sign her in resembled Rose; both had an air of authority that seemed to emanate from a mysterious source. The older European actress look.

"Tell me," the woman said when they'd handled the basics, "what kind of fill do you prefer in your pillows? If you like, we can keep that on file for your next visit." She didn't blink when Andie had no idea what kind of fill or at the fact that she'd made no reservation: "Just an impulse," she couldn't stop herself from explaining. She must remember to tell the operator to fend off any phone calls, admit to no one that she was here.

"Not uncommon," the woman said. "Several of our regular guests come on impulse, from any part of the world. When they're needing a respite." At a barely perceptible nod, the man appeared again, awaited Andie's permission to move the crate.

She got to her feet to accompany him, Henryk, slipping into a more feminine walk, as if she had on slingback pumps and a narrow cigarette skirt, as if her hair were smooth and she weren't wearing khakis and a nothing-special shirt, the sweat dried to salt on her skin.

Like the lobby, the hall was an art museum with the feel of a gallery in the Frick. On her first visit here, when she was still a student, she'd have been able to name the paintings. Startling to realize she hadn't remembered all this was here: Gainsborough, Reynolds, Van Dyck. She pictured her Billy portrait up there among them. She'd like that, but with a little disclaimer beside it saying the artist did not support the views of the subject. No, that wasn't necessary. Nobody cared now what Van Dyck thought about politics.

"Who acquires the art?" she asked Henryk. The two of them

were the only people in the elevator.

"Our curator," he said. "The collection is quite remarkable."

"I see that."

Another lean young man in livery stepped in at the next floor. He nodded to each of them with a pleasant glance, murmuring without irony, "Good afternoon." Two young guys who must know each other well, yet there was no banter, nothing that excluded her.

From here, she thought, the outside world, even Pinehurst, felt harsh. This was a haven. Had she appreciated that at eighteen? Yes, indeed, she had. This morning on the plane, when the first cart of drinks toddled down the aisle, she'd remembered and known that this hotel, before she'd chosen the city, was her destination.

The room he showed her to was a suite. Even larger than the one where she'd spent those nights with Mom and Zack.

She waited until the bellman was gone, then situated the painting in one of the walk-in closets. She wouldn't be able to shut herself up in this closet and bang her head, the space was too big, the walls too far apart. But she was through with that. Coming here was rounding a corner, she was sure of it. In this city there was room to move around and nothing was considered bizarre.

In the doorway between the living room and the bedroom, she turned in a circle, to take it all in. This was not going to be her last visit here. Next time I come, she thought, I won't be on the run. All my pieces will be selling for $100,000 and there'll be no backtalk from the customers. I'll come here for regular time-outs, "respites", like the woman downstairs said. I'll be as alive as I was on that one day in the studio. And I won't be alone.

She started filling the tub, then picked through the basket of bath products. She sprayed a bit of the scent, just to have a whiff. Her skin, sticky from heat and travel, would soon feel clean and smooth. She eased into the tub, felt the water and steam taking over.

She emerged from the bath brand-new, confident and extraordinary. Already she felt able to manage the problems back home. If Billy were here now, she'd persuade him that this portrait would give him and his causes extended life, would reach people long after his retirement that his political rants never could. People would sense his complexity. He would be won over to her view, he'd be grateful and his eyes would take on that ambiguous shine.

The way she felt now, she might well decide to stay here and skip the meeting with him. She could get word to him, if she felt like it. It might be the wisest thing to stay away from him.

Only mid-afternoon. The towel felt pillowy against her fresh-shaved leg.

From the windows of the bedroom and living room, she could see the river, about as wide as the long upper stretches of the Ganges in dry season, the forward motion somehow with a sinuous feel, though the water moved straight past, slipping beneath the wide yellow sheen of sun on the surface. Seeing it move, her skin prickled, first on the backs of her legs then over her body, as if every tiny hair were touched by rising bubbles of carbonation. She shivered, yet her mood was exultant. She drew her attention back into the room, finished her unpacking.

The rest of the city was on the other side of the building; she imagined it quietly turbulent and full of deep currents, far more so than the river. Marian would say it was crazy to choose this town with its decadent vibe, out of all the places she could have gone. But what did it matter? Living in Pinehurst hadn't kept her out of trouble.

Stepping into her pants, she hesitated. The fabric felt heavy as duffel bag cloth, not in keeping with her current situation; she'd go shopping for something more appropriate to wear, more feminine and gorgeous and free.

There'd been logic to her thinking about why she'd done right to come to New Orleans; but it had slipped away from her. For once in her life she was acting on healthy instinct. Like any other animal. An image flashed of her face on the dog's head. No matter. Just now, the primitive within her didn't scare her.

The sidewalk on Canal Street felt like a boardwalk. Gaudy gift shop windows, a lot of litter. A fan was blowing feather boas out toward the street in the doorway ahead. In the window, a battery-operated gizmo: a pair of fat plastic dolls having jerky intercourse, the guy grinning back over his shoulder.

She turned off the broad thoroughfare into the French Quarter, headed a block north toward drunken touristy Bourbon Street. From ahead she heard music. Getting louder. Coming from just beyond the next corner. She felt ditsy and light, as if she had a caffeine high. The moment she stepped past the last building on the block, live brass blasted out of a door across the street, a huge golden sound. A group of couples drifted across her path, drinks in hand, the man nearest with a wide straddling gait. Mostly the foot traffic felt ordinary, except for the aimless pace and the plastic cups in hand. Sour garbage smell hung over a patch of pavement. Standing in a recessed doorway, a plump cheerful girl faced the pedestrians, wearing only a seafoam-green satin slip. "Hey there," she said to the man ahead of Andie. He moved away from her, shook his head no; she offered the same perky hopeful greeting to Andie.

"Hi," Andie said as she passed. She couldn't help laughing; the sight of the girl's fresh-faced approach was somehow relieving. No guilt there. And such beautiful milky skin she had, great lingerie; she didn't look beaten-down and drug-addicted at all.

From an open window onto the street, a sustained wavering note on a horn, sound she heard as yellow. Again came the feeling that her every hair was moved by bubbles in a gritty silty liquid.

Up and down the street: the trolling clumps of young guys, many in bill caps that half-shadowed their faces. Still she could see expressions: grinning, furtive, expectant, doubtful, boastful, sliding toward drunk.

A transvestite, tall and coarse-featured, hurried along the sidewalk, crossing to the other side. She/he was the only person who seemed to be in a hurry, striding, face and one free hand in a dither, carrying on an argument, saying apparently what she wished she'd said earlier.

Andie felt not the slightest desire for a drink. She seemed to be reaching the edge of the district, the part with a festival feel; at this end the strip clubs were more obvious. A pink column supported a glass case of still photos: live sex, the women slack-mouthed with pleasure. Couples Welcome, the sign said. A photo at eye level showed the man's penis on the verge of entering the woman. She tightened her thigh muscles, let go; did it again: squeeze and release, the pull of that narcotic rhythm. She was playing with danger. Didn't care. No doubt the spell of the city, the momentum of her rush to get here, were making her reckless. She couldn't bring herself to worry. The break from constant fear felt so sweet she could cry.

Sets of feet on the sidewalk behind her, coming closer. She stopped all motion. They were walking slowly, strolling. She hadn't been doing anything obvious. Though nobody in this neighborhood could get too judgmental about her sexual adventures, at least not while they were here. She turned back in the direction she'd come, heading toward the other end of the street. A couple of the men in the pictures had appeared to be amateurs, selected from the audience maybe, wild disbelief on their faces. The women had more the porn star image.

She imagined lying spread under the man with bony shoulders who grinned open-mouthed into the camera. The scenes might be fake, like in movies: photos posed in a back room to bring people in for the liquor and topless dancers. She crossed onto the next block and each doorway she passed raised the volume of sound, which gradually fell away until she came to the next bar entrance. Everywhere doors were open, but a woman entering alone, even in daylight… For the first moments inside she wouldn't be able to see. She'd have to stand and wait, a blind target, until her vision adjusted. The girl in the green slip wouldn't be scared to do it. Thank God, I am. She was glad to discover it.

A gift shop drew her, bright with a glass front full of T-shirts and visors, pink-sequined halter-tops strung on a clothesline. This place was open and full of light; this she could handle. She wandered in. The display of Mardi Gras beads along one wall was like a candy counter, mouth-watering color and shine. She stopped, ran her fingers through the strings of beads, gathered two fistfuls. The man from behind the cash register stepped to her side. Dark-haired and elfin, scrawny like the guy in the photo, eyes full of warmth and tease. "These would look very beautiful on you," he said.

"Yes? Which ones?" She let them flow across her hands. The beads of the purple strands were made in the form of tiny gleaming dice, bright purple cubes with dents on each side. He made a loose dance-y movement to the beat of the music across the street.

"All of them." Beads and nothing else was what he meant. Maybe some of the strands were longer, would swing against her, brushing back and forth all the way down. His smiling gaze into her eyes did not stop. She had to look away. Intimate and sweet, she thought, when the moment had passed. That was how it felt anyway, whatever he intended.

He lifted a few strands of beads and placed them over her head, around her neck. Running his hands down the length to straighten them, the backs of his fingers traveled across both her breasts. Done before she could stop him and then his hands were gone. "Look in the mirror," he said. "You will see a goddess."

She saw a woman whose face held all the brashness and doubt of those fellows in the bill caps. Beside her the dark-haired guy with delighted eyes. Again the thought: in the library that day, she could have been the one escorted out by the security guard, for brushing her fingers along the neck of some boy in a T-shirt with a backpack. Though a boy wouldn't have rushed to the counter to complain. At least she hoped not. She moved to make the beads swing side to side, a dance in itself, her nipples two hard points.

"You see?" he said, giving a shimmy to his narrow hips. "You rouse the voodoo queen."

"I'll take these," she said. "The purple dice too."

"Of course, the dice. To remind you to take chances."

"I don't need reminding." They had moved to the counter, he was ringing up the sale. His hands were short-fingered with bitten nails.

"How long are you in town?"

"I'm not sure." He had in mind, she could see, to reach again for the beads she was wearing. She shifted away, to her slight surprise. Tonight, though, she would put them on against her bare skin, wear them as she lounged in the decorous art-filled sitting room of her suite. That was only slightly more reckless than taking a bath.

"Thanks," she said, gave him a wave, half-dismissive and wandered out the door.

Walking faster, she left Bourbon Street, roamed through other streets of the French Quarter. The section was small compared to the maze she remembered: she'd gone exploring alone a lot that first trip. The Quarter still full of alleys and vines and hiding places. The city these days had other hipper districts and other seedier streets.

She got an oyster po'boy in a noisy restaurant, drank a Coke, felt relaxed and satisfied, as if she'd done well on a test, or met a deadline. Across the crowded dining room, waiters ran back and forth, lots of tables of jocular people. She watched a couple her age with their two middle-school kids. The woman seemed tired from having to look disapproving.

Not yet fully dark when she came out of the restaurant. Unless she decided to sit in a bar and listen to music, there was no reason not to go back to her hotel and go to bed early, in that bed with mahogany posts, wake up fresh to figure out a plan: two plans, one for the painting and one for herself, for finding what she needed here.

Her return to Windsor Court was an easy walk except for crossing Canal Street,which felt slightly sinister in an impersonal way, less companionable than the street of drinks. The genteel world of the hotel lobby welcomed her once more, dozens of yellow roses massed in one arrangement on the gilt baroque table. A different set of doormen, courtiers every one. She was glad to be back.

Upstairs in her suite, she switched lights on in every room, then went to the closet. She shouldn't uncrate the canvas. There was no reason. But the need to see it tugged at her. The sturdy metal nail file in the bathroom would pry the boards loose and a valet would bring her a hammer, in fact, do the work for her, when she wanted to put it back together.

She freed the portrait with a couple of satisfying cracking sounds and carried it out of the closet. Without the protective container, she moved the canvas carefully. It wasn't dry. Or finished. She leaned it against the side of the bed, sat down on the carpet, level with it.

A figure at a desk, an interior with light angling in from one window, a less direct light from the other side. He seemed almost to vibrate. The bits of gesture she'd gathered from him, taken all at once made a turbulence.

Billy was staring, not at the viewer, but at some unseen object. He seemed to see her with his peripheral vision. She stared, demanding his eyes turn full on hers. There was no change in the effect: of his seeing without needing to look.

She pulled the knit top over her head, shook out her hair. Then unhooked the bra, let it fall. Barechested, except for the beads, she was sitting in that office in front of him, the leather of the wing chair sticky against her back. She shook her shoulders, her breasts still in swaying motion even as she stopped. Holding the undersides, she watched her nipples turn from lavender-pink to scarlet. She could stop, get up from the floor and put on her shirt, act like a normal person. Or, and she felt a smile light her face, she could ride this boiling wave.

She unzipped, shoved a hand into her pants, four fingers raking through her pubic hair. Billy was watching, that fire in him whispering at her like an open furnace window. Her eyes fell almost shut. She'd soak her fingers and wipe them across his face, wet-lipped already, full of beckoning.

But, no, she wasn't going to stay put in a hotel room, no matter how fancy, when nighttime New Orleans lay outside the door. She yanked her hand out, zipped with fingers still dry, rushed the canvas back into the closet. Grabbing her shirt, she left the bra lying on the carpet, its straps a nest of snakes.

Down the corridor toward the elevator, tucking the key card into her pants pocket…the walking made a tugging motion, a rhythmic ache. She stepped into the elevator. The drop pushed up against her inner organs, lifting, then letting go. She leaned back, woozy, against the wall of the car.

The door opened. A blond man in a suit stepped in. He nodded, glanced a second time. At the lobby level, they walked out without speaking.

One doorman. She had the thought to face him and lift her shirt, in Mardi Gras tradition, yell out some primitive cry across this pale gold lobby.

"Good evening," she said, in answer to his quiet greeting. "No cab. No, thank you." The streets were dark. She took the river route, past the big casino. Did women standing in the crowd around the glittering roulette wheel, "show their tits" for a string of beads as they did in the streets at Mardi Gras? She felt the ache from the inside of her pubic bone around to the back side of her asshole. She wanted to straddle a man's back, as if he were a horse.

A left turn, the walk seemed much longer, the traffic lighter on the broad Canal Street. Maybe she had missed the turn. Couldn't have. All that light and music. She hiked on. In the hotel, she'd forgotten the weight of the humid air. Now the craving was dying down. A wave had carried her here and then started to withdraw. Across the street and up ahead, she saw the yellow-white glow of the party. She crossed and in moments was in the midst of the crowd, neon flashing, sudden shadows, making it harder to see faces. So many people, and music pouring out of every door. She pressed forward, as if she had somewhere to go. A shoulder in the jostling crowd bumped hard against hers. She looked around, confused.

The man was grinning, he'd done it on purpose. Young and dark like the guy this afternoon, but tall, rangy, half a dozen strings of beads around his neck. "Where are you going?" he said. "I'm Troy. I'll walk with you."

She hesitated, a sign she'd returned to normal.

"But," he said, with mock-alarm, "you have nothing to drink." He pushed his drink into her hand. "Have some of this," he said, "and I'll be back with a nice… Wait, let me guess. Either margarita or Scotch and water."

"Gin and tonic," she said. "With a twist."

"Righto," he said, "very refreshing," as he backed toward the open door of the nearest bar. "Don't go away."

The cup he'd handed her was nearly empty, cola-colored. She sniffed: bourbon, fittingly. She took a sip. The first taste, as always, felt as if she were swallowing something alive. She relished the sensation that trailed down into her center. After the first sip, the rest was just drinking.

The street felt festive, the mood a bit forced, like New Year's Eve. A grill across the street was bright-lit, menu up on the wall: a change from all the bars, people needing a relatively cheap hamburger to soak up the alcohol.

The guy, Troy, should be coming back if he was going to. He might not. She wasn't sure she'd recognize him. He should have escorted her inside and then ordered the drink if he were interested. Standing here was stupid, as if she were waiting for a school bus.

She walked. The inch of a drink was just enough; let him have her gin. The space of the street was smaller than you'd expect, a narrow rectangle overhung with balconies. A plain-faced man standing by himself on a corner looked as if he had paddled the length of the Mississippi to get here and now didn't know what to do. She could understand his uncertainty. That's who she should have a drink with, find out what wave dropped him here.

In the shop window at her side stood a mannequin with a pair of pralines stuck on the chest to look as if she were wearing two big brown pasties. A praline, with a swallow of bourbon on Bourbon Street: that ought to complete the stereotypical out-of-towner image. She could already taste the sugar and pecans crumbling in her mouth. She headed in the door. Then she saw the clothesline of haltertops, stopped. This was the same store she'd been in this afternoon. At the cash register, though, a different guy, husky, pale with a military haircut. She glanced around the small spacebut no, the other guy was gone. Just as well.

"Where are you keeping those pralines?" she said to the bulky-shouldered man lounging at the register. "Like in the window."

He smiled, as he unfolded out of his waiting position. He had the compact build of a piece of heavy machinery, a crawler tractor, or a motorcycle. "I can get that pair for you," he said, "if you'd like to try them on." Sexual innuendo was no doubt part of everyone's job description here. His T-shirt sleeves were tight around his biceps, his eyes seemed weighed down by his heavy forehead.

"Not what I had in mind," she said. Each breast, loose under her shirt, felt defined as if he'd drawn a circle around it with a wet Magic Marker, dabbed a bright dot in the center.

"You sure now?" Still smiling, he'd sized her up, eyes lingering. "Pralines are right there." He nodded back toward the door. She'd walked past a bushel basket, full and overflowing with the cookie-sized candies. He stepped out from behind the counter. The guy here earlier had been sweet, boyish. This man's heavy jaw was thrust to the side as he picked up a plastic-wrapped praline, ran the tip of his finger around its perimeter. The skin of his hand was hard and nicked, as if he worked construction, or stayed out on an oil rig for days at the time.

He waggled the praline by one edge. "You know the saying around here: show me your tits and I'll toss it to you."

"That's for beads, during Mardi Gras." She'd seen the pictures, drunk college girls, braless, holding their T-shirts up to their chins. She'd left her beads behind in the hotel room. The excitement, though, was coming back.

A customer was coming in the door, others following. A man in wide plaid Bermuda shorts. Then from behind him: Troy, with his pile of dark hair; she hadn't properly studied him before. He was holding her drink up over his head, like a boy at a keg party.

"Found you!" he called out, unhesitating triumph in his voice, even as he saw the burly sergeant-type. She could smell the gin, its fresh juniper breeze with an odor like the glue on Scotch tape. She took a sip of the drink as Troy himself, of all things, introduced himself to the clerk, who had made no move toward withdrawing.

"Cap," he said his name was, didn't offer a last name.

"Like captain," she said.

"Exactly." Next to Cap, Troy seemed like a young boy eager for his dawdling parents to hurry up. Though his face was showing the start of doubt about what was going on.

"Tell you what," Cap said. "I think I need me a drink too. We got a little wet bar in the back here in the stock room and a boy I can send out to work the register. Come on," he said. She hesitated, then followed, Troy behind her. Okay, so the three of them would have a drink.

The back room stretched across the whole width of the store, but was only a couple of yards deep. Everything in this tunnel was the color of cardboard, including the pair of old chairs and the sofa that sloped worse than hers, except for the coffee machine that burned its little red light on a counter. And a tow-headed 19-year-old unloading a box of merchandise, who stopped what he was doing, unpacking an assortment of raunchy flesh-toned toys and checking off a list. Without speaking, he passed the three of them and went out to the front of the store.

"Have a seat," Cap said. He motioned to the two chairs, as the white square of refrigerator light for a moment darkened everything else. The fabric of the seat felt bristly under her hand. Troy, 25 probably, but more an impatient teenager, was tapping his heel on the floor, glancing around the room, at her, at the other guy. She felt a little protective of this boy.

She took a sip of the gin, then put the drink aside. The buzz inside her was starting again. She felt it in her crotch: a heated spot, like the tiny red bulb in the coffee machine. A sweet radiance; she'd sit for a few minutes and enjoy it. Billy's face appeared before her, the image of him watching her. That face of his was formed by lust.

Cap's back, his hard Marine butt were still turned her way; Troy tried to get her attention with his eyes. She ignored his invitation to leave. This was crazy and dangerous, being here. But she'd come out of the hotel stalking trouble, madly ready to grapple with the beast that had hold of her. Brain awash in desire, she was slipping into a state of don't-look-back that took away any fear.

In a slow, deliberate motion, she came up out of her chair and stepped across the narrow space to the sunken brown sofa. Easing down onto the cushion made the flesh of her face feel warm and heavy.

Troy watched. He was getting a hard-on. She wanted both of them pressed close, Troy at one side of her, Cap's solid heat at her other side, the three of them in a huddle.

Troy, over there in his taut jeans, cock-proud, sat too far away. He had a gentleness to him that was appealing, the way he'd come to find her, carefully carrying her brimming drink. If she had on a skirt, she'd open her legs. She wanted to give the kid whatever he wanted. He took a swig of his drink and pulled a string of beads from around his neck, tossed them in a pile in her lap. "Show me your tits." Her heart was beating in the sides of her neck. On the other side of the wall, the bright-lit public space of the shop.

"You first," she said. She could feel herself trembling; taboos loosening, all the barbed wire falling away.

He unzipped. In one glance, she could see penis and face, his eyes warm and glazed as he gave it a loving wag. "Tit," he said. She unbuttoned two buttons, exposed one breast, let her hands fall to her lap. Her own breath brushed across her bared skin; she couldn't look down.

"Mighty pretty," Cap said. Troy was heading for the sofa, condom in his hand. He dropped down beside her, bent over her breast. Inside her, needles flew from her center toward his mouth. Pressed snug between their two bodies, she felt thrilled – she felt safe. But how could that be?

Cap's hand brushed her hair the same second his lips found her other breast. "God!" rose up in her throat. Anyone could hear, in the store, on the street. But it didn't matter; they all were her friends.

A small typhoon was turning in her middle. She let Cap shuck her out of jeans and thong, and with his full weight, roll her out on the couch, smell of mildew puffing up from the cushion. Troy's warmth still near, her face pressed against the side of his leg. She was swamped with love for him, for them both. She was home, where she was supposed to be, breathing Cap's breath as he went into her, already the feel of pleasure growing wider than her body, a haze of sensation pouring off the edge of the sofa, spreading across the floor, tears leaking from the outside corners of her eyes.

Cap slumped, then dragged slowly off, watching her face, as if...what was he seeing? The chill on her damp body eased as Troy hovered, narrow-chested and dark, over her. "Hello darling," he sounded husky, almost tender; she wrapped her arms around him. Then lost track of him; where is he? where are we going?

A burning started at the base of her spine, roared through her to the top of her head. And beyond. A yell started out, pushing her head back. With the force of her whole chest: another. And on...until the sound broke her into pieces, and every spinning atom of her dispersed into the crowd in the street and out across the night; warm waves of her rushing, eager and joyous, to everyone, anything that would take her.

# 26

In the morning, she sat with her room service breakfast, sections of the *Times-Picayune* scattered around her on the bed. The man who'd brought her tray had just bowed out of the room. She lifted a steam cover. Hot eggy aroma. She sank into the first bite. Excellent. The right choice. She'd ordered big: all the specialties. "Perfectly poached eggs topped with sauce choron and caviar, nestled on slices of smoked salmon…" Beside the plate, her dishes of jewel-colored marmalades. She dabbed at the topaz one with her finger. Tart. For dessert, here was her baked apple ladled with double cream. She dipped in a spoon; the cream was better than ice cream.

Yesterday she'd hardly eaten at all. Today she felt healthy, invigorated. Settling down in her pillows, she attended to the business of eating. At this angle, she saw through the window only sky, imagined it both brighter and hazier above the river. Cap had given her a souvenir: a hurricane glass. Fitting that she'd come to a city prone to storms, though it hadn't had a hurricane since before her teenage visit. The whirlwind of a glass sat on the counter in the bathroom, her toothbrush in it.

Even now she felt a little sexy. But not on the prowl. When the valet, in his spiffy uniform, had arrived with breakfast, she hadn't been tempted, though she was freshly bathed and wrapped in the hotel bathrobe.

Finished eating, she kicked off the covers, rattling the plates on the tray beside her. Sitting up on the side of the bed, she waited out a dizzy moment from caffeine and the sudden motion. Lazy and peaceful as she felt this morning, she wasn't going to lie here musing all day. She had a portrait to deal with. Questions to answer. And power beyond anything previously imaginable. She picked up the phone, called her voicemail.

"You have two messages," the recording said.

"Andie, my dear," Tripp's smooth voice, her stomach

tightened. "Need to talk with you. How about giving me a ring soon as you can." Click. She certainly wouldn't be calling Tripp; if she did, he would know where she was.

"Andie, I know you're checking your messages." Marian. Andie flopped back, lying crossways the bed. "You've been gone all day and you're not at home and I'm worried. Give me a call and tell me where you are; I don't care if it's ship-to-shore radio. Call me."

Marian has turned into my savior. Not that I'd have chosen to go through all this just to be better friends.

She drew the Pinehurst area code on the hotel notepad. Made the 9 into an even more elaborate design: electric numeral, adorned the way a monk would do it, with gilded lilies, a couple of fat cherubs holding a banner.

She dialed Marian. Not home. The voicemail came on. She started to click off, then hesitated.

"Marian," she said at the beep. "I'm okay. I decided to take a few days away. Would you call me at this number if you see anybody looking for me at my studio? Find out who it is and do not say where I am." She paused. "Call me anyway." Hesitating, "I seem to be in a new phase…" But the recording cut her short before she finished her sentence. My new phase is…she searched for the definition…tranquil determination. Tranquil and unstoppable.

Her mission, or one of them: new clothes, a fresh start. And a task that was just now coming clear: Saint Louis Cathedral; though she wasn't sure why. She'd pictured it on the flight, the massive white three-steepled church at the heart of the city in the midst of the street circus of fortune-tellers and sidewalk artists. She could feel it tugging at her, insistent.

Even in bright midday sun, the alleys and sidewalks near the cathedral seemed a place where no one could find her. Her shopping bag held her old clothes. She'd worn the new ones, hastily purchased, out of the store, this diaphanous skirt of uneven lengths that made her feel like a woodland sylph. She was a little cooler, though, air filtering through the weave. Each touch of the fabric against her legs made her aware of herself, as if her skin were new and something to pay attention to.

Here in front of the cathedral was crowded Jackson Square: the fortune-tellers and portrait artists and mimes. The man working at the nearest easel was drawing a child whose parents hovered, watching. The guy was good. He could have done Billy. He could, or she could, for that matter, paint a copy of the canvas, blurring the upsetting details of him. Give him one with a bland mask on; he'd assume she'd changed the first one, not started over. The true face would be her property, a preparatory study that did not belong to him.

She was walking toward the cathedral, out in the full blast of sun, leaving behind the charcoal artist, the sweat-soaked back of his neck and shirt. Not a bad idea. So she had one game plan for the list: she could do the portrait for Billy here in her hotel room and reappear with it. At the back of her mind, though, she'd known she could make a duplicate before skipping town. She hadn't needed to leave town to come up with that idea or to do the work. But to start again, copying stroke for stroke, would take her far longer than Billy was going to allow.

Through the foyer of the cathedral, the central space ahead huge and hushed, a muted directionless light, thick, she imagined, with dust motes of dull gold. Surely there were priests around for hearing confession. Though she wasn't Catholic, and this morning for the first time in these weeks that seemed like years, she didn't feel guilty. At least a priest would let her ask him her question, which she hadn't yet figured out how to word, about God and sex. Why, in her current peaceful state, she was still searching, she wasn't sure. Except that it felt necessary, urgent, and now she was at her bravest and most capable.

A docent was approaching, with a welcoming docently smile.

He could tell her about confession...this elderly effeminate man...and could probably also relate lots of livelier facts about this town than the age of these pews. "I was on the cusp," he said, "of giving up on a group for my 12:30 tour. And here you've arrived."

"Good timing," she said.

"Or I could simply answer any questions you might have, business being slow today. I seem to have an eternity on my hands." He gave a charming little chuckle.

This was going to be far too easy, not awkward at all. "Here's my question. Is there a priest around who can hear confession?" She could say she'd sinned sexually and that the experience, degraded as it surely was, had felt transcendent. The priest would then say this was the devil beguiling her. And she'd say no, it wasn't; but what was it? And did he know about a serpent made of pure life force that can climb up through your body to your highest *chakra* just overhead? Maybe she'd speak of it by name: *kundalini*. She felt self-conscious even thinking the word, but it was time to talk about it, and to keep asking as long as she needed.

The docent frowned. "I'm afraid there's no priest available just now." He hesitated. "You're Catholic?"

"Episcopalian." At the wall was a dark cabinet with full-sized doors, big as a mausoleum. But this one structure surely wasn't enough for a congregation, instead more a token decorative confessional.

"When will a priest be available?" She could sit with him for a moment in one of the back pews, no booth necessary.

"I'm afraid I'm not really the person to ask about this." He hadn't even offered a phone number. "I can tell you that the Sacrament of Penance is offered at 4 p.m. on Saturdays. But the thing is, my dear, a priest cannot grant absolution to anyone not in full communion with the Catholic Church."

It would do no good to tell him she wasn't seeking absolution.

Time to give up on this foray. "Sounds like I'm in the wrong place. I guess you get a lot of folks tumbling in here wanting morning-after forgiveness."

He laughed. "We have the occasional reveler."

Outside, Andie stood at a corner of the square, damp with sweat again already, waiting for the slow traffic to pause. Where would you go to find someone who knows esoteric religion, someone accustomed to hearing sordid tales, who would take seriously the idea of sacred sex. Rose had said she'd run across the *kundalini* idea here: you could find anything in this town.

Two men in Renaissance clown costumes had set up a box in the middle of the street and were putting on some kind of play. Pedestrians gathered. Cars sat still. The snappy mini-drama that she could only half see brought a laugh from the crowd, and just as quickly the men and the box were out of the street; a boy in clown suit followed them, passing the hat.

Halfway down the length of the square, she came to a narrow door into a bookstore, Faulkner House. Surely a book person would be able to give her a lead. She leaped up the step, hungry for the AC as well. Inside the door, she lifted wet hair back off her face, shaking her damp shirt away from her skin. She felt fevered. It couldn't be this hot. At the end of a counter an ownerish-looking woman in half glasses and gorgeous sexy heels was turning through a stack of paperwork. "Hi, I have a question," Andie said.

The woman cast a slow look in her direction. "Yes?" in a husky jazz-club voice.

"I'm looking for someone who knows about *kundalini*."

"Good Lord," the woman said. "Blowing in here like there's some kind of antiquarian book emergency. Sit down." She motioned to a dining room chair that stood beside a bookcase. "Cool off. You're all over-heated and agitated."

Andie sat, refraining from leaning her sweaty back against

the beige-on-beige-striped silk upholstery.

"How long have you been in town?" She'd gone back to checking order sheets.

"Couple of days."

"Obviously not long enough."

Andie leaned back in the chair. When she'd left the hotel, she'd thought she'd felt calm. The high ceiling, high walls of books soothed her some. They kept out the weather.

"What's this scavenger hunt you're on?"

Her agitation, now that she noticed it, felt like the faint whir you hear underwater, ambient universe noise. "The serpent power. You've obviously heard of it. And don't tell me to look it up or do a web search. I need to find the person who can show me how to grab it with my hands."

"You walked right past all our local experts outside on the square."

"The fortune tellers." Of course. She'd passed one working at a card table not 10 feet from the door of the store, next to a pastel portrait artist.

"Exactly. They're famously adept in all kinds of occult matters. And if that doesn't work, you might check in at a voodoo temple. Or one of the herbal stores."

"I wasn't thinking. Haven't been for days."

"You came to the right town then. Would you like a glass of water, by the way? Or a drink? You look like you need it."

"Can't stop now, but thanks," Andie said, moving toward the door. Outside lay the rich hunting ground of Jackson Square, its four long sides lined with psychics and seers and painters and card readers.

"I don't suppose you know who'd be good to start with," Andie said, nodding out the window toward the square.

The woman shook her head. "Let the vibes guide you," her tone ironic.

On the doorstep of the store, Andie looked down the shaded

sidewalk to the right. Under a live oak nearest sat a big woman with long grey hair, selling potpourri, oils and divination. Next a young girl supervised by an older man. The girl seemed to be the guru, talking in a glancing way to a customer who followed every move of the child's stubby face. A little child shall lead them. Though maybe not in the case of my particular problem. At the corner she smelled dope mixed with the manure of horses that had just passed down the street. An earthy, loamy combination. Made her proud of her sweat; she wished she were dirtier, stickier. She sat down on a stone block, half in the sun, to watch the traffic, to see who settled at what table and how they looked when they left. The nearest man, slack-faced and thin-bearded, had no traffic; he didn't look healthy, that was why. He was trying to catch her eye; she wouldn't let him.

She walked on. At the next consulting table, the girl's brown back was brushed by her ponytail. "He lives with his two aunts," the girl was saying confidentially to the big-bellied man across from her who was laying out cards. Tarot. The brash yellow of the nearest card caught her eye. "I can't see why a 31-year-old man would do that," on her thin arm a fine gold bracelet. "I think it's a convenient excuse really."

"Let's see what we have here," the man murmured. His beard was monk-like, a frizzle around the edges of his round face, his voice from deep in a whiskey barrel. He mused over the cards, one and then another, gave the girl a soulful, searching look and returned to his study of the table. The incense, a breeze of patchouli. A feel of decay in the air, she half expected seeds to sprout in the cracks of his hands. Close as she was, she could hear his snuffly breath, the rustlings of the girl's quick movements. The man had taken in that she was there, his mutters were louder. He was was sinking his hook in her, his next customer. "The Empress card," he said, "is the female principle. We keep returning to that."

"I know but..."

"Here's what you do," he said. "I want you to take this card with you." He pulled a card, by feel, from a box at his feet. "Every morning, study this woman and her bare belly with the stars back there behind her. Once more before you go to sleep. Every day and night. Just look. Don't fret. Don't think. At the end of 3 months, I think you'll find that you've resolved what you want about this man."

He'd placed his hands on the table top, leaned back, in a your-time-is-up manner. The girl, who apparently had been crying, wiped her nose as she studied the card, started to slide from the chair. "Okay," she said. "Thanks."

Andie inserted herself into the old library chair the instant it was empty.

"Motivated," the guy said. His grin had turned smarmy, less circumspect than with the fine-boned beauty who'd preceded her.

"Highly motivated," Andie said, not bothering to smile. Closer, she saw the Phi Beta Kappa pin on the frayed neck of his T-shirt.

"Name's Jules." He was gathering and re-scrambling his cards. He waved his hands across them as if shooing flies. "Throwing off the energy," he said, "starting fresh."

"Good idea." Once not long ago she'd have at least flickered a snide thought. That snarky tone might be something she was leaving behind; she was no longer qualified to judge, since apparently anything was possible.

"So what's the burning question?"

She gazed out across the sun-blasted green center of Jackson Square. The park was merely fringed with the artists and New Agers. Out there in the middle lay grass and light and simmering air; the vendors along this row sat with their backs to the glowing center. She wanted to scoop up that light-infused yellow-green as if it were Jell-O and glob it into her mouth with both hands.

"The question," but she hadn't formed the sentence in her mind, "is…how do you...?" An impulse to fill in words crossed his face; he held back.

"I'm looking for someone," she said, "who has felt, out of nowhere, a racing electric shock inside and gone off the rails and then recovered. I need someone who can tell me how you do that, how you recover," she remembered the book's threat: loss of sex forever, "without being damaged. How to be sure you're in control again, but still be able to reach the sort of," she hesitated, "expansive feeling."

He cut his eyes to one side, then the other, laughed without confidence, uneasy as if she'd asked him about buying drugs. "That's quite a question."

"I see you know what I'm talking about."

"The magic snake," he said. "What some of the Hindus and Buddhists call *kundalini*. Different names for it in different religions."

She felt a surge of hope.

"Not that it's a household word," he said. "But Saint Teresa described the same kind of experience, light rising up through seven layers of her, and she's not the only one. Call it *kundalini* or *chi* or the Holy Spirit, same damn thing in my book."

He pushed the pile of cards at her, turned face down. They weren't real cards; they were made out of pasteboard, hand-painted on each side, the backs all slight variations on a complicated dragon tattoo that he wore on his forearm.

"Pick one," he said. Her hand hovered over the mess of them. They looked as if a child had left them this way.

"I don't believe these are your regulation tarot cards," she said, waiting to see where the swinging magnet of her fingers would stop. "You painted them?"

"I did. Took me almost a year."

"That's devotion."

"You're considering too long," he said. "Just grab one. Waiting isn't going to make your choice righter."

She took the card closest to her ring finger, flipped it on its back.

Jules crossed his arms and leaned over to examine the catch. "What do we have here?" he said, his twinkling smile back.

"You tell me," she said.

"That's not the way this is going to work."

The card was the face of an old man, a Da Vinci knock-off pencil portrait touched up with watercolor. In the middle of his forehead was a third blue eye, narrower and more bloodshot than the other two. "This means I'm supposed to ask a wise old man? I'm not interested in gurus." An image flickered of Rose, who came from this place, then the dream: her mother with the gift in her hands. "Consult my third eye? Too vague. I've tried all that, more or less."

Jules settled back, arms still crossed, made a dismissive move with his chin.

"You know best," he said.

"You talked to the woman who was here before me. You were giving her advice. I heard you."

"You don't want advice."

"I want a remote control I can point at myself and turn off and on and manage the volume and change channels however I want." Last night she'd been holding the controls, after a fashion.

"I'd like to have a gadget like that," he said.

Yielding to her sexual fury wasn't the answer. She had to know she could count on herself, to behave like a regular human, resist if she needed.

"Take another card."

She touched the nearest, the dragon on the back had color smeared until it looked like a bruise. She turned it over. Color flared: yellow. A dancing youth, in brilliant yellow boots, his profile against a matching yellow-gold sky. She blinked at the shock of the color.

"Did you make this up?" she said. "This image?"

"Nope. That fellow goes way back. The Fool. I copied him."

The fool, she thought, looked happy. "Is there some reason the sky's that color?"

"You tell me."

"A parasol full of light." Like her umbrella: a taut canopy of blazing yellow fire above her head, a protective firestorm of energy. No wonder working on it was frightening. She pushed damp hair back from her forehead, tried to focus her mind. "I thought there might be something archetypal," she said, "a standard tarot answer."

"All answers custom-made," he said. "By you."

"I have a painting built on this yellow. Working on it is what started the magic energy snake to moving. Or maybe it was the other way." He shot her a look of serious interest. For a second, she could see him, as if through the eyeholes of his everyday mask. That quick glimpse hit her as hard as the radiant yellow of the card.

"But if this is supposedly holy," she said, "in any way…"

"Look," he said, "I've read about this stuff, that's all. Couple or three voodooiennes here are the ones who know about *kundalini*. Some say it happens more to women over 40, so maybe I'm at a disadvantage. You been by the Voodoo Museum?"

"I walked past. It was closed, looked a bit touristy."

"Don't let that deceive you."

"What are you suggesting?"

"Go by there when they're open and ask for Clarice. Tell her you want a *gris-gris* bag made; that's going to cost you about thirty bucks. And then while she's setting up that ceremony you engage her in conversation."

"What do I ask her?"

"Tell her what happened to you. Tell her the snakes have gotten loose, run amok, and you don't know what to do."

"Is the place open now?"

"Maybe. They're not running on linear time around there."

"Not here either," Andie said. She laid cash on the table, the

$20 his sign asked for.

"Come back by," he said, "and tell me what you learn."

Risen, she paused at the side of the chair. "So have you talked with Clarice about this stuff yourself?"

He canted his head in a yes-no. "I wanted to stir up the snake."

"Think twice about that. It's a nightmare."

"Except when it's going wrong," he said, "it's a good thing. Best thing in the universe, I hear."

Andie walked and ran toward the street where she'd passed the museum, so certain she knew where it was that she hadn't checked the street name. The old townhouse she'd seen earlier, balconies laden with vines, wasn't where she'd thought.

Damn! She was probably no more than a block away, but the search wasn't as easy as walking along the ends of grocery aisles, peering down each one to see if it was there. "Sir," she said to a youngish blond man out strolling in a three-piece suit in this heat. "Can you tell me where the Voodoo Museum is?"

He laughed and twirled what looked like a phone card in his fingers. "Who you in a hurry to hex?" he said. Closer, she saw spots on his lapel.

"Who hexed you?" she said.

The man laughed his hooting laugh that sounded as if he were trying to act black. "Aren't you a sassy girl," he said. "You need some voodoo."

A walking cane would complete his look, with a gold head that unscrewed to reveal a little flask inside the stick. He probably wasn't much more than twenty years old.

"So are you going to tell me where it is?" she said.

He pointed. "This direction. I will escort you."

She didn't want an escort. "Only a few doors away," he said. "I will leave you at the doorstep." New Orleans was full of regular people who weren't in costume. Not everyone here was obliged to be such a character. But she had chosen this guy to ask.

"Oops," he said as they stepped into the shadow of the balcony. "Not open." He gave the door a shake. "You should wait here until someone comes from the back to let you in. They're probably all in the courtyard." He was still rolling the phone card in his fingers as if it were a coin. "I'll be going on," he said. "You take it easy."

She nodded, gave him a wave, examining the door as if she might try to break it down. The wood was thick and ridged beneath the paint, like timber off an old ship, not the flimsy rectangle they'd had at the mental health center.

She was the only person visible on this block now. She took a seat on a low concrete bench and leaned against the wall. The bricks felt like thick wedges of heat. She listened with her backbone and her ribs to the interior of the building: not the slightest rattle or creak.

She sat, almost crouched, like a sidewalk vendor in India. People straggled past. She let her eyes close and open again. She hadn't had much sleep last night, even late as she'd slept. After what must have been an hour, she unfolded upward, painfully stretching out her cramped legs. The sign in the window claimed they were open, but she wasn't sitting here any longer. She wasn't giving up either. Tomorrow she'd get the concierge to call.

She walked into the walled enclosure of the hotel grounds, irritated to be back. She'd set out this morning on a hunt and found what? Some new clothes, a place to call tomorrow. Plus, the tantalizing hints from the tarot man in the square. Not a lot, it now seemed, but she was on the right track.

The cool cave of the lobby beckoned. She was glad to be walking in here after all. Too wilted, though, to make eye contact with the cadre of gentleman-bellmen. It was going to be nice to lie down and contemplate dinner, pick up the phone and dial

Marian again.

Inside at first, she couldn't see, blinded for a second, as if she'd stepped out of the sun into a bar on Bourbon Street. People were rising from one of the sofas, coming toward her. She saw motion and direction but not faces. For me? she thought. Am I under arrest?

"Andie."

"Otis?"

Marian was stepping out from around him, shoulder bag still in her clutch.

Andie felt herself grin like a 5-year-old, startled and thrilled. "Good," she said. It was more than good. A sensation of joy was traveling in crazy circles inside her, a frisky puppy racing one way, then another. "I'm immensely happy you're here," she said. "Let me get a shower and then we'll find somewhere to have dinner and talk."

# 27

"So why did you come?" Andie said, leading Marian and Otis into the sitting room of her suite. Marian took a seat, half-facing the river that was catching late afternoon light. Otis remained standing, hands behind his back, sentry stance. "Your buddy Tripp," he said, "showed up at the studio yesterday."

Andie put out a hand to steady herself against a chair. "You talked to him?"

"He wanted to know how to get in touch with you. Said your client was wanting to see you."

"To see me."

"'To expedite matters' is what he said."

"I'm surprised Tripp would say that much."

Marian turned fully toward the room. "Tripp had a man with him, Andie, wearing work clothes."

Andie felt heat rise all over her head. "He brought a man to carry the canvas out. And Tripp thought I'd let it go? He knows nothing."

Otis's face was expressionless. "He was asking for the building superintendent."

"Good God! He was going IN?" She held to the chair.

"No chance of that," Marian said. "Mayrelle told me nobody is walking through that door. Especially not Billy Sylvester's man. Besides, you're the one who has the painting. They go in that room all they'll get is a yellow umbrella. Right?"

"The umbrella? He wouldn't! That would be outright burglary. Oh, surely not. Why would they?" Andie dropped down onto the arm of the chair. "You came all this way to tell me this? You could have called."

"We came," Marian said, "because we love you."

Andie glanced at Otis who, solemn, met her eyes and nodded. "You guys," she could hear her voice husky with emotion, "you're champs to do this, coming all the way down here."

"Come back home with us," Otis said. "There's a flight first thing in the morning."

"Are you kidding?" getting to her feet. "No."

"Hiding out like this," he said. "It's crazy. It's not going to work. You need to deal with the guy, not be down here by yourself getting into trouble."

By trouble, he meant sex.

Marian said, "I feel the same way, Andie"

"I don't care if it's crazy," she said. "I'm doing what my instincts tell me to do."

"Alright then," Otis said. He went over and flopped down onto the sofa. "Fine. I've said my piece."

She looked away from his disgruntlement to Marian. "So," she said, "as soon as I take a quick shower, we can all go out on the town. You might as well, since you're here." She ventured a glance back at Otis, who made no response.

Standing on the cool bathroom tile, half undressed, she resisted going back to the other room, to say she was fine and Marian and Otis didn't need to worry. She stepped into the tub, under the shower spray. Here she was, once again, on a trip with two people who were trying to make everything right for her. She'd never wanted to leave that life, the vagabond threesome, never turned rebellious the way kids were supposed to. Well, she'd turned rebellious last night. *That* was a threesome. She let the water pour over her lukewarm, then almost cool.

How dare Tripp think he could walk into her studio? He wasn't above the law.

The water felt soothing, was starting to wash her thoughts away. She ran conditioner through her shampooed hair with both hands, until the strands felt fat and slippery. She let the spatter sprinkle her face, then lowered herself to sitting in the tub. Flipping the lever, she closed the drain and watched water, half-inch by half-inch, start to rise. She leaned back, so that the spray on her face was barely more than a mist. Back and back, until she could feel the drops pelting at her throat, stretched and percussive as the head of a drum, the impact vanishing into her bones.

In this position, neck arched, she was a wolf showing surrender to a dominant animal. She could sleep this way, she was deeply comfortable…

When she woke, or came out of her daydream, she didn't move. The water was over the tops of her knees. Her body was still breathing in the manner of sleep; her eyes were open, as if she were sneakily watching herself sleep. Around the outline of her body, something like a blue shadow, though not a shadow. It was a shining blue haze. She watched. It didn't seem to change except to move with her movement, the edges soft but distinct, reaching out maybe 2 inches above the surface of her skin, a radiant sock around each foot. She smiled, or felt her eyes warm, anyway.

"Andie," Marian knocked as she called out. "Are you alright?"

"Mmmmh." It was an effort to speak. "I'm alright."

"You've been in there forever." Marian had stuck her head in the door. Andie could see her shape and the change of light through the translucent shower curtain. One or both of them, Marian or Otis, might need to use the bathroom. She sat forward, shook herself out of her stupor. The blue haze was gone.

"Where are you guys staying? You have reservations? I didn't think to ask you. I'm going to pick up the tab, by the way."

Marian's laugh was uninterpretable. "Six blocks away, a budget chain with no Caravaggios in the lobby. It's a different planet."

The three of them rode the elevator down, uninterrupted by stops at other floors. "I'm going to check with the concierge desk," Andie said. "I've been trying to find out when the Voodoo Museum is open. I keep going there when the place is locked."

"Voodoo," Otis said, with a grimace. "South Carolina would have been closer."

In the lobby he and Marian waited while she talked to the same Jeanne Moreau-like woman who had checked her in. "I need to make an arrangement," Andie said, "to see a woman named Clarice at that museum. For a *gris-gris* bag."

Jeanne Moreau, picking up the phone, didn't blink or show a flicker of amusement.

"Hello," she'd at least gotten someone to answer. "I'm calling for a guest here at Windsor Court." Scattered across the quiet lobby were clusters of three or four here and there, blazers and dresses for dinner, the room with the feel of a party in the first half-hour when most of the people hadn't arrived.

"If you can be there in about 20 minutes."

Andie turned her attention back to the woman at the desk who was speaking to her. "Tonight?"

"Yes, they're having some sort of gathering there later in the evening. Clarice will be able to see you if you go now." She paused, smiled in an offhand backstage way. "She told me, and this same woman has said this to me on the phone before, that the word concierge in French means 'with candle'." She laughed, embarrassed.

Andie made a bow of deference with her head. "Thank you for lighting the path ahead," she said. This is what a guru should be, a soft-spoken gracious guide.

With Marian and Otis, she slid onto the back seat of a cab.

"A voodoo museum," Otis said, "is not what I call 'out on the town'."

"That's alright," Marian said, "we can just keep Andie company on this errand."

"My chaperones," Andie said, with a touch a pride in them. For that purpose, at least, she didn't need them. Or so it seemed, because the panic was gone, burned out. No way, though, to explain that to them without talking about last night, causing more alarm. On either side of her, she could feel the arm resting against hers, Otis's hard and warm, Marian's warm and soft. Her throat tightened with feeling at their huge effort on her behalf.

On the right, passing the casino, bright-lit. Billy's money was diminishing; already it would be a struggle if she were to try to pay it back. The thought made the cab seem not in New Orleans, instead on the road from the airport back into Pinehurst. She made herself get located, taking note of the night scenery sliding past. They were in the Quarter, full of balconies and dark-massed vines and the sax player on the corner ahead playing a wild "Onward Christian Soldiers". The air pouring into the back seat with the music felt smooth and soapy, air to wallow in. She wanted no intrusive thoughts, no interference.

The taxi was pulling up at the curb; here was the museum, the front wall she'd leaned against. A row house with a downstairs shop window and the voodoo shingle hanging out. The two of them trooped after her. Inside at a desk sat a pleasant-faced young woman with drab brown hair and freckles. "I've come to get a *gris-gris* bag made. By Clarice. Someone just called here for me to arrange it."

"Oh, sure thing. From the hotel."

A woman in a white turban was browsing the packets and jars on the shelves. The room felt like an old-fashioned general store. "Hang on," the receptionist said. "Clarice's in the back."

The three of them stood in a clump, waiting. Otis said, "I don't know why I'm in this place." A shuffling footstep: all turned. The curtain over a doorway behind the desk parted. Tall and black, red-lipsticked, short flapper hair slicked down in spit curls, the woman emerging was eating a loosely assembled BLT. "Hey there," she said to them. "This is Clarice. One of you wanting a *gris-gris* bag?"

"Me." Andie stepped forward as if the other two were going to try to beat her to it. "And I need to talk with you."

Clarice nodded, casting a thoughtful eye over her, as she

chewed and swallowed another bite. "Fifty dollar," she said. "*Gris-gris* bag and talk."

Andie handed over crisp cash to the girl at the desk, as Clarice rewrapped her sandwich. "Come on back this way," she said, leading into the hallway lined with old portraits, then a fast turn into a darkened room of African masks and an altar. "This the museum," Clarice said, as they passed blue candles burning under a primitive painting of a head-wrapped woman with haughty eyebrows and big hoop earrings. She could see the Billy portrait here, too: in fact, this might be the perfect place for it. "Marie Laveau," Clarice said. "Voodoo Queen. You come look later."

Andie cast a backward look at the candles, at a skull, its wide empty sockets. Marian and Otis would hang around, no doubt, walk in the neighborhood. This appointment likely wouldn't take long. Passing through a narrow open courtyard, she could hear a rooster, though it was night. "Here we go," Clarice said, stepping up into a room off the patio. The light was as dim as in the museum, but with a rosy-yellow tint, less formidable. Andie took a seat on one of the worn velvet Queen Anne sofas, as Clarice behind her began to set up on an old sideboard spoons and jars of what looked like spices. The mantel with its candelabra seemed high; the room had a feel of faded Old World grandeur. She leaned back against the hard upholstery.

"A tarot-reader said I should come and talk to you."

"Him," she said. "I know that boy. He is good to me."

The thought of kickback crossed Andie's mind; she didn't reach out to seize the idea. "What are you doing over there?" Andie said.

"Making *gris-gris*. Means grey, balance between black and white. What you want this bag for?" Her style of speech felt Caribbean but she had no accent. A put-on, Andie thought; that didn't seem likely either somehow.

"Lately I haven't been under control the way people are

supposed to be. It started suddenly a few weeks ago. I want to know what I'm dealing with."

Clarice looked her over. "Control? You're not fat, honey. You got a nice little shape."

Andie laughed, which momentarily made the room look brighter, more yellow. Clarice, standing with her hands on her hips waiting, was a tall column of a woman, 180 pounds at least, and handsome.

"Not food," Andie said. "Sex."

Clarice gave a dismissive hoot the way the white boy in the suit on the street had tried to do. "People wanting voodoo for sex," she said, "they don't come in here talking about control. No, ma'am, want to get it, is what they want. And keep anybody else from standing in the way. That's right," she said, drifting into a sort of singing: "'When do I get laid? When do I get paid?' That be what they asking."

"I don't want to give up sex," Andie said. "But I need to be able to say no, and have the sense to stay out of dangerous situations. I've been lucky not to get hurt…"

Clarice laughed again, more rueful than derisive. Whatever she was mixing Andie could smell from the sofa, a medicinal cherry smell strong enough to make her blink. Clarice was packing the mixture down into a red flannel bag no bigger than an egg, tying it with black string.

"Stay sitting right where you are," she said, turning, lighting a match to a smudge stick. The cherry cough syrup smell was mixed with burning sage, the stinging fruit odor still stronger. "You just pay some mind," she said, "to what you feeling in all your parts. I expect you won't have trouble doing that."

Andie took a quick survey of her body, her genitals no different in sensation from the back of her legs. She coughed at the smoke. Clarice was singing or chanting in what sounded to be an African language, facing the mantel holding the smoking stick, the red bag and a sort of castanet that she clicked to the rhythm of her boogeying movement. Light from the candles on the mantel flickered and brightened from the movement of the air. She sang, her back turned, then moved to sing facing the next wall. Sitting, not seeing the woman's face, her eyes, Andie felt left out and useless. She could have called and had this done if this was all it was. She wanted the castanet or whatever it was in her own hand. And the fire and that reeking bag. The room was as hazy as the bathroom had been less than an hour ago, the smoke winding both of them inside it. After facing in the fourth direction, Clarice stepped back toward the center, dropped onto the love seat across from Andie, her eyes showing a shiny glaze. "Put this in your hand, now," she said, placing the sack into the socket of Andie's palm. "Take this home with you. Make the sign of a cross on it." And she covered the red flannel with two streaks of resin-smelling oil from a vial she produced out of a skirt pocket. "Hold it in your two hands when you think about what you need to think about."

Andie opened her mouth to ask about the word *kundalini,* the talking part of her $50 tab. What was it? What did it have to do with sex? How do you keep some kind of grip and manage it? But talking about anything felt drastically wrong.

A sound at the doorway and Clarice glanced that way. A straw-hatted old white man had pushed open the door that had stood slightly ajar to keep them from suffocating in smoke. She glanced at the bony-chested guy, then looked again. Around his neck looped two fat snakes, big heavy ropes of muscles. Andie could see the surface of one of them barely moving; the scales seemed miraculously shifting shingles. The man nodded at Andie's stare. "Boas," he said, with a touch of reproof as if she'd been gawking at someone disabled.

"Ah," Andie said in the tone of one perfectly comprehending. She couldn't take her eyes away from the snakes.

"Folk arriving," the man said to Clarice. He, like the boy on the street, seemed to be trying to sound black.

"Alright then," Clarice said. "Get on from here, let me finish with this lady." The man shut the door. Only then did Andie feel a ripple of aversion to the snakes: a creeping sensation around her neck and, in her tailbone, a shiver that made her come up off the sofa to her feet, as if the cushion beneath her was stirring.

"Hold on now," Clarice said. "Those serpents gone down the road and we almost finished here."

Andie felt a ghost snake winding its way up her spine and her head jerked back.

"That's right, baby," Clarice said, her voice taking on preacher cadence. "Yes, Lord."

Andie tried to speak. Her tongue moved in her open mouth, she made no sound. Her head pulled back in a way that felt spastic; she was staggering, about to lose her balance. She reached out for the furniture. Clarice had her by the arm, steadying, walking her as if she were drunk. Andie felt tears coming hot from the outside corner of each eye, heading back into her hair. The spasm in her neck let go. She straightened, reached a hand to her back: nothing felt different there.

"What's going on?" she said to Clarice. As if to a doctor: tell me straight. "What is *kundalini*?"

"The goddess she goes to meet the god," Clarice said. "Same way in any man, any woman, if they lucky and keeping good watch." She was humming with a swelling sound that was about to rise and take over. "Earth touch sky," she said. "God-within touch God-outside."

"This is good?"

"Good like fire, like fast water. Good if you ready to wake up, see what you and everything made out of." Andie waited, shaky still. Clarice smoothed her skirt over her hips, let her eyes fall near-closed. "All us part of great Bondieu," she said. "Can't be no separate."

I never wanted to be separate.

"Only makes trouble," Clarice said. "What they call 'wrong

rising'."

"Wrong how?" Heat was coming up in her face again.

"You breathe easy now, girl." Clarice swayed as if calming a baby. "It go wrong if you not prepared, not knowing and getting good help, that's all. Too much fire and flood, going off everywhere."

"How do I get hold of it? So I don't have to worry again." She saw herself chopping with a hoe at the tangle of snakes. Swinging until it was a bloody writhing mash that kept moving after it was dead. "What could I have done different in the first place?"

"Nothing. It would have took years to be ready. Can't get ready afterwards." Clarice humming and rocking, eyes closed, held Andie by the arm. "You blessed, child."

"But my old life is thrown out the window. I'm on the run."

"You finished with running. You caught. Stay tonight here."

"My friends..."

"Friends can stay."

By 10 p.m. torches blazed at the sides of the narrow courtyard, and the group was gathered in the open space. A dreadlocked drummer was patting a soft warm-up beat near the side wall. She felt stunned and calm from the talk with Clarice, like the exhausted aftermath of being sick: depleted, but once again able to think.

She searched with her eyes for Marian and Otis. There: the two of them standing off to the side. They fit in nicely here, Otis black, Marian a middle-aged white woman in full flowing skirt. She pictured Billy in this crowd. He fit too, but for different reasons: his charisma, easy walk, his physicality, his nod to the possibility of violence, everything she'd tried to show of his deceptive high-wattage charm. The kind of force you could see in him should only be allotted to the good. Not to everybody, not to people like him and me.

She walked over and joined her two buddies, as if she'd

stepped away for only an inconsequential moment.

Otis was taking in her face, her stance, apparently noting changes. She couldn't tell if he thought they were an improvement.

"Did the *gris-gris* lady tell you anything?" Marian said.

"Yeah," she tried to swallow, but her throat wouldn't. "My life force has gone off like a fire hydrant and there's nothing to do about it."

"That's you talking," Otis said. "Not her."

"Accurate translation, though. I guess I must have been holding it back too long."

He nodded, making clear he knew that too.

"Clarice says we need to stay for this party. I don't know why. I'm pretty wrung out."

A woman near them turned. "Three people tonight," she said, "will have the Lave Tet, washing of the head. To cleanse and renew." She nodded toward three mismatched wooden chairs that sat near the wall across the courtyard from the drummer. Near them were several large bowls and a larger shell.

"Do the three know who they are?" Andie said. "This isn't a surprise for them, is it?" God, she hoped not. Surely they wouldn't pull people out of the crowd. But her heart had already picked up speed. She glanced across the gathering of thirty or so wearing every sort of braided fabric turban or brocade African cap. Probably the three were off somewhere getting ready.

The woman canted her head in a way that was neither yes nor no: "These three, they have prepared a long time for this night."

"Might not hurt any of us," Otis said, "to cleanse and renew." Andie glanced back at him. He was serious.

The drummer hit an emphatic bump and another, then let silence fall. The murmuring crowd quieted. Andie noticed for the first time the night sky overhead, stars paled by the lights of the city. When all were still, the drummer, joined by a second, took up a steady beat. A woman, unseen, called out a musical line:

"Aaaah-Shay Ah-Shay." From a door of the surrounding museum building, came four people; she counted as they emerged onto the courtyard, dancing, progressing slowly into the center of the circle, pausing and gyrating near the chairs. A thin girl with determined little shoulders, a man with his chest shining in the open neck of his dashiki, two older hippie-looking women.

It was the girl with the shoulders who emerged as the leader, she could be no more than twenty, with dark, dark skin. Head turning in a half circle with each swing of her arms and upper body. Her eyes, bright with the torchlight, seemed not to see. On either side and across the yard, others starting to dance. The crowd seemed to sway in the flickering torchlight; the girl herself the flared head of a snake, invisible body descending through brick and clay and mud. Snake as water. Snake as motion.

Weak as she felt, Andie noticed her body starting to twist, upper body moving on the stem of her hips, as if a fresh power source was slowly kicking in. With rising delight, she let its current carry her. Her arm brushed Otis's on one side, then Marian's, then Otis again until a space had opened out around her. Still she could feel each of them dancing, their humming presences, both after only a moment dancing: Marian expansive, shimmering; Otis compact and barely moving.

The middle of the group seemed stirred by one current. A wild scream. My God! Like a cat. It was tall Clarice, doing a shimmy all out of time to the drums, which sped to catch up with her. Clarice in dark glasses that were knocked awry, crooked on the tip of her nose. Andie slowed as she watched, her own motion sobering. Clarice, who'd been so calm, now feverish and blank-eyed, the flesh of her face shaking side to side, all normal consciousness seemingly gone. She had to look away.

On her other side, the three initiates, the ones to be cleansed, danced in a manner that seemed labored, striving. Seeing them, a note of pleasure rang in her chest, at how she felt her own body moving. Snake-like. Smooth as a stream. You blessed, girl, Clarice had said. She didn't want to be blessed the way Clarice was. But this flowing medium place where she swam, this was good.

Now the three took their seats in the chairs, led and pressed into place by the snake-girl, the music keeping the other dancers going, some crooning and rocking. At a metal patio table, a thin-shanked man with crossed legs watched as if he were taking notes. Into a big mixing bowl, honey and thinner liquids, woman in white stirring. A drink? No, to wash with. The first of the three people, seated, tipped back his head; the honey mixture, like fire in the firelight, poured through his hair, along his neck, falling to make dark puddles on the pavement: Blue! Pouring and spreading, a radiant night-blue. As if the force moving all of them was spilling out, frighteningly potent, beckoning.

Now she wanted to be in one of those chairs, at the center. A whiskey bottle passed among the dancers; a fast swig and on to the next hand, quickly empty and tossed aside. She didn't need it, alcohol or the washing. Her body moved on its own like water roiled, water piling into waves.

The chanted names changing with every washing, Ogoun, Grand Bwa, La Sirene. Andie shook her own head, her hair, until she was dizzy and thought to pause and eat the honey, shining and impossibly blue, off the pavement and feel the grit on her tongue, take in the power pooling there. But couldn't slow her reeling dance. It didn't matter. The feeling of her twisting muscles from ribs to pelvic bones was everything she needed: the delicious fullness and freedom of this. Stretching and pulling in an untiring motion, basking in the heat of her own blood and muscle. She smiled, though her face felt sleepy. Sleepy, sleepy smile. The ghostly current slowly rising.

Climbing higher. Keep going! She felt herself start to strain. I can do this. But the moment was sliding away.

The washings were done. Soon the drumming would stop. She saw Otis, Marian, across the courtyard. She'd traveled without knowing it. The tide had left them scattered here on these bricks, moving slower and slower, the ocean color…had she only imagined it?…drained away. Snake motion slithering backward into hiding again.

She gripped her middle with both arms, held on. Bent double over her arms, so nothing of her could escape. She needed to keep on, yet felt herself depleting. Life leaking out of her, out of everything, and there was nothing she could do.

"Don't go." Was that aloud? Had she screamed it out like Clarice? Had she wailed? She might have; in those minutes, she'd have felt no shame. But then she'd let her scrambling effort, her self-awareness bring her down.

The music slid past, glassy, unnaturally calm, the hum of it no more than a soft broom swishing. She saw across the top of the crowd, two arms upraised in a turning V. A living snake stretched between the woman's two hands. One of the boas. Her eyes moved, but slowly, across the crowd to the other. There: draped like a heavy shawl across a dancer's head and shoulders, the weight of it slowing his dance. Andie felt her own bulk pulling her toward the ground, paved uneven with bricks, lure of sleep pulling her, running out of gas, giving up for now.

She woke lying on dirt she could smell. Birds and human voices crying out sounded sharp but softened by too much space. She opened her eyes. She was outdoors, the sky grey and damp reaching from horizon to horizon, lying on her side on an open stretch of riverbank. Her creaky mind searched. Half asleep she'd ridden here in the night in a van, singing all around her, air coming in the open car windows.

Lifting up on one elbow, she saw she'd been sleeping at a tilt, head higher than her feet. Feet down toward the water that was a darker grey metal than the sky and slurping at the layered mud edge of bank, just beyond the jumble of stones. So thirsty her head hurt. Marian and Otis…but she didn't see either of them among the scattered sleeping bodies. Down near the water: the voices she'd heard, three of the dancers still at their praying, their murmuring chant. The moment, the night of abandon, was ending even for these last singers. The birds sounded like the cries of her own sadness, let loose in her sometime in the night.

She lay back, her hair in the dirt that smelled like plant rot, rain on tar. They'd come a distance to get to this place: the far side of the Mississippi, downtown New Orleans a cityscape on the other side. She'd come a distance. She could sleep some more, or crawl a few feet further and put her hands into the murky river, wet her face and try to wake up.

She let her eyes fall shut, imagined pushing dripping fingers back through her hair. A baptism, a *lave tet* to wash away grief: so much of her life already wasted and gone. The weight of the sadness held her where she lay. So many years busy but unengaged, her heart in neutral. The knowledge of that wasn't going to rinse off.

No strength now to move anyway. Getting herself there to the water's edge wouldn't take her to what she wanted: to be full and surrounded like last night by extraordinary life, for that feeling to rise and go on and on. Here on the bank of this muddy river, that flow seemed lost. But at the same time it was close, quiet, almost silent, yet as vivid as if she saw it with her eyes: the rushing glittering bioelectric energy of life.

She wanted to touch it, didn't know how, except for the yearning in her chest that almost spoke with a voice, the desire sweet in itself, its very strength taking her closer. Her eyes squeezed tighter shut, as she leaned inside toward the vast presence. Why a symbol as off-putting as a snake? When the force was this living sinuous river of light…she sensed it so near, yet still out of reach…this wild upsurging river of cobalt blue.

# 28

A van ride back into the city; then in the gris-gris room, Andie found her sunglasses on the dark sideboard where she'd left them, in front of the row of herb jars, unlabeled, the glass clouded on the inside.

Outside the door in the courtyard, Clarice and one of the men were talking in normal, full-volume voices that jolted the tender edges of her brain. "Somebody's got to lead the cemetery tour," the man was saying. He had been the one hitting a wood gong.

"Two groups this morning and at least three this afternoon."

She peered back into the big closet behind the sitting room.

Shelves of huge glass jars, and everything the color of dried leaves. There had to be water somewhere. She could drink the whole wide mouth of the morning's river. The night's blue visions made her want water, that same electric-blue, physically touchable and tastable, breaking forth in daylight. Not that it would quench the kind of thirst she had, for the force she'd sensed and almost seen. There was something in the Bible about the water of life. That's what I want, all the unlived life flooding in. At the same time, she was simply dehydrated from the sweating and dancing, insanely thirsty. She didn't stay to search long in the back room. No lavatory in sight.

She glanced once more across the heavy furniture of the sitting room. Marian and Otis had been gone since about 2 o'clock in the morning, according to the man who'd driven them back in his low-cruising station wagon. He said she'd practically commanded them to leave without her when she saw they were both ready. He seemed to think her authority had been something powerful to behold. "Lord, yes, child. You been seized by the spirit. Those friends could never have gone against you. No ma'am."

Dancing had broken open, or at least located, the tight jars of sadness inside her...she knew that much...and then, hours later and with no great fanfare, had flickered before her an image of the invisible universe. She feared that the memory, her understanding of it, would deconstruct and vanish; she must not crush it with her grasping.

She put on her shades before going back into the now-bright courtyard. Almost 8 a.m.

In the back of the taxi to the hotel, she held against her face the cold bottle of water that Clarice, all business, had handed her as she left. Clarice didn't seem to think the night's events were anything special.

In her imagining, the night, or the sunrise, was still in progress on the river. If she let it come clear in her mind, she'd be carried bodily by the force of it through the window and back there.

She poured ten seconds worth of the icy water in an arc down her throat. This was what she needed: water, the feel of its flow restoring her. For seconds, anyway.

She paid the cab driver, crammed the empty plastic bottle into her bag. On the hotel steps, she made a weary acknowledgment of the closest bellman. He smiled.They were used to her now. A mystery guest. Woman not-quite-of-a-certain-age, alone, coming and going at odd hours. If the bellmen were as attentive as they seemed, they might note in her a curious calm this morning. Exhausted as she was, she felt enlarged, enough to allow for the unexpected, enough to carry her newly felt sadness without being swamped.

The air-conditioning of the lobby hit her face, made her almost moan with relief. She imagined the chilled, tempered air filling with the cherry smell of the fat flannel *gris-gris* sack in her pocketbook.

Someone had called her name. She looked around.

"Andie," in a voice hardly above normal speaking volume. Marian was waving from behind the open rail that marked off the hotel restaurant, trying to do it discreetly. She headed to where Otis and Marian had taken a table behind the greenery.

Otis, napkin in hand, got to his feet, leaned to pull out a chair for her. The plates were a mess of crusts and remains. "You started without me," she said. "Which one of you wants to pass me your glass of water?" Both glasses were plunked before her. She started on the fullest first.

"You're just getting back now?" his tone on the verge of accusing.

"I'm glad you didn't insist on staying." She cast a glance at Marian who cocked an eyebrow at her over the rim of her coffee cup.

Andie felt her scalp shift with the shock of a startling thought, a possibility. She put down her glass, stared at the greenery, the brass rail, before letting her eyes slide over to Otis.

He, she could see, was waiting for this glance, yet pretending not to be: he was too aware of the way he set down his coffee cup.

She wanted to pull back from the table, have a second to look from a distance and take this in. The two of them, Otis with Marian. They'd spent the night together. A chasm opened in front of her, dizzying.

Marian was talking, saying…what? She couldn't follow: "…3 a.m.…taxi…Canal Street…" So now I'm the third wheel. Unnecessary and in the way. She couldn't take it in, Otis with Marian, had never thought… Marian was so much older, 20 years almost. The two of them sat opposite each other at the table, like a million other times, Marian still talking. But as a couple? together?…the image bounced away from her.

Otis said, "I've been to last night's kind of party before," his voice bringing her back. "Around the homeplace in South Carolina. Did it do you any good?"

"Yeah, it did." She cleared her throat. "Seems it did you guys some good." Amazingly, her heart had slowed enough for her to be offhanded, to speak at all.

Otis looked away, rubbed the center of his chest with one hand. He had on a fresh, stiff-from-the-clothesline-looking T-shirt. No longer would she be able to flirt with him. No longer were they three friends of equal standing. She was an extra, interrupting their honeymoon.

And Marian…Andie felt tears start into her eyes. Marian had wanted this so long; here she was finally, sitting with her coffee, looking quietly pleased. No maneuvering or managing or presiding the way she usually did. She gave Andie a sweet, how-about-them-apples little smile, with the lazy ease of someone who has just caught up on her sleep. No one spoke. Wouldn't do to hug her here, right in front of him; though maybe Otis had known her feelings all along.

The two of them a pair… I need a little time to get used to it. She pushed back her chair, got to her feet.

The first heat of midday was coming up out of the pavement pores. It was the right thing to give them time to themselves. And she did have business to take care of; seeing them together had only sharpened the desire. Though all she knew of it was the craving for water, to see again the shine and motion, to feel her spirit move like the light on the bottom of a swimming pool, then sense a flowing connection she couldn't fully imagine. At the moment, she felt connected to nothing and no one.

She'd had a look at the hotel pool, before coming out. Silly, but water was water and she was simply going where she felt pulled. She hadn't stayed long. The air had been full of chlorine, a couple of women paddling and drifting, careful not to get their hair wet.

She'd walked a block or two then along the riverfront: nice enough, but a replay of the early morning wasn't possible. She'd felt no hint of what she sought, had thought instead about the new couple. Of course, they might not last any time. Impossible to predict.

Back on the sidewalk, heat lay thick as if she were swimming in it, this wave-billow of mugginess. Maybe the river she wanted was here in the air all around her. That would make church sense: the Kingdom of God is before you and you do not see it. Her chest and back were damp with sweat. She kept walking, flowing with the slow crowd.

Or perhaps she was taking the water craving too literally. But it was pulling, pulling... Like a smell. She was a thirsty, blind dog trying to find its way.

Nothing to do but stay in motion.

Or sit and wait. There were benches up ahead to the left. How could the city be alive and stirring in such heat? New Orleans itself was a species of animal, tropical and aquatic, crawled ashore to sun itself in the damp mud.

A child bumped into her head-on, an uneven line of them coming down the sidewalk, brushing and darting past, six-year-olds. A class field trip. She turned to look where they were going: the Audubon Aquarium. A patient teacher, standing as tall among them as a lighthouse, guided them in the door.

Without hesitation, she followed the class in: through the entranceway in the wake of the kids, then into the crisp cool of the aquarium building, pausing to let them go on ahead, their tinkly voices moving into the distance around a wall. She hadn't taken a second to think, but now knew she was where she was supposed to be. She smiled. I might be starting to get a knack for following hunches.

In the entrance she looked this way and that for where to go first. Amazon Rainforest or Shark Touch Pool? What did her instincts say?

Nothing.

She walked on, hesitated at the doorway to the Caribbean Reef. Not here either. She kept moving and sensing, though she wasn't sure how she was doing it. Then with a surge of certainty, she rushed ahead, against the flow of traffic. She was traveling on a current now; it was that strong, what was pulling her.

She kept walking. Around a corner. There! The sight stopped her. A great window onto an underwater world and inside, slowly rising and falling, bubble shapes with their trailing strands. Jellyfish! Chillingly primitive. Before her, one was rising, a pale blue-tinged moon in early evening light, streaming tendrils barely there. Water riffled the purplish edge of another creature, a breeze touching the lightest of curtains. This live thing made of little but water.

Her urgency, her upset, she couldn't remember the feel of it. She too was floating in a cool clear medium. She felt the coolness inside her head: this is what the deepest part of my mind is like, the hidden underside, floating living bits, prehistoric and weird. Now I know…

They could sting, these creatures, though they didn't mean to; even a dead broken-off tentacle could wrap unseen, poison-tipped, around a swimmer's leg. She'd seen the snaky awful scars. But watching them now in bright light felt easeful; she let her shoulders drop, her chest expand.

So many hours she'd spent sitting in view of Charlie's fish tank. She'd missed it, though she hadn't thought of it until now. Watching the blue acara that wasn't blue at all, the big shy keyhole cichlids, the firemouth that ate smaller fish and had to be removed. That lighted box of water was the heart of his house. No, he was the heart… Gratitude, and pain, flushed through her for Charlie, for his careful chemistry and feeding, for all the thousand mornings he'd made her tea with two sugars, for his thorough, methodical care that she had been too numb, too distracted to feel.

In the ache of that loss, she felt movement inside her. It was gratitude that lifted within her, to Charlie, Mom and Zack, Marian and Otis, the first-graders, everyone… Surging and halting and moving up again: liquid emotion, love itself, released to rise, pushing through the oldest dry layers of fatigue.

Joy swept the length of her body, touching her tiniest hairs, seeping out beyond her until she was commingled, with everyone, everything. She too was water floating in water, all edges and limits, for this moment, gone. This was the dissolving she'd so frantically sought.

She leaned her forehead against the glass, the stream of energy, liquid blue flame, the *kundalini*, reaching from deep in her bones up through her middle, and this time not stopping, but cresting, invisible as sunlight, ecstatic, high above her head. She stood and let it take its natural upward course, then soften and spread wide.

Outside on the sidewalk, she felt giddy, stumbling around in ordinary yellow daylight. After what just happened, she ought to be lying spent on a bed. Cars crawled past. She waited. No wonder mystics were portrayed in a state of slack-jawed bliss. Reflected in the glass of the aquarium, she'd seen her lips and eyelids engorged and heavy. Finally, the sublimely sexual surrender…and without need of strangers in a backroom.

No one had been near, fortunately, to observe, or to interrupt. Though when she'd turned finally, she'd seen one of the first-graders, a sturdy little girl, big-eyed, watching her from a distance.

A break in the traffic. She started across the street. A horn blared. She jumped back onto the curb. She'd almost stepped in front of a car pulling out.

She sat down at the edge of the sidewalk, dropping straight from where she'd stood. She'd sit here and wait until she got her bearings.

An ambulance was passing slowly, sirens off, bumper to bumper with the cars front and behind, the guy riding shotgun bobbing his head to music she couldn't hear. This pavement was warm as beach sand. Pedestrians passing: the frowning, hurrying young man dressed in plain white shirt and tie like a Mormon missionary, the unreadable face of the old woman with slow heavy feet, wide-strapped red sandals. From the ground, her angle of vision gave each person huge importance. Or maybe she was viewing them each differently.

"Ma'am?"

She looked up. A policeman. She saw overhead his paunch, then his face with a slight, worried smile. "Everything all right, ma'am?"

"Everything's fine." She felt touched that he'd ask. "Am I doing something bad? Is it breaking the law to sit here?"

"Well, maybe not, but you're worrying me." The man had a kindly hefty face, his body tight-packed into his uniform. "You're sitting too close to the traffic. We have some nice benches." He gestured down the sidewalk.

She unfolded her legs. "That's alright," she said. "Thanks. I'm ready to walk again." She got up slowly, the heavy police belt catching her eye; the only submission she could imagine desiring now was to the force she'd felt upwelling inside her. If what that force wanted was surrender, she had surrendered.

He laughed. "Being a tourist," he said. "It'll wear you out."

She smiled. He thought she had a hangover. Perhaps she did, of a sort.

She turned to go back down the waterfront, leaving him rocking on his heels, surveying the street and the Goth kid who was, of all things, skipping along the sidewalk, a drugstore shopping bag dangling from his fist. No, this route was the way she'd come. Instead, she crossed at the corner, looking carefully this time, and headed straight, further into the city.

When she woke, she was lying on a park bench, on her back, her feet sticking off the end. More than an hour since she'd sat down here to "rest a minute". The snow-cone cart had moved on. A murmur of voices near. She twisted her head to look, neck stiff from using her pocketbook for a pillow. Yards away, a couple of homeless-looking men were sitting on a low wall, talking, eating the roasted chicken that one held on crumpled tin foil in his lap.

She smiled and let her eyes close. Lying out here in this park, and nobody had bothered her. She felt the smile on her face lingering. What did the Buddhist say to the hot dog vendor? Make me one with everything.

She put her hand up to touch where half her face felt sunburned. Her skin radiated heat, ordinary out-in-the-sun heat. She pulled herself up to sitting. One of the guys on the wall nodded. She nodded back, then straightened her clothes, ran a hand through her hair, got herself more organized and presentable.

Alert again, she started walking. Her legs had lost the rubbery feel. She felt strong. Healthy. A perfectly-made animal. She swung along with pizzazz to her step. If she were wearing a flippy skirt, like a kid or a twenty-something, she'd flick the edge of the hem as she sashayed through these streets and there'd be no danger to it.

This melting-hot city had been waiting to help her all along. She wanted to return the favor, strew gifts on all the passersby. What she'd been doing, struggling against compulsion, searching for God, now felt selfish and solitary. She could certainly find a good cause for some of her Billy money here.

In the window of the perfume store: rows of alchemical-looking bottles. Ten more paces and she was in front of a tobacconist's, the sweet peach aroma drifting out as the door fell shut behind a burly suspendered man disappearing into the darker interior.

I do have Billy still to deal with. Walking was supposedly a good way to think, find answers; she'd heard it worked. She'd never been sure how a person went about thinking, except for letting ideas drift up. Certainly after this morning, her channels were open. She was ready.

Passing a shop for children's clothing, no, these were coats for dogs and cats, in this blazing-hot climate.

An hour of walking, and she still had half the afternoon before she was to meet Marian and Otis.

Would she try to explain to them what happened? The *kundalini*, the exploding life force, an eruption of compressed love, risen from the base of her spine up and up toward God. Or was the force itself God? Her friends wouldn't laugh, either one of them, outrageous as it might sound; they'd both seen enough these recent weeks to know better.

All that had happened would mean nothing, though, without a change. She would not let herself slip back to the way she'd been living. No more dodging her real work out of fear, or wasting herself in memories of childhood, or in a romance that had stopped making anyone happy. One moment fully alive and she couldn't go back.

Well, that wasn't exactly true. This change could easily slip away like a New Year's resolution, turn into nothing but another memory to wallow in. But after what she'd been through, she couldn't allow that, she'd dedicate every moment to making sure that didn't happen. She'd stay awake. Her friends would help her.

She crossed at another intersection. Stoplight. Another block. Another light. Another dozen blocks, with the constant slow alteration of the angle of sunlight on the heads and faces and shoulders of pedestrians.

She was tired: from the walk, from everything. A strained feeling had developed along the outside of her left heel. She'd passed numerous huddling tour groups, the long white wall of a cemetery, bars and restaurants and street after street of old and indistinguishable buildings. Late afternoon, and she'd wandered through Faubourg Marigny, and Louis Armstrong Park, the central business area, the rough-looking housing project behind the Quarter, likely the place she'd been lost and frightened long ago, all the way to the streets of tangled gardens, big old homes.

She took a rest on the grass at the edge of a yard. The lawn felt dewy and cool underneath her. The house was set far back, the residents wouldn't even notice her from there.

When her legs and feet had recovered, she checked the time again. Almost 6 o'clock, and people were coming home to these houses, cars slowing to pull into the drives, finished with their work days. She felt fond of them, all of them, returning to their various folds. This *kundalini,* when it wasn't rising wrong, was both a reservoir and an upward stream of love.

Almost time to meet Marian and Otis at Pat O'Brien's, the famous old bar. Marian wanted to drink the restaurant's trademark Hurricane. Otis said he wouldn't mind having one either. She was to accompany them on their date.

They were waiting for her when she arrived, only 10 minutes late, at the entrance, a brick-walled carriageway. "We already went in and checked out the possibilities," Marian said.

"I'm with you," Andie said. "Lead on." Through the arch, under crossed muskets hung high, they passed a doorway where a rowdy crowd pressed to get in. Inside around a stage with two baby grand pianos, people sang in a rambling drunken chorus. "So good of y'all to come down here and supervise my entertainment," Andie shouted ahead to Marian, "to make sure it's wholesome."

Marian laughed, called back over her shoulder "Maybe you didn't need us."

"I need you," Andie said, but wasn't sure Marian had heard.

At a table in the main bar, Otis made a point of pulling out chairs for both of them. With their glances and little smiles, he and Marian were now so clearly a pair. They'd probably be surprised to know how much it showed. Sitting here watching them, she asked herself: do I feel like an extra? A child? She didn't: neither tagalong burden nor part of their private magic. She did feel a mess, though, from the day's hike in the heat.

"Back in a sec," she said, when they'd ordered drinks, two of the rum Hurricanes, hers a virgin Cyclone. She sure didn't need any alcohol.

She left to find the ladies room, wash the afternoon's sweat off her face and neck. The turn she took led her into a courtyard: more tables, more crowds, a night-lit patio. Out near the center was a fountain, a pan of fire glowing behind the smooth sheets of falling water.

Brushing against the shoulders of seated diners, she came to the edge of the stone circle and looked up. Here for all to see was the image Clarice had hinted at: fire and water together, the unearthly joining. And so like how she felt: a state of liquid glowing calm.

Stooping at the edge, sprinkle and mist hitting her face, she put her hands into the bottom pool, let them dangle there. No one at the nearby tables seemed to find this patio fountain so entrancing. Of course it wasn't, unless everything was.

In the rush of the water above her head, she felt the whisper of an idea.

# 29

In the airport, she started making phone calls. First, Billy's office. Of course she wouldn't reach him. She jabbed at the numbers, chagrined that she knew them. Fourth ring. She'd only get voicemail, since it was closing time back east. All she wanted to do was to confirm, to announce the news that she would in fact show up in his office as planned.

Marian and Otis were shopping for pastries and coffee at the foodery next to the gate; she'd given them carte blanche in choosing for her any lush sticky chocolate-oozing goodie.

"Hello?" the tone tentative, dubious.

Andie hesitated, a rolling pause, the sound of her greeting already in her throat. "Is this Senator Sylvester's office?" knowing it wasn't. Couldn't be.

"Um, yes?" Throat-clearing. "How can I help you? This is Alison, the senator's assistant." Andie could picture her lifting the blonde strands of hair away from her face with one sweeping motion of thumb and ring finger.

"Oh," Andie said. "You're still there. At the office."

A rustle at the other end. "Well, hello there," Billy having seized the phone, his voice pouring warm oil into her ear. "You and I have an appointment coming up. Tomorrow, is it? I'm counting on it." He broke off, came on again. "Tried to reach you. Sorry,the reception on this phone is practically nothing inside this building."

So she'd inadvertently dialed his cell, and Alison had not sounded as if the two of them were at work. What was she doing picking up on his cell? Reckless.

"Senator," she shouted. "I'll see you tomorrow," and clicked the phone off. Over her head a flight was being called, the voice authoritative with a trace of weariness: "…will be boarding… Passengers in rows...may now…"

She watched the press of traffic passing the gates. A frazzled woman hauling toddlers by the wrists, clusters of pilots and flight attendants, all clean-cut and uniformed, looking far down the corridor ahead of them as they talked to each other and grinned. That's how I wanted to be, she thought, crisp and clear, easy-going, in charge. What a foolish hope that was.

Marian had spotted her; with their paper cups and sacks, she and Otis headed this way. Her mind, underneath the surface flurry of the phone call, felt still as a pond. She watched as they crossed the passenger avenue, Marian, who'd searched out Andie's particular snack, holding it forward as they came closer. The two of them, and that crumbly piece of baked goods, whatever it was, a sudden sharp love for both of them felt like a burning deep behind her collarbone. "Thanks," she said taking the loose-wrapped sticky bun.

"Did you get hold of Sylvester?" Otis said.

"To my surprise, I did."

"Yeah?"

"We're on for tomorrow, as planned."

Marian blinked her eyes tight shut, as if to avoid seeing a crash. "What're you going to do?"

"Show up and talk to him."

"Take the canvas with you?" Marian's face showed she already knew the answer.

"Nope. Empty-handed." She smiled with satisfaction at the prospect.

Otis shook his head, steering them into the flow of traffic toward the gate. "You're holding out on us."

"I won't know what I'm doing until I get there," she said. "The plan is still forming."

Andie dozed with her head propped against the inner window, a blanket stuffed into the angle of window and seat. Now and then she'd hear some murmur of Otis or Marian in the row ahead.

Sleep was overtaking her breathing again. The drink cart

came toward her, moved past. Images of Billy rolled and tumbled, as if in the wire cage of a rock polisher. The portrait was packed somewhere deep in this plane.

Without shifting position, she let her eyes come open, stared out the window. The far edge of the cloudbank in the distance made a second horizon against the clear sky. Such blue-and-white clarity. She imagined the spirit of Tim roaring and leaping across the pillowy cloud surface on his monster motorcycle, humming like the jet engine. Tim wasn't gone. He was part of the cobalt blue river and the upward stream; like everybody else, he always had been.

# 30

With the portrait set up in Elliott's studio, she centered his digital camera on the shape, long-ways. It almost perfectly fit the vertical frame. Night outside, the room wonderfully lit with Elliott's best-lightbulbs-on-the-planet track lighting, just the right overhead to take out any shadow.

"You could do studio photography in here, Elliott," she said, squeezing off another couple of frames on the camera.

"I work a lot at night," he said. "Because of my office schedule; and, you know, I photograph nude models here after dark."

Her fingers hesitated on the back of the camera. "Anyone I know?"

"I keep it a secret."

"Elliott, I'm sorry I couldn't tell you where I was going. It was something like a whim."

"More substantial than a whim," he said.

"A rip tide then."

"I've read you have to swim across those things to get out."

"Or let them deliver you where they will," she said.

"These photographs," Elliott said. "Are they what you're keeping for your files before you give Billy the face he wants?"

"I want these in the can, safe and sound, no matter where I let the rip tide deliver me next." She looked at the image on the back of the camera, close in on Billy's face. Perfect. She could blow it up big as a poster if she wanted, make it look like a Post Office wanted-criminal flyer. "Elliott, do you know anything about Billy Sylvester's involvement in intelligence-gathering?"

"All I know," he said, "is Billy's always been on the intelligence and foreign relations committees. Last week he was ranting in favor of the death penalty for that guy Hanssen, the FBI agent they say sold secrets for years to the Soviets."

"I missed that."

He nodded. "Didn't read the papers on your vacation."

"You think he would see classified information?"

"Him? He'd have access one way or another."

The thought dragged her shoulders down.

At Billy's office, Shawan was at his station. Behind the desk a beep, muted and discreet. Shawan picked up, gave her a nod toward Billy's door. "The senator," he said, "will see you."

In the open doorway, Billy: handshake and mutual appraisal, as they moved into the big room, the door shutting solid behind her. She dropped into the wing chair. His face was neutral, as if his performance were still an hour away and he was reading his mail backstage in a bathrobe, eyes as yet unshined.

"So," he said. "You come all the way over here to see me and you're empty-handed. Or is the masterpiece out in your car?"

"Not in my car," she said.

The neutral expression hardened. "What's the status of this project, Andie?" The use of her name felt ominous, raised hairs on her arms.

"The project's not finished. I thought it would be better to talk in person." A look of disbelief traveled across his face. He leaned back in his chair, as if pressed there by the force of a laugh, but he hadn't laughed.

"Why, that sounds almost romantic, talking in person," a sarcastic spin on his words. "But then you artists are that way. You untamed people. I suppose you make a point of ignoring a deadline, being rebellious and unreliable." She saw a further change in tone coming. "What exactly," his voice cold, "did you come here to tell me?"

She gave her head a slow shake. "All I can tell you is I'm not finished."

"You have a plan? Anything specific to offer at all?"

What she had mainly was a feeling, brought home from New Orleans, that the outcome was up ahead of her and what she had to do was stay on course until she had let her thoughts, sparked beside that courtyard fountain, fully develop.

"My plan," she said, "is to finish the work, let nothing else get in the way. It's no more than a matter of a few days."

"Not 3 days," he said, "not 5, but 'a few.' Well, Andie," as if he were continuing an inevitable sequence of thought, "I've got something I want to show you."

"What's that?"

"My pictures," he said.

"Your pictures?" She pictured a pasteboard box of newspaper photos of Billy at press conferences and ribbon cuttings.

He was on his feet, buttoning his suit jacket. "That's right," he said. "My collection. The house is 7 minutes from here, we're going to ride over and take a look. I want your professional reaction."

His house. Bad idea. Billy was gathering keys. She was curious to see where this was leading. She'd never pictured him driving a car. His not having his driver meant just the two of them.

The house itself was in an old neighborhood of Raleigh, big, but no bigger than the others nearby. Set far back from the road, among huge old trees, the drive led down a slight hill, which was so far the only surprise: that he wouldn't locate himself on a rise.

He'd said almost nothing since they got into the car. A glaze over his face warded off interruption.

The perimeter of the house was bare of shrubbery, only low flowerbeds and ground cover, which looked odd. Of course the arrangement left no place for a John Hinckley-type loony with a gun to hide. He always seemed relaxed, though, as if worries about that sort of thing were occupation for lesser beings.

He cruised the Lexus into the garage. She felt a flutter in her chest as the door rolled down behind them.

She stepped out onto the smooth concrete, not waiting for one of his ceremonial moves, his coming around to open the door. She stretched, though she didn't need to, as if recovering from a long drive. The full upward rush of the *kundalini* had not driven away awkwardness or uneasy fear.

"Hope you don't mind trooping in through the kitchen," he said. "The inside air-conditioned route, as opposed to going out front to the quaint winding flagstone path my wife put in. The layout she and the fellow settled on would baffle a bullfrog."

Andie laughed, her shoulders letting go one notch. "The kitchen's fine." He could have had his portrait painted with his wife, his family. Men like him often did. She pictured the woman she'd seen in a few newspaper pictures, curls set close to her pale severe face. This was a mistake, coming here: I should know better than this by now.

Through the quiet chilled rooms, no one home, she heard only the sound of someone running a vacuum cleaner upstairs. Billy punched in a code at a door that looked as if it would lead out to the backyard, or into the Pentagon. A click, and he led the way through.

A long gallery/living room opened in front of her. Thirty or more paintings hung high and low in a space that was dim except for the spotlighting on each one. The canvases, so many and so close, formed themselves into a larger composition before any one of them could jump out. She sank down into the nearest chair, low to the floor and muddy yellow; she needed to sit. Looking up, she felt herself a supplicant before the portrait in front of her. A Sargent?

Billy had been watching her, she felt it, and felt him look away as if to give her a moment of privacy. At the edge of her vision, she could see he'd taken a seat, was sinking into contemplation too. Yes, it was Sargent, the woman in lavender. She let her eyes travel to get the whole situation before coming back. American Impressionists mainly: one of Childe Hassam's flag studies, a Frieseke woman with a parasol that looked like fire hovering overhead, like her sunlight-yellow umbrella.

And over on the right wall… "George Washington," she said, half aloud. "One of the Peale brothers. Right here in your den." The long slab of face was yellowish, picking up the yellow lapels of the uniform, with thin lips and incongruously rosy cheeks.

Billy, his hands tented in front of him, was paying her no attention, his gaze fixed on a stunning idealized vista of mountains and water in light. Hudson River school, either Bierstadt or Cole. Tripp had said long ago: he has an eye, favors the Hudson River boys. It didn't take an eye to do that. What he had was a lot of big-ticket sure-bets. All that took was cash. But, no, here on part of one wall, were unknowns. Up-and-comers, all from North Carolina too, Lowry, Filene, Martin, Knowles, all somehow representational and, like the others, all suggesting transcendence. Tripp was right: good stuff. Nothing of hers here, though: no college presidents or news teams.

"This," Billy said, as if feeling her gaze drifting back to him, "is what I wanted you to see. This picture right here."

The canvas he nodded toward, one of the Hudson style, was framed as if it were the door of a cathedral: of clouds and snowy ragged peaks, one cold cataract pouring out of a rough cliffside, light lying across an expanse of flat water. The light seemed to be up ahead, at a spot you could reach if you paddled hard enough across that smooth reflective arm of a lake.

"There ain't no place that looks exactly like this," Billy said. "Nowhere but inside this rectangle and a few more that are scattered across the world."

She held back the questions: how had he gotten this, how could he pay for it?

"What I'm saying is: the painter made the place, if it exists at all, look a lot better than it could possibly look." From his semi-reclined position in the armchair, he raised a hand toward the painting. "And you see the result. Right there: a sight so sublime it restores your faith."

"I should make you look that good?"

He laughed. "Well, darling, not that good. I'd be putting the movie stars out of business if we did that."

He reached with the same hand he'd waved at the canvas, ran his fingers between her fingers lying on the arm of her chair. Then lifted away, as if he'd stroked a comb through hair, once only, then back to the arm of his own chair.

Her cheeks, lips, eyes went hot, as she moved her hand to her lap, out of his reach. He *had* caressed her hand; this wasn't something she'd imagined. Her eyes fixed on the wall thermostat, she could feel still where he had touched, all the way to the joinings of her fingers to her palm.

"I don't have a movie star agenda," he said. "I don't approve of those people." His tone no different than before, but that one move… And now the air against her skin felt oily and electric with sex, as if both of them were leaking.

"That's America right there," waving toward the canvas, as if pressing her to drink, get drunk on the sight of it. She *felt* drunk. She didn't dare look at him or move. She heard him shift, then settle himself in his chair still as if nothing had happened. "Yes, ma'am," he said. "This is our best self, and I say that in all sincerity. Looking at the best, it brings out the best." He jerked his chin around toward her with such insistence that she found herself turned, looking at him head on. His face was close, his features too large. "What you want to do," he said, "is inspire people to do better, be better. Pure and clean and majestic."

She turned and stared again at the cool reflection in the painted water, the cloud-misted mountains. She swallowed, testing with a murmur in her throat whether she could speak. Because of last time, because of her rubbing herself against him; don't think of that now. "This is what you want in your portrait then?" she said. "That's what you're telling me?"

"I'm saying, show me as a man who aspires toward the best. You can see my better self. You have from the first minute. That's one reason we clicked real nicely. We work well together. You can't deny it." He laughed. "Much as you'd like to."

"I don't deny it." Her heartbeat was still pumping heat into her face, her crotch, the little knot there making her want to rock, back and forth, up and down. Oh, please, not with him; not with Billy Sylvester, his wedding ring on that hand that lay on his leg, his jaunty talk jogging on.

She licked her lips, which felt parched. "Get me a glass of water, please."

He laughed as he hopped to his feet. "Yes, ma'am. The lakes and rivers in these pictures make a body thirsty," he said. "It has happened to me more than once in here." Passing behind her, he skimmed the palm of his hand across the ends of her hair; she felt the contact in her pores. His footsteps stopped. He stood behind her, not touching or speaking.

"Billy," she said, without turning.

His hands were coming down the front of her upper arms, his arms wrapping around her.

Her whole body humming inside… She prayed. Help me stop. I don't want this. Her crotch pressed harder against the chair cushion, the bones of her pelvis pulling wider apart. A hand brushed across her breasts, breath damp on her neck. She couldn't…

She felt the lift of power inside her. In some hot center of herself, she felt her will go calm. She took hold of his wrists, one in each hand, and unwrapped his arms from around her. As if she were taking off a coat.

He stepped back.

She turned her head to the side, in his direction, knowing she could barely see him

"From here on, Billy, let's keep it to handshakes. Both of us." She *had* led him on. God knows she had.

She sensed him not moving, watching her. Then he turned and went on through the door.

Alone in the room, she got up, walked to the canvas: stood with her face close enough to heat the cracked oil of that blue-gray-green-gold lake. Closer than any museum guard would allow. Her muscles felt near to collapse with relief: she'd held out.

And she almost laughed: no worry about sex being destroyed.

She was back in her chair by the time he returned with a tall sweating tumbler of water. She ventured a quick glance at him: his face blank, eyes calculating. "Your beverage, ma'am," he said, handing it to her with a napkin. He had brought nothing for himself. He took his seat.

"You know I have the utmost respect for you," he said. "Your work."

"Thanks." She held the cool side of the glass against her face. Then took a sip.

"And the work you can do," he said, "that's way beyond what you've done in the past."

She felt her face harden. This was none of his business. He was taking his revenge.

"You have to admit I know what I'm talking about. I have discerning taste."

If she spoke, wild emotion, unpredictable, would erupt.

"All I want," he said, "is for you to put your hand to work making an image for me that will inspire. Is that unreasonable?"

"No, it's not." She put the water glass down on the table, on the coaster that was waiting. She got to her feet. "Let's go, Billy," she said and managed…pretty well, she thought…a smile. "I believe I'm clear on what you're asking."

After dark, every light in her studio on, she set up the fresh canvas, same size, same shape. If anyone were out there in the night to watch, she thought, they'd see her as she'd seen Charlie's fish, rippling and holding steady in bright-lit water.

The finished portrait sat propped against the cabinets to her left. She punched in the African drums tape she'd bought at the voodoo museum, sketched onto the primed canvas the basic shapes: desk, flag, head, torso, legs. On top of that outline she made a different set of marks, the cone of light from his office window, soft scratchings showing its outer edges of influence within the room. Like an Annunciation, she thought, stepping back, that blast of light from the window, a call from God. To Billy Sylvester. Turn in your path, my son.

What she was going to do was copy the original except for the face, which would have to be different, somehow uplifting to the viewer yet without deifying Billy. In the state she was in these days, she could do it fast.

To make two paintings, this much of a plan had come to her quickly, her first day in New Orleans, and even before. It hadn't seemed serious or plausible then, had been simply too daunting. But now she knew where to find in herself what she needed to be able to do it. She'd started to catch on at the fountain at Pat O'Brien's: that she, like everybody else, was both a reservoir and an outpouring. That she'd been pretty stingy all these years about what she'd poured out.

Soon she'd have both portraits: the more idealized image she was speed-painting onto the canvas, and the finished original, as unsettling in its way as that hybrid, dog-headed woman reflected in the car window weeks ago.

After 9 a.m. Andie woke, unshowered. The bedroom was hot, the windows open, a mile-away chainsaw whirring like an insect. She pushed herself up, still in last night's underpants. Her mouth felt as if she hadn't brushed her teeth. She had, though; she remembered doing it, meeting her own eyes in the mirror all the while.

With background and shapes roughed in presentably, this morning she could do the tricky part, Billy's new face.

She stepped into clothes, eager to get there.

In the studio, she walked up to the canvas, Billy #2, and went straight to work, without a glance in either direction.

This second face. She laughed. This one was going to surprise him too.

It was true that a kind of tension was gone; his expression had none of the turbulence from before, the sense of wild water crashing repeatedly against rock. Yet here in this calm, thoughtful pose was his mouth, the curve of the eyelids carrying the weight of his pensiveness. The image was smoothly admirable; no one could argue. And yet there was still force to it that said: look twice, think again.

The work hadn't been difficult, she'd stopped worrying and striving, instead made way for the still-scary energy; steered it, simply by her intent, into what Billy would refer to as her best self. Second by second, dabbing with tiny strokes, she felt no hesitation. In fact, she could paint a few more of these. She could paint three or four versions if she wanted. Make him sublimely ambitious, make him inspiringly powerful, make him seductive. Let him choose which one to claim. Then she'd have all the others.

In only minutes she'd placed another Billy face in the correct position on a third canvas, noting now and again as she worked an exuberant force inside of her. She pictured a flashing torrent, a fountain, unfettered and full of fiery life.

# 31

"Here's what I'm going to do," Andie said. Otis and Marian and Caitlin sat around the diner table. Marian carefully choosing a French fry from Otis's plate, lolling it in his puddle of ketchup. "I'm asking Billy to come to my studio."

"He's not going to come," Otis said. "Not without a month of security preparation."

"He'll bring his guys with the wires. He's still hoping, Billy is, that he's going to get the picture he wants."

"At this point," Otis said, "I'm hoping that too."

Marian's body settled slightly toward his as she let her gaze drift off. The two of them an item now, everyone had taken notice, and noted as well that both seemed different, quieter. People also seemed to think that Andie had changed. More cheerful, they said. Warmer. Looser. Life, and painting, did feel enticingly unpredictable; lunch with her buddies, cozier.

"So what are you asking Billy to do when he gets here?" Caitlin said. She alternated, these days, between hyper-attentiveness to conversation and not seeming present at all.

"I'm asking him to look at some possibilities. The new face I just did. And a third one I've sketched."

"How've you made him look bad in the third one?" Marian said.

"He doesn't look bad. He looks the way he likes to look: powerful, charming. He'll love it. Or he should."

She put the last touches to yet another version of the too-familiar face. This was the final one she intended to paint. Billy's eyes, looking out of the canvas at her, showed the same touch of wicked insight as when he'd told her she could do better work than she'd ever done. Moving back to the window, she could take in at once, in a blur, all of the five faces of Billy she'd painted. Two full paintings, and the other three located within a rough sketch on an otherwise empty white canvas. Not the whole of him, only the face and head, with the outline of torso, to show for each what the overall effect would be.

The work, for this stage, was done. She dropped into her desk chair to make the call, without pausing to clean up.

"Shawan," she said. "This is Andie Branson."

"I know who this is, and I don't need any caller ID."

"I guess that's good. Any chance the senator is free to speak with me?"

"He has been expecting to hear from you. I can make an appointment."

"I'd like to talk to him now, please."

"He's in a meeting."

"I'll hold."

The line switched to music. Andie leaned back in her chair. Paint was smeared across one pants leg, diagonal across her thigh, the ruddy cheek color she'd used for him. Red as a brick in places. He looked over-heated. Likely he hadn't opened that meditation book again; one morning she would read that he'd been taken in for tests, when the truth would be that he was in intensive care if he was alive. When that happened, she'd feel it, some sadness, some loss. She didn't like to think so, but it was true.

"Andie, my dear," he came on the line. "So awfully sorry to keep you." She pictured him grinning at his own sarcasm, tilted back in the chair. No doubt two or three aides, their laps piled with papers, were seated around the room.

"No problem," she said. "I need you to come to my studio." She paused long enough to take note of his silence. "I've produced a group of pieces for you to look at."

"A group," he said. "Paintings?"

"Most of them just the face, or head. Different expressions."

"Well, this feels like progress indeed."

She could almost hear him smile. "They're set up in my

workspace."

A pause. He'd have to be assessing what was involved. "All the way down to Pinehurst," he said. "To call on the queen in her castle."

She waited.

"I can be there," he said, "at 8 tomorrow evening. Wouldn't mind getting in a round of golf before dark."

"Good. Do you need any special arrangements here? For security, privacy, that sort of thing."

"My folks will take care of all of that. You and I don't have to worry about a thing."

"I'll have the canvases ready," she said, as if they weren't already crowding the room.

She was wearing a dress for her encounter with the yellow umbrella, a loose floral summery thing that felt like nothing around her, as softly bright as the morning's light. On the rack of the easel, she placed the *gris-gris* bag, still smelling like cherry cough syrup. If it was magic, she didn't know it. But it had taught her something. Grey-grey, the phrase meant: neither black nor white, good nor bad. Like *kundalini,* she thought, as amoral as a fountain of water, a force to be channeled and used for better or worse. Billy had used a lot of his for worse; he'd probably say the same thing about her. Though the truth was, she mostly hadn't used hers, used her life, as she could have. Surely the sharpness of that loss would ease.

Except for the little red sack and her uncommonly feminine garb, going back to work on the umbrella felt surprisingly ordinary, normal. She herded together twisted paint tubes, started to wipe a brush that was still rosy with Billy paint. She hesitated, then left the color, refrained from wiping the brush clean.

In the room full of Billy faces, she stood in front of the canvas, squaring herself as if in front of a golf ball. She took three steps back, unfocused her eyes and let the image go straight into the back of her brain, a melting yellow glow, a celebratory sunburst, a thousand-petaled lotus, a spinning *chakra*. Showing through the shadows still: the powerful base coat of cobalt blue, which she now believed she might remember painting.

There wasn't much left to do, not as much as she'd thought, touching up a few places, getting rid of that barely-visible yellow crossed circle that warned: Don't Paint. Within minutes, she'd fallen into an easy rhythm, her hand doing what was needed. Once she heard browsers outside the door whispering loudly, as if they knew she was in here and shouldn't be disturbed. She mucked together yellow and white on her plate. Three years old, she was playing on the floor by her father's armchair near the open window, looking up to see his wrist as he reached with his cigarette to the ashtray on the table, then brought it back to his mouth. She could hear her mother's voice, the sound of it a balm, with such deep and crisscross notes. The sound of their talk settled down around her as she played on the floor by herself, smelling the good sharp smells of coffee and the dust of the rug with the murmur of their voices making a canopy over her.

She stepped back from the canvas, looked at what she'd done. One shadow was too sharp. She softened the line, muddied it, stepped back to look once more.

That's it. She tossed the brush onto the table.

Done.

The room was quiet. A murmur of conversation from down the hall, a door clicked shut and then opened again. She walked in a circle through her studio, taking a tour, letting her glance fall on everything: the scraped and paint-stained table, the racks of canvases.

How could it have been so hard to paint anything as simple as a yellow umbrella? How could the doing make her feel so splendid and grand, as if she were a welcome part of Creation? Her heart was on the verge of lifting her off the ground. At the same time, she felt the fatigue it had left in her, as if a huge tree had been pulled slowly up out of the ground and she was the ground and the tree and the one who had done the pulling.

Billy had showered, she noted as he walked in, changed from his golf clothes to an almost-hip, drapey shirt his public would be surprised to see him wear. His aftershave she could smell as soon as she got in handshake distance.

The room, lit for night, felt bright and festive, easels set up and waiting for him in a semi-circle.

"Good Lord," he said, when he saw the sheer number of canvases, before his eyes had paused on one. "Now how do I begin to look at all this?"

"You can handle it," she said, pointing him toward the chair she'd set out for him, her own a little distance away. She rolled it back further as she took her seat.

"I'm in a house of mirrors," he said.

"You are."

He cut her a glance. "I'm told that when a painter paints a portrait, it's always a self-portrait."

"There's truth to that too." She still wore the flowered dress, as if this were a date she'd dressed up for.

His attention was locked on the second canvas: the wistful one, though to call it that was greatly over-simplifying. She could tag them all if she wanted: triumphant, thoughtful, plus the one safely in storage with its dark undercurrent and the one that was, if not transcendent, at least most uplifting. Again, it would only be a shorthand for the different sharp mixtures of expression on each face. As if in each, he was two colors of house paint, or ten, poured one into the other, not stirred. So many separate currents, each barely tinting the other. She'd long kept herself divided into segments, some well-hidden from herself.

She recrossed her feet, ankle over ankle, let her eyes run quickly across the row of faces, stopping at the wall, the corner of the cabinets. Allowed her eyes to rest there in the empty neutral space, giving him plenty of time to look, trying not to be aware of him.

This might be the last time she'd see Billy. She certainly would not be attending any installation ceremony, sitting on a dais hearing speeches on his so-called "achievements", the damages he'd done in his long career.

"Well," he said, a barbed wire jab in his tone, "I expect you're feeling like a clever lady about now."

She waited.

"Very clever indeed," he said. "No one would argue about that."

"Do you see what you're looking for here?" she asked.

His gaze stayed flat and cagey. "I see what you're telling me."

"What do you mean?"

"That there's no stopping you. You can make me look any way you want any time you want to. Take one image away and here come a dozen more."

"You look good, though."

"In a couple of them, that's true. The one there on the end and the one beside it. Either of those..." he paused. "Terrific. No question. What I'm saying is: you're a loose cannon. I take one of those and leave you the rest? To do what with?" He jabbed a finger in the direction of her face, holding the lock on her eyes, the hard tension in his lower lip. "I gave you access to me," he said. "All those hours."

"Anybody with a tin of watercolors could paint your portrait, Senator, going by a newspaper picture. Besides, there are lots of pictures of you around, cartoons, magazine covers."

"Those are temporary, and," he searched for the word, "superficial. I want all these pictures, every one of them."

"That's not our deal."

"What I'm looking at here was not our deal."

"You wanted a portrait. You have your choice." She pointed to the most recent face, dashed off in under an hour. "Take that one. You look robust, ready to take on the world. It's you."

"I want all of them."

"Billy," she said, "Unless you arrange to bury me under the courthouse, I could, as you said, always paint more."

He made no sound, the shine in his eyes going full blaze, two fingers of one hand twitching where he gripped the arm of the chair. He said, "I'll have a look at that contract."

"I already looked, Billy. It included no gag provision, no confidentiality clause or limits on how many pictures I paint or what I do with them."

She was on the verge of shaking, hard enough to wobble the joints of the chair. She could feel, second by second, the trembling storing itself in her thighs: Billy, Senator Billy Sylvester, was plotting fast as he could how to choke her off, how to stop her. When she'd only just now let go of her death hold on herself.

"Billy, take whatever time you need. I have snapshots of these I can send home with you, then let me know which one you want."

Something like a bitter smile crossed his lips. "Long time ago," he said, "I decided I wanted you to paint this picture, whenever the time came. I got to tell you: my feelings are hurt that you'd do me like this."

Her eyes closed: he was monstrous. And yet he harbored that long room full of cool blue ideals, the Hudson River landscapes, the Cassatt of a woman in a long white dress reading. She hardened herself against any charm he could use, any display of decency.

"Billy," she said, "choose one." She reached for the packet of photos waiting on the table, handed it over to him. "Then let me know which."

He laughed, a genuine laugh. "I'm truly sorry," he said, getting to his feet, "that you're not on my team. Just imagine the great things we could accomplish."

At the doorway, he paused, looked back; his phalanx of guards had already begun to close in around him. "About the umbrella painting," he said, nodding with his head. So he'd seen it over there, where she'd moved it well out of the way but, boldly, not into hiding. She felt a ripple of fear as he took one step in the direction of the canvas.

"That!" he said. There was menace in his tone and the shine of his eyes. "That's the one that's sublime."

"Thank you," she said. "That means something, coming from you."

"Easy for you to be all smooth and gracious," he said. "You've won this skirmish, slipped away from me."

Had she? His saying it made her doubt it. His lawyers could find a thousand ways to come after her, if he decided to take that course. But then she didn't think he would. "Maybe we're both going to come out alright on this, Billy. Call it even. That would be my preference."

He gave her a long discerning glance before he vanished out the door.

Just after sunrise, Andie took a seat with a glass of iced coffee on her front steps that needed repair, a coat of paint or stain, a board knocked back into place. Her legs felt jumpy. The inside of her mind was a sack of crawling things.

But then, from what she'd read these last few days, the *kundalini* rising was only a beginning. And she wasn't the only one who'd ever got hit hard by it; she'd laughed when she ran across the line: "…may sometime experience moments of sexual promiscuity…"

She'd expected calm today, after being decisive, taking charge yesterday. Not even 15 minutes after Billy had walked out of her office, Tripp had called. They were choosing the second one, he said, his voice as warmly elegant as ever. It was the only one of the new ones she'd completed. Good. Her work on this project was done.

Easy to understand why Billy had picked that picture: he could see what he was getting. With an unfinished one, they'd be giving her a chance to make more trouble, though she had no interest in doing that. At some point, maybe years from now, she'd know what to do with the real portrait. For now, it was safe.

With the cup in her hand, she got up, gave the slightly shaky board a stomp with her heel, ambled out to the corner of the house. The place needed work everywhere she turned. Neglect was what she saw in the cracked paint and the places a board had split away from a nail, wood deteriorating on the sash of her bedroom window. Maybe she'd throw a renovation party; ask everyone to bring a hammer or a paintbrush. She reached up a hand and felt along the ledge at the top. The whole frame needed replacing. Dust and leaves, splinters of cracked paint, drifted down around her. She wanted to be buoyed, not salted with dust.

She turned her back on the house, walked to the edge of the field beside her lot. Weeds grew tall across the land that stretched out open for acres. In front of her, close, the grass was thick, with taller reeds making a second thinner layer above. Hidden insects whirred. Nothing moved but the feathery tops of the tallest grass. It was like looking out across ocean.

She put her cup down on the ground at the edge, walked in bare-legged, as if wading into surf. Bugs, grasshoppers scattered in every direction as she kicked through vines. The early morning heat itself held a low steady sound. Here where she'd come to a stop, the thick growth was over knee-deep, an old beer can held inches off the ground in the tangle. She sank down to sitting, taller reeds batting her face as if she were paddling in white-capping water.

In the distance, a car passed on the highway, a high-pitched zing as the tires whizzed past. She rolled back and lay down. The sky looked white with the looming heat, a steaming white towel coming down over her face. She stretched out one leg, then the other. Each hand clenched a rooted fistful of stems. She closed her eyes and gripped tighter, holding the rail of Mike's boat that was pounding over waves: the rail slick, water rushing up onto the deck. She clung on in fright, the boat plowing farther into rising seas. Slipping! She was thrown flying, legs flung wide, toward Archie, Cap, engulfing them all as she hit down hard against the water, felt it close over her head.

She sank fast as if she were weighted, broken months and years piling up on her, struggle useless. She watched the silvery underside of the surface disappear overhead. So quiet. Defeated, she drifted down, light from above quickly growing dim, a trail of grief following her. Buried in water that was dark, barely moving. The weight of it hurt her. She wanted breath to sob. Nearly 40 years of life gone, the romance of her childhood finished. Such bright promise, always on the verge of a break-through, any minute, soon as I have time.

Fathoms deeper, letting her last breath out in fat silver bubbles that raced, with the last cry of her voice, up and away from her. She sucked in the water, couldn't keep from it, pulled it into her lungs.

But she was alive still, inhaling, exhaling water, pain humming as she drifted deeper. Bumping to a stop, her feet touched bottom. Bare feet planted on sand, clean and smooth against her soles. Loss of all she might have done, and hadn't, bore down on her. Held fast on the bottom, pushed to her hands and knees in the sand, she breathed in what she had pushed away. Drew in the breath that could drown her. Arteries pounding inside her skull, pumping her heated blood, her wildness, her sadness and rage, blood so thick and dark it was black.

Face, bones, muscles loosened, knots inside her flying loose, one after another… Losses mourned. All her gifts accepted.

She came up on her knees and let her arms drift up, hands waving like seaweed. A wash of joy bathed her brain. She felt her breath making its whispery trip inward, lifting her chest, the air easing back out, damp and warmed, into the world again. She opened her eyes. She was on her knees in a sea of weeds: in love with every drop and twig of the universe. Born again, probably not for the last time.

Roundfire Books put simply, publish great stories. Whether it's literary or popular, a gentle tale or a pulsating thriller, the connecting theme in all Roundfire fiction titles is that once you pick them up you won't want to put them down.